The Baby of Belleville

Originally from California's San Joaquin Valley, ANNE MARSELLA now lives in Paris with her husband, a jazz musician, and their son. Her previous books are an acclaimed collection of stories, *The Lost and Found and Other Stories* (NYU Press), *Patsy Boone* (Editions de La Différence) and *Remedy* (Portobello, 2007).

The Baby of Belleville

Anne Marsella

Portobello
BOOKS

Published by Portobello Books Ltd 2010

Portobello Books Ltd
12 Addison Avenue
London
W11 4QR

A CIP catalogue record is available from the British Library

9 8 7 6 5 4 3 2 1

ISBN 978 1 84627 223 3

www.portobellobooks.com

Text designed by Patty Rennie

Typeset in Minion by Avon DataSet Ltd, Bidford on Avon, Warwickshire

Printed in the UK by CPI William Clowes Beccles NR34 7TL

For Sue

'The people in a fiction, like the people in a play, must dress as nobody exactly dresses, talk as nobody exactly talks, act as nobody exactly acts. It is with fiction as with religion: it should present another world, and yet one to which we feel the tie.'

— Herman Melville, *The Confidence Man*

'I often think that people wouldn't have children if they knew what it was like, and I wonder whether as a gender we contain a Darwinian stop upon our powers of expression, our ability to render the truth of this subject.'

— Rachel Cusk, *A Life's Work: On Becoming a Mother*

Chapter I

*On how Jane de La Rochefoucault née
Maraconi spent her first weeks with the baby
Honoré fortifying herself with Prince Rupert's
vitamins and coping with the heatwave while
her husband, Charles de La Rochefoucault,
freestyled through pestilent waters etc.*

'Why is this place *still* such a mess? Just look at all these boxes!
And all this laundry... didn't I fold it last week? Didn't I wash
it? And what have we here? Dirty troubadour socks? Oh for Christ's
sake, Charles, don't just sit there, do something! Pick 'em up!'

Normally, Charles de La Rochefoucault, my husband, will do
anything for the sake of the Lord, but now he just looks up at me with
glazed eyes, his forelock dangling limply over his brow. He is sitting
on a low stool, his favoured troubadour socks with their woolly
ecphrasis of trumpeting medieval musicians, lie at the foot of the
boxes filled with our books and musical scores, our winter clothes and
bric-a-bracs.

1

'Sit down, dear,' he offers, pointing to a rather large carton. When on automatic pilot he is always polite. Charles has been trained in the glorious tradition of chivalry and consulted the fine print of *The Order of the Garter*. He is my knight, my good husband, a man of noble birth who, with quixotic integrity, averted his eyes to my humble Italian-American background and my family's shady affiliations the time it took to tie the knot. There are moments, however, like when I was giving birth and grabbed the trainee midwife by the smock to rough her up – she refused me pain relief after all – that Charles fears my morganatic claim to the de La Rochefoucault name is being usurped by some bullying Comorra claimant.

'I can't sit down, Charles! *J'ai les fesses en choufleur!* And this damn whoopee cushion… it just won't work!' Tears well in my eyes. My poor bottom really does feel like a cauliflower and could use some assistance. The whoopee cushion in truth is an inflatable rubber ring which is supposed to allow me to sit on a chair without agony, but flatulently releases its air after a mere five-minute sit. Most of the time I am forced to nurse Honoré standing up.

'Do something about it, Charles. I must have another one.'

'Where would I find such a thing, Jane?'

'God knows – ask your mother! She's the one who brought it over. Or call La Leche League's new mothers' hotline. They seem to know everything. And here, take Honoré for a moment.' I hand him Honoré, milk drunk and ephemerally content; by the time I get back from the loo, he will be fussing again. It is ten thirty at night and sleep is still hours off – if sleep we are to get, for the past six weeks have turned us into owls, nocturnal predators not of mice but of slumber, that priceless, unattainable prey. Our once wise and widened eyes have narrowed, our feathers are ruffled and annoyed from the deprivation and heat. Only Honoré gets some shut-eye, a morning and afternoon nap which occur on condition I carry him in a baby sling up and down the Canal St-Martin and the Canal de l'Ourcq until I attain a kind of transcendental state that coats me in salubrious indifference. I become impervious to the fatigue, to the hopscotch of avoiding dog shit, to Honoré's fussy awakenings if I attempt to rest on a bench, to the stifling, sticky heat. How I would prefer to take a nap alongside my babe with a rotating fan at my back, but he will not have it. Newborns, of course, have the last word; their life depends on it.

I do believe he finds contentment in having his forelock gently bounce against his smooth, calendula cream-smelling brow like Charles and Charles's father, the late Count Hubert de La Rochefoucault, both of whom had (or rather have – in Charles's case, *ma foi!*) a prominent kiss curl that requires taming with Dippidy Do hair gel. Perhaps Honoré already has an intuition that as with Samson and rock stars and even Jesus Our Lord Himself, hair will be the source of his strength. As for my own, it is falling out in packets. My lustrous long ropes, my dark-as-dawn Maraconi locks snake along the bathroom and kitchen floors beneath the broom. I've never swept or shed so assiduously. Charles, for the moment, is pretending not to notice my capillary crisis; it really would be too much for him, I believe. He holds my hair in the highest esteem, has bought me ribbons and clips and sequined barrettes to adorn it, props for our favourite game *A Knight Caught in Her Tresses*, the rules and objectives of which, for the sake of modesty, I shall not reveal in these pages.

What I *can* say about this game is that it is invariably played to one of Charles's musical compositions that aired on Radio France three years ago to mixed acclaim, *Ode to G.S. in F Minor*. The ode in question pays tribute to what the de La Rochefoucaults call the Great Sensibility. I should explain that if one were to climb the branches of the de La Rochefoucaults' distinguished family tree to where the tippy-top branches brush against the heavens, one would discover that a common congenital weakness for the flights of Poesy and the Holy Spirit united the tribe, a weakness fortified by a captialized moniker: the Great Sensibility. For the Arts and *L'Amour* there is no better ally, but in matters of housekeeping even a broken broom would make a better friend.

'Charles? Can't we do something about these boxes, dear? It's impossible to find anything! And where on earth are the Prince Rupert's?' I implore upon return from the WC, a bit frazzled from having just pushed the fire-breathing switch of our electric toilet. We are hoping one day to afford an electrician and a plumber, for with each flush the switch spits out a flash of lightning and makes attending to our basic needs most distressing. The phone rings, before Charles can answer my query. It's my mother, calling at last! From Ranger Roger's station at Pine Flats, no less. Ever since she left my father to become a full-time shepherdess, she's been taking her herd of sheep up the mountain in the summer for good grazing. She spends three months in the High Country on a horse named Pinesol, leading her sheep from one grassy pasture to the next. And while her flock chews the day away, she paints watercolour landscapes, bakes sourdough bread in the ground, fly fishes, gathers wood and filters Giardia out of the water to make lemonade; she tirelessly labours on the mountain and easily forgets our encumbered world below.

'I've had my baby, Mom.'

'You have? Well that was quick, darling!'

4

'Six weeks ago, Mom. I've been trying to reach you…'

'You know I'm not reachable up here, dear.'

'But you were supposed to be at Wawona Hot Springs by the first of August, weren't you?'

'We got detained. Six of our pack llamas caught the flu and we were stranded at Bull Trout Meadows for ten days. Manuela and Carlotta were too scared to go off on their own and scout out for help. You can't blame them; it's so different from the Pyrenees here, what with the grizzlies. So we had to wait it out.'

Manuela and Carlotta, I should explain, are two Basque girls my mother imported from Spain to help her with the herd. They are orphans from Pamplona, have never set foot in the Pyrenees, and are symmetrically pierced on the face – Manuela on the right side of her nose, mouth and chin; Carlotta on the left – so that when positioned next to one another and viewed at a certain angle, their features perform an optical illusion, making their eyes, noses and mouths converge. Two girls: one face. Which I believe is why Mother often addresses them as Mani-Carla in one breath. In truth, I think she sees them less as individuals than as ideas to be perfected. Manuela and Carlotta know virtually nothing about herding and are dying to get to California, but Mother is obsessed with them both and has become dependent on their incessant mistakes, which she corrects with a giddy patience.

'You know, Mom, you really should take someone experienced with you. Someone who knows the business and the mountain; you are running great risks! Charles and I worry about you!'

'I want these young women to learn Self-Reliance, one of our great American values. When they return to Europe one day – if they ever do – they will do so as New Women, Daughters of Emerson…'

Now, I might rightly protest against my mother propounding these high ideals, which she must have picked up from a cursory reading of the Emerson fellow for the benefit of Mani-Carla, as these very principles were clearly away vacationing in Massachusetts during my upbringing. If I learned to cook (paramount for Self-Reliance) it was thanks to Grandma Maraconi; if I learned how to write out a cheque, balance a budget and hem gym shorts it was thanks to my dear Home Economics teacher Miss Maybelle; and if I have acquired a degree of self-confidence in performing the actions this life and its job markets require of us, it is thanks to Charles who believes in me one hundred per cent. Indeed, perhaps the only transmission I can credit my mother with is a passing down of her talent for elaborate make-believe. She has always lived in a fantasy of her own invention, a reality painstakingly created, sometimes from things as banal as Tupperware bowls, as when she became a Tupperware party consultant for mobile-home parks, or inspired by paintings or books she loved. I remember well her Picasso blue period when she persuaded us that she was truly blue inside and produced pee of this hue to prove it. In the end the unruly, whim-spun narrative has been her gift to me and I make of it what I can as a playwright. When I was giving birth I remember saying to Charles, 'Go now and rest. In the morning our babe will be born,' which was in fact a line from my historical rock opera, *Away in a Manger*, based on Marie Antoinette's acting out of the Virgin Mary's *accouchement* in the barn. The production ran for four nights at one of New York's more confidential off-off-off Broadway venues a few years back and would have continued on three more nights had not the leading actress developed a hay allergy that made her neck swell to twice its normal circumference. Such are the hazards of making one's heroine a guillotined queen, I suppose. The literary rock opera genre has yet to come to the fore, but when it does, and I am certain it will, *Away in a Manger* will be a major contribution to the form. How grateful I am to Mother! But let us go back to the here and now where our telephonic conversation is nearing *fini*.

'Would you like to talk to Honoré, Mom?'

'Oh, is that his name? Is it after Balzac?'

'Not exactly. It's Charles's great-great-grandfather's name. But he was a poet and a friend of Balzac's; they drank pots and pots of coffee together and then raced to see who could get to the WC the quickest.'

'He must have been a remarkable man. Say, Janie, how's mother-hood treating you?'

'Just grand. I haven't slept in six weeks, my bottom's on fire, Honoré's too hot, we're all too hot! I think I would feel like I was falling in love again if only I could remember what it's like to fall in love, but my memory's shot. And I keep forgetting to take my vitamins. I don't know if I'm going to make it, Mom.'

'Sounds good, Janie. Just like it should be. Hang in there. Remember, I hung in there for you. *Embrasse Honoré de ma part*,' she added in French before our connection was cut, probably by some squirrel gnawing the makeshift line set up by Ranger Rogers.

So now Mother knows the news. I'm certain she would have expressed a desire to see us, to hold little Honoré in her arms, if only we hadn't been so rudely disconnected by a rodent. In a month she will be back at her ranch and more easily reachable; I think we will invite her to come for a stay. A Christmas trip perhaps? Unfortunately, right now we are not equipped for overnight houseguests. We've only been in this flat for three weeks, having moved from a tiny studio we had been renting on the rue Mouffetard. Our new abode is a three room affair that belongs to my mother-in-law Mathilde, or, rather, it belongs to her Association under the Law of 1901, Catholics For Communism, of which there are now but two remaining members of the original five, Mathilde herself and an ancient Armenian *résistant* she calls Komrad Kerkorian. While I make no claims to possess the qualities required of real-estate agents – a friendly, optimistic disposition even in the face of collapsing porches, an ability to micro-manage nit-pickers, a wardrobe of power suits and Latex gloves, a knack for picking locks, a diviner's rod – I would like to give you a brief tour of our lodgings if you would so agree to follow me. Shall we begin?

To arrive *chez nous* you must get off at the Colonel Fabien métro station and walk towards the Communist Party Headquarters. Then turn left when you reach its gates and are nearly face to face with the great and mysterious white egg dome that sits upon its rolling lawn, a dome modelled, judging from the size, upon the eggs once laid by Soviet hens on steroids. Next cross the street, continue on past Le Café des Dames and Le Longchamps, onto the rue de Meaux. Half a block down, stop at the shiny red door (there is only one of this glycerol hue), type in the code AB 1970, push the door and hit the light button on the left, for if you do not, you will feel like a blind man at a Chinese restaurant. This pitch black closet of a foyer is steeped in the chow meins and curries stirred up in Madame Li's restaurant to the left; her kitchen ventilation pipes, which run through our entrance, are full of little holes patched with band-aids. Once the lights are on, however, you will find this narrow entryway strangely charming. The lights in question emanate from a Venetian chandelier, which once illuminated the boudoir of a certain Mademoiselle Mimi at a minor château in the

Touraine. It was given to Mathilde and Hubert, Charles's parents, as a wedding present by a member of the de Jouveny family but was never hung in their home for reasons unclear to me. I believe that Mathilde's hanging it at the rue de Meaux was at heart a Communist gesture, an individual attempt (she is excluded from communal efforts for reasons you will learn soon enough) to spread the wealth, to provide the nation's proletariat with the light of a lustre. But her generosity did not stop here: the walls of this chamber are covered in wainscot and royal blue velour wallpaper with a crown-bearing lion motif, a Pierre Frey covering left over from an interior decorator friend of Mathilde's who had just finished refurbishing Madame de Pompadour's *cabinets* at the Petit Trianon Château. The effect of the chandelier's lights upon this luxurious wall covering, the way it sets the golden lions a-twinkling against the deep azure velvet, is redolent of certain depictions of Our Lady, and this in turn inspired the Dos Santos family on the second floor to affix upon the wall facing the mailboxes a statuette of Our Lady of Fatima, dressed in a Plaster of Paris gown and cape with finger and toenails polished in pink. Madame Li, joining in this spirit of donation, contributed a lovely Miss Taiwan calendar and two red New Year's lanterns which hang from the ceiling, their yellow tassels teasing the heads of those tall enough for the tickle. Charles is six foot four and gets tassel-tickled every time he walks through because he has his head in his symphonies and forgets to duck. For those of you who are tall, you've been forewarned.

Continue on now up the staircase to the right, and do take it easy because you have six flights ahead of you. The former headquarters for CFC (Catholics For Communism) is on the fifth floor, which when converted to US weights and measures, becomes the sixth floor. The wooden banister and stairs are cleaned with savonette and waxed once a week by Dolores Dos Santos (of the second floor, as already mentioned) who unfairly complains about the hygiene of the Chinese (Wang, Li and Tseu familes: of the first, third and fourth floors respectively), an unsavoury prejudice that dates back several centuries to Vasco da Gama and his shipload of sinks which he tried to trade in the Far Orient for precious metals. How presumptuous of him to think those porcelain potties were worth their weight in gold! The Asians sniggered and poked fun at Mr Vasco's sanitary wares and his retinue of Jesuits who demonstrated their use, but in the end it was Mr Vasco who had the last laugh. History is a ruthless story indeed. I do wish that Dolores would review the sins and follies of her forefathers and quit ranting about the duck meat and dried fish hanging in Madame Wang's window; if it is her pleasure to cure her proteins in the Parisian air, then so be it.

But let's continue on up the stairwell, which smells of savonette on Mondays, Tuesdays and Wednesdays, of nothing in particular on Thursdays, of fried cod on Fridays, and of muttony olive stew on Saturdays and Sundays. You'll notice that the doors are all painted fire-engine red and that the walls are covered half way up with 1960s style Portuguese tiles. Their purple and brown abstract motif was common it seems during the Salazar period when the Dos Santoses made their exit with a truckload of ceramics, and, if I am to believe what I heard from Mathilde who heard it straight from her decorator friend of Trianon fame, the fashion is now making a comeback in some of Paris' most influential kitchens. Imagine yourself then, if this facilitates your ascension to the fifth floor, as Catherine Deneuve's personal chef (on Fridays this does help to sublimate the smells) preparing fritters for

Yves Saint Laurent (alas! He has passed!) and the Grande Dame herself while listening at the door for kiss-and-tell secrets. With a bit of luck and depending upon your taste for the flights of travesty, this jejune exercise should painlessly bring you up to the fifth floor (US 6th) where the three of us now reside.

Our flat is a recently whitewashed two-bedroom apartment, which on the western side looks out over the city's tiled rooftops to the breasty, Byzantine domes of Sacré Coeur on the mount of Montmartre. It was this view, I believe, together with the remarkable proximity to the Communist Party Headquarters that convinced Mathilde to purchase the flat some twenty years ago for the purposes of her unorthodox organization. She saw it as a kind of holy coop annexed to the majestic roost down the street and believed it would be a shoo-in, a way to get her sneakers through the doors of the great communal Hen House. In a sense, this worked, she did manage, her arm pretzeled through the card-carrying Komrad Kerkorian's, to reach the reception desk, but she never did get further than that. The choice was made explicit to her: she must either renounce her nobiliary lineage and Catholic affiliations or her Marxist aspirations. Since neither option was conceivable, Mathilde became, by dint of personal necessity, a self-appointed Communist dabbling in Liberation Theology and an odd variety of mystic materialism, including the practice of babysitting Jesus (more on this later). But, excuse me, please, I must interrupt this visit briefly to take my Prince Rupert's vitamins and I am still waiting for Charles's answer to my earlier question as to their whereabouts. Let us hear what he has to say; perhaps he knows something we do not.

Charles: 'I believe I saw them somewhere... let me see... yes, it seems… could it have been… in the kitchen? Perhaps by the sink? Do have a look…'

Clearly Charles is preoccupied with some musical equation far more interesting than the sum of my daily nutritional requirements. I am to take two of these foul tasting liquid nursing vitamin vials a day, morning and evening, upon the advice of Mathilde's holistic councilor, Dr Delamancha. I believe they have cod liver oil in them and live algae too, plus sweet tasting pollen, which only adds insult to the gustatory injury. Imagine eating sugared fish livers! I must clothespin my nose to take this dreaded dope.

Jane: 'But Charles, we don't have a kitchen!'

It is simply inadmissible that Charles will not admit we have no kitchen! As you will see once you have quickly admired the view of Sacré Coeur and made your way through the maze of boxes embarrassing our impressionable living room, that there is an adjoining room of about 9m² which contains a mini-bar with a single hotplate on it. Next to this is a gold-leaf tap topped by an oxidized copper partridge (a Trianon left-over) jutting from the wall. Below it, on the floor, there is a blue plastic basin whose purpose is to catch the water cascading from the golden spout. The fact that Charles calls such a transient set-up a kitchen is only proof of his dedication to music, of his ability to live almost exclusively in the sonorous, snaking cavity of his ears. Forget cupboards, sinks, man-sized refrigerators, ovens and four-burner stoves; to Charles, a kitchen is not the sum of its Whirlpool appliances but an idea. An idea from which springs by way of an almost associative magic an assortment of dishes he delights in eating. Needless to say, it is Jane Maraconi who mans the hotplate, who not magically but by the sweat of her brow cooks up the one-burner Neapolitan dishes, the *spaghetti con le vongole* and the *pesce all'acqua pazza*, and even, if Honoré generously allots her an hour's respite (very rarely, indeed, almost never), chicken diavola, Charles's favourite dish.

It is difficult to say when we will acquire a proper kitchen or at least a sink (perhaps the Dos Santos could be of help?) though when Charles finishes his job at the car wash and the pay-cheque comes in we might be able to manage it. I emphasize *might*. I mean, how much can one expect to make soaping up Renaults? But perhaps you are wondering what a composer is doing with his hands in the suds. Let me explain, bluntly if I may. Our finances have been rough of late, ever since Charles's royalty statements began dwindling after his *Suite #2 for the Holy Spirit and Three Harps* was panned by a *Le Monde* critic. He was thus compelled to take the first job he found, which happened to be a two-week stint at a highly confidential 'car show' washing Vegans. Vegans, I should explain, are revolutionary vehicles, hopefully soon to be manufactured by Renault. As their name suggests, they are vegetarians of a sort, running on methane biofuel made from farmyard manure rather than the standard mixture of hydrocarbons and dinosaur bones. The prototype, both sleek and unfathomably lightweight, was designed by a team of France's most prestigious engineers, all graduates of the Ecole Polytechnique with a specialization in Automotive Esthetics. Charles had to undergo a background check before being hired, for the event is so wrapped in security and secretiveness – the car being truly maverick and not yet marketed – that the employees serving it had to be given clearance before gaining entry.

Perhaps we should be proud, in light of our freshly founded parenthood, to participate in this ushering in of an ecologically sane car, even if only by way of soap and sponges. It pains Charles to spend

13

all those hours away from his compositions, but there is a very good chance that the rhythms of washing will inspire a new oeuvre, as they once did for the blaxploitation film *Car Wash*; perhaps even a hit will come of it? This is what I tell Charles to encourage him on as he dutifully leaves the house at 7.30 a.m. for work, though I needn't. He brandishes the bubbles quite bravely indeed from 8:30 to 5:30; it is only when he returns home that the Great Sensibility makes its forceful comeback and melancholia, that misfit of the soul, manages his motions. This explains why he is now sitting amongst our haphazard boxes, despondent: I believe he would like to find *Suite #2 for the Holy Spirit and Three Harps* but has no idea where it might be; none of our boxes are labelled or numbered.

But now Honoré is colicky, fussing, we are all sweltering and must get out of the house and take a walk. The sun has gone down but Madame Mercury is still up painting the town red. I have just found the Prince Rupert's buried in a package of diapers but can't find the clothespeg. The very thought of taking this pollinated fish liver concoction with live seaweed in the heat makes me seasick.

'Charles, the clothespeg!' I call out to my captain. Honoré is now wailing; his *aihn-gee, aihn-gee* plaint reminds us of Mick Jagger's 'Angie', a song which gave its singer the key to the City of Angies. He accommodated an average of 1.5 Angies a day while the song remained in the charts. We are not at all sure this augurs well.

'How come I can never find that damn clothespeg when I need it?'

'Here, *chérie*, I'll hold your nose if you like.'

'Please do, Charles. I hope I can get it down. It's dreadful stuff. I'm beginning to wonder if the taste of it isn't getting into the milk. Maybe that's what's making Honoré so fussy.'

'Nonsense!' says Charles, who holds Dr Delamancha's prescriptions in highest esteem ever since he cured him of a ringing in the ears with belladonna drops. I squelch my suspicions therefore and down the contents of the vial whilst Charles pinches my nose. Honoré, who we sat in his baby chair to perform the operation, has turned up the volume on his jaggers. I sputter, nearly gag but do manage to get the stuff down.

'Look, Charles!' I point to Honoré, having shuddered off the vile vitamin flavour. Our babe's disposition has undergone a radical transformation. The storm of jaggers was merely a flash flood, over and done with in a jiffy. He is now wiggling quietly in his chair, smiling at us both. Very drooly and sweet. 'Maybe you're right about the Prince Rupert's after all. Why, he's so calm all of a sudden.'

'As Dr Delamancha always says, to treat the child, one must first treat the mother.'

'Yes, perhaps he has a point, Charles. I've noticed that when Mathilde does her birch tree syrup cures, you seem to get rejuvenated too. Or at least more regular.' I bend down to pick up Honoré, who needs changing now, and sing him the little diaper song: *Wet, wet, wet, now don't you get upset. Let's get you dry, dry, dry, before you start to cry.* How he loves to be changed! To look up into the adoring face of his parents as they clean and dry him, medicate his rashes and re-diaper him. And sometimes he does surprise us with a little spurt of fountain, making the event somehow festive and gay. I change the diaper and dress him in a clean onesie. It's too hot to add any layers; he will take this walk in his underwear. How lucky he is, little Honoré. Charles and I would like to go out in our skivvies too, but we are much too modest. Already, with our clothes very much on, we do make an odd couple, a bit like Jack Sprat and his wife, though I am by no means fat, just short and with fifteen extra pregnancy pounds saddling me about the hips. Next to my five-foot-one, pear-shaped frame, Charles's totem-like stature, his lean verticality makes for a marked contrast, which does not go unnoticed. If Charles never pays attention to the rather rude comments that sideswipe us in some of Paris' rougher arrondissments, it is because he does not hear them; I on the contrary do, and I fail to appreciate the crude allusions to our supposedly awkward lovemaking. How wrong they are to assume such a thing! How *culotté!* The only clumsiness, if one can so call it, that might disrupt our embraces would have to be hair related and nothing a thick-toothed comb cannot correct. In short, this unfortunate situation hardly encourages us to strip down. Though others do so without so much of a blink of an eye.

Such as Mr Li and his cronies who are seated in their underwear along the banks of the Canal de l'Ourcq drinking Tsingtao beer. We spot them from across the canal and wave. Charles is carrying Honoré in the baby sling and I am walking alongside in black, stretch-waist pants and a spaghetti strap floral print mini dress, trying to hold my belly in and failing. But how can I possibly win that battle; it is effort enough just to filter in the oxygen from the mucky, heat infested air. Honoré is crying again; he is baking in the sling. I take him out and hold him up in the air so that he's facing outward toward the stinking, sluggish waters of the canal and the huddled groups having a midnight happy hour along its banks.

'Look, Honoré, that's Mr Li.' I point Honoré Mr Li-ward just as the gentleman arises, showing off his red and blue striped briefs. He poses for a moment as his friends clap and cheer. Honoré kicks his wee legs with joy. How quickly he gets into the spirit of things, a regular reveler.

16

Though most likely he doesn't see these men in briefs on a bender. What he senses from his maternal post across the canal is their merriment. Babes are emotional barometers; their telepathy traverses rivers and streams, great lakes and oceans. In this case, a putrid canal, a narrow, microbe-infested reservoir of urban wastes but with amusements on both sides. Honoré is picking up on the Chinese merrymaking. I turn us around to look for Charles who seems to have receded towards a game of *boule* being played behind us. Then I hear a splash.

'*Ce n'est pas vrai!*' Charles has moved up next to me again and is pointing to the water where Mr Li is now dog-paddling about in the liquid filth.

'Oh, Charles, do you think he will die? All those diseases in there…'

'Not if he goes and gets shots.'

'But I'm sure he won't. We must tell him. He doesn't know the customs here.'

'We'll tell Madame Li when we get back. She seems to be a sensible woman.'

'You know she really is, Charles. She's the brain behind their all-you-can-eat lunch buffet and the three euro supplement on shrimp and crab dishes. We really should eat there sometime. Once the pay-cheque comes in that is. Oh my God, Charles! Look! Mr Li seems to be drowning!' Indeed, our neighbour's dip has taken a turn for the worst; he is now flailing his arms and sputtering, his head bobbing in the lurid waters.

'Oh, Charles! We must do something!'

An Algerian family camped nearby around a tabbouleh salad has moved to the edge of the quay, shouting out in a shrill mixture of

17

Berber and French; they've twisted their tablecloth into a rope and have tossed it out to Mr Li. But Mr Li is unable to reach it and now it has become a soggy, sinking thing. Honoré has got the jaggers again, unstoppable ones; he has just telepathed in the drowning man's angst. Oh my poor dear! He's too wee for such woes! I hear yet another splash, this time right below us. It is Charles and now he is freestyling his way to Mr Li. And *ma foi*, he's got his head in that filthy water! Oh but he is fearless like those leper-licking saints! I try to pray his way to safety, but Honoré's jaggering has filled my head and its little chapels. I can't supplicate from within so yell out: *Holy Shit! Help! Un Noyé! Au Secours!* My call gathers the petanque-playing hipsters to the canal's edge; the twenty-somethings look curiously across the waterway towards the opposite bank where none of the picnickers knows how to swim. They are foreigners, from countries where municipal pools and natation instructors are far and few between. The banks of the canal, you see, are distinctly divided in their populations. If your back is to Place de la Bataille de Stalingrad, and you venture up the left bank toward La Villette, you'll encounter The World. If you take the right bank, you'll meet The Scene. We usually begin our walk up Scene side and end it down World side though I'm sure the opposite trajectory is equally pleasant and I do wish we had taken it this evening; saving Mr Li directly from the left bank would have precluded this hazardous swim through the mire.

'Look there! That's my husband!' I shout proudly to a girl next to me as I point to Charles and try hard not to think of the slime he's swimming through. She turns her ruby pierced belly button his way.

'Is he going to make it?' she enquires. The ruby is twinkling in the light of a *lampadaire*.

'Well I should think so!' I appropriately respond. Initially, my faith in Charles does not fail me. True, his crawl has considerably slowed down, but he is nearly there. Just a few feet away… four more strokes…

Suddenly faith grabs a little air: 'Call the fire department! Call the firemen!'

I'm screaming at the top of my lungs while faith holds her hands up and fear's readying to throw some lead. Chalk it up to my centuries-old Maraconi survival instinct evolved from mobstering at the foot of a live volcano. Like any self-respecting capo, like my Uncle Al, one of Boise, Idaho's best, I've got a gut that gets it right. My gem of a neighbour is quick to it, on her cellphone dialling for do-gooders, those fellows superbly versed in the saving arts and calisthenics, men who express their love on ladders, their helpfulness with hoses. Here we call them *pompiers* because they are always perfectly pumped up. Not only do they save lives daily and for free, but they keep themselves ship-shape. How often Honoré and I encounter them in the Buttes Chaumont park whilst they calisthenicize, generously exhibiting their tax-funded goods, their brilliant buns shining through tight rayon shorts or tattle tales as we used to call them in St Mercy High gym class. Just thinking of them usually makes me sigh a bit, I admit, though not in such a dire moment as this. Charles is trying to get an arm wrapped around Mr Li, but is having trouble. Mr Li is pulling at him madly, grabbing for dear life, which is what drowning men do to the detriment of all concerned and why it's best to knock them out cold as any self-respecting life-guard knows.

'Good God, Charles. Put him out! Giv 'im the old one-two!' But he can't hear me over the jaggers, my voice won't carry that far anyway. The firetrucks too, drown out my coaching.

'They're here,' informs my neighbour as the siren suddenly stops. 'I hope they reach him in time,' she says nonchalantly.

I want to give this doubting Thomasina a slap.

'That "him" is my husband! And they sure as hell are going to get him in time!' Her ruby flickers as she turns away from me frowning. Luckily for us the fire station is but a block away; the men file out of the truck in record speed, decked out in tattle-tales and wet suits. Four wet-suited saviours jump in and begin wrestling with Mr Lee, disentangling him from Charles though it is hard to narrate this intervention from across the way. I can only see the outlines, not the fine lines. I do believe however, that they prick Mr Li with a tranquilizer, for he goes limp all of a sudden and is carried away in the hefty arms of a *pompier*. Waterlogged, Charles too is taxied to the ladder at the canal's edge, then lifted out of the canal by the boys on the banks. Honoré and I wave to him energetically but he doesn't see us. His clothes are drenched and dripping, clinging to his thin frame for dear life; he looks like a man-on-stilts emerging from the sewers with a rat on his head. But it is not a rat really, just the forelock stiffened and gobbed up with canal slime and god-knows-what. The bell-bottomed pants are now stuck to the peg legs. His trick is up. The World sees that tonight's hero is merely a long-legged man attempting to reach beyond his height. And thank goodness he did; if it hadn't been for Charles, Mr Li would have gone down to join the sludge sucking carp before the firemen arrived, that is for certain. All heroes reach beyond their height of course, some succeed in making the stretch, others fail; Charles did a bit of both.

'Darling, I'm coming!' I shout across the water, but Charles is being taken into the fire truck. He turns around and waves to us, letting us know that he will return when he can, once he has been washed and given his shots. I head back home jogging to keep Honoré bouncing and happy. He giggles and seems to have put the aquatic drama behind him. He also senses my relief.

'Let's try to sleep tonight, Honoré. That way Dad will come home all the more quickly. What do you think?' I should add here that since Honoré's birth, indeed, perhaps even prior to that momentous event, I've noticed that my son is quite of a different mind than me, that in fact our ways of being and thinking have precious little in common. The most telling example of this is bedtime, of my needing sleep at night and his not. There is also my need to be alone with my thoughts and my body at least occasionally, and his constant need to be in my mind and arms. There are mothers who love to nurse as much as their babe loves to suck, mothers who perceive their wee one as an extension of themselves, as adorable, adoring mirrors of their own emotional and nutritional requirements. Honoré has not allowed me the comforts of such an illusion.

Which makes it all the more astonishing that he seems to have seen the wisdom of my suggestion for sleep. Why this is I'm at pains to say, perhaps his father's bravery has wiped away night's anxieties, frightened away its Caspars and other hapless ghosts. Be what it may, Honoré and I sleep with our three-speed fan on high from 1 a.m. to 6 a.m., that is to say a salutary five-hour stretch of slumber so deep and opaque that there was nothing to remember of it but its abysmal deliciousness. Oh thank you, my boy! Thank you, my little love, for letting us sleep through the night – or at least a part of it – I say to him. I'll be a better mother for it, you'll see!

Chapter II

Which recounts the visit of the magi, the offering of a Koranoblaster and more.

It is now 8.00 a.m. and I am nursing Honoré as I slug away at my Turkish coffee (two spoons of sugar, three of coffee, brought to two foaming boils in a conical brass pot) a practice discouraged by La Leche League, but which I adhere to entirely. Honoré will jagger and get antsy with or without the Turkish delight. Now that I'm the Mother of Honoré there is a proscription on days-off, siestas and even, *ma foi*, going to the bathroom, that is, when Charles is not around to take over. Such as this morning when the Constantinople coffee is quick in getting me there. I have no choice but to set Honoré down in his little box, which I should add is nothing like the 'box behind the stove' imagined by Faulkner in his lurid *Sanctuary*, but rather a nice wooden box that once contained six bottles of a very fine Aligoté, sanded and painted by Komrad Kerkorian and lined with soft cushiony fabric, a pillow for a mattress. The box is light and compact and therefore easy to move around, unlike most cribs that you can't fit through a doorway. I am thinking that if Honoré stays with me in the bathroom, he will feel like a participant too. Could this even be perhaps a form of precocious potty-training? So now here I am indecorously seated upon the fire-breathing throne with Honoré propped up in his box facing me. For thirty seconds or so a relief-enhancing calm presides, then Honoré begins to thrash his arms and legs and the jaggers start. 'But I'm right here, Honoré! I'm right here!' I wave to him frantically, hoping my wagging will distract him, but see it is going to take more than this. I launch into an energetic round of 'Itsy-Bitsy Spider' replete with all the hand gestures. This seems to do the trick, but in the meantime, on my side, nothing is happening. No relief in sight. And worse, as soon as the song ends, Honoré is clamoring for the next round. So I go on with 'Frère Jacques', first in French, then in English, hoping this musical interlude will buy me a few moments more. Next comes 'Sing a Song of Sixpence' followed by 'The Muffin Man' and 'Hey Diddle Diddle'. Honoré is enjoying it all immensely, but as soon as I stop, the jaggers rise up in rebellion.

'Oh, Honoré! A minute's peace, for Christ's sake!' And just as I mention the Lord's name, the front door opens and shuts; we both hear Charles's steps approaching. He stands in the doorway now looking in at us; his long face gaunt with fatigue. And *ma foi*, he's wearing hospital pyjamas!

'Excuse me,' says my knight, seeing me seated on the throne. He discreetly moves away to give me my privacy.

'Come back, Charles. We're so glad you're home at last! But tell me, why are you wearing pyjamas?'

'My clothes are still wet, I'm afraid,' he waves a plastic bag that must have held his canal-drenched slacks and shirt, undies and socks.

'Did they give you all the shots you need, love?'

'They did,' he says rubbing his bum. 'They were very efficient and tended to me well.'

'I'm glad to hear it, dear. Maybe you should take a Prince Rupert's just in case. I think it works as a detox agent as well.'

'Yes, perhaps tonight. I'm running late now as it is…'

'Are you going to the car wash? After all you've been through, Charles?'

'I am, Jane.'

'But don't you think you deserve a little break? My God, you nearly saved Mr Li's life, you know. Listen, you're late as it is. Just call in and tell them you're waterlogged.'

'I should go, Jane.' Charles is about to head to the closet to get dressed but I catch him just before he turns his back to us. His sense of duty, I'm beginning to think, is almost as strong as his Great Sensibility.

'Well then before you go, Charles, could you help me out here? Take Honoré please. I need a few minutes alone.' As Charles lifts Honoré out of the box I notice his nose twitching, picking up a scent.

'What is it, Charles?'

'I believe he needs changing.'

'Well then change him. And shut the door!' Charles's announcement sours my humour on the spot. In truth I am feeling a tad resentful though it certainly isn't flattering to admit this. Shouldn't life's ironies be fodder for laughter? And shouldn't mothers applaud their wee one's clearances? Even if they are at the expense of one's own? But emotions rarely mirror the 'shoulds'. And thank goodness for that really! Live an emotion fully, I say, then it will leave you in peace. And so I allow this resentfulness to express itself in the style of my Maraconi forebears, that is to say with loud threats of the kind my mother had always washed from my mouth with Dove soap in my formative years. Moments later, I emerge from the bathroom. I am now back to being a mother-in-love.

'Have a good day at the wash. And don't forget to wear rubber gloves!' I take Honoré's little mitt and wave it at Charles as he heads down the staircase. It is already getting hot and stuffy. We'll have to go out, maybe to the Buttes Chaumont park where there's some shade? Oh if only Honoré will let us park somewhere and relax a bit! I'm beginning to feel like I'm on one of those walk-till-you-drop marches.

'Shall we go, Honoré? I'll take a blanket and we can take a nap on the grass? How does that sound?' Honoré responds with his irresistible smile, the same one he gives the girls behind the counter at the boulangerie causing them to shriek with pleasure. He is not really responding to my suggestion, only pretending to. His key desire is to get me out and walking ASAP, and he's willing to crack a smile for it. So I begin gathering our things – the baby sling, a bottle of water, the whoopee cushion just in case he lets me sit – to go outside, but am interrupted by a knock on the door. Then another.

'Who's there please?'

'*C'est la police.*' Oh dear. The word police in any language quakes my Maraconi bones. If only my late great Uncle Al were here, he would know just how to breeze these johns off. He turns up occasionally, you see. In my times of need. The first appearance he ever made was when I was giving birth to Honoré: he stood next to me as I lay on the gurney, with the golf club he was holding when he was bumped off by his boss, Enrico Dececco. He had two weaknesses, Uncle Al: girls and golf carts. He never failed to accommodate a lone girl in a lone golf cart, a gallant proclivity that in the end did him in. The last golf cart he ever mounted belonged to Dececco. The girl did, too.

'Don't open that there door so quick, Janie-girl. Take your time…'

'Is that you, Uncle Al?' I gasp as I always do at our miraculous meetings. I sense him now just as I had on the gurney.

'You betcha. How's my Janie-girl?'

'A bit worried about those flatfoots on the other side of this door. Isn't there a way to just make them go away, Uncle Al?' I pull Honoré close, take a deep breath.

'You just stand your ground there. They'll go away when they see you mean business, Janie. But remember, you gotta be polite… we Maraconis are known for our extra-special hospitality,' says Uncle Al before shrugging off. I sense his presence suddenly evaporate like water splashed on a hot griddle, though without any crackle or swoosh of smoke. He never stayed long anywhere, Uncle Al. Not even in a golf cart though he was forever hopping in and out of one.

'I'd like to see some proof of identity, please,' I finally muster, encouraged by Al. My eye looks through the peephole to identify the knockers. Two men are standing in front of our fire-engine red door; one with brown curly hair wearing a jean jacket and black T-shirt, the other, slightly taller and blondish with a white button-down shirt and khaki sports coat tossed over his shoulder. I recognize them immediately.

'Oh Honoré! It's Starsky and Hutch! They've come to visit us! Can you believe it?!' Honoré smiles as he sees my hand reach the knob to open the door. He is drooling quite profusely, a sign of good humour and healthy teething.

'This is an honour!' I gush out in greeting. But neither Starsky nor his sidekick offers me a hand. Instead they both pull out IDs from their jacket pockets and flash them so quickly that all I can make out is the *Préfecture de Police* insignia sitting atop several emphatic black lines. 'How may I help you?' I change my attitude from one of admiration to service. When on the job, this duo gets down to business.

'We'd like to know, Madame, if you've seen these men?' Monsieur Hutch holds out three photos depicting men of North African descent in their mid to late twenties. Of course I have seen them before; they are our magi – Charles's co-workers: Samir, Rachid and Ahmed. But I wasn't going to admit this to Starsky and Hutch! Samir, Rachid and Ahmed were over for dinner just last week, charming young men bearing Levantine gifts for Honoré. Now as far as I'm concerned, anyone who eats at our table benefits from our protection; it's a Maraconi rule, part of our Italian table etiquette which is so unlike the de La Rochefoucaults' with its emphasis on folding lettuce leaves three times with the aid of a fork and knife so that the large foliage fits into the mouth like some origami edible. And then there is the cheese platter and how one must cut the Camembert, but I won't go on, for a description of the de La Rochefoucaults' table etiquette merits an entire chapter alone.

'Sorry, officers,' I shake my head.

'Is your husband here?'

'No, he's left for the car wash.'

'He wasn't there this morning,' says Starsky, trying to catch what he thought was my lie.

'Oh no, you wouldn't have seen him,' I shoot back, swallowing my surprise. 'He just left twenty minutes ago. You see, he spent the night in the hospital after having saved Mr Li's life, or almost saving it…' And

I went on to give them a *compte rendu* of last night's and this morning's episodes (minus choral practice in the loo!), filling them in with all due honesty, only refusing to recognize publicly the men in question. I must say that actually dealing with this distinguished duo in real life is quite different from watching them as a bystander on Channel 6. They are much more personable on the tube; perhaps it's those extra ten pounds supposedly added to the body when it appears on screen?

'If you hear from any of these men, you're under obligation to inform us immediately,' warns Monsieur Hutch. So they think I'm going to be a snitch, do they? A 'Huggie Bear' in a nursing bra? They have no idea they're dealing with a Maraconi!

'Now why would I hear from them, officers? You aren't trying to tell me I'm in some kind of danger, are you?' I feign a look of horror, as if my imagination were suddenly prancing off on the horse of suggestion, heading for some creepy horizon where evil men pick off Mothers of Honorés.

'If you don't inform us, you could get yourself in some serious trouble,' butts in Starsky, who is trying a bit too hard to be a tough guy. The overacting does not become him; perhaps he should try platform shoes. The additional inches could help.

'You shouldn't menace a breast-feeding mother,' I chide him. 'It can make the milk turn.' At this Honoré starts in with the jaggers, the mere mention of sour milk is just too much for him. I throw inspectors S and H an exasperated 'see-what-you've-done-now!' look which effectively sends them on their way, back down the six floors to their red and white Ford Torino. I bounce Honoré as I go to get the keys; his darling forelock flips and flops.

'We're out the door, now! Shall we stop by St George's to say three

29

little prayers for Rachid, Samir and Ahmed?' As soon as I shut the door, Honoré's humour is back to humming, and so I tell him the story of the Three Little Prayers which is really a spin-off of the Three Little Pigs, with of course Prayers taking the place of Pigs, and a ranting and raving demagogue named Ousama Ben Falwell replacing the huffing-and-puffing wolf. Honoré likes this little tale, particularly the part where Ousama Ben Falwell gets so filled up with his own hot air that the last little prayer has but to prick him with a diaper pin.

As I walk us to the park, up the Avenue Mathurin Moreau sweating a little, I try to keep my mind off the mounting heat which by the afternoon will be unbearable even in the shade. Instead I steer my thoughts to our evening epiphany last week, the arrival of the magi and our lively celebration around the table. I had prepared marinated artichokes, chicken diavola and a rum baba, which Madame Li generously allowed me to bake in her oven. We fashioned a table out of boxes, covered with red-checkered cloth, and set little tea lights around it for atmosphere, but also for light as our one light bulb was (and still is) some forty watts short of providing proper living-room illumination. Charles was in an exceptional mood, and even set up his three metre-long Alpine horn for the occasion. He intended to greet our guests with a blast of this elongated bugle.

Rachid was the first to arrive. Decked out in a roomy white and silver Nike tracksuit and matching babouches, he appeared in our humble foyer like some desert potentate having transited through Detroit, luminous with a sunny-citrus aura and metallic overtones. I would have thought he'd be steaming in a tracksuit, but he seemed fresh and cool and mint scented. A gold chain charmed at his throat with a Fatima's hand the size of a silver dollar.

'Enchanted, Madame,' he greeted me, having been ushered in by Charles and Honoré. 'And here is a something for the baby.' He held out a small package, really just a padded envelope, which made it easy for Honoré and me to open.

'Why look, Honoré, baby trainers and tracksuit! Size six months!' I held them up for all to admire. They were two-tone, baby- and grey-blue. Printed on the athletic wear jacket was a rather odd encouragement that read: 'C'mon gout!' Oh dear! I thought to myself. We certainly want none of that! Isn't gout reserved for royalty? But I kept my apprehension to myself, thanked the first of our magi for his kind offering, never mind the preposterous call to the paroxysmal disease.

Another knock on the door was followed by a second honk on the Helvetian horn; Samir and Ahmed made their entrance and expressed their enchantment. Samir stepped in first: his Kool-Aid green tracksuit and bumblebee striped trainers reminded me of an Idaho birthday party. Back home we always celebrated ours around the Iraberry source, a rectangular pool of emerald green water that was man-assisted but no less miraculous, for its water changed from hot to cold according to some mineral whim. It was our yard's centrepiece, a crater of liquid warmth or cool in a surround of swampish meadow. Bees abounded, stung hands supinated for succour, children and adults alike grew suspicious. Every party was torn into by screams and wails.

Relief swept over me when Samir bent down to untie his shoes. 'Yes, leave them next to the door. That'll be fine.' Ahmed, entering behind Samir, slipped out of his white babouches, smoothed the long white robe he wore over a pair of jeans. He had a face that seemed carved out of beard, as if his barber, in the gardening style of Le Nôtre, mowed his

31

woolly visage into decorative patterns; on each cheek a crescent moon sat with symbolic weight but offered little illumination. I noticed over the course of the evening that he would scratch the left one when trying to remember something, a gesture that made him seem contemplative and stern with revelation. Recall failed him all the same.

'Asalaam Alaikum,' I greeted him, his beard-moons reminding me of my manners.

'Please, Madame. This is for the child.' I was handed a two-foot-long box wrapped in green and red Christmas paper.

'It's from Ahmed and me,' added Samir to whom I had just passed Honoré, prompted by his great green open arms.

'Oh you shouldn't have!' I exclaimed, tearing the paper off the box. Honoré drooled with excitement, wetting one of Samir's pant legs, deepening its verdant hue.

'Goodness! What have we here?' I enquired, full of wonderment at what appeared to be a toy boom-box shaped like a great gilded book with a golden speaker on each side. The many buttons and Arabic calligraphy adorning it gave me a clue as to its purpose.

'Could it be,' I asked hesitatingly, 'a Koranoblaster?'

'Look, Madame,' said Ahmed, fumbling with the gilded toy, pushing one of the primary coloured plastic buttons that lined up in rows below golden Arabic script.

'Do call me Jane.'

'Does it need batteries?' enquired Charles. The answer came in the boom of a bass line; a standard rap rhythm tolled darkly as a Koranic caller wailed scratchy sounding verses, rolling out the *tajweed*, as it were, the prayer of the faithful. The strangulated voice lifted then dropped, in serpentine undulations: *Allah u Akbar.* God is great, God is good, let us thank him… No, nothing hokey. Here there is no god but God. Ruler of a rhythm box. Charles pressed a green button and the rhythm shifted to a salsa beat. Ahmed hit a red one. The opening verses, the *Al-Fatiha* moaned with mysterious meaning. I took Honoré's index finger and pressed it down on a blue button, for we were curious Christians being offered a lesson in Islamic recitation: a peal of women's ululation rang out to greet us. With delight we found that with each push of a button a door opened into the chambers of an inspired, battery-operated chapter of the great Mohammedan book.

'Astonishing!' Charles, I could tell, was listening with his composer's ear, yet what he was making of the tinny, muffled muezzin voice, compressed into a plastic prayer-box I could only guess. His forelock dangled upon his brow, his eye enlivened, perhaps, by some fantastical vision of an orchestra made up of extra-European divinity toys.

'Remarkable, truly remarkable!' I agreed, nodding my head in amazement. 'It's a kind of Sura sing-along, isn't it? A memory game for mini Muslims?' Ahmed bowed with solemn dignity; his crescents, with his head inclined, seemed to possess the ubiquitous, grinning snigger of the Cheshire cat.

The doorbell rang yet again.

'Are we expecting someone else?' I asked Charles, just as I realized, informed by the uncanny, femiform wires of intuition, that the finger at the bell belonged to Mathilde. Yes, Mathilde. She and I are like two roads leading to Charles from opposite directions, meeting at an overpass that runs above his head. Charles has no inkling of what goes on between us; his ear is not attuned to our roars and rumbles.

'Why, Mathilde!' (my instinct was right) 'What a lovely surprise! Do come in and meet our friends.'

'I shall only stay a minute, *ma chère*.' As she gave me the *bise* on both cheeks, her eyes narrowed in on the goings-on in the living room.

'Has Charles been at the horn? How lovely! Please Charles, would you honour your mother with a hoot?' Mathilde was wearing her usual uniform: a basic black A-line dress with an indigo blue Maoist jacket. As always, she was shod in blue Keds.

'Brilliant! Lovely!' she chimed and clapped her hands as Charles offered her a blast that could have shoved a herd down the mountain. 'Now where's the Sacred Child?' Samir, who was still holding Honoré, handed him over to Gran. I wish that Mathilde would not call Honoré the Sacred Child; it's a bit much and might even lead people to think he was divinely conceived!

'God bless you, my Sacred Child,' she said crossing Honoré, initiating him into Romish gesture, a preliminary to patty-cake and other hand games to follow. Honoré cooed, looking up at Mathilde's four-inch bun; it perched upon her head with astounding permanence, as if it were fastened with mortar rather than pins. It is all real hair, shimmering silver in colour. Perhaps Honoré perceives it as a magical mountain, one that the Itsy-Bitsy Spider would willingly climb and ring-around-a-rosie on. He adores Mathilde even if she burdens him precociously, and uselessly I might add, with a messianic mission. The Sacred Child, indeed!

Mathilde then looked out at our magi, at last registering their presence. 'Welcome, brothers. Here you are God's guests,' she said, expansively opening her one free arm. The three kings touched their hearts in the manner of North Africans, before offering their hands for a shake. I made the introduction while Charles lifted the amazing toy for his mother to see.

'Can it be?' exclaimed Mathilde, her hand pressed against her heart. 'A Koranophone! I have not seen one since Constantine! Not since my days with the Moorologist, Père Piccoli, at the birth of the Liberated Algerian nation!' Ahmed, pleased that his gift had ignited Mathilde's enthusiasm, pushed two buttons for a brief demonstration. The introduction to some surah, unidentifiable to a Christian or a Jew but surely rudimentary to a Mohammedan was sung with a solemnity enhanced by the static, as if radio waves were carrying the verse from a distant minaret.

'Perhaps not quite a Koranophone,' Mathilde corrected herself, 'but similar. Why, *ma foi*, it's rather extraordinary and I believe it will serve the Muslim nations well.' Samir, eager to impress Mathilde further, changed the rhythm section to a reggae beat. Clearly, the toy's ambition was to make Islam appealing and accessible to all including the dreadlocked babes.

'The Muslims are light years ahead of us in these things. No wonder our children are no longer learning the catechism. If only John Paul II had left us the legacy of his voice in a box, Oh if only we had captured his vocal enlightenment – the seven sacraments in seven languages, expressly for young apostolic learners!' Mathilde now directly addressed our three kings. 'I am a communist and could not abide by our late Pope's condemnation of a system based on Christian ideals of fraternity and equality, but I held his tongue in the highest esteem.'

'Maybe one day it'll be a relic,' I suggested.

'If so, it will certainly be shipped to Poland,' Mathilde replied. 'He is greatly loved there, by his people. And they will want more than his tongue.'

'Madame?' enquired Rachid.

'Really, please do call me Jane.'

'Madame Jane, please, I would like to wash my hands…' As I led him to the WC, Honoré, guided by Mathilde, began pressing the buttons, changing chapters and rhythms at a reckless speed, deforming the divine so as to better witness it. I tried to warn Rachid above the Pentecostal cacophony about our electric toilet and the lightning problem. *Faites attention à vous-même. Bonne chance, mon ami!*

Our dinner, by all accounts, was a success, the chicken diavola was served in seconds and thirds, the bottles of wine and Fanta soda merrily emptied, the ambience convivial; no-one seemed to mind Honoré's jaggers, which intensified up till dessert when Mathilde entertained us with a story that had the amazing effect of appeasing the colic. Though she hadn't meant to stay so long (Let us remember her words: *I shall only stay a minute*), Honoré's giggles and a nice bottle of Baume de Venise convinced her otherwise. Moreover, her uttered intention was apparently incongruent with her inner one, for she pulled from her bag as our cocktail commenced, a package of angels-on-horseback, a savoury of oysters wrapped in bacon which she brings to every feast or fête. Unfortunately our halowed guests could not enjoy them because of the ham. I served them a mixed-nut medley instead and marinated anchovies too.

By the end of Mathilde's story about a renegade Algerian girl, shunned by father and fiancé because of her love of Allah – a rather agile transposition of the Virgin Martyr narratives – Honoré was fast asleep in Charles's arms. I got up to make our guests some Turkish brew. Ahmed pulled at the whiskers of his left moon. Rachid, who ignores the prophet-imposed prohibition of his faith, poured himself another glass of Baume de Venise while Samir gazed wistfully into the empty orange bottle of Fanta. Perhaps I shouldn't have doused my rum baba with orange flower water to trick the law-abiding Samir and Ahmed into eating it. My ploy worked; they indulged, ignorant of their crime. Rachid sucked up the rum and kept quiet about it. There's no harm done I'm sure. We avoided ham which is the main thing, nothing cloven in this kitchen if you don't count the bacon on the angels-on-horseback.

'Uncles under the One God,' Mathilde addressed our guests. 'Have you ever in your life tried to imagine yourselves as women?' Her question would have taken us by surprise had not the preceding story, a feminist plea of sorts, prepared its way. Still, the magi now grew conspicuously quiet.

They looked uneasy. They shook their heads.

'Have you ever asked yourselves who your sisters really were?' Mathilde went on, encouraged by their bafflement. I could tell from the way her voice dipped rather than rose at the end of her question that she was about to launch into one of her manifestos. I say 'one of' because Mathilde expounds widely, her range of subjects increasing rather than diminishing over time.

She continued: 'Have you looked keenly at that mask of treachery that they've been made to wear and divined from its contours the truth of the woman behind it? I tell you that until you have peered into her, you will remain in ignorance of yourselves. In a world where family honour is still invested in the panties of its maidens, women are handy metaphors, likened to earthly ideals and commodities. Shrunk down into symbols they are more easily exploited. Poetic devices should serve the feminine cause but instead they have been turned into a sword against it and for this reason we must issue a new poetic license to

37

mystery. Let it be our chauffeur in our drive to explore the female heart. Can a mystery enlighten a mystery, you ask? I'm afraid this is the only way to go about it. To see the dark, one must use darkness as a guide, for by turning on the light, the darkness dissolves.'

'My sister Yasmine… my closest sister, beloved…' began Samir, lost in his thoughts. 'She left my parents' home to live with an atheist in Holland and I tell you, I had it in my mind and heart to murder the man. I could not bear to think of her corrupted, polluted by the demon-loving Dutchman.'

'I do not doubt you loved your sister dearly,' replied Mathilde. 'But I'm afraid you did not see her, for if you had, you would have noticed certain changes in her comportment prior to her flight; perhaps she flapped her arms before dinner to test her wings or maybe she dieted on asparagus in spring to lighten up and prepare for love. Did she ever complain about mending your clothes and tidying your room? Did she ever invite a fly into the soup she prepared for you? Such things must be observed.'

'You talk of shrouding women in mystery. But is this not what we Muslims do with the veil? This unfathomed nature of women you speak about is honoured and protected by it,' said Ahmed.

'Yes, I believe you are right. But I have always felt that the veil should not be opaque as they so often are, not so tightly pulled about the face. Rather they should be shimmering and transparent, made of fine silk, or if rayon, only of French make. And they should fall gently around the face, caressing the woman's cheeks, never rubbing or pulling against them. Irascible custom rather than God has erased the true purpose of the veil.' Having said this, Mathilde pulled up the cloth napkin that had been resting on her lap and affixed it up on her head to demonstrate her vision of veil wear, but the height of her bun and the small dimensions of the square checked napkin made it look instead like she had an Alice-in-Wonderland-style red and white mushroom on her head.

'I have given you a poor example, but I trust you see what I mean.' Mathilde, ever erect and elegant, did not flinch as Charles pulled the napkin down. Honoré woke up from his short nap, jaggering for milk. I took him in my arms and put him discreetly to my breast in the dim nursery just off the 'kitchen'. Through the door I kept my eye on our table; the magi, Mathilde and Charles sat in silence, contentedly, not needing to converse. The pause was not awkward but poised like a dancer in the spotlight: her performance has culminated and yet the atmosphere is ripe with possibility. For a short moment it felt as if a bright star flushed our table with light, separating us from the greater surround of night. Certainly it was not our little tea lights that provoked this sensation of being so suddenly incandesced; a feeling that some inner light in each of us fused with this larger source of illumination so that we became like matchsticks, lighting up in glowing flashes.

When all our guests finally left to find their beds, we regained our own blinking in the dark.

'Close your eyes, little Honoré,' I cooed to him. But his eyes were blinking too. And so we spent the rest of the night, like owls who widen their pupils to see all of the dark.

Chapter III

*Which recounts the malady called Laughing
Breasts Syndrome, the case of the stolen Vegans
and a secret assignation.*

Honoré is now sleeping in a wrought iron crib, a de La
Rochefoucault heirloom, which Mathilde dug out from her attic
at Thrushcross Castle. But the important change is not the going from
box to cot, but from a restless refusal of shut-eye to a genuine
enjoyment of slumber. He seems to have reached a minor age of reason,
in any case, he sleeps five-hour stretches now including a two-hour nap
– all in the crib. I am delivered of the daily marches, of my twenty-four-
hour diner duty. We've survived the chaos of chain feedings and have
settled into a rhythm that suits us both, though the Great Sensibility
continues its lactic journey, leaving my breasts forever itching and
irritated. Not even Dr Delamancha, our remedy man extraordinaire,
has a cure for this *inconvénient*. Upon Mathilde's urging and generous
offer to foot the expenses incurred, I at last made an appointment with
the thaumaturge for a Friday morning. At 8.00 a.m. Honoré and I

traipsed across town to his 16th arrondissement *cabinet,* ready to display our faultless latch-on technique, ready even to offer of squirt of milk for the purpose of scientific analysis if such a sample were required. But nothing so demonstrative was asked of us; Dr Delamancha, whose moustache is a superbly groomed replica of Gustave Flaubert's in his middling years, caressed the curling ends of it between two fingers as he looked at me. If he weren't Mathilde's trusty doctor, I would have thought he was undressing me with his brown beady eyes. Indeed perhaps he was, but to give him the benefit of the doubt, let us say that he did so with the intention of viewing the source of my ill underneath the tee (in this case a purple sleeveless from Tati), which was tight-fitting and thus demanded he sharpen his gaze all the more pointedly. After nearly five minutes of this inspection, during which I had no choice but to sing 'Itsy-Bitsy Spider' to amuse Honoré who has no patience with medics, *ma foi!,* a light seemed to go on in his head, radiating down to his fingers which began typing furiously at his computer's keyboard. At last he spoke:

'What you have, Madame, is a very rare manifestation of what we call in our colloquial French *le rire aux roberts.*' Here he gave us a smug, suggestive smile that made both Honoré and me blush. 'It is a pathology that afflicts the highly sensitive, the highly strung and the high tempered. Saint Catherine of Sienna, who as we know, frothed at the nerves, suffered from this same complaint during her bouts of spontaneous lactation. It is likely you will have such irritation as long as you nurse, but I will prescribe something that should help you along. Remember, Madame, it is better to have them laughing than weeping.'

I nodded my head in agreement, trying to imagine the sagging slope of jaggering breasts and accepted the homeopathic prescription he had made out for belladonna and nux vomica, and another I had never heard of – *ricinus communis*. So now we all know the truth: I have what is called Laughing Breasts Syndrome (LBS) and it is as irremediable as it is irritating. Try imagining any part of your body constantly in stitches and I think you'll get an inkling of just how annoying this is. And Lord knows what effect it's having on Honoré: will he develop a natural taste for the comic's trade? Will he rise as a stand-up comedian, a mouth full of chuckles? It is hard to imagine anyone named Honoré de La Rochefoucault performing live at the Yuk Yuk Club, but of course he could always take a *nom de guerre* which is what Jerry Lewis did with spectacular results in France.

But to return, dear reader, to our current predicament, which is hardly a laughing matter. If you remember, Honoré and I were visited upon by plainclothesmen Starsky and Hutch the morning after Mr Li's near drowning with mug shots of our magi who I purposefully failed to recognize, sending Messieurs S & H noisily down the six floors and out to their Torino, never, I presumed, to return to our flat on the rue de Meaux.

As it turned out, I presumed wrongly.

Charles returned that night from work, his face drawn with fatigue, his forelock too pooped and drenched in sweat to bounce against his brow.

'Darling, you look just awful! Come and have a seat on Jinn-Jinn.' I pointed to one of our cardboard boxes upon which I had set a round, pink candy-striped cushion, a hand-me-down from my mother who acquired it during her *I Dream of Jeannie* phase during which she tried to make the house look like the inside of Barbara Eden's bottle with two pin cushion sofas and lots of pink poufs and purple pom-poms;

everything was low on the ground, including my father who constantly tripped over the floor cushions. 'Oh Master!' Mother would cry out, pulling on her harem pants and pretending to care. That was not one of our brighter moments, but I'm glad I've kept Jinn-Jinn all the same and am thinking of renaming it Little Miss Muffet for Honoré's sake. Honoré flailed his limbs in excitement at seeing his papa, but I held him back, for clearly Charles needed a rest before being handed our babe. He sat on the pouf, but it failed to bolster him up; his shoulders drooped inward like a thirsty leaf.

'Let's get your father something to drink, something to perk him up, shall we?' I suggested cheerfully to Honoré, whisking him away to the room we call the kitchen where, in a *Bébé Cash* diaper box on the right, we keep the booze. 'A little gin-and-tonic for Papa? With a slice of lime?' Honoré gurgled the way bartenders sometimes do, when they've just bent down under the counter to take a slug on the sly. We prepared this cordial single-handedly as mothers with babes-at-breast are wont to do and brought it out on a platter – still using only right hand – with a bowl of pistachios.

'Thank you, dear,' said my knight as he absently lifted the G&T to his lips but aimed the glass too high so that he snorted the cocktail up his nose.

'Wrong substance, love. Here, let me help you.' I lowered the glass between his lips; he looked befuddled but was now positioned to drink. The liquid seemed to do him good, for he winked at Honoré and tapped his knees, inviting our son to sojourn there for a time.

'We had a visit today, Charles,' I began, measuring my words so as not to upset his cocktail hour unduly. 'Two inspectors dropped by. They were the spitting image of Starsky and...'

'I know who you mean,' he cut me off.

'Do you?'

'Apparently they were at the car wash today. My co-workers filled me in.'

'With mug shots of Ahmed, Rachid and Samir?' Charles nodded his head in response. I looked at him carefully: his bent shoulders were not simply slack from the *après-coup* of life-guarding; they were weighted down by a burden.

'Three Vegans were stolen yesterday. Samir, Rachid and Ahmed have also disappeared,' he offered at last.

'I see. But this could also be a coincidence, couldn't it?'

'I am certain it isn't.'

'So our wise men are car thieves?'

'No, not car thieves,' corrected Charles. 'But they have taken the cars, yes. No doubt.' It is so like Charles not to condemn his friends; as we Catholics know, it is far easier to repent when one says 'I have sinned' than when one proclaims, 'I am a sinner.'

'Listen, Charles. If they did steal them, I'm sure they had a good reason for doing so. We must have faith in our friends. Remember the rule of St Ignatius of Loyola: do not change your course of thinking when pursued by doubt, for the evil spirit is making an attempt to obstruct the good direction.'

'They have stolen the cars,' repeated Charles to himself.

'Their stealing the cars is not a problem in and of itself. It's the word "crime" that's weighing on you. It's pulling you down, Charles. But the notion is too general for our purposes. We must use discernment, try to understand the motives, and until we know more, mum's the word.' Charles nodded in agreement and began bouncing

Honoré on his knees, clearly relieved. I had given him a new perspective, shifted his focus from the climes of criminality to a clearer comprehension of the context.

As a Maraconi, I'm inclined to view events such as this with a high degree of relativity. It is as with determining the percentage of fat in unfermented cheese; one does not consider its brute weight but must subtract its water weight to get the exact measure of milk fat. In the case of crime, the underlying motivation is like the cheese's water; it keeps the crime afloat. And not until it has been subtracted and scrutinized, weighed for what it is, can we ponder the true nature and import of the improbity. The Maraconis have long taken this casuist perspective, perhaps because we are just small-time mobsters, rinky-dink Idaho players. Not one of my uncles ever took his racketeering to Chicago or New York. My cousins have extorted no farther east than Kentucky. We work the weighing stations, divvy up the degrees, for we don't have the choice; we cannot afford to dispense with our scales unlike our formidable brethren of the Cosa Nostra.

Two weeks went by after that first visit from Starsky and Hutch, during which we had no sign from our magi. Charles turned in his rubber gloves and sponge. The job had ended. We set up a makeshift desk in Honoré's room for him to compose upon while I took Honoré on morning and afternoon walks either to Buttes Chaumont or to Belleville, stopping at the Café Chéri(e) along the way for a mint tea. Honoré, I must say, loves cafés and has already had the pleasure of sipping a *grenadine* and a *menthe à l'eau* directly at the *zinc* where we take our drinks as if we were on the run and *sans le sou*, which most often we are, busy and broke. A series of salutary rainstorms then came and pummelled the heat down to the ground, clearing the air. This change in weather, of course, affected us most sanguinely; the daily business of taking Honoré on walks, grocery shopping and cooking on a single burner no longer oppressed us quite like before and required far less deodorant. In a word, our lives had at last, since the birth of Honoré, calmed to a reasonable extent, even though our sleep deprivation had us seeing double, even triple and Charles was dyslexifying his notes and had to return to rudimentary verbal compositions.

It was at about this time, after the rains, that we began to perceive odd noises, first the faint, cracking sound of a wood floor as if someone were tip-toeing on the planks above our heads in the vacant, sixth-floor apartment. Whoever this was, he had taken care to remove his shoes so that the wood creaked and popped as little as possible. We heard his footsteps at night and in the early morning but never the opening or closing of the door.

''Tis strange,' I said to Charles. 'There must be a new squatter up there, but how did he get in? We never heard anyone break the lock. In fact I went up there and the lock hasn't been changed. Should we try to call the owner?'

'Call Mathilde, then, to find out who the owner is. Of course she'll be delighted to know there's a squatter.'

'Yes, she is a firm believer in free-lodging and justice for all, isn't she? Remember how she battled to set up a tent-city on the parvis of Notre Dame for penniless pilgrims arriving for the Feast of the Assumption?'

'That was a courageous exploit indeed. And it would have worked had the Entreprise T.P. not reneged on their offer to donate the necessary port-a-potties. My mother has a generous heart.'

'She does, Charles. But I think we need to know who is living above us. What if he brings his family and relatives to live with him? And then we'd have ten people above us frying fritters and flushing the toilet at all hours. The noise would be terrible for you! How could you possibly compose? And just think about my nose!'

This final consideration pushed me to pick up the phone and call Mathilde. I am almost unbearably sensitive to odours, and the scent of deep frying, which is traditionally the preferred *mode de cuisson* of squatters according to a recent study published in the *Guardian Weekly*, makes me as woozy as the piscine perfume of Prince Rupert's vitamins.

'*Oui, ma chère. Tout va bien?* I was just about to call you, in fact…'

'You were? Well, it looks like I beat you to it! Everything's fine here, Mathilde, but we're wondering if you would happen to know who the owner of the flat above us is? It looks like someone has moved in…'

'I have no idea I'm afraid. But I'd like to see my *chéri.*'

'I'm sorry?'

'*J'aimerais voir mon chéri, à l'heure convenue.*' I was about to pass the phone to Charles, the '*chéri*' to whom I presumed she wanted to speak, but the persistent, enigmatic way she spoke hinted that she was trying to tell me something else entirely. The queer sensation this provoked in me brought back a particular memory of my grandfather, Pops Giuseppe. He was a musician, Pops, and not directly involved in his brother's shady dealings, but he shared his agile twists and turns of the mind. I remember one afternoon I spent with him at the park; I must have been only eight or so. I was skipping along beside him in my Mary-Janes, delighted to have my Pops all to myself. He kept singing in his mock Sinatra voice: 'Round and around she goes, where she'll stop nobody knows,' snapping his fingers in a jazzy kind of rhythm. I assumed he was referring to the park's Ferris wheel, which I adored and couldn't wait to get to. But then he made a sudden turn out through one of the gates of the park, pulling at my hand to follow. My heart sank but I didn't protest; I was hardly the apple of his eye – he was indifferent towards children – and knew I had to mind my manners to keep in his favour. We crossed the main avenue alongside the park, then turned onto a side street lined with warehouses. Pops kept singing his ditty, chuckling from time to time as if at a private joke between him and the song. At last we turned into a driveway that ran alongside a grey-blue brick building wreathed by dusty oleander bushes and weeds. Pops knocked on one of the screen doors; a woman's voice invited us in. She was probably in her late twenties, with very tan skin and an amazing blonde afro demonstrating a remarkable back-combing technique and the uncanny strength of maximum hold hair-glue. There was something harsh about her face, her features were too filed down and pointed for softness, yet she radiated with an almost unnatural vigour, an energy that seemed to make her sizzle irresistibly. She was seated, wearing a clay-spackled apple-green minidress, her bare feet firmly planted on either side of a potter's wheel. I remember her matching panties flashing like green light between her legs, and the wheel turning round and round while her hands molded the soft, wet clay into a chalice. Her name was Claris and she invited me to try the wheel, which I did, and while I did, she and Pops went into an adjoining room to take care of some 'business'. I may have been young, but I did realize as I splattered myself with clay that the business was rather sweet between Pops and Claris.

What I found out much later was that my grandfather, in addition to playing trumpet in the Laurence Welk Orchestra, had a vocation to reform prostitutes by training and hiring them to work in his pottery studios. I won't say he did this out of altruism or a deep desire to facilitate redemption; he was probably getting back at Uncle Al by stealing strumpets from his bordellos in Boise and Salt Lake City – there was always a skirt-chasing rivalry between them. But he had a remarkable deal really: all the sweethearts he wanted (for the repentant potters accommodated him freely, I was later told by my cousin Guido) and a thriving pottery business supplying post Vatican II Roman Catholic Churches with earthenware folk-mass utensils. He began the painstaking process of redeeming the Maraconi name, which my own father continued and culminated by becoming a tax lawyer, an honest gentleman by all accounts, who supports the local symphony and the shopping addiction of his second wife Shirley.

But the point I'm trying to make is that it was during this afternoon I have just described that I became aware of codes, of their secret nature that banded together those privy to them. A code erects walls around itself, it is a fortress if you will, meant to keep out foes and fools. Pops was testing me with his song, lowering the drawbridge, then pulling it back up before I could scramble to cross it. I was thinking Ferris, he was singing Claris. When my eyes at last alighted on the potter's wheel, I giddily marched across the bridge and into the citadel, joining ranks with Pops and Claris and all the other girls at the wheel. It is only now I realize this was a valuable lesson for me, one that I drew upon as Mathilde uttered her queer request.

'Very well, Mathilde. I will see you then, *à l'heure convenue*,' I replied before hanging up the phone. I was pensive for a moment, trying to decipher her message.

'Pray, what did Mother say?' asked Charles.

'She wants me to meet her at the Café Chéri(e) it seems, on Friday at eleven, after her monthly CFC meeting.' Much to my surprise, the answer to the riddle came spontaneously as if of its own volition. 'There is something she wants to tell me in secret. Goodness! Do you think our line is tapped?'

'I should certainly hope not. No, no, you know how she dislikes the phone. If she has something important to tell us, she prefers to do so in person, without the distortion of wires.'

Two days later, on the Friday in question, I put Honoré in a kangaroo pouch and walked us both down the Boulevard de La Villette, past the Communist Party Headquarters and its astounding egg, to which we waved a red hankie, past the Café Narval Tabac and its hirsute tic-tac-toe players, past a primitive portrait of Cleopatra on the Café Cairo's window, past the Doner kebab Turk with its shaggy wrap-around roast on a skewer, until we spied the endearing red walls of the Café Chéri(e) and its rows of rain-damaged school tables out front. It is a homely place, really, with aluminium rimmed windows and a grey, concrete floor riddled with grime-filled fault lines, but someone took care to put up mock crystal chandeliers, retrieved probably from the Montreuil flea market, to light up its great red arena. Honoré and I went up to the counter and ordered an apricot juice. The barmaid Adèle, whose three mutts trail behind her in a mangy cortège as she serves and tidies tables, and whose little white apron matches her blanched, short clipped hair, not only in hue but amazingly, in shape as well, treated Honoré to a round of *Ainsi font font font, les petites marionettes*. This added to the fun of being up at the bar, but when she left us to serve her tables, we realized that our wait had grown long. At 11:20 Mathilde still had not shown up. Ten minutes later I found myself cursing her under my breath and knew that I had to get the pent-up rage out of me, for once it started to churn, it became too lethal to keep in. Adèle kindly agreed to hold Honoré and let her jealous dogs yip and yap while I skipped to the loo. Therein, I turned on the tap full blast, flushed both toilets simultaneously before cursing Mathilde at the top of my lungs, for there are few things that anger me more than being stood up by my mother-in-law. Fortunately no-one came seeking relief in the WC as I ranted, but I am quick at purgation. It took me no more than three minutes to vent and atone, which really is astounding considering how long most people spend in the bathroom! I returned to the bar, quite energized really and had to hide my giggle when Honoré drooled into a customer's beer; he was hanging over Adèle's shoulder happy as can be, right above the four *pressions* she had just milked from the tap. It'll bring them good luck, I thought to myself as he dropped another pearl of drool in the Kronenbourg. And I sighed at the thought of our wee one's purity; his poop is but buttermilk, his drool fresh as dew. Thoughts only a mother-in-love can harvest. Then suddenly, the jaggers!

'Oh Honoré, what's wrong, love?' I held out my arms and took him from Adèle's shoulder. 'Did a fly land on your nose?' But I could tell it wasn't that; Honoré needed his milk fix and fast. I placed him in the football hold position and sprinted to the black vinyl seats in the very back. The foam stuffing was popping out like the spongy innards of a French cheesecake, the kind that are burnt on top on purpose. But neither Honoré nor I minded the lumpy sofa; our main mission was milk, which we got to very quickly. A bit of fumbling at first, but then Honoré latched on to his laughing source of sustenance. While I can't say I find nursing pleasurable, it never fails to relax me, to loosen the grip of daily pressures and concerns. It limbers the mind, loosens the joints, paves the way for transcendence or sleep. I do wonder what particular illuminations Simone de Beauvoir or Virginia Woolf would have had, had they written under the milky spell of breast-feeding. Might they have spawned a new literary genre or movement? Imagine us now referring to Boobsbury or Breastentialism. Heavens! One can only speculate of course, but in my case, just as the hind milk came flooding through my breasts with its vitamin-packed nutrients, I felt a door in my mind open, and standing at this threshold appeared the true meaning of Mathilde's code.

'Oh my God, Honoré! We've got it all wrong. What she meant by *Chéri* was the Holy Sacrament! Which means the meeting time is at 5 p.m. at the Eglise de Saint Gervais when Mathilde baby-sits Jesus! Why, of course! How did I get so off track? Well, it doesn't matter, does it, Honoré, let's go home for a little nap. Mother makes mistakes when she's too tired.'

At four-thirty, after a blessed two-hour nap I might add, Honoré and I rode the métro to Hôtel de Ville. Saint Gervais church, our destination, faces the back end of the Town Hall and flaunts it buttresses at the Seine. The upkeep and maintenance of this minor Gothic jewel is assured by a charismatic order of brothers and sisters of which Charles's Cousin Constance is an associate member. Cousin Constance is a confirmed virgin and wears a rope and a rosary around her waist. When she is not vacuuming the tatami floor of Saint Gervais, she administers to circus gypsies at the Porte de Pantin. Mathilde is particularly fond of her and feeds her as often as she can at Thrushcross Castle to make up for her poor diet of merguez sausage sandwiches, which is what the circus folk eat. As we walked along the nave to the ambulatory, I kept my eye out for Cousin Constance, but there was no sign of her or her hoover. It must have been one of her gypsy days.

The chapel of the Holy Sacrament is protected by an elaborate iron gate with gilded spikes at the top so that in good Gothic fashion the devil would be speared up the bum if he ever tried to land thereupon. Its door was open for the daily Adoration Hour. Inside several worshipers in white robes knelt before the Lord who lay, transubstantiated, in unleavened discs in the golden illuminated ciborium. Mathilde, kneeling on the stone floor, her back as white and straight as a pillar of salt, was clearly in the lead. Though all these prayerful souls were racing to get closer to the Lord, it was a seemingly static race, in which the spirit did the moving. If you watched closely enough, however, if your eye grew attuned to the spiralling subtleties of the spirit, whose very mobility agitated the immobility of these worshiping salt pillars, you would notice that Mathilde was nevertheless advancing toward the Lord at a faster rate than the rest. To illustrate this, perhaps it is best to think of snails, who without legs or any sensible means of locomotion, slither imperceptibly in their race to the Leaf, their innards needy of Sustenance.

I hesitated to enter the chapel, apprehending the effect this particularly intense vibratory context might have upon Honoré, who was liable to come down with the jaggers at any minute, but remembered that Mathilde had stressed I meet her *à l'heure convenue* by which she meant Adoration Hour. I looked at my watch; there were only ten minutes left of the sixty. I would have to take my chance. With Honoré in the pouch, facing outward, towards Jesus, I knelt down beside Mathilde, swaying every so gently so that Honoré could adore the Lord to-and-fro. We waited while Mathilde, transfixed, made her imperceptible journey to the ciborium. I was beginning to think it very possible that she simply did not sense our presence, when suddenly, I found in front of my knees a missalette which seemed to have journeyed to me as invisibly as Mathilde herself was travelling to the Almighty Host. She had clipped a message on it scribbled in red ink and punctuated with exclamation marks:

Our magi are fine and well! The cars are kept quiet in the stable! There is no squatter upstairs by the way: it's the police! You are being watched! Careful! Come to Thrushcross on Sunday! Make sure you are not followed!

The worshipers began rising, crossing themselves before leaving the chapel. Mathilde remained, however, as she always does, until *Père Hublon* came to fetch Jesus for mass consumption. She cannot bear to leave Him alone, unattended. Perhaps she fears He might fall from His golden dish, animated by the same imperceptible force that advanced her towards Him.

'Mathilde,' I whispered, pointing to her scribbled message. 'What on earth does this mean?'

'Just what it says, *ma chère*. Everything is fine, really, but we must be careful. Komrad Kerkorian, my staunch Armenian ally, has been of inestimable help; he has turned the oubliette into a dormitory, which works nicely. They all have beds.'

'*Ma foi!* Do you realize the risks!' My whisper rose, grew raspy. I made Honoré whimper. Mathilde looked down at her watch.

'It's ten after. Please stay here with Jesus while I fetch *Père Hublon.*'

'I don't know if Honoré will be able to handle it, Mathilde. He's getting antsy.'

'Tell him about the Blessed Mother,' she advised as she crossed herself with great solemnity.

For the next fifteen minutes I sang nearly the entire repertoire of my rock opera *Away in a Manger* into Honoré's ear, giving him the whole story as it were, from Saint Anne giving birth to the immaculate Mary, then to Mary's visit with Elizabeth, the birth of the Baptist, and finally Jesus. All in the presence of Jesus himself, who never once butted in to correct me on a misleading detail. Honoré did seem to enjoy it all, particularly when I tickled his toes, which is what Marie Antoinette does to Louis XVI in the opera as she breaks the news about the holy bun in her oven. When Père Hublon finally relieved us of our baby-sitting duty, we returned to the nave to find Mathilde. But she was again on her knees, singing the psalms, eyes shut, hands stretched out. There was no reaching her. Up at the altar, I saw Cousin Constance, not with the gypsies after all, but here amongst us – she is prone, I might add, to make uncanny appearances and disappearances like sages and Blackfoot Indians do. She led the singing in her high, angelic voice. I do suspect that she levitates, that without that rope and rosary anchoring her down, she would walk six inches off the ground quite contentedly. Yet for the sake of the superstitious circus gypsies, who were unlikely to see the hand of God pulling her up by the top of her head, and surely to avoid osteoporosis, which can be kept at bay by increasing foot-to-ground impact, she wraps the rope around her waspish waist every day.

Constance is an attractive girl, petite, blonde, though she definitely needs to use a better moisturizer. She has adhered to the ways of the gypsies but forgets that she does not have their oil. I don't care how hard you pray, the Lord just does not provide anything better than Nivea cream and if Cousin Constance used just a blob or two, it would be an improvement. Her flaking skin aside, I must say her best asset is a cherry-shaped bum, which I was privileged enough to glean last

Christmas at Thrushcross Castle when I unintentionally surprised her in the bathroom just as she was lifting her treasure from the tub. How quickly she covered it with a towel, yet still I was witness, perhaps the sole ever, to this delightful tush that has sadly been given an early retirement. Is it possible that the pleasure of levitation equals or surpasses earthly pleasures? Alas, I shall never know!

Honoré and I genuflected before sneaking out on the psalms. 'Wait till your father hears about this, love,' I whispered in his ear. 'But not to worry,' I reassured him, sensing the jaggers coming on. To be honest, I was near to jaggering myself, but held strong for my son and added with as much confidence as I could muster:

'Your gran has a plan.'

Chapter IV

Which recounts a surreptitious visit to
Thrushcross Castle, a meeting with the magi
and Cousin Constance's run-in with
the wash-and-dry.

On Sunday, Charles, Honoré and I left the flat at around ten. Our destination was Thrushcross Castle, but we made it appear that we were going for our Sunday walk along the Canal St Martin with our usual stop at the Café Chaland, where the owner has earned himself a reputation as *Monsieur Propre* (of cleaning detergent fame) though he sometimes changes the gold hoop earring for a two-centimetre diamond stud. His toilet bowl, incidentally, is always impeccable. In fact we did head toward the Chaland, but then turned on the Passage Delessert, and again on the rue Pierre Dupont where Charles had parked the car the night before, in preparation for this getaway. No sign of Starsky or Hutch. As Charles pointed out quite rightly, our upstairs neighbour could well be an entirely different cop. After all it is hard to imagine either Starsky or Hutch tiptoeing *en point*.

Thrushcross Castle lies at the edge of the forest, though it seems to be a prolongation of it, for the grounds are in fact a great woodsy terrain, without any formal French garden. There is, however, a substantial vegetable plot and a rosary, which Mathilde tends to as an afterthought; it is wildly overgrown with weeds, but the roses, when they begin their bloom, do so with an angry abandon and according to a vital insouciance that brings their beauty to a disconcerting pitch of colour and whorls. I don't believe I've ever seen Scarlet Fires so deeply red, or Manuelas so richly carmine. The flowers unfold with such wild violence that Mathilde will only go near them wearing the protection of apiarian apparel. As for the vegetable garden in the bailey outside the kitchen, it is looked after by the homeless and rehabilitating women, or *demoiselles d'honneur* as Mathilde whimsically refers to them, who lodge in the belfry; they tend to it well, for the fruit of their labour – the cabbages, carrots, Swiss chard, courgettes, potatoes and tomatoes – is what feeds them. The demoiselles cook all the castle meals under the supervision of Anoushka, a Russian émigré whose former incarnation as a ballerina is evinced by her outward pointing toes and the extreme perpendicularity of her feet to her legs. Mathilde is convinced she will not advance in life outside the castle unless she learns to point her toes northward and out the postern door. The demoiselles also keep chickens in the dovecote, and a sty of hogs which provides the necessary bacon for angels-on-horseback.

The castle itself is a *Château Fort*, that has long housed Charles's ancestors and protected them from various barbaric invasions, particularly those occurring during the Hundred Years War. While it is a fine example of medieval architecture, it was never intended to be a showcase-style hunting resort as were its seventeenth-century counterparts that dot the French countryside like celebratory cakes erected in stone. No, Thrushcross is a beautiful but serious castle, one that we even might consider, with a stretch of our imaginations, as having communist connotations. After all, it has always housed the needy in simple but adequate style. The fact that it is sadly dilapidated, that its murther holes spit unruly splays of morning glory and nasturtiums and that its crumbling *échauguette* presents a hazard to passers-by below, reflects Mathilde's predicament: without funding from the Communist Party, how can she possibly maintain the upkeep of such a commodiously accommodating fortress? Certainly, her name alone, no matter how noble and well-meaning, cannot adequately foot the bill, which is what Mathilde has long been arguing in her missives to the *Partie*. It is simply remarkable that Mathilde has kept this stately commune alive by hook and by crook; but then, she has a remarkable gift for delegating tasks, which only those of true faith and confidence possess, and for inspiring the total devotion of those she helps.

When we at last pulled into the chestnut tree lined drive that cuts through the forest to Thrushcross, we spied Komrad Kerkorian who, with the lingering but persistent force of his eighty-year-old sinews, was pushing a wheelbarrow full of wood towards the castle.

'Greetings, comrades!' He set down his load for just a moment. 'Your mother is waiting for you. Go on now. I'll be there in a minute. We'll be needing to light a fire this afternoon…' Komrad Kerkorian is forever at work and always lighting fires in the fireplace no matter the weather. He runs permanently cold, due to some unmentionable torture inflicted upon him by the Nazis when he was caught as a resistant in the Maquis. He was only fourteen when all the heat was siphoned from his body, but he was lucky and clever enough to have escaped with his life. Charles got out of the car to give him a hand and I was about to skit my way over the gearshift to take the wheel, but Komrad Kerkorian was determined to wheelbarrow his way back to the castle alone. He keeps himself warm through incessant labour when not seated at the hearth.

'Say, Charles,' I remarked as we parked the car next to Mathilde's decrepit *Deux Chevaux*, pointing to two cloaked figures walking side-by-side toward the stables. 'It looks like your mother has some monks as guests.'

'It could be Frère Jacques, or even Frère Pierre-Hugh. It's hard to tell from here.'

Just then, one of the hooded monks turned around and waved at us energetically. He pulled on the other brother's arm, and they both headed our way.

'Goodness! That looks like…'

'Frère Jacques?'

'That's not who I see… or at least who I think I see…'

The monks approached quickly; it was impossible to make out their faces, but their walk was distinctly St Denis; they moved with urban attitude, the cocky strut of rap stars who thrust hips forward to take the world on with their crotches.

'Asalaam Alaikum,' Charles greeted them, holding out his hand. 'I'm glad to see you're well.'

'We're good,' said Samir from beneath his hood 'Your mother's taking care of us. Can't say we like these Christian robes much but I don't suppose we have a choice, do we? Ahmed refuses to dress up as a

Nazarene so he has to stay underground in the oubliette. I couldn't do that myself. I need air and sun. Life!'

'Not to mention all the girls living here…' added Rachid with a smile that a holy brother is only allowed to issue at the mention of good brew.

'You're monks, remember?' I warned. 'Play your part and forget the girls. They are homeless which means they can make their home anywhere, with you or with the chief of police.'

'A man never lost his life from looking,' replied Rachid.

'I'm sure you're wrong about that,' I said, and nearly launched into the story of Orpheus who lost not his life but his wife, by attempting a forbidden glance, but Mathilde came scooting out on her Keds, white wisps of escaped hair freeing her face of its usual severity.

'Where's Honoré?' she cried out, causing unnecessary alarm, for he was asleep in his car seat, happily dozing. Charles went to fetch him and set up the pram. 'Thank goodness!' she sighed with relief. 'I was afraid one of the demoiselles had already got to him before me!'

One of the things I appreciate most about coming to Thrushcross Castle is all the feminine arms, loving and eager, that reach out to hold Honoré, sharing in that primordial maternal task. I do perform it lovingly, but I also need respite from holding the baby, allowing me a brief moment of empty arms. Mathilde, on the other hand, while taking great pains to infuse her sorority with a spirit of sisterly comradeship, nevertheless confuses her outreaching daughters for competitors; I do believe this is the only instance where such a blight to her principals holds sway. Could it possibly be that Honoré brings out the closet capitalist in her? Perhaps we should not go so far. She is after all Honoré's grandmother; and why shouldn't she be given first dibs?

Mathilde gripped the pram's handlebar with proprietary pride as she pushed Honoré into the Grand Hall. I followed behind, while Charles went with 'Brother Robert' and 'Brother Samuel' to check on the Vegans in the stables.

'We're having a private lunch today, exceptionally,' Mathilde explained. 'I told the demoiselles we had family matters to discuss. And… Now, how are we going to do this?' Mathilde looked up from the pram at the narrow helical staircase that led to her quarters in the donjon.

'No problem, I'll just unhook the seat and carry him up.' But as I fumbled with the latch, I shook the pram a bit too roughly causing Honoré to arouse from his comfortable morning nap. And as always, upon waking – we must remember how hard it is for wee ones to be sharply snapped out of milky (I assume there is a great deal of this involved) dreamland – he offered us an impressive round of jaggers amplified by the castle's peculiar acoustics, for the thick stone walls seem to draw out and expand the sound from its source before absorbing it entirely, in a callous asphyxiation.

'Oh dear,' said Mathilde, 'I can hear them coming!' Busy as I was trying to console Honoré, I only lent Mathilde half an ear, though I was a tad annoyed her focus was not with me in my efforts to comfort. 'Up the stairs! Up the stairs! *Ma foi!*' she sputtered looking over her shoulder. The sound of women's bantering and laughter emerged from the left corridor behind us. 'We must go *now!*'

'But I can't, Mathilde! Don't you see that I'm about to change his diaper!' I was struggling to pull a diaper out of a Tati bag, but my one operational hand was unable to extract it from the coil of violin strings Charles had tossed in. 'And I could use some help, damn it!'

'Certainly,' said Mathilde, responding promptly to my profanation. She took Honoré from me – and just in time. For the demoiselles were upon us, or rather their hands were, waving at us like that multi-membered Indian goddess forever armed to the hilt with bracelets and bangles. Though these girls were bare-wristed, their hands were scented with parsley and lemon and something else hinting of peppery sweetness – perhaps paprika? Honoré's little head and brow were anointed by fingers fresh with ingredients, his skin lightly oiled by olive fruit in this pagan baptism which Mathilde tried to fend off, dipping and ducking as she did. But the sensate novelty of the adventure – the scents of home-cooked food, of female baby high (yes, this too has a smell, like pancake batter) – took Honoré from jaggers to giggles. A contagious chorus of laughter rose and protracted ecstatically before fading out in ghoulish waves of distorted echoes.

'You will have your turn later,' Mathilde told them as she at last managed to dart up the stairs with Honoré bouncing on her shoulder. '*Ma foi!* I've barely had a chance to hold him!' The giddy hands returned to their apron pockets reluctantly; there were sighs and moans of dismay. I, of course, could not afford to douse their desire; their arms were for me a haven, one that offered those last lingering vestiges of Jane Maraconi, the person I was before I became the Mother of Honoré, the possibility of momentary revival. Without a babe in arms, I was afforded, if even for a half an hour, the illusion of blossoming once again into that carefree narcissus. To think that once upon a time I could spend a leisurely hour in a foaming bath adding and subtracting water on a whim whilst sifting through the pages of *Glamour* to find out the true Secrets of the Slim! and *Gourmet* to eschew all calorific constraints for the sake of culinary sublimation! To think that I would submit myself to nearly every fashion fetish and mutation of the pedestrian jean and then worry endlessly about panty-lines (still a bit of a problem)! Or that I worried excessively over the epilation of my eyebrows! Do I miss that old Jane? I do, though certainly not enough to harbour any ounce of regret about the birth of the Mother of Honoré; revisiting old Jane from time to time suffices. Perhaps this appears paradoxical: how can you terribly miss something yet be satisfied to return to it only at specifically designated visiting hours? But transformations are never the clear-cut affairs we expect them to be; they might be unalterable, yet they are hardly disconnected from their prior incarnation. Mathilde likes to say that anyone who looks at the butterfly and doesn't see the chrysalis in its nervous flutter has only the flattest faculty for the ontological. But then she is coming from Catholicism which holds that the Word is made Flesh and that the Flesh is there for us to eat. And while we celebrate transubstantiation for the perk it is, we also remember that in the beginning was the Word. As simple as that: the Word.

But as I was saying, it is always in my best interest to keep on the good side of the demoiselles if only to get that occasional glimpse of the word I once was – Jane – before fleshing out triptychly (five extra pounds for each part of the name) into the Mother-of-Honoré. Incarnation I'm afraid, inevitably adds on the pounds.

'He'll be right down,' I assured the demoiselles. 'He's dying to see you! How about after lunch…' But my voice was swallowed up by the stone coil of the stairwell and the handle of the Tati bag had just broken, obliging me to concentrate on finding a way to grip the slippery pink-and-white checked plastic. I hadn't managed to change Honoré but now, in his grandmother's arms, he didn't seem to care a bit.

Mathilde led me to the main room of her quarters, a spacious, sparsely furnished hall the family called Sans Peur in tribute to the fourteenth century Duke of Bourgogne, Jean sans Peur, who once, as legend has it, caused a great scare therein by setting his wet breeches too near the hearth before bedtime; they caught fire and nearly burned down the castle. There even remains from that era a long, wooden table with lion's feet that has valiantly weathered the devastations of time, with the help of expert refurbishing and beeswax. Mathilde keeps a white linen cloth on it at all times and a bouquet of her garden roses, all the more heady from being beheaded, releasing their perfume with the generous desperation of a threatened skunk. Apart from the ancestral table, an impressively large monastery wardrobe and a wood scriptorium, the few furnishings decorating the space make up a mish-mash of styles and epochs. None of the chairs sitting around the table at their own stately banquet match. Their styles range from Louis XIV, to Napoleon III, to Bauhaus, each one in its way a silent historian of the comforts and discomforts of the human behind. Then there is a burgundy leather sofa, and four duchess armchairs, all hand-me-downs from Mathilde's designer friend of Trianon fame. For floor coverings Mathilde has opted for herbs in the medieval tradition of her forebears; between the stones, in that sliver of space, the earth makes up for its meagreness by growing dwarf varieties of lavender, germander, sweet fennel and mint. Needless to say, this vegetal tapestry adds to the dampness of an already dampish abode, which is why the large fireplace once overly fond of John-without-fear's trousers, is kept alight most all year round, expect of course during heatwaves. At the height of summer it is also incumbent upon Mathilde to water twice a day with her Barbès teapot. As in the grand hall below, this vast chamber has ten elongated bevelled windows on the east and west sides; they were added some time in the 1700s when Rousseau was twice entertained in the very room by the poetic recitations of Charles's ancestor, Guillaume Edouard de La Rochefoucault, on the Holy Spirit's influence on the mores of converted animists – such were the issues of the day. I, however, had my own concerns.

'What is going on here, Mathilde,' I queried as I changed Honoré's diaper on the couch. 'With the stolen cars…'

'There's nothing to worry about. Now tell me, is Honoré getting enough milk?' The enough-milk question, as any nursing mother will agree, provokes in the maternal provider, that industrious twenty-four-hour diner, a strong desire to slap the offender silly. But I controlled that instinct and instead, turned the question differently.

'Does the Lord get enough love? There is no way to measure that, but certainly He thrives.' Putting it in catechism terms, as a matter held in the hands of faith, conveyed my point to Mathilde.

'Well, he is looking wonderfully well,' she corrected herself. 'He takes after Charles, long and lean.' I set a blanket on the floor and lay Honoré thereupon on his back. He kicked his spindly legs with gusto, gurgled happily.

'Just assure me one thing,' I returned to what was worrying me.

'*Ma foi!* What is this now?' Mathilde sounded annoyed; her chin jutted out defensively, its subtle cleft trembled in protest.

'Just tell me you're not trying to convert our Muslim friends.' To be honest, I normally would not have suspected Mathilde of plotting a conversion scheme, but with the sight of Rachid and Samir in monk-wear, cloaked like Capuchins on their way to a hops harvest, this possibility flickered at my consciousness.

'I would have thought that by now,' she replied, with great *sérieux* calibrating each word as befits a Countess, 'having joined our family four years ago, you would come to understand our ways and our values. Of course, we do not expect you to comprehend everything right away. But what you have said pains me, for it manifests such disregard for our convictions.'

'I meant no harm, Mathilde. Don't take it too roughly. It's just that you get these Muslims dressed up as monks. I mean, for them, it's a kind of heresy. I can't understand how they've agreed to go along with it.'

I was speaking *en connaissance de cause*, for prior to meeting Charles I had nearly committed myself to a Mohammedan; a man who though only a mild practitioner of Islamic ritual, refused to enter cathedrals and churches, even the state-owned wonders of Notre Dame and Chartres Cathedral, fearing Christian contamination. For him I happily gave up ham, grilled the meat of beasts whose throats were slit to the cry of *bismillah*, and even wore a potato sack (he kept one in his car) over my mini skirts whenever we visited his family on a lark. None of this I minded, and in the end it was not the contradiction of our faiths that parted us, but his livid jealousy of my rock operas. Certainly this is not the time to expand on my failed interfaith romance; suffice it to say that his companionship afforded me an inside view of Muslim sensitivity to the perfidiousness lurking in the infidel habitat. Imagine missing the wonder of Chartres' stained glass glories, the gothic, candle-lit organ concerts of Notre Dame for fear of catching Christianity! But so it is, and this is why I could not help but suspect Mathilde of being on the conversion track, for how else could she have managed to monk them up?

'*Ma fille*, it is not me you have underestimated but the Holy Spirit,' Mathilde replied, her delicate nostrils expanding as air coursed through them. 'The de La Rochefoucaults do not convert; we have no need to. We are quiverers, tuning forks by which the human pitch is attuned to the Holy Spirit.'

As odd as this sounded, I had an inkling of what she was talking about; I have often seen Charles taken up in quivers at his composing desk before putting pen to paper.

'So it's a bit like the quaking of the Quakers or the rolling of the Holy Rollers.'

'Heavens no! Nothing so crude or orgiastic! This quivering is a way of fine-tuning the fractal experience of the divine, of following the minute increments by which the logic of faith is made manifest. It is painstaking not charismatic; its principle device is discernment, the caterpillar's quiver. You must review your St Teresa of Avila, Jane.'

'Yes, I suppose I should. Didn't the devil break her arm? I'll look it up… but, how did you, *tu sais*, get our magi in those hoods?'

'This is precisely what I'm trying to explain to you. Tell me, how did Teresa manage to steer her way through the tangle of treacheries, the lies of suspicious prelates and jealous Ecclesiastes? It was because she was able to determine that exact degree of the heart's escarp, where it falls away and fails its divine purpose. In a sense she was a geometer, inching her way over the terrain, so that she learned by stealth, how to transform a clod of earth into the cornerstone of her castle…'

There was, of course, no response I could offer to this. When Mathilde begins talking alchemy and inchworms I simply listen. Like so many things about my mother-in-law, how she managed the Muslims will remain a mystery. I bent down to give Honoré a tickle under the chin, his little cleft quivering ever so slightly. Oh dear, I thought, they do start young in this family. And I suddenly saw Honoré as being so completely other than me, a beneficiary by birthright of the de La Rochefoucault gene pool and secrets, its geometers and tuning forks.

'It is an excellent disguise, Mathilde. I commend you on getting it over their heads.'

'It seems to be working well,' she replied pragmatically just as the sound of someone approaching caught our attention.

'That'll be Padre Las Vegas,' she said interpreting the footsteps in the stairwell. 'Cousin Constance might join us as well,' she added. 'It all depends on if she finishes in time at the encampment – the gypsies are cleaning out their campers today and she's giving them a helping hand. She is very dedicated, you know... the little ones are due to make their First Communion in April; and she's started a rosary circle that's working quite nicely; the women pray with chapelets of peas... Oh Padre, do come in. Come in, come in! You must see Honoré!'

Mathilde picked up the baby and held him facing outward, towards the priest whose cheerful arrival was hampered by a limp; he advanced with the physical apprehension of a man stepping down off a bus with no railing for support. A small, wiry fellow with high Indian cheekbones and a long Spanish nose, Padre Las Vegas acquired his distinct disability in an El Salvadorian militia attack. The four other priests who had been with him on the doomed mini-bus that hit a Claymore mine had given up the ghost at the sacrificial occasion, but Padre Las Vegas was spared. He got off with a shattered hip-bone that was locally repaired by a medicine man for whom the Holy Spirit is said to transform into whatever surgical tool is required – in this case bone-glue. His good fortune continued as Mathilde, through her various

71

Liberation Theology contacts, learned of his plight and helped to have him imported fifteen years ago. He has stayed ever since, preferring to contribute to social justice from abroad, by giving PowerPoint presentations throughout France and Spain on how Jesus (primary sustenance of the poor, peppered with Marx and salted with Hegel) has empowered the powerless, given hope to the hopeless. Unfortunately few attend his lectures, for this is the Old World where folks are not so accustomed to the shake-and-bake doctrines of the New World, to our highly seasoned attempts at fashioning our inheritance of hybrid genes, Enlightenment and Socialist Christianity into a pie with equal proportions for all. May he carry on valiantly, Padre Las Vegas, and while he does so, I shall return to my narration of his appearance among us.

'Would you like to hold the Sacred Child, Padre?' Mathilde uncurled Honoré's index and middle finger, held them together by the tips as in the icons. My babe obliged her with this sleight of hand; he was in good humour, perhaps sensing that his role in this tableau vivant was the leading one. He played it with quick, efficient passion and then curled his tiny fingers back into a fist to suck on.

'It is a beautiful child. Looks much like the father,' said Padre Las Vegas as he gently tugged Honoré's kiss curl. 'Where is Charles?' he asked, glancing around the room.

'Away…' I began, then hesitated, not knowing if Padre was in the know. 'In the manger,' I went on, encouraged by a nod from Mathilde. '*Con los hermanos moros…*'

'*Muy bien, muy bien.*'

'Constance! Why, you made it!' exclaimed Mathilde, seeing beyond all three of us to where the new arrival appeared in a dreadful state, her usually blonde hair now an ashy hue from the accumulation of dust and soiled hay that clung to it; her face and white robe smeared with grime and what could very well have been animal dung – it certainly smelled like it.

'Are the campers spotless?' asked Mathilde.

'*Tout à fait*,' she replied. 'I swept their entire encampment, including under the trailers and around the elephant cage. *Ma foi!* The smells were alarming but Saint Francis narrowed my nostrils. I was not so bothered after that.'

'Now please take yourself, Constance, to the wash-and-dry; we will sit down to eat at half past.'

'I thought the wash-and-dry was out of order,' I remarked as Constance disappeared, for the last time we stayed at the castle this unusual shower contraption of outsized sponges and vibrating towels, motorized to clean and tickle a body dry at amazing speed, was shut up in its garderobe, gathering rust.

'Samir, I am happy to say, has successfully repaired it. He is a superb mechanic. He has now put himself to work inventing a portable wash-and-dry for the feet ablutions required of Muslims before prayer. The feet are the most difficult part, what with washing between the toes. Many a man is late for the prayer because of this.'

'Speaking of the devil…'

'Do watch your tongue,' Mathilde reprimanded. And she took her vaporiser of eau de Lourdes and sprayed some at Satan, or rather my mention of him. Just like Saint Teresa of Avila who used holy water similarly whenever she sensed the devil sniffing around.

Samir arrived with his hood thrown back; his long, narrow face exhibiting both an alarming candour and opacity, the expression of a young man caught between love of home and love of freedom, in short, a boy puzzled by both his larger and immediate predicament. Did he think Mathilde was going to wet him too?

'Come and join us,' encouraged Mathilde as Charles and Rachid followed behind him. 'We'll be sitting down to lunch once Constance has been wash-and-dried. *Ma foi!* I do hope she finds the shampoo.'

'More importantly, Mathilde, I hope you left the Nivea cream where she can see it.'

'I don't believe I did… it seems to me I gave it to Padre some time ago… for his dry elbows.'

I fumbled in my Tati bag for Honoré's calendula cream.

'You don't mind, love, do you?' I asked Honoré, holding up the yellow tube. 'It would do Cousin Constance a world of good.' Honoré, now in Charles's arms, gave me a gummy smile full of generosity and the drool it induces.

'Be right back!' I kissed his wee forehead before taking the stairs up to the next floor to find Constance. From the hallway I heard the shower being turned on and the motor of the wash-and-dry starting up. I wondered if I should wait, or knock on the door but as I was debating the best course of action to take, there came a piercing scream. Then:

'*Seigneur! Au secours! Au secours!*'

'Cousin Constance! What's happened?' I burst into her private cabinet, the door to which she thankfully had not locked (most unusual for a Virgin!), and found her caught between the two huge body scrubbing sponges of the contraption. They were closing in on her, or trying to, propelled by the motor, which was grinding with the effort. Why she had not entered the wash-and-dry sideways, but frontally, I have no idea. Perhaps for reasons of modesty? To avoid the touch of the brush on her most private regions? However noble and worthy of a Confirmed Virgin her motivation may have been, the brushes were nevertheless squeezing her mercilessly.

'Turn it off! Turn it off!' she screamed.

'But where's the button?' I looked frantically for the switch.

'There! There! Over there!'

'But where's there?' Unable to point, for her arms were locked against her sides by the machine, she nodded her head to the left. I scrolled my hand down the left side of the metal frame, but there was nothing that remotely resembled a button or switch beside the knob to turn on the shower.

'Oh God, Constance, I can't find it!'

'Help! Help!' Though I could not see her face, for she had her back to me, I could tell from her muffled, inward-reaching cry that she was not calling on me for succour, but upon the Holy Levitator, to lift her from this perilous place. Would He be able to succour her? With the showerhead raining down on her hard, I had my doubts. Even planes can have trouble taking off in hailstorms. I ran quickly down the stairs to look for human help.

And back up them again with Mathilde and Samir in tow.

'I don't understand... why... you can't find... the switch!' Mathilde scolded me between gasps for air; she was running out of breath as we took the stairs two by two.

'It's on the wall,' said Samir.

'On the wall? What ever do you mean?' Mathilde stopped dead in her tracks.

'Come on! You can't stop now! Constance is getting crushed!' I insisted.

'I'll show you,' said Samir, pulling at Mathilde's arm. But he needn't have; by now we could all hear Constance's crying and responded by breaking into a full run once we reached the top of the stairs.

'Here!' shouted Samir, as we reached the bathroom. He flipped off what I had thought was a light switch on the wall of the garderobe. 'I rewired the electricity. It's much better to have the switch on the wall, no?'

'There? Why I…' Mathilde was stunned. The rasping, grinding screech of the frustrated motor subsided in a downward crescendo as its bristled arms parted. Constance was now released from that harrowing embrace, and yet she stood still, perhaps engaged in post-panic orison. She did not move for several moments, which gave the three of us time to marvel at the splendour of her backside: the darling curve of the small of her back, leading as if in tempting preview to the plump but firm mounds below, milky white and shaped in the perfect rounds of an inverted heart. From the corner of my eye, I glimpsed Samir. His jaw dropped and he held his hand to his heart, manifestly overcome by this vision of loveliness.

'Stunning, such perfection… to think that… she'll never share…' I whispered to Mathilde.

'Never share… no, she will not, 'tis a pity to think… perhaps if she had… never mind. The Lord will… love it better.' Then she turned to Samir. 'Please leave, brother. We will take care of things from here. May this aperçu of the virgins you will one day encounter in your Mohammed's heaven, inspire you to the highest pursuits. And thank you for rewiring our apparatus. Now that we know where the switch is, we shall not have any more trouble.' Samir took leave, coughing to cover up his embarrassment, for Constance having re-emerged from her metaphysical pause, suddenly turned around to find the three of us there. She shrieked and covered herself like Eve, with her hands. Mathilde grabbed a towel from one of the cabinets and tossed it to her.

'Take cover, Constance, and dry yourself well. Lunch will soon be on the table.'

'Here,' I said, handing her the calendula cream. 'Feel free to use some of this moisturizer. It does wonders for your skin. Why, look at Honoré…' She took the tube and studied it for a moment with polite acknowledgement, then handed it back to me.

'I'll be fine,' she said, with the watered-down smile of those who self-abnegate on an hourly basis. She seemed so calm now, so composed after her little peep show.

When we were at last gathered around the table, Mathilde and Padre Las Vegas at the head, Charles, Rachid and I on one side, Komrad Kerkorian, a blushing Samir and wash-and-dried Cousin Constance facing us with an empty seat between them where Ahmed would not be joining us, for he preferred to dine in the oubliette where he was comfortably ensconced, we bowed our heads in an ecumenical blessing invoking that charming tautology and monotheistic affirmation so dear to our Muslim guests – There is no god but God – adding to this a *Rahman* and a *Raheem* as in the introduction of *A Thousand and One Nights*. Komrad Kerkorian, an orthodox Christian so reformed as to have the 'Christ' removed entirely from the appellation, keeping only the suffix 'ian' so dear to the Armenian people, lifted his fork with a convivial *bon appétit*. We dined on red sea bream, steamed potatoes and green beans sautéd in butter and parsley, accompanied by a Sancerre. Or perhaps I should say they dined; every time I tried to sit down, Honoré would jagger and fuss until I stood back up and swayed him around. It was playtime for him, lunchtime for me. And this divergence in our respective timetables had me eating on my toes, grabbing a nibble here and there, a sip of Sancerre, a pinch of bread dipped in salted butter. I should have just brought along a peanut butter and jelly sandwich, that staple of American motherhood, but I wished to avoid scandalizing my French relatives. None of whom, I might add, offered to put their plate on hold and relieve me of recreation duty. Not even Charles, *ma foi!* I had to give him the Maraconi chop-chop, a benign but efficacious punch on the back of the neck to get him up out of his seat. He coughed up a green bean, but got the picture. And I arrived at the table just in time for the cheese, which I cut faultlessly, respecting Mathilde's criteria for width and angle and would have received her full approval had I not poked the virginal Saint Marcelin with my knife before discovering it a tad too ripe for my palate, which incidentally is often the case for cheese having attained sainthood.

But what concerns us most here is not the food or family dynamics of our table, revealing of character and custom as these are, but our pressing case of the stolen Vegans, the discussion of which enlivened our luncheon and the events that ensued, which shall be faithfully documented in the following chapter, god-be-willing.

Chapter V

Which recounts the plight of the magi and their involvement with a man named Woo while ending in a traffic jam made tolerable by a poem.

'Inshallah…' Samir's voice tapered with reverence and that hint of doubt at the heart of every avowal of submission.

'If we want God to will it then we must first be very clear about what we have willed, Samir. When you say the Chinaman will be here next Friday, has the appointment been made and confirmed?'

'It has. Mr Woo be here Friday, inshallah.'

'Very good. I should hope his trucks can hold all three.' Mathilde preferred to air her doubts without the god-be-willing bit. 'Have you assurance that he will pay your price?'

'It has been agreed. He will pay the two hundred thousand we are asking, in cash. Inshallah. Otherwise he will not get the cars.'

'This sounds like the kind of fundraising we do back home, the Maraconis, I mean,' I butted in. Their project to sell stolen goods to a dubious entrepreneur at extortionate cost reminded me of a typical

Maraconi manoeuvre largely practiced by Uncle Al, whose 'land-reform' projects (picking up flailing farmland for a tune and 'donating' it to golf course developers) brought him a great deal of non-taxable revenue.

A raised eyebrow from Mathilde.

'Shall Padre and I bless the cars before their journey?' Cousin Constance offered.

'No need! Ahmed will take care of that. No need!' Samir stuck out his hand flat like a stop sign. Can it be that in Algeria, cars may not be blessed by women with beguiling buns? That's certainly how we sell them here!

'Speaking of Ahmed, I think the best way to get him out of the oubliette would be to allocate a portion of your proceeds to buying him a pilgrimage package,' Mathilde suggested. 'The prospect of Mecca would surely lure him out.'

'It is for older men with the wisdom of age to do this. Ahmed is not yet wise enough,' said Samir shaking his head.

'But in Ahmed's case, such zeal and excessive piety have earned him early hajjship. I daresay the stampeding crowds and lack of proper latrines and sleeping quarters will awaken him to the pressing need for betterment of faith-inspired logistics, for I believe the seed common to all reformers lays in abeyance in his breast awaiting proper irrigation,' opined Mathilde.

'Can you get to heaven without becoming a hajji?' I asked.

'A hajji is given a better reception,' explained Samir.

'A few more lovelies, better dates?'

'More of what is good, certainly.'

'Cousin Constance, could you fetch the platter of dried fruits that

Komrad Kerkorian brought us. By the way, Komrad, where did you come upon these sweetmeats?'

'My cousin Aram sent them from Hollywood.'

'A dreadful place but the fruits are quite nice... maybe a bit shiny... the dates. Not like the *deglet nour* of Algeria.'

'They melt in your mouth, not in your hand.'

'Hand me a couple, love... the apricots there...' Charles said, lifting Honoré up and down above his head like a fifteen-pound barbell. Honoré squealed with delight, drooled and danced. I popped an apricot into Charles's mouth.

'*Hey-soos* is for you a prophet, for us the Son of Man... *creo que*... we can, eh... strive together, nevertheless, for the social justice with the model, eh... of *Hey-soos*...' Padre Las Vegas could be overheard in deep discussion with Rachid, who looked at the priest with an expression of near horror, for there is nothing that displeases a Muslim more than such combining of theologies with a religion that has three gods: Father, Son and Holy Ghost.

'What I'd like to know is,' I began, returning to Mathilde's initial concern and query, 'how did you find this Mr Woo? Are you sure he's reliable? I mean, how do you know he's not going to drop a dime? Or that he won't just run off with the two hundred K?'

'We think he's good,' said Rachid, relieved to have this distraction from Padre's inclusive *Hey-soos*. 'Our common source is reliable.'

'Maître Jian,' added Samir.

'A great kung fu master... our master. We have studied with him for fifteen years... The Arab world is not lacking in champions,' Rachid interjected in response to our surprised faces. 'There is the Egyptian Master, Lightening Abd-al-Kader, who fights at fast-forward speed and the Algerians twins, Toufik and Tahar. It is said they possess the strength to destroy the mountain and so live in Holland now where it is very flat. There they are less of a threat though no less admirable. And then there is the Syrian, Mohammed "Chin-Chin" Beyoumi and...'

We listened with interest as Rachid recited a litany of illustrious Middle Eastern martial artists. We had never dreamed that such men existed, that the practice of wei wu wei fortified by five prayers a day was the key to championhood at the Temple of Shaolin. But the upshot of Rachid's revelation, which matters most to us now, was that the Mr Woo in question, a longtime associate of Master Jian at the Wushu Institute, now works for an ambitious Shanghai entrepreneur operating out of Nigeria who we'll refer to as Mr X and whose project it is to mass produce biomass-run diesel engine vehicles modelled on the Vegan. This capo has been granted monopoly rights by his shady government connections to exploit the stolen prototype to his heart's content. We can reasonably assume there are huge profits to be reaped from this venture by Mr X and his cronies. And our magi's meagre demand for 200,000 euros does seem but a pittance; in the long run they might regret not having taxed Mr X's affairs as Uncle Al wisely did Frankie Bonadelli's country clubs. Let us trust they have calculated carefully and that the proceeds will suffice.

As it transpires our magi are thumping the Korans of the grass roots organization, Muslims Without Borders. This group apparently sprang from the discontents of the Saint Denis suburb where many Muslims huddle in the run-down, rationalized housing blocks surrounding Christendom's first gothic cathedral, inaugurated by the headless St Denis himself. According to Ahmed's summation, the purpose of Muslims Without Borders is to protect the interests and security of Europe's Muslim community. It provides outreach programmes, legal services and counselling and has plans to open satellite branches in London and Brussels. We visited him in the oubliette after lunch, as the demoiselles kindly looked after Honoré, their arms ready to rock and lullaby – bless them! In all truth I could not have taken dear Honoré down into the depths of that little dungeon of a dormitory where our friends have been residing. Mathilde has done her best to cheer up its damp walls by hanging large swatches of leftover fabrics on poles, a silk and brocade patchwork of sumptuous autumnal hues that lends a regal prestige to the quarters, yet the lingering medieval ghosts, once enemies of family and state forcibly shoved therein and duly forgotten about six hundred years ago, can give us the spooks. Ahmed and his comrades, however, appear to be immune to any bad business these apparitions might conjure up – being of different blood and faith, you see.

Ghosts or no ghosts, Ahmed has established the oubliette as a headquarters and is reluctant to leave it. Mathilde, in her infinite generosity, had a satellite dish installed, enabling our three kings to watch Al Jazeera news 24-7. Which Ahmed does, when he is not praying or doing business on his phone. He takes two meals of fish a day in front of the TV, haram meat being out of the question what with the difficulty of procuring halal viands in Fontainebleau, and even if such meats could be found, Mathilde would not send her cooks to fetch it for fear of raising suspicions. He sleeps little, and always in the eerie blue glow of the television rising and subsiding, for he is taking the temperature of the world, finding the best route through its fevers and contagions. The Chinese colonization of Africa could be counted in Celsius; he has come up with a hopefully accurate thermometric estimate for Nigeria where Mr Woo is to lead the convoy of Vegans. The risks of this transaction should be short lived: there will be five critical hours when Woo and his men drive the Vegan-carrying trucks to the outskirts of Brussels. There, Mr X's cargo plane will await them at his private airport. Ahmed has been going over the route's coordinates meticulously with one of Woo's scouts, Mr Jet Li. Li has made the journey four times to pinpoint where the gendarme posses tend to set up their blockades. He has been observing the border patrol, noticing who works when and which of the officials lets trucks roll on through the checkpoint without so much as a wave of the hand. Ahmed has taken note of every potential danger and threat to their mission.

These were tense times for our friends, and I believe that Ahmed's squatting and thermo-calculating in the oubliette helped anchor the common cause in a way. The unifying purpose of our magi's mission, which I have neglected to limn in its full attire – please forgive me, dear reader – would be best recounted by Ahmed himself. If only Ahmed could write for us here, yet as he cannot, I will opt for conducting a short interview with him – a pure creation on my part, modelled on the interviews of the French daily, *Libération*, which Charles sometimes reads in the WC when he has the time, *ma foi!* – in hope of illuminating the magi's intentions.

Sitting lotus style on the diwan, Ahmed el Medhi scratches his temple beneath his white skullcap, while his beard, trimmed into a likeness of breakfast croissants, twitches as if some raw nerves were jumping for cover beneath the skin. He lowers the volume on the TV with the remote and turns my way. His smile is parsimonious, given in a flash. It is quickly replaced by a frown of pensive displeasure.

Ahmed: In the name of Allah, the most Merciful, most Beneficent…

Jane: Yes, Maker of Heaven and Earth; of all that is Seen and Unseen... *(The Nicene Creed earns me a raised brow)* Now, can you tell me, Ahmed el Medhi, about your current rescue mission at Muslims Without Borders? Is it true that the forces of organized crime have been holding your Muslim brothers captive? Using them as slave labour in the fields?

Ahmed: Such is the truth. A terrible one – revealed to me first in a dream. I was buying meat at the Islamic butcher shop: a shoulder of mutton for making a stew. But I did not take it home as I had planned; instead I went to my cousin Ali's and gave it to him.

Jane: Was he... expecting you?

Ahmed: No he was not, and this is just the point. Such a dream announces hardship for the person to whom the meat is destined.

Jane: I don't believe I follow you.

Ahmed: It is written and explained in Ibn Sirin's manual of Islamic oniromance.

Jane: Oniromance? Pray tell...

Ahmed: The interpretation of dreams. It is all explained very clearly in his book to which we are greatly indebted. Truth transcends time and what was true of dreams in the seventh century when Ibn Sirin was inspired to write his treatise, continues to guide us today.

Jane: So no revisions by Freud?

Ahmed: No revisions whatsoever. Not now, not ever, inshallah. Shall I go on?

Jane: Please do.

Ahmed: I understood that Ali was in distress. I then called his home in Algiers and got his wife. She began weeping when I pronounced his name, it seemed he had left to find work in Italy and she had not heard from him in two months. And so I told her that she must accept Allah's will next to which our own has but the strength of dust, but that I had been sent a dream which surely meant that The Merciful One would offer us His aid. A week later this proved true with a telephone call from Ali. By a stroke of good fortune the gangmaster had left his cell phone unattended and Ali quickly put in a call, risking his life doing so I may add. He told me that he and eleven other Muslim brothers were being kept as slaves, driven to work the fields from 4 a.m. to 10 p.m. and living in a shack with four to a licey mattress, no running water and only enough gas to cook five meals a week. We are starving, he said. We are being worked to death. And other words of such distress that my heart was committed to their rescue. I now had the gangmaster's number. Our negotiations began.

Jane: Any more dreams? Trips to the baker? Or the candlestick maker?

Ahmed: Yes, another dream. Just two nights ago. In it I was taking a bath at the hammam. Usually this is a sign of worries caused by women, but in this dream I relieved myself in the hammam's waters.

Jane: Perhaps you could explain further?

Ahmed: But is it not obvious? This is a presage that I will soon be relieved of this burden.

Jane: I don't see it… what women are involved?

Ahmed: Beneath every burden that a man carries you will find a woman; she is the root of our worries, always. If Ali's wife had not insisted he bring home more money, he would not be in this dire predicament.

Jane: And if his wife were allowed to find work and bring in more money herself, she would not have asked him to leave.

86

Ahmed: This just shows how little you understand. Tonight I will surely dream of the urge in a hamman again, but this time without relief.

Our interview shall end here, dear reader. There is no use in reporting futile discussions, and perhaps you think me unkind to project such opinions upon Ahmed. I'm afraid the mind of invention has had its way. But now at least the whys and wherefores of our magi's mission have been revealed and you are in the know.

In the meantime, they must all stay in hiding or with hoods on. Charles, after lunch, had a man-to-man with Samir and Rachid in the barn, telling them that for Mathilde's sake they must leave Thrushcross Castle after the transaction so as not to put her in further danger. They agreed, though they insisted on remaining a few extra days, the time it would take to get hold of the French passports they had ordered from Better Identities, a catalogue of fake IDs put out by a clandestine Turkish company. Samir even suggested Charles procure a Swiss passport for Honoré (pages: 10, cost: 2,000 euros), which is always a good thing to have (neutrality), as one never knows just how this world shall turn.

We left Thrushcross Castle even more on edge than upon our arrival, our minds preoccupied by the stakes and our implication, particularly Mathilde's, in them. Honoré's barometer picked up on our angst; he jaggered a good part of the way home, unable to find solace in a worried breast. We made four nursing stops at various Elf stations along the way, but Honoré just grew fussier with each feeding. Fortunately there was recourse to be found in my memory bank of poems. The Jesuit poet, Gerard Manley Hopkins's verses –

World-mothering air, air wild
Wound with thee, in thee isled
Fold home, fast fold thy child

– came to mind, just in time, for Charles's nerves were readying to snap. The poem offered us all a new perspective on the Holy Mother, likening her to the air we breathe – minus the greenhouse gases. We caught our breaths then, and by applying our awareness to breathing in and out the mothering air, grew calmer somehow. In any case, we made it through a forty-minute-long traffic jam at the Porte de La Chapelle without uttering a profanity; we kept the mothering air pure. And by the time we finally manoeuvred our way out of it, Honoré was fast asleep.

Chapter VI

*On the sudden insolvency of Jane and
Charles, the looming threat of an all-grain
diet, a post-Pimm's request and more.*

The week that followed, however, afforded us little time to think
about our magi's predicament and plans. We had a crisis of our
own that required every ounce of our attention, if such insubstantial
things can be measured in terms of weight. Angels have the scales to
do so. Our crisis arose on Monday as I went out, with Honoré in tote,
to the ATM at the Place du Colonel Fabien. There was a crisp blue
autumn sky and a slight chill to the air that wrinkled the changing
leaves of the plane trees around the circle, ageing them overnight. The
sight of these crinkly leaves made me think of my own skin, which the
past four months of mothering on too little sleep had weathered almost
as ruthlessly. A desire for the pricey miracle creams sold at the
Marionnaud perfumery began waving its red flags at me. I wanted
those time-shield potions with their biomimetic peptides, collagen-
inducing liposomes, micro-encapsulated actives, never forgetting the

plant and sea extracts that firm, regenerate and reduce the visible signs of photo-aging. This craving hit me hard as I passed the great Communist egg, and arrived at the threshold of the Banque National de Paris. I stood before the machine trembling a bit, and fumbled to get my card out of my pocket, which wasn't so easy because of the baby sling. Honoré squealed as I lifted him up with my left arm so that my right could slip into the pocket; for him there was the thrill of elevation, an amusement park high. And while he marveled at the sensation, I retreated into my own world of concerns and nervously considered the luxury cream splurge; I pictured myself slathering my face in ludicrously expensive botanical creams, my pores drinking in the precious ingredients like mother's milk, my complexion lightening, my skin texture tightening. The transformation from drab mien to peaches-and-cream certainly justified the price. I remembered a Marionnaud saleswoman once explaining to me that 'only the most botanical brands go *into the flower* to extract its substance.' My mind's eye imagined nectar-extracting bees in white coats and their clever syringes. No wonder, I thought, that these creams are so divine, so tonic and firming: they are propelled by the petal mysteries. I rapidly found justifications for plunging into those petals myself: Why, hadn't I gone through the agonies of birth, nursed and nurtured non-stop? Surely I deserved a treat, a pick-me-up! Not only did I deserve it, it was owed to me, like Loréal owes Claudia Schiffer – *parce que je le vaux!* Because I'm worth it!

As the voice in my head shouted this last affirmation an internal siren went off, alerting me to a danger I knew all too well: it was the SLYMP – Sounding Like Your Mother Patrol – ringing my ears.

'Oh Honoré, It's Mother again! She gets me carried away at times,'

I admitted to my son, who had not yet met his grandmother, but perhaps would one day if she ever left her sheep. 'Luxury botanical cream will be for another time. When Dad or I get a job, or some nice royalty statements come in. In the meantime we'll have to shoot for a bit less. Maybelline, maybe?' I turned my attention back to the cash machine and tried to take out one hundred euros, but was refused. I reduced my request to eighty and was again refused. Then, I tried sixty but the money machine would not concede. I lowered my request by twenty until I reached the lowest denominator, twenty euros – barely chickenfeed enough for minor groceries and Nivea cream – and was refused even that!

'Oh my God, Honoré, there's nothing in the bank!' I perhaps should have kept this grim fact from my child, but I preferred to be upfront with him as much as possible, seeing that my own parents never were with me. Money was as taboo a subject as sex and the Maraconis' mobstering. I walked down the Boulevard de La Villette, as dazed as I would have been had the Mammon machine possessed a robotic hand and punched me in the face. Slaps in the face do not awaken you to hard reality by the way; they take your wits away and leave you reeling like a tottering top. I found my way to a bench on the Boulevard's promenade before I toppled.

'Have we really spent all the car wash money?' I wondered in disbelief, as I pulled Honoré out of the sling before he could start crying, which he invariably did whenever I sat myself down for a rest. I held him facing outward under his arms so that he could watch the parade of passers-by – a motley crowd of Chinese sweatshop workers on lunch break, hooded fellows from the nearby projects playing raï hits on their cell phones, Tunisian ladies talking with their orange hands, and the neighbourhood transvestite with her pink poodle and the tight T-shirted boyfriend she calls Sam-the-Man – while I collected myself and tried to think things through. We had had no great expenses, but it was true that we had been living for a month off the lingering remnants of the previous month's minimum wage salary. That couldn't have been strung out very far even if we'd been eating an all-grain diet and drinking screw-cap wine, hardly advisable fare for a nursing mum. Pangs of fear and dread plucked at my chest; I thought of the congenitally indebted Mr Micawber in *David Copperfield* and his grandiloquent speeches blanketing the shame of his empty coffers, the barren cupboards. Would we too have to compensate for our deficit with longwinded greetings, uphold our dignity with overwrought rhetoric? I tried to imagine Charles laying our case bare before the banker in some such interminable, sympathy arousing terms: *'My dear Madame, this is indeed a meeting which is calculated to impress the heart with a sense of the instability of all human existence before the vagaries of supply and demand, as so evinced by my wife and our babe who derives his sustenance from Nature's founts – in short…'*

Yes, in short this was not our style at all; moreover, it did not behove Micawber either, except to expedite his extradition to Australia (Chapter LVII). I tried to put that overpopulated Victorian family out of mind, for whenever they appear, they exacerbate the impression I have in times of uncertainty of being rootless and roofless – plucked from the earth and left without shelter overhead. They are my insecurity gauge as it were, and now that I'd registered just how far we had plunged, they could return to Dickens' story and go on enlivening that tale with their endearing misery. Practical solutions were needed. An inventory of the kitchen cupboard, a list of possible money-lenders, an appointment with our banker, Madame Dupont, a call to the unemployment bureau…

A chill wind whipped towards us from the east, slapping our left cheeks. I turned us both around as I got up so that it would slap the right one too. 'It's what Jesus said to do,' I told Honoré, whose face reddened from the blow. 'Life is not tit-for-tat, my little love. We must be bigger than that. The wind cannot hurt us – I promise you.' Honoré's kiss curl was flying like a flag of surrender. Perhaps these strong sensations of wind-might overpowered him, for he began to jagger with all his heart. 'There now, Honoré,' I cooed as I tucked him back into the baby sling, 'trust your Mother. I'll take care of everything. I always do, don't I?' I rocked him in the sling as I walked down the boulevard to help him settle. But it was a cacophonic cavalcade of police cars screaming around the Rond-point du Colonel Fabien that cut the jaggers sharp. Honoré turned them off respectfully to listen to the honks and sirens, his head tilted at 45° just like Charles when he listens to Boulez. As for me, I could not help but shudder. My Maraconi instincts told me to dodge, to make a run for it. And while normally I would reason with such a rash impulse – for what motivation did I have to run? – motherhood has quickened my instincts to such a degree that they slip right over the blunt edge of logic. I spied the alley to the left of the Communist Party Head-quarters, where the commies keep their recycling and sprinted, my arm wrapped around Honoré to keep him from bouncing out of the sling. The surge of adrenaline coursing through my breast seemed to do him a world of good, seemed to give him the ego boost he needed after turning both cheeks. He giggled, he drooled, he gave a happy grunt and pooped. I squatted behind a five foot wall of stacked crates full of emptied wine bottles, ready for recycling, and waited until I heard the sirens well on their way to Stalingrad. 'They're gone now, Honoré,' I reassured him. And I intended to stand back up when one of the bottles in front of us caught my eye. A 1986 Clos des Lambrays Grand Cru! 'So that's what the Communists drink! You'd think they could spread the wealth a bit, or at least pass us along a bottle in our time of need!' I pulled out others and found them to be more of the same; there must have been some 200 dead bottles, probably left over from a post-Soviet caviar reception inside the great white egg. The *partie communiste*'s extravagance hit me like an insult.

'The cost of four of those bottles, Honoré, could feed us for a month – if we skipped the veal scaloppini. Frankly I think they've done your grandmother a favour by not letting her in. What would she say if she saw such abuses! Why, her bun would come undone!'

Honoré looked pensively at the bottles, then gave me a quizzical glance. I think he suspected, like me, that if Mathilde's chignon truly did come down, it would, by some metonymic manoeuver, unravel the ties of ideals and sensibilities that unite our family and strengthen our peculiar vision of the world. Imagine the Great Sensibility itself pinned up in that pinnacle of softly silvering hair and you will then see it through our eyes, for the beacon that it is.

'No worries, my little love. We won't say a word about what we've seen. Maraconis keep their secrets – we call it Omerta – a vow of silence – and this is as good a time as any to learn about that. When I was little my Pops trained me, you see. He'd say, "Come over here now, Janie-girl, I got a secret for you but you can't tell no-one. Swear you won't tell no-one." And when I solemnly swore, he'd say something like, "Your cousin Tony's got a big red ant in his pants and it's gonna bite him on his behind. Don't laugh! And don't you go telling no-one!" And you know, Honoré, I never said a word – I didn't even laugh – even though I knew Tony was going to get bit on the booty. That's the hard part about keeping secrets. The devil in you wants to crack them like an egg on someone else's head. Like Humpty Dumpty, Honoré – he's one big secret, and once he cracked it was all over. That's exactly what Pops was trying to teach me.'

It's tricky to discern how much Honoré gathered from my explanation as to why secrets must be held like babes at the breast – never dropped, never shared – but he remained uncannily quiet as we headed back home, bouncing against our empty wallet. We stopped at the statue of Our Lady of Fatima in the foyer of our building and peered at her pretty pink toes. For some reason they made me think of Mother in the seventies when she wore lots of frosted make-up. It had the strange effect of lowering her IQ. She enrolled in a course offered by the Junior League called 'Colour Your Rainbow' and spent hours upon hours playing solitaire with colour swatches. To ascertain the vibratory value of the different hues, she would clip them to her clothes and hair, and sometimes, when she cooked, they fell into the food. She just kept stirring. Fortunately, when she switched to matte make-up, her smarts came back. That's when she started up her Tupperware consultant business.

Our Lady's toes are not frosted pink, I should add, and this reassured me as I began my prayer, for I needed the help of a Holy One with as High an IQ as possible. We had to get from broke to stoked. We had to shake the money-maker. And quite frankly I didn't see how we were going to do it. Unless Divine Intelligence coughed up an answer. Here was our prayer:

Oh Holy Mother of God! We have no more car wash money in the bank! We spent it all! But only on diapers (Bébé Cash brand – not Pampers) and food (veal just once a week) which you know we need. I'm not asking you for a miracle, only to intercede on our behalf at the foot of your son Jesus, Our Lord, to help us find a sustainable way to make our living in the long-run (regular royalties would be best), and in the short, someone to float us a loan at absurdly low interest!

Having finished this personalized petition, we went on to say five Hail Marys and would have gone on to say seven had Mme Li not walked in at that moment, smiling and bowing her head. *Ca va bébé? Ca va bébé?* She dipped her hand into the sling to tickle Honoré under the chin. He cocked his head, gave her the coy smile of cherubs; she giggled with glee, tickled him again. Then she stuck her finger in his mouth to fish for teeth. *Y a des dents? Y a des dents?* Honoré clamped down hard on her line. *Oh là là! Bébé mord fort!* She seemed to derive even greater delight in being bitten than in being smiled at with celestial grace. But I have found that people from all corners of the world enjoy these displays of strength in babies. Perhaps the most common of common denominators amongst us all is this pleasure we take in our wee ones' wholeness, the uninterrupted freshness of their force. When Honoré released his bite and Madame Li retrieved her finger, we bid her goodbye and headed upstairs. I managed to glance quickly over my shoulder and saw her ripping the page off her Miss Taiwan calendar: a new month had started. And we had nothing in the bank! And only rigatoni and canned peas in the cupboard!

Charles was working on his new symphony when we walked in and I could tell from the position of his forelock – dangling over his right eye (he uses his left when composing, for he is left-eyed and right-handed) – that he did not want to be disturbed. I have an immense respect for artists-at-work, for I know myself, as a writer of rock operas, how vividly the heart, soul and mind are solicited and engaged in the effort to create something from nothing, but unlike Charles, for whom the pleasure of music suffices to quell the angst of poverty and hunger, I am also pragmatic and incapable of stringing the simplest of sentences if I am not certain that ahead of me lies a balanced meal composed of the Three Marvellous Food Groups: Veal, Pasta and Wine. In other words, I have a stomach. And my mind will not work properly unless it is guaranteed its fill at regular intervals. In this way I resemble Honoré who lets the jaggers rip if I'm five minutes late for a feeding. This is considered quite normal for a baby, and I suspect we should outgrow the tendency. Charles clearly has. Why I have not, I'm not sure. But perhaps this has to do with Mother's refusal to nurse me. She handed me over to Frau Gerber, a stout German nanny whose nursery practices were predicated on the teachings of Dr Daniel Gottlieb Moritz Schreber, a pre-war paediatric pedagogue who incited parents, including Mr and Mrs Himmler of Heinrich fame to *crush the will* of their children, *establish dominance*, and *permit no disobedience!* Fortunately for all of us, she only stayed a month, but during that time she managed to convince mother that breast-feeding was deleterious to my delicate digestive system and instead formula fed me on a strict schedule, setting me down on her knees to do so. This position appropriately rendered the cuddling so sharply proscribed by Dr Schreber impossible. I have a photograph of Frau Gerber, holding me just so and looking into my father's camera with a stern, triumphant expression, taking delight not in me, but in her own exacting fortress of post puerperal maintenance. She kept me alive, I must credit her for that.

When I turned three weeks, she had her metal spoon poised to stuff porridge down my wee throat: imagine that! Feeding solids at three weeks! This would make any right-minded mum or paediatrician gasp! Like a journalist flashing the camera at the horrors of the world, my father duly stood by documenting my early days with Frau, rather than taking me from her arms. Why he trusted this overbearing nanny (even the Germans got rid of her!) over his own instincts, I suspect has something to do with tax law. He was in it deep and it smothered something good in him. And where, you're probably wondering, was mother while Frau Gerber diapered and fed me with her draconian drive to drown out the lights of nursery love? She was in the hospital undergoing a series of operations the nature of which she has never clearly specified, though Grandma Maraconi once told me she was 'getting her matrix moved'. It seems odd now that I never questioned further, never asked either Grandma or Mother what it meant to move a matrix, nor where her matrix had resettled once it had been moved.

But all this is an attempt to explain, first of all, why I remain a scheduled eater to this day and have never been able to skip a meal without experiencing a panic attack, and secondly why I found Charles's engrossment in the nimble notes moving across the page of his perforated *cahier de musique* so unbearable. How can he be all ears and no stomach? Why, he doesn't care if we have lunch or not! There was no use telling him we would go without our daily bread (unless Madame Li let us dine on credit). I needed to drop the news in his ear, without letting my own stomach get in the way. I dug through one of the boxes – yes, I'm afraid we still have not unpacked those – and pulled out my megaphone, a former prop in my rock opera. Louis XVI (played by a Jimmy Hendrix lookalike named Lewis with an epiphany crown pinned into the wild Brillo pad of his afro) used it to recite a laudatory poem about Versailles to the plebe called 'Mirror Mirror on the Wall'. I always felt it was one of the highlights of the show; there was a funky *Electric Ladyland*-like guitar riff in the background, and hundreds of hand mirrors suspended in the air around Lewis as he dittied into the megaphone. One critic (actually a journalism major at Cornell writing for the campus canard) described it as 'the scene that really rocked the house'. I kept the megaphone as a souvenir of the heights my show had reached and I've used it once or twice, to get across an urgent message to Charles – and these desperate time called for desperate measures.

'We need your attention, please!' I shouted through the megaphone. Honoré was not sure he liked this but instead of jaggering, supported me – he is a dear! 'There is no money in the bank. I repeat: there is no more money in the bank!' Honoré and I waited for Charles's response. We held our breath, expecting him any minute to flip back his forelock and stand to attention, as men are trained to do in times of trouble. But Charles merely turned our way with a sigh of annoyance.

'What on earth...?' His forelock was still a-dangling as he looked at me.

'Once again,' I spoke into the megaphone, 'we are broke. Entirely broke. There is no money in the bank! I repeat: no money in the bank!' At this point I broke down and dropped the megaphone. Charles rushed over to me, taking Honoré from my arms. 'Yes, take your child. Soon he will have nothing to eat; his mother's milk shall dry out.'

'What are you talking about, Jane?'

'Good God! Do I need to tell you again?'

'Are you absolutely sure?' Charles at last pushed back his kiss-curl. His voice had shrunk as if put through a sudden, vigorous wash of reality. He stood there, holding Honoré, forlorn. Like me he knew what this meant; that the long, fruitful days he had been spending at the composing table were numbered; we would have to find work as quickly as possible – and any kind possible – be it waiting tables at MacDavid's at La Chapelle or working the halal fryer at Paris Fried Chicken down the street at Stalingrad. And until we found a job, we would have to burrow down to the lowly grade of borrowers. I looked into Charles's eyes and divined what he had in mind from their hazel dread, their golden specks of determination.

'Edward?' I enquired.

'I'm afraid so.'

'Can we reach him now?'

'I believe he plays polo on Saturdays.'

'Then let's try around six. After he's showered.'

'Seven is better; after he's had his Pimm's.'

Charles knows his cousin Edward far better than I, of course, and so I went along with the plan. Yes, after a Pimm's cocktail it was. Edward is Mathilde's brother's son, a first cousin, and like the car, sports the name de Saab. Mathilde is fond of recounting stories of how he and Charles adored each other as children, how they would play elaborate games based on the Three Musketeers and studied *escrime* on the weekends together. Charles played the role of the melancholic Athos, Edward that of the proud Parthos, affecting the gestures of a giant. They seemed to share one heart and mind, to inhabit an imagination so peculiar to them both, one they had sworn to such secrecy that they were sure it set them apart from the rest of the world. Then Edward crossed the Channel to spend a year in an English boarding school: and it was here that he met John, who was to misplay the part of Aramis and become the jagged tooth saw that cut through the bond uniting the cousins, shattering their fantastical kingdom. It was John who turned Edward away from his poetic inclinations and convinced him to adopt the mercantile persuasion in which his country formidably exceeds. In other words, he descended from the highlands of sublimation to the flatter lands of money-making. Edward followed John to HEC, France's foremost business school, while Charles entered the conservatoire. The rift between them mended over the years, but Edward, a high-end banker at a private Italian bank is certainly not above making thoughtless cracks about our royalty statements. I believe he is secretly envious of Charles for running with the Great Sensibility, for flying it high like a kite, no matter the weather; for taking risks with only feeling and rigorous aesthetic standards as capital. But we both knew that he would loan us the money we lacked, if only we could swallow our pride – which we could.

As Charles and I were discussing how much we needed to tide us over, the phone rang. It was Marion, a friend from down the street near Belleville. She happens to be a librarian but has never heard of the Broadway musical hit *The Music Man* or Gary, Indiana for that matter. She's French and a functionary and will go on strike at every invitation to do so. Her timing was perfect, for we needed a mini loan to get us through the weekend till Monday when Edward was likely to accommodate us.

'*Salut ma belle, ca va?*'

'*Pas trop…* Things are a bit rough, Marion. We just realized we're… well… broke! *Complètement fauchés… Sans un sous…*' Why is it that shameful things are easier to utter in French?

'How much do you need?'

'Oh you're too kind! Well, just enough to get through the weekend. Enough to buy some bread, and some artichokes. And maybe some… veal. Oh, and a bottle of wine too. We have some pasta left and a can of peas…'

I was grateful to Marion for getting the measure of the situation. For not asking too many questions and limiting the humiliation, even the kind that is accidentally provoked by a thoughtless slip of the tongue. It was agreed that I would stop by at around six, which suited me quite well: to be honest I didn't want to be at the house when Charles called Edward. Was this cowardly of me? Perhaps, but I had already requested a tide-us-over loan from Marion and saw no reason to sit in as a bystander to our second, more daring demand for subsidy. Moreover, I didn't care to witness the uneasy telephonic scene between a Pimm's-less composer and his Pimm'sed-up cousin.

After making a luncheon of Rigatoni with Peas and its Ten Drops of Olive Oil (all that was left in the bottle alas!), nursing, and napping a bit, I said another little prayer to Our Lady of Victory. This time I supplicated for a small professional *victoire*: a part-time, home-based, stint that would pay the bills and the cost of a vacation or two, on the holy day holidays. This rigatoni-fuelled prayer was more focused and pointed than my previous attempt. After all, feeding rather than fasting straightens my spiritual aim (which may be due to some dyspeptic anomaly resulting from the Frau Gerber era). I had the strong sensation of being heard, of receiving an affirmative nod of Her holy head. It is simply not possible for me to explain such things except to say that entering into this kind of communication is a bit like speaking to a mute friend on the phone; with attunement, you can sense the exact expression and reception of your interlocutor. Maybe we could call it telepathy, but I find the term and its pseudo-scientific pretensions quaint; any self-respecting believer knows that prayer is one big telepathon, with lines working 24/7. No-one is busier than the Divine, no-one can even fathom such dedication. You can't blame the holies if they get their lines crossed from time to time, or if sacred squirrels bite through the wires. Blame can only be fairly put on Free Will, or rather our inability to practice it wilfully and freely.

I asked and I received.

Chapter VII

*In which Jane receives the extraordinary summons
of a lady of great repute and discovers the artistry
of a Muslim plumber named Momo etc.*

It was on Monday that Our Lady answered my prayer, which was sooner than I had even hoped for. This response came, quite appropriately, by way of a telephone call at 9.00 a.m., just as I was cutting off the bottom seam of my moisturizer tube to get the last dab of cream, while simultaneously swinging Honoré in the baby-sling across my chest. There was not enough cream really to cover the expanse of my face, but it was the best I could do until Charles returned from his appointment with Edward, the loan funds in pocket. But the phone rang before I could even smoosh the last dollop into those wrinkles running across my brow, furrowed by the night plows of motherhood. I feared it was a wake-up call from Madame Dupont, our banker, and I trembled as I reached for the phone, expecting to hear her clipped, critical voice, that way she had of remonstrating me like a child, as if banking had anything in common with motherhood! *Ma foi!* The voice, however, was a man's I did not recognize.

'Excuse me for opportuning you, Madame,' it began in a sententious French badly translated into English. 'I do hope that I have not deranged you. May I have the honour of presenting myself?'

'Yes, please do,' I insisted. Clearly this was not someone in banking. Bankers have no qualms about deranging you.

'I thank you for this, Madame. I am called Fabrice de Fontanelle, secretary of Madame K_____ of the Third University and I am rejoiced to have the honour of calling you on her behalf to convoke you to her office tomorrow.'

I was thrilled by this honourable invitation to convoke and nearly dropped the phone at the mention of Madame K_____ (please, dear reader, due to this great lady's celebrity, I prefer not to reveal her identity, for the sake of her privacy and to avoid judiciary prejudice in the event that she should pan my portrait of her), a woman whose reign from the illuminating tower of France's philosophical citadel has earned her renown throughout the old and new worlds. Why, I had read her work when studying at Cornell, wrote a dissertation on her semiotic masterpiece *Heaviotiks*, defended her good name against an obscure group of campus bio-feminists who declared her a fraud for writing with her mind, not her body. Her radiophonic appearances on *France Culture* accompanied my cooking, her articles in *Le Monde* stimulated our soaks in the tub. My God! Thought I. How could this be? Madame K_____, requesting me?

'Pray tell,' I queried, regaining my poise. 'Why is it that she wants to see me?'

'She is researching an English secretary, Madame, one who can translate her essays and correspondences into…'

'English, yes, I see. I'm American so English is not a problem, in theory.'

'Madame said an American would be fine. She will be honoured to receive you at five o'clock tomorrow in tower number twenty-four, tenth floor.'

'Yes, yes! Five o'clock sharp.' I hung up the phone in a daze, looked down at my babe who nestled in the sling, listening in. 'Can you believe it, Honoré? Such a windfall! Our Lady of Victory certainly came through for us! I was dreading the thought of your father working at Paris Fried Chicken's halal fryer. All that grease! Even if it *is* blessed!' At the thought of his father's forelock sodden with trans fats, Honoré's mouth contorted into a menacing pout. I swiftly lifted him from the sling and held him against my chest, swaying away the jaggers.

'You can always count on Our Lady, Honoré. My goodness! I was imagining she'd get me a part-time stint in a bookstore at best. Never would I have imagined employment with the likes of Special K!'

The moniker Special K came just then in a flash of inspiration and surprised me with its appropriateness; not only was Madame K_____ a special lady indeed, she was to provide our daily bread, our source of sustenance, the cereal on our breakfast table as it were.

'Let's give it up for Special K!' I rang out, clapping Honoré's hands. He giggled with delight at the play of his palms. Honoré was picking up on my relief as the threat of future insolvency lifted. 'Wait until Dad hears about this! He might need some cheering up after his meeting with Edward. We'll be ready for him, won't we?' Honoré and I then went into the closet to find something to wear for the appointment. I brought out three pre-pregnancy items: a black, no nonsense Ann Taylor dress, a faux Chanel suit of a pinkish weave, and a red wrap-around dress with Berber embroidery around the décolleté. 'OK, Honoré, let's play the dressing room game!' I tried to sound as cheerful as possible as I set him atop a comfy stack of pillows on the bed. He was not a baby who tolerated being out of arms for long. I would have to work quickly. I stepped out of my peignoir and pulled the black no-nonsense number off the hanger and over my head. It slid down aided by a silky lining over the mounds of my chest and belly, but hit the ground hard at my hips and would slide no farther. The dress, once an elegant sheath, bloomed out preposterously at the waist leaving my bum exposed in yellow primrose-print panties. Tug as I might, there was not enough stretch to pull it down over my newly acquired rear and the expanded east to west range of my hips. I whipped it off with disgust as quickly as I had slid it on, and grabbed at the pink suit. But Honoré caught a whiff that something was wrong all the same. I dipped into our Itsy-Bitsy Spider routine while stepping into the faux Chanel to get him off my track. How multi-tasked my fingers have become with motherhood, buttoning, zipping and spidering all at once! The pink suit fit more or less, but something wasn't quite right; the skirt, already a mini, was made even shorter by my wider girth. I didn't care to call so much attention to my short neo-Neapolitan legs and doubted that Special K would appreciate the display. 'That won't do either, Honoré,' I explained to him in an optimistic voice, though I was feeling less than sanguine. 'But no matter. I never was very fond of those rags. Let's try that little red number – the one we call Miss Haiwa!' I waved the dress with a toreador's flourish to build up some excitement, which is what every dressing room needs. Then I slipped my arms into the

108

dress and wrapped it around me, tying it on the side. It seemed to fit fine, to fall gracefully over my augmented curves. It certainly didn't make me look thinner than I was, but it also didn't exaggerate my extra baggage. And the Berber décolleté accentuated my full breasts prettily, surrounding them with a buzzing energy of machine-made stitches. Miss Haiwa it would be!

I picked up Honoré before he got bored on his kingdom of cushions and we whisked ourselves off to the living room. I was pleased that Honoré had had this glimpse into the ladies' dressing room and had seen I was a worthy role model; I did not let the downsizing discourage me, but pursued trying on the next frock, never once berating or lamenting my rise from size 12 to 14. In a word, my comportment was stoic, and I hoped it would rest in Honoré's pre-verbal memory and later unconsciously aid him in choosing the right kind of wife. I believe this is what is meant by the adage that it is the mother who chooses her son's wife. A mother must never forget that she is training her boy how to spot a potential spouse; that the manner in which she includes him (or not!) in her daily activities, from the most menial (washing spuds, using the lavatory and cleaning it, sweeping hair up off the floor etc.) to the more triumphant (a home facial, or a reading aloud of *Wuthering Heights*, or even salsa dancing to Eddie Palmieri's orchestra), will contribute to shaping, years down the line, his life's romantic arc. He will believe he's made a choice when in fact the brick path has been laid by a mighty mason (i.e. mother) inclining him to 'choose' a brick (i.e. girl) that fits the established pattern. So much for free will!

When Charles returned, somewhat sheepish as so many of us are when we've just been handed a loan, Honoré and I broke the good news.

'Is this true? *C'est vrai?*'

'Oh it is! We got the call at around nine. I'm to meet her tomorrow at five o'clock. By the way, you'll have to go with me and take Honoré on a walk while I'm talking to her. We'll be cutting it close between feedings. He'll need to be fed either right before I go in or right when I get out.'

'You know, I have met her before,' said Charles looking inwardly to recapture the meeting. 'It was in Dr Delamancha's waiting room. She was reading *The Interior Castle*, highlighting passages here and there, and I couldn't help but broach the subject. At the time I was working on my *Symphony of the Seven Dwelling Places*... yes, I remember telling her a bit about it... In the end we exchanged calling cards. I think I may still even have hers.'

'So she goes to Delamancha!'

'He has many high-profile patients. Pop stars and such. He gets them off heroin with homeopathy.'

'Does he really? Do you think Special K goes for rehab too?'

'Maybe she just needed a liver cleanse or something to clear out her sinuses... Really, Jane, that's none of our business.'

'Oh yes it is, Charles! Now that I'm to be her secretary, I need to know. The body–mind connection being what it is, if I'm to translate what's in her mind, I need to understand the state of her soma. I need to know what substances she's on.'

'Let Delamancha do the understanding. She's in good hands. I don't think you need to worry about her health.'

'I'm not worried! That's not the point. Well, anyway, hand over some cash. I need to go shopping.' I sat down in our one armchair and let Honoré feed before we headed out, for I hate making nursing stops on street benches. I shook my head at Charles, who was pulling a few bills from his red wallet; his absolute faith in Delamancha precluded him from getting my point, which is that by knowing of a person's physical state, her pains and symptoms and the treatments taken to alleviate them, one is privy to her particular manner of somatizing and hence given a key to her psychology, which in the case of an employer– employee relationship is indispensable. From a theatre course I took from the late Stan Herivosky in New York, I learned to tell a great deal about a person, for example, simply by observing how they stand: there are those who lock their knees and groin (chastity belt effect, expressing fear of libidinal drives, of the risks of creativity); those who thrust out their booties and sway their backs (common in females, this posture shows a reticence to move forward, a tendency to focus on the rear view); those with hiked up, high security shoulders (reveals a wounded person who has overcompensated in defensiveness and has trust issues); those who thrust their heads forward like chickens (aka the disembodied head syndrome; the outstretched necks of these folks make them look as though they're running from the guillotine. They have a morbid tendency to conflate personal guilt as if they were gods, responsible for everything; they offer their necks but never risk them); those who collapse at the diaphragm and slump shoulders (this reveals unresolved emotional issues that defeat the person; they collapse in on themselves. Common in females and males with overbearing wives). Now, if you can gain such insights into a person just from observing posture, imagine how much you can learn from looking in her medicine cabinet! It's quite extraordinary! I didn't go on about this, however, because I already had my mind on groceries and cooking a nice meal for the evening to make up for the last few days of make-do rations. I thought I would prepare an osso bucco with green bean salad and risotto alla milanese. For dessert, maybe some poires au vin, which are really quite nice, particularly if you can afford to soak them in the kind of wine the communists next door drink. We could not, but I thought a nice Saumur would do well. As I was mulling all this over and changing Honoré, I heard footsteps overhead.

'Charles, did you hear that?' We both silenced ourselves like pensive statues listening in. The footsteps, which were barely audible, continued above us for a moment, then stopped entirely as if whoever was up there had plopped himself into a comfortable chair.

'They're back again!' I whispered.

'Let's not jump to conclusions,' warned Charles. 'Maybe there is a new renter after all, what do we know? I'm going to go up and knock on the door. If it is the police, then they'll know we're on to them. If it's a new renter, I'll invite him over for a drink.'

'Yes, I suppose that's not a bad idea. We do need to find out what's going on. But if it smells bad up there, think twice about the cocktail invitation, would you?' Honoré and I listened to Charles's heavy footsteps marching slowly up the stairs with purpose, then to his knocking on the door followed by – to our surprise and fascination – the opening of the door. Then we heard a meeting of voices, Charles's Cary Grant baritone and another man's tenor. Our upstairs neighbour stammered quite a bit, and there were pauses during which he seemed to be fetching his words from a limited lexical stock on one of the higher shelves of his brain, difficult to reach. Clearly he was a foreigner, but from below with the door shut I could not surmise his origins.

'So what's the word?' I asked Charles, who returned to the living room with a round box of Oolong tea.

'A very affable man, Chinese, I believe. Dressed quite remarkably – like the David Carradine fellow, only without the western satchel. He doesn't speak French really but seems to understand it. I invited him down for a drink tonight.'

'Did he give you that tea?'

'He did. Very neighbourly of him.'

'It's dreadfully diuretic. Which reminds me that it's about time we get that fire-breathing toilet fixed. Too bad we can't ask Samir to do it…'

'No, he'll have left Thrushcross Castle by now I should think. He'll be somewhere down in Naples if all's gone to plan.'

'Maybe if we call Muslims Without Borders we could get a referral? Give it a try, Charles. We're going out now to hop and shop.' I made several small leaps in the direction of the door with Honoré in the sling. He loves it when we hop together down the stairwell and skip to the store. I'm not a particularly youthful mother – at thirty-eight I'm definitely on the ripe side – but skipping pokes a tongue at time, plays havoc with its march forward. I skip us back to my eighteenth year, becoming one of those high-school mums about whom the neighbours exclaim, 'Why, she's just a babe herself!' a fledgling mum with a jobless husband whose immaturity is her best asset. Honoré revels in this joyful surge of youth and recklessness. In all frankness, I do think a young mother would have suited him better, one who could wipe off the fatigue of sleepless nights with a splash of water on her face, one who saw the future as an open book awaiting her pen, a lass whose hide-and-seekness surrounds her with an aura of dynamic mystery. As it is, Honoré has to compete with my basic need to replenish a diminishing energy supply through sleep and heaping plates of food, and to produce theatrical works right now, not at some hazy distant hour on the horizon. At thirty-eight, I am antsy to put my plume to paper; the open book is currently under my nose, tsk-tsking me at my desk. Mercifully for both of us, hop-scotching down the street flies us above the prejudices of clockwork. There is something about leaping in the air, that defiance of gravity, that makes us merry, suspends anxieties and the jaggers they engender – if only for the time it takes to get groceries.

When Honoré and I returned from skipping and shopping, out of breath from the five flights and laden with bags from the butcher's, the Monoprix and Mme Su-hun's market garden produce, as well as a small light blue bag from Marionnaud perfumery filled with fragrance samples and a new Dr Hauschka moisturizer (I had to look good for the morrow), we nearly collapsed in the doorway. Thankfully, Charles arrived to relieve us of the packages. He was looking pleased, as if he had made some fresh musical discovery that would propel his work forward to the tippy edge of the avant-garde. And yet, as I was about to find out, the source of his pleasure was situated elsewhere entirely – in the john, to be exact. I heard several grunts then the sound of metal hitting the tile floor in the bathroom to the left of the entryway.

'Who's here, Charles?' I asked somewhat alarmed.

'The plumber, Jane dear,' Charles replied triumphantly.

'Where'd you find him?' I walked into the living room to be out of earshot, took Honoré out of his pouch.

'At the Café Chéri(e). I met him in the lavatory this morning… he was unclogging the toilets there. The clubbers clog them up every weekend – God knows what they stuff down there. One of the toilets coughed up a Stabilo highlighter, several address books, a tube of depilatory cream… Anyway, I asked him if he could stop by our place after work – he calls himself Momo… which is short for Mohammed, you know.' Charles was all the more pleased with himself for having found a solution to our WC problem as he so rarely helps with the household, and his lack of contribution has calcified into a bone of contention between us. Momo was his way of making it up to me. He was like a Mother's Day gift I suppose, practical, handy around the house, a reminder of my burdens.

'Hello,' I said entering the bathroom. 'I'm Jane, pleased to meet you.' I didn't extend my hand, for it's best not to when your interlocutor is a plumber, but gave him my welcome smile. The truth was I really needed to use the toilet, and was going to suggest Momo take a coffee break, have Charles invite him to a bit of Turkish brew in the cucina. But when I peered into the loo's little alcove and saw the state of our once fire-breathing throne, I gasped. Simply put, the toilet had been dethroned, and now the hideous projections of its mute Adam's apple caught in mid-swallow shocked me with its porcelain obscenity. The rainbow coloured electrical wires which once fed the fire-spurting switch were now tied into a topknot, a galvanic coiffure, that swung ominously when Momo's head bumped it.

'Don't look,' I instinctively commanded Honoré, turning around so that he wouldn't have to witness the dismal sight.

'Oh dear!' I said to Momo over my shoulder, 'what on earth are you doing? What has happened to our toilet?'

'Nothing to worry about, Madame,' Momo replied with several rubber joints clenched between his lips. He was a small, bow-legged fellow with a wide, square forehead traversed by deep lines that read like a road map. These latitudinal furrows hinted at a life of travel, of round trips from Tangiers to Paris, by bus and boat, not for leisure but to eke out a living.

'Momo will do the necessary. Say, Madame, you wouldn't have any, eh, cement, would you?'

'No, I'm afraid not.'

'Any plaster of Paris?'

'No.' Momo shook his head at our incompetence, at our lack of building materials which any self-respecting home-owner is to keep on hand. I wanted to tell him that we had all these things back home in Boise, Idaho, in the backyard shed. I wanted to redeem myself, if only transcontinentally. But of course there was no point. And in any case, who knows what Mother kept in that shed these days. Maybe it was stuffed with left-over party favours from the Tupperware days.

'I'll have to go out now and get the materials. I'll need some...' Momo made the French gesture, rubbing the tips of his fingers against the tip of the thumb, signifying money, a word nearly offensive to the French and thus best replaced by Gallic finger-speak. Though Moroccan, Momo had spent enough time here to know how things were done.

'How much will that be, do you think?' Momo's brow rose and his eyes looked to the east as he made his quick calculations.

'Give me fifty.'

I left the bathroom quickly and went to sit down in the living room to nurse Honoré before I headed down to Café Chéri(e) to use the WC. Charles advanced the money without so much as a question, which made me question him.

'How much is this going to cost us, Charles? Did you get an estimate?'

116

'He said he would give us a friendly price. That it wouldn't be too expensive…'

'A friendly price! Good God, Charles! Do you know what that means in my family? Extortion, for Christ's sake!'

'Please, Jane, your language…'

'Do you realize how much this might cost us? Now the toilet's all in pieces and we're just going to have to pay whatever he asks!' I tried to keep my temper down as Honoré was nursing and there's nothing worse than spiking the milk with adrenaline. 'Listen, Charles, when he gets back, you're going to have to get an estimate, make him be upfront with you. We're in no position to be robbed blind by a man named Mohammed.'

Honoré had finished his milk and the smile on his face was almost smug with contentment, not unlike Mick's perhaps in an analogous Angie situation.

'You stay here with Honoré while I go out. And think about inviting Momo to dinner. That just might get the price down. I certainly bought enough food.'

I then gave myself an indulgent two-and-a-half-hour break from motherhood; after visiting the WC at the Chéri(e), currently relieved of Stabilo pens and tubes of Neet thanks to Momo's plumbing techniques, I wandered around Belleville, down the rue du Faubourg du Temple, stopping at Tati to check out the deals: a package of ten pastel wash-gloves for two-fifty; three yellow cotton onesies with an *ours brun* motif for three-fifty; a bottle of Voilette Beauregard eye makeup remover for one-twenty. With the cheerful pink-and-white checked Tati bag tucked under my arm, I went back up the street until I reached my favourite exotic food store. I bowed my head to avoid the long salted tongues of dried fish and the green, pickle-sized bananas hanging in the doorway and entered its cave-like intimacy. Not an inch of space is wasted. The shelves display items for cooks and shamans alike: African peanut butter in tins, skin bleaches, cocoa butter creams, sweet potatoes, plastic bags of white manioc, as well as teas that relieve the entrails, infusions that promote priapism, herbal remedies for happy sleep, yellow and green powders to flavour fish and lamb, pili-pili pepper necklaces, cinnamon sticks and the usual yellow label Espig brand spices. Stocky burlap bags squat on the floor stuffed full of grains and beans. Every hue and texture of legume imaginable can be scooped up into a brown paper bag, weighed by the grumpy Chinese shopkeeper specializing in African and Island fare, paid for at the register at wholesale rates. I replenished our stock of white beans to make *pasta e fagioli* and picked up some turmeric and cumin, indispensable for the tagine dishes which I was intending to prepare.

I stopped by Marion's on my way back; she was in the midst of a transcendental meditation, but seemed to welcome the interruption. She lives alone and doesn't work on Mondays, when the library is closed, and I think she meditates because she's not sure what else to do. Like many people, including Charles and I, who used to trans med together before Honoré was born, the idea of meditation appeals to her but she finds it somewhat boring once she lotuses down to do it. We had tea and chatted on about the recent translation of *Moby-Dick* and about the King James Bible and the inherent difficulty of translating such Saxonity in French. I was going to say something about Chapter XL of *Moby-Dick*, in which Melville sets his international group of harpooners up for a lyrical verbal slam that would make fantastic rap opera material, when suddenly I felt the pressure of the milk arriving, that ache and swirling feeling of all the vessels and ducts singing out in lactic unison. I excused myself and made a run for home.

My shirt was wet by the time I arrived at the rue de Meaux – fortunately I had a raincoat to cover it – and Honoré, jaggering away in Charles's arms, was ready to latch on for dinner.

'Where on earth have you been?' enquired Charles accusingly as I nestled Honoré under my shirt. I pointed to the packages I had dropped on the floor in the hallway.

'Taking care of the family,' I replied self-righteously. 'Mothers don't write symphonies in their spare time, we don't have that luxury.' My jab annoyed Charles, who forever feels pressed for composing time. Still, when push comes to shove, he gets more hours at the keys than I, and as the first inklings of a new theatrical piece were becoming perceptible to me, along with the desire to get them to paper, I felt a tad resentful. Yet mostly I was frustrated with myself for not sitting at a Café Chéri(e) school desk with a notebook and pen to sketch out my incipient inspiration. Buying beans and sundries would indeed contribute to our well-being and comfort, but in doing so I had foregone the call of artistic imperative, cheated myself out of a rare chance to indulge my plume. Beans can always wait in burlap bags (though their preparation does require foresight, what with the soaking overnight), but art will die on the vine if unattended. Perhaps I had only myself to blame, but I'm no martyr and I was glad to have a guilt-prone target at my disposal. Charles made no reply, though I could tell by the way his kiss curl grew almost taut that he was annoyed. He went to the bathroom to see how Momo was getting along.

Our Chinese neighbour never did stop by for a drink, perhaps he had misunderstood Charles and had nodded his head in agreement to a proposition the nature of which we will never know. I put our burner to work during Honoré's nap, preparing the osso bucco first so that it could slow-braise, then the pears in wine. And Momo continued to clang his tools, past cocktail hour (which he declined, though he did accept a glass of apple juice), past dinner (which he also declined though he accepted a slice of toast spread with Kiri cheese), past Honoré's bedtime at ten. He didn't close his toolbox until near midnight, at which point he ushered us into the WC excitedly. If he were tired from his long hours of toil, he certainly didn't show it. He panted with the nervous expectation of an artist anxious to pull back the sheet covering his latest tableau before his benefactor. We followed his signal to position ourselves at the proper distance and angle so as to gaze most propitiously at his creation. And there it was! Three stairs tiled in a mosaic of Oriental ceramics and jewel-hued glass shards of blue, gold and green led up to our toilet, now perched on a veritable rather than a proverbial *throne*. This royal alcove where the toilet now reigned was done over in peacock-blue tiles from floor to halfway up the wall; a golden frieze ribboned its way around the three surrounding walls, just at the height of one's head (mine more than Charles's, it should be said) when seated at the throne, like an aureate crown, though square, not oblong in its glory. The electric flushing apparatus with its topknot of wires had been removed for good and now sat in a plastic bag, pestilent in its retirement, awaiting disposal by next day's green coated garbage men. Propped up at this extraordinarily regal height, the WC which of necessity had previously required the Saniflo unit to flush, no longer had any need of the electricity-generated grinding and crushing for the riddance to happen; now gravity, like the greedy gullet of a force-fed goose, would pipe it all down to the Parisian sewers.

'Why Momo, this is simply extraordinary! It's glorious! And that horrid switch is gone for good!'

'We certainly didn't expect this...' Charles added, trying to overcome his speechlessness. 'The mosaics are... exceptional. We had no idea you were... an artist, *ma foi!*' I could tell that Charles's mind was filled with hesitant wonder at this strange manifestation: before us was an artisan who transcended the coprolitics of his trade, that hands-on with the pipes that embrace human detritus (including the highlighters and address books of crapping clubbers) by designing kaleidoscopic creations of beauty. Of course this alchemical journey from the abject to the sublime is more than familiar to the artist; and yet the crude realism of Momo's point of departure – toilets and their tubes – and its symbolic deficit made the transformation all the more remarkable and rare.

'Watch!' Momo commanded us. Hastily, with his cowboy stride, he walked up the three bejeweled stairs, leaned over the throne and pulled the flushing device. A rush of water accompanied by a great gurgling swallow and the fainter, melodious tinkle of the tank refilling delighted us with its acoustic novelty. Gone was the electric cackle and fire spurt of the Saniflo unit before its engine revved and its rotating blades tackled their task. We sighed with relief.

When the tank had refilled, Momo flushed it again. Perhaps to give us added proof of its high performance, perhaps simply for the pleasure of hearing waterworks. Charles was not insensitive to the music, and left us for a brief moment to jot down some notes at his composing desk. Momo flushed a third time before stepping down from the throne.

'It's very good now, Madame, is it not?' he enquired with rhetorical

121

flourish, convinced now that we, his benefactors, having expressed our awe and appreciation, were readying to make our offer.

'It's more than good, Momo… it's beautiful. And you must tell us now how much we owe you.' I was willing to play into his expectations only so far. I felt in no way capable of making an offer. Had he been simply a plumber it would have been easy to bargain down the price – I'm a Maraconi after all, and have learned the mercantile manners of my ancestors – but the art part threw me. I knew that no artist likes to put a price on his work, that he sought its value in the eyes of others, inwardly supplicating those peepers to make the highest bid imaginable. Momo frowned to reprimand me. He became impatient, nervous. The highway lines of his forehead crumpled accordion-like into a treacherous alpine road of hairpin turns.

'Please, Madame, a pen and paper…' he said at last with a closed-mouth sigh that pouted out his lips. This was a French sigh which had caught on in the North African colonies years ago. I went to Charles's desk, returning with a Post-it pad and a pencil. Momo began jotting down something in Arabic, writing rapidly from right to left; then there was some multiplication and division, perhaps more addition. In the end he came up with his sum, the fruit of this mathematical word problem, and circled it.

'I'll get that for you,' I said, relieving him of the Post-it pad and returning to the living room where Charles was just finishing up.

'Can you spare two hundred euros, love?' I ask Charles. I felt tears coming on and tried to fight them back by breathing deeply. The truth was, I was being pulled by two contrasting emotions – the tragedy of spending two hundred euros on a toilet and the unforgivable slight of paying an artist so little for so much. I went into the kitchen and let

Charles handle the *règlement*. Though plumbers work in wetness, they abhor soggy bills, which ours would have been had I stayed around a minute longer. Digging out a Tupperware bowl from one of the kitchen boxes, I filled it with a generous helping of osso bucco and risotto, sprinkled parsley on top for freshness and sealed it shut with that emphatic pop-in-place sound which always brought such personal satisfaction to Mother. This image of her, nearly fulfilled and suddenly self-confident thanks to this percussing plastic, helped me regain possession of myself. I returned to our company in the living room.

'Please take this dinner with you, Momo. There is nothing haram in it to offend your confession. Just veal and rice.'

'Thank you, Madame.' I knew of course that artists love to be fed Tupperware dinners, homemade meals they could heat up at their convenience, thus avoiding the creative drain of dinner socializing.

'Did you tell Momo that we have friends in Saint Denis?' I asked Charles, having overheard Momo from the kitchen talking about his parking garage near the cathedral.

'Used to have friends in Saint Denis,' he replied tensely, waving his hand to dismiss my comment.

'They work with Muslims Without Borders,' I added, ignoring Charles who I felt was being absurdly cautious. 'You've heard of them, right?' Momo nodded his head as he set the Tupperware into one of his plastic bags.

'I've heard of them, Madame. I heard the police shut down their headquarters.'

'When was that?'

'A couple of days ago. They operate some kind of terrorist unit, they say…'

'That's nonsense of course! Has someone come to their defence?'

'I don't know. It's the Algerians who run it.'

'Yes, yes, you're Moroccan... I see.' So much for the great Muslim fraternity, I thought to myself as I admired Ahmed, Samir and Rachid even more for persisting to promote brotherhood across borders against such odds. Even their Moroccan neighbours eyed their solidarity as merely supposed and styled for Algerians alone. Muslims Without Borders had a great deal of work ahead of them, uniting Moroccans, Tunisians and Algerians as well as Sunnis and Shiites and their conflicting schools of jurisprudence. In my heart I wished them well. God-be-willing their unity will one day be restored.

When we bid Momo farewell, it was half past twelve. Honoré was sleeping but would surely wake in two hours for a feed. Charles went out like a light, but I could not get to sleep. Not only was I anticipating Honoré's cry, I was beleaguered by worrying thoughts of our magi: Did they make it across the border? Might they have been caught and now be locked away in an Italian prison? Or what if something went wrong with their meeting with the capo? Did Mr Woo make away safely with his convoy? I counted catastrophic scenarios, each one surpassing the former in the extent of disaster. Try as I may, I could not get my mind to counter these dramatic denouements with sanguine reports; my spirit darkened with the expanding night around us. Mercifully, an idea at last came to me like a parental hand plugging in a nightlight: if I called Mathilde I would surely get some news, or at least obtain an appointment to hear the latest. Due to the hour, I could not phone of course, so I said my special Prayer of Conveyance, a kind of wireless plea. It went something like this:

News, news must get to you
Even if you are in Timbuktu.
Listen closely, open your ear
So that these words come crystal clear…

My dear Mathilde, you know we worrry
About our magi and if they curry
Favour with the capo, or carabinieri
Or if they've been locked up and said 'sayaneri'

Give us the scoop as soon as you can
We are all concerned with the plight of Man
Those held in thraldom and their saviours
Of whom it is required such radical behaviours.

Near the Kingdom of Naples, the Comorra crew
Have with heinous treatments made our Wise Men stew
Their stirred-up anger must with righteous industry quell
The evildoers of the fields – may the magi sound the knell!

My dear readers of the atheistic branch, friends and followers of the Dawkins fellow, you have surely by now chalked up our zealous faith and prayerful practices to anachronistic nonsense. And yet you must at least concede the therapeutic benefits of such seemingly futile efforts, for having uttered this orison beneath the blankets of the conjugal bed, beside my sleeping spouse who mercifully slumbers without snoring, a calm descended upon my mind, cottoning the litany of disasters in a fog that decreased their visibility to vanishing point. My mind was peaceful at last. I slept for three hours, until Honoré woke, later than I had anticipated – God bless him – then rolled back to sleep until his six o'clock feed. When Mathilde called at 8.00 a.m. and proceeded, without my enquiring, to deliver the news my prayer had put at the heart of its inquest, it came without that pinch of incredulous surprise that follows coincidences.

'Ahmed just left two days ago,' she began her report. 'I confess I was sorry to see him go. The oubliette seems so empty now, so silent without the television running… without the telly imam calling to prayer. I went without a watch while Ahmed was here, I relied on these prayer calls to situate the hour; how little I cared about the increments of seconds and minutes! It was enough to pin time down five times a day and release it after the last *Amen*. I was concerned about Ahmed in truth… he never reversed his decision about the monk's disguise, which only compromised his safe departure. Padre Las Vegas and I managed, after lengthy eschatological discussions, to persuade him to trim the moon from his sideburns, to remove his little skullcap and the white Islamic robe he so favours. In the end it was the Apocalypse of Saint John that came to our aid. That lively inventory of hell's horrors, its seven-headed beasts with diademed horns, its ponds of fire and looking-glass harlots somehow ignited Ahmed's cause and made him more cautious. "My Highest Duty" he reminded himself over and over again. "Accomplishing Allah's will…" He is now stationed near Cannes, where I found him a position as a convent cook. The prioress owed me a favour, you see. Remember when I took those three decalced – by which I mean barefoot – sisters in for rehab? I returned them sober as stones. Put Keds on their feet. Ahmed, by the way, took the television with him.'

'Have you heard from the others?' I enquired anxiously.

126

'Only that they reached San Marco in Lamis, where the San Matteo monastery lies; Padre Las Vegas accompanied them there. They'll be using it as a base for their emancipation operation. Rachid called me upon their arrival, they were nervous about the charcuterie and the crucifixes, which is only understandable... I suggested an educative entertainment to engage and lift their spirits – a bit of monkey-see monkey-do, I told them, "study your Nazarene Brothers closely, amuse yourselves at the art of imitation." Of course I assured them that they wouldn't have to eat cloven-hoofed flesh, that the monks would happily scramble some eggs to replace the rillettes, or offer a platter of cheese rather than proffer prosciutto. "Remember," I told them, "that the Koran sanctifies Christ as a prophet... does it bother you so to see the Son of Man nailed to a cross? God bless you, my sons! Your dismay is a sign that you suffer along with the Great Sufferer. Your life-saving exploit will set you on equal footing with your Hippocratic homologues at Doctors Without Borders; you shall vaccinate your brothers against the scourge of slavery, amputate the tools the field masters have sewn onto your uncles' hands. But unlike France's medical mercenaries, hubris shall not limit your range in reaching the human heart, for suffering is not outside you but within you." This seemed to have cheered them up.'

'It sounds like they're all a bit uneasy about this, Mathilde. You haven't heard anything from the police, have you?'

'We did have a little visit, yes. Two plainclothesmen drove up the other day. They were greeted by the demoiselles – a bit too excitedly, I might add. By the time I arrived the fellows had shed coats and shirts – the blond one was stripped down to his *marcel* and the shorter gentlemen bare to the waist – he was terribly furry. I daresay you know how the demoiselles are... gentlemen callers being so rare at Thrushcross... I cannot be held responsible for their conduct – I provide for them, rehabilitate them, teach them the catechism and hygiene, but can do no more... I am a Frenchwoman, you know, and would never inhibit a healthy appetite.'

'But what happened? Did they come looking for the magi?'

'It took me a moment to find out... they were enjoying themselves you see. It's the Polish demoiselles – too pretty – they were, how should we say it? – delighted to accommodate these gentlemen callers with relaxing rubs. I honestly did not want to interrupt this display of hospitality, but as the proprietor, I felt it my duty to greet them. "What brings you to Thrushcross Castle, my dear men? I see the demoiselles have made you feel at ease..." I announced. The swarthy fellow had a bit of a time wiggling himself free of the arms around his neck though the blond man extricated himself more quickly and had his shirt back on before I could see if he had chest hairs. He flashed his police ID and announced his procedure. I was asked to look at three photos and identify the men therein represented. I told these gentlemen that with all due respect I could do no such thing. I explained my fundamental difficulty with the trickery, the widespread *trucage* which has corrupted photography today and turned it into a deceptively democratic art – by which I mean that its very democratization falsifies representation and cheapens the élan to render the truth by way of a singular vision – and that this *malheur* is due to the fact that it is practiced for the most part not by truth-seekers, but by vacationers and advertisers. Because of this, I explained to them, I would not be able to honestly identify the men in the mug shots even if I did know them (which I certainly did not) for already, in the very rending of their faces, dishonesty and dissimulation were at work. The darker one – a presumptuous fellow, *ma foi!* – then took to threatening me, claiming I could be charged as an accomplice. "An accomplice to whom? And to what?" I replied. "For I cannot identify these men and even if I claimed that I could, I would be lying, for the photos are in themselves a lie." The upstart then flashed the photos at the demoiselles who smiled, shook their heads and oiy-oiy-oiyed at the handsome faces of our fearless trio. Fortunately the demoiselles hadn't the slightest suspicion about the monks, whose hooded heads were all they saw, never a face, never a lock of hair. I kept the brothers at a distance. And the girls know better than to disturb men of prayer with their undernourished libidos. Particularly the Polish demoiselles, whose reverence for John-Paul II extends to all habit-togged brothers.'

'Oh dear,' I said when she paused for breath. 'Starsky and Hutch again. Those were the same men that came to see us, Mathilde. It bothers me that they are on our trail.'

'I assure you there is nothing to worry about; the police have been suspicious of me for years. Suspicious of my dormitory filled with Eastern émigrés, lasses tired of turning tricks, Mary Magdalenes on the run, pooped pill-poppers, broken legged ballerinas – they stop by occasionally, you know, to pay their respects. I don't think our plain-clothesmen actually believe the magi transited through Thrushcross; but they were intrigued and wanted a treat from the demoiselles. A rub-a-dub-dub…'

'Three men in a tub. Who do you think they'll be?' I took the cue from Mathilde to ring a rhyme for Honoré. He was getting antsy, waiting for me to finish on the phone. We'd have to wrap it up.

'One more thing, Mathilde, and we need to make it quick – Honoré's in jagger mode – what about Mr Woo?'

'An extraordinary man! He came to us before the light of dawn, dressed in a flowing white silk suit… there was something so supple, almost immaterial about him, you see – and he reminded me of a wave of moonlight on a pond, rippling with night breezes. His movements were feather-light, his energy razor sharp. When he raised his arm to guide his convoy of trucks to the stables, an arc of quivering light followed his wing, then shot its rays across the sky, illuminating the Vegans. The flash was explosive, it lasted but several seconds and ended in a brilliant splintering of light cascading over the vehicles. They were light-washed, you see… transformed from ruminating Renaults into… what shall I call it? Yes! Sedans-of-Wonder, *ma foi!* I am unfamiliar with the Asian principles of such pyrotechnics, but I will venture to say that this was a kind of benediction…'

'But do you have any idea if he made it to Brussels?'

'None whatsoever. But I have asked the Sacred Heart to inform me.'

'And?'

'I haven't heard back yet.'

'What about the demoiselles? How did you keep this secret from them? Did they get a whiff of any of this?' At this point, Honoré started jaggering, a serious, full-lunged wail, which only a nip of milk could quiet. 'Hold on a second… Honoré needs to nurse.' I set him on my breast, his satiny head cradled against my arm with the trust of the famished. I put the speakerphone on. Caught Mathilde in mid sentence.

'…I added it to their goulash. I was sorry to do so but it had to be done…'

'Added what?'

'Why, the bromides! Dr Delamancha assured me they would be harmless – and they didn't seem to affect the taste of the dish, at least none of the demoiselles complained the paprika had soured. They slept soundly that night, not a peep… Not one of the girls arose to use the ladies' room. In any case, I had locked the dormitory door just to be safe.'

'Sounds just like a St Mercy High senior year sleep over. They used to lock the girls in the gym once we had our nighties on… and there was this girl named Tara – she was a majorette – who did a striptease in front of everyone. She was shameless and had the most amazing dye job… her pubic hair was hot pink like a fluff of cotton candy. She was really proud about showing it off. You can't blame her really…'

'I've never cared much for show-and-tell, Jane dear. May I have a word with Charles please?'

'I'll call him.' I didn't call Charles, however, but waited it out a bit. Mathilde could hold. How I dislike it when she cuts me off like this! Particularly as we had been confiding in one another like good friends, or so I thought. Just as I was perceiving a loosening of the 'law' which titularly joined us upon my marriage with Charles, Mathilde tightened the title. Mother and daughter *in-law* we were, and as such, our attempts at amity would always run up against the roadblocks of jurisdiction. Charles came into the living room. I pointed my toe at the phone.

As I shall never be privy to the conversations between Charles and Mathilde (he took the phone into Honoré's room for privacy), nor shall you, dear reader. But let us not be concerned then about what is denied us. Instead, may we focus our transcendental energies on supporting the magi, who are soon to liberate enslaved men and perhaps risk their own lives in doing so. I shall leave you now as I myself am going to embark on a new chapter of my life as a working mother. Bringing home the bacon and wrapping it around oysters. Wish me luck. God-be-willing we shall meet again soon in these pages.

Chapter VIII

*In which Jane de La Rochefoucault says a
few words on the topic of Maternal Madness and
joins a circle of international nursing
mothers at the Café Chéri(e) etc.*

Honoré is now nearing seven months. He sleeps through the night when not in the throes of teething, which of course he often is, poor dear. On these nights of dentition Charles runs to the crib armed with Dr Delamancha's chamomile drops to cool the smiting and bring the jaggers down. Honoré now takes a morning and afternoon nap during which his mother knocks out translations on Special K's favourite subjects – not the daily allowance of vitamins and iron, but sublimation and Mother Madness (more on this in a moment). His musical aptitude hardly surprises us of course; already he plucks out *Au claire de La Lune* on the piano guided by a paternal hand and sings in his crib, a budding baritone, following in his father's vocal range. As a tribute to the grandmother he has never met, he tosses Tupperware tops, after wetting them thoroughly in that university of infantile knowledge – the mouth. Do I sound now like a fawning, adoring mother, ever admiring my son? Yet perhaps to say I watch my child with wonder would be to lie. Motherhood has not allowed me such tender distance or the refreshment of a leisurely gaze; my overwrought nerves, the heated substances coursing through my blood on the hormonal highway, preclude the cool flush of wonderment. Forget the frisson. None of that amorous chill for the Mother of Honoré. Yet there is another kind of love that threads the hearts of the demanding babe and the flustered mum – it may not be as tender, but is certainly as sure. I feel as if I've been in the front line since day one, attending to Honoré's non-stop needs as if my life, even more than his own, depended upon it. Am I enjoying this adventure? In all honesty, I'm too harried to relax into the transports of delight. Do I regret it? Not for a moment. Is it worth all the wrinkles? It is worth the world.

Special K is currently at work on a book entitled *From Motherhood to Madness* (I believe, or is it the reverse?) and I have been able to glimpse some of the pages. She writes that (always putting the important points in caps), the violent emotions of the mother, HER PERVERSION AND MADNESS (I love you/I hate you; I feed you/I eat you etc.) her manic states and emotional outbursts (If I have to Palmolive another sticky Tupperware top in this goddamn bucket of a shitty sink I'm going to…!!!) can be worked through if SHE DIVESTS HER PASSION/MADNESS THROUGH SUBLIMATION which in turn allows her to RETURN TO TENDERNESS and the child to CREATE HIS TRANSITIONAL SPACE. I suppose this is another way of saying it's best not to be overbearing. Also, that if you have some means to transform your mother-angst into something useful, be it scrapbooking or writing librettos, both you and babe are better off.

Do I feel this madness? This maelstrom of gusting love giving way to – God help us – the sadistic thrill of hate? I confess that I do, at times. Honoré can try me to the point where my reason departs in an act of self-preservation. Madness, yes. My poor boy! He has every right to be demanding, after all. When the calm returns, I readily take the blame for these drifts; such departures to the extremities of the self create an absence at the centre. And is it not PRECISELY THIS CENTRE HE DEMANDS? (Special K).

Do not judge me too harshly, dear reader. I have been ungentle but not harmful, quick-tempered but never abusive. I have never given Mother Trouble the upper hand, though admittedly, I've come close to being toppled. Perhaps my best asset in this no-win business is my knack for SUBLIMATING (Special K) or rather creating. I do this almost obsessively; in its most minimal manifestations, sublimation requires merely a bit of olive oil, vine ripened tomatoes, a clove of garlic (for making Grandma Maraconi's prize-winning pomodoro deluxe), or a fine-point pen (preferably black) and the back, blank side of a bank statement (for jotting down lines of my libretto), or even a broom (which stands in as a waltzing Charles). This might explain why Honoré can lie in his crib for an hour, fully awake, perfectly content to shake the daily trappings of his five senses into his six-month-old imagination, that vast transitional space wherein he has, to his credit, INTERIORIZED THE ABSENCE OF MAMAN. Suffice it to say he has taken the cue from me. He keeps time with my jejune sublimations by operating his own. Though I'm as faulty as airport security equipment, I am not nannyish. Perhaps I might after all qualify for Winnicott's good-enough-motherhood? But let's not jump to conclusions too soon, *ma foi!*

I've been working for Special K now for several months, translating her international correspondence and conference papers in which she caps the essential. I first met her in the 25th tower office to which I had been convoked and whereupon she hired me after a cursory nod at my résumé and a question regarding a literature course I once taught at the art school Parsons Paris entitled 'Art and the Real'. Mercifully it was a 'yes or no' question, which spared me the embarrassment of explaining how the course literally imploded when I had my students play characters from *Dorian Gray* and conduct a mock trial of Oscar Wilde. A homophobic marketing student with a sixth-grade reading level was the instigator of this mutiny, which in the end cost me my job.

Unsurprisingly, Special K is a striking woman. She arrests your attention with an authority both natural and earned combined with an astounding light – not in the least accounted for by her platinum bob – radiating from her person in bright stabs. One wonders how she can throw so much sun around her, brushing it aside as another might push back her hair, or darting it forward with the intention of sizzling you. Her starry aura envelops, consumes and tricks you into feeling blessedly chosen to sunbathe in her presence, while you are in fact drafted into its service with as little consideration as a master gives his slave. On first meeting her, it took me a moment to recover from my initial daze and actually perceive her face, which is surprisingly small though quite wide from temple to temple. This is due to her broad set of cheekbones, seated high and prominent in a face that bespeaks a distant, Asian ancestry. Her opaque brown eyes sink into a sliver, but can open wide with emotion or revelation, rising into the shape of a camel's hump. During our interview she perched on a regal swivel-chair at her industrious desk within a surround of towering bookshelves, one of which was lined with copies of her impressive *oeuvre* and its translations into some thirty tongues. Unlike the others, this particular bookcase was protected by glass doors and could only be opened with the aid of a key.

When I made some admiring comment of this impressive display, she went over to it and removed a copy of her latest philosophical novel. I was struck again though this time by the sensual fullness of her now upright body, the way she nonchalantly rolled her hips. Certainly I hadn't imagined this illustrious member of the intellectual Star Academy, a woman of some sixty years, to display such earthy voluptuousness. I had always thought of her as a Head, as a great Mind inhabiting the helium heights of high-pitched Metaphysics, but there she was strapped in a cross-your-heart bra like Jane Russell, her bottom wide and sassy. When she came over to hand me the book, she did so standing beside me, pressing herself into me as she held out her novel for both of us to admire, and I could not keep myself from inching away, crab-like, from the insistent cushion of her body. What came to mind just then were the rumours I had heard about her celebrated *ménages à trois*, her bisexual exploits with libidinous doctoral students and ambitious admirers on Continental campuses; and, as if to prove this graduate school gossip true, her own boasts of *libertinage* as a defiant form of resistance to bourgeois monogamy. *Ma foi!* I wondered, *is the Special K coming on to me? Is it the Berber décolleté? The matador-red of my wraparound? Or is she turned on by the subtle pheromones associated with mother's milk?* I took a little leap to the side, hugged the book, as I expressed overly enthusiastic thanks. The phone rang just then, calling her back to the desk with its piles upon piles of erudition. I made a curtsey and took my leave.

Cradled in my arms was her novel *La Pendule de Pénélope*. Its back cover sported an emphatic puff from a prominent *Le Monde* critic: *Ce roman est un livre entier! Un festin métaphysique du mal et du bien, il annonce la littérature du troisième milliénaire.* Goodness! As I headed down the stairs, I flipped it open to read Special K's inscription. What she had written proved pure and prudent: '*Pour Jane, avec mes amitiés, K*'. So it was agape, not amour that she was pressing into me! I'm afraid my inbred Maraconi suspiciousness deluded me unduly, tricked me into believing my patroness had unwholesome designs when her behaviour merely resembled that of many fleshy females whose bodies, like bumper cars, craved collision. I'm a bit cushionny myself these days. Did she weary in the late afternoon and require a pillowy assistant to rest upon? Lord help me if my stern ever saddles down low like my Neapolitan forebears. Grandma Maraconi – God bless her! – had hams that started below her knees. Her thickness came not from the plates of pasta she ate twice daily before her meat course as my father always claimed, unforgiving as he is of the overweight (who incidentally are soon to inherit the Earth, or at least the United States of America), nor did obesity and its gelatinous revenge on the flesh plague her. With Old World dignity Grandma Maraconi grew wide and wilful, firm not fat. She flanked herself with heftiness to withstand Pops' skirt chasing, to belittle it with the girth of her fundament, to watch those chasuble-making maidens dwindle down to bite-size nothings. Pops never lasted long with any one of them; they may have been tasty but could not compete with Grandma's fortified sturdiness. They were but anchovies, she the iron anchor. Once reformed at the potter's wheel these mini-skirted minnows finned southward to the Great Salt Lake. Taking a wad of cash from Pops' wallet. Perhaps some of them went on to be mothers?

There is something about motherhood, if I may go on about the subject, that brings the focus of existence back to the body, to its fundamental needs, which are largely but not exclusively biological. Bottoms must be wiped, of course, burps require special care and positioning, tiny nails must be clipped with utmost precision, but if the child's mind is engaged in lively exchange, he will forget the discomfiting heat of his diaper, he will smile at the bewildering pangs of indigestion. In other words, I have learned as the Mother of Honoré, that the secret intelligence of the body comes to bear its fullest fruit when the imagination joins it as playmate. Maternal love is the bond that makes this playtime possible. A loveless child falls short of the bloom; a child smothered by inordinate love ripens too quickly, which rots the potential. Mother Trouble would be responsible for these unfortunate drifts, as Special K carefully explains, for the madness breeds excess – takes mother and child to the outermost reaches of themselves where life rattles them brutally like salt shakers low on seasoning. And no mother is exempt from this treacherous navigation through the field of folly…

I have found that I am happiest as a mother when I am amongst other mothers; and it seems to me that the lifestyle best suited to my maternal disposition would be a communal one, with many mothers on board to raise a horde, cooking and tending the wee ones together. I delight in the idea of this mum-utopia, but there is no way of making such a reverie real, especially in Paris where even the Communist Party fails to come together, as the ousting of a potentially prime player like Mathilde so clearly evinces. The best I have managed, and through no particular effort of my own, is to be acquired by a nursing circle. What exactly is a nursing circle, you ask? Roughly sketched it is a meeting of minds and mammae. But perhaps the way to describe such an unusual phenomenon is to take you directly to where it transpires: the Café Chéri(e), Wednesday mornings, 11.00 to 12.00. Shall we?

(Sitting with babe at breast in the far right hand corner of the café on vinyl armchairs and a dubiously stained brown corduroy sofa, in a section where smoking is prohibited by law, but allowed by long-standing Gallic tradition, the mothers of the nursing circle convene, always as if by surprise, for the circle came about with the concentric randomness of water hit by a negligently tossed stone. Ours is a globe-trotting group: from Athens to Milwaukee, from Boise to Agadir and Berlin, our breasts have traversed oceans, braved continental drifts, married outside the bounds of nationhood to arrive at this outpost in the 19th arrondissement. Here is Artemis the Athenite foodie; Myriam, the Moroccan who has overcome inverted nipples but continues to have a tag problem; Tracy the Milwaukeeian, a La Leche League consultant who nurses eighteen-month-old twins; Bettina the Berliner who boasts an E-cup nursing bra; and of course, Jane the Boiseian who has given up as much sleep as she has milk.)

Artemis: You take the mackerel and fry it till it's almost black. But you stuff it with rosemary first, salt it of course, but cook it good. My daughter loves it, it's a fatty fish, not farmed… she eats it with her fingers… your son will like it. You must feed him fish… how come you don't make him eat right?

Myriam: I don't know if I should go to the doctor, don't I? Felix a bit sick, I think. He vomit this morning and a something green came out, isn't it?

Tracy: Nurse him. Just keep nursing him! It's the only thing they can digest when they're sick… I call it kill-germ juice… *[ringing of cell phone – the Disney tune of 'It's a Small World']* Hello? Yes, this is La Leche League, Tracy speaking… What makes you think he's not getting enough milk? Uh huh… have you been pumping? Yeah? Well, stop. Put him on your breast and nurse him. Give him the real thing and as much as he wants it. You've got to get your supply up and he's demanding. Get to work, mama… What? Uh-huh… Listen, you just forget what that Frenchie doc said. In France they don't know diddly about nursing… here a woman's breasts are the exclusive property of her husband – it's part of the Napoleonic code…

Jane: I'm going to try to keep this up for twelve months… I think… but I've, uh, got this problem… a kind of, well, itchiness…

Artemis: Why don't you feed him fish? Does he eat fruit? Will he have apples? My daughter loves shrimp in tomato sauce. You can buy the shrimp frozen, not farmed, be careful not to get the farmed ones. You make a nice tomato sauce, with olive oil, some thyme maybe… And be sure to take the seeds out of the tomatoes, or it gives them the shits. My daughter…

Bettina: Fish sticks, that's the easiest… with some chips… Dieter loves that… *[Sudden look of distress]* You know, I think I'm coming down with something… Do you see any red slashes here?

[Pulls up her top far above Dieter's head, revealing an E-cup mamelon, swollen hard but slashless.]

Jane: What's wrong? *[Twists her neck to take a look.]* You think you might have mastitis? I don't see anything suspicious there…

(The entire circle is impressed by the Teutonic breast but pretends the contrary, for milk supply is not contingent on size but only proper demand-style feeding. All mothers are potentially equal and the non-competitive nature of the nursing circle depends on an understanding of this scientific fact.)

Artemis: Try putting a cabbage leaf on it… I swear to you it works! But it must be organic… and green, not the purple one.

Tracy: Did you know that breast milk has even more antibodies the second year you nurse? *[She receives just then another call. The twins are now sleeping in a stroller, drugged with calcium.]*

Myriam: Perhaps I give my son something bad yesterday… something green… but I don't know… I don't give him green things to eat, only sometimes a pea, isn't it?

Jane: Like I was saying, I'm going to try for twelve months, that's my goal, but this itching… it's just driving me crazy… and I'm not sure I can…

Tracy: You've got an estrogen problem, Janie… *[She puts her hand over the phone's speaker.]* No, I was talking to a friend right here… now what were you saying? Doc said to stop and use formula? How's that? We've got to do something about this damn Napoleonic code problem!

Bettina: If I were you I would have given up by now… I don't believe in suffering as a mother… and really organic formula is not a bad way to go…

Artemis: Maybe he ate something off the floor? Or do you have houseplants? Athena is always trying to eat my ferns. Once I found her with a whole leaf in her mouth, I had to stick my finger down her throat to retrieve it.

Myriam: Nothing on my floor would be green, won't it? I don't have houseplants, only a bonsai, a so tiny one, isn't it? And this is green, like a pea… I don't understand…

Jane: Apparently there's nothing to do about the estrogen imbalance… I'm stuck with it. As for organic formula – I've got nothing against it, Bettina. The thing is, there's no way Honoré is going to give up on nursing. He's loved it from day one.

Tracy: You're going to have to grin and bear it, Janie – it's for the worthiest cause in the world. But hey, listen, you can drop me a line whenever, even in the middle of the night. I'm usually up feeding the twins anyway… Just give me a call when it gets too tough on you…

Jane: I appreciate it, Tracy, but it's not really like that… I'm not in a crisis, only it's irritating, you know…

Bettina: Listen Myriam, would you like the name of a good paediatrician? One who does homeopathy? Felix does look a little off, I mean, he's been sleeping all morning.

Myriam: Yes, you think I should take him to the doctor's, should you?

Artemis: I've never heard a baby cry like your Honoré. I'm sure he's hungry…

Jane: Yes, he sounds like Mick Jagger, doesn't he? You know, when he sings that song 'Angie'…

Tracy: I always hated that song.

Jane: Well, it can't be such a bad thing to sound like Mick, can it? *[Puts Honoré into the sling and swings him wide from left to right. Goes around circle planting kisses on both cheeks of each mother.]* I'll see what kind of fish they have in the market. *[Faces Artemis, who raises her bow, arrow ready to shoot its dietary reasoning. Steps aside of the target, excuses herself from the circle.]* Farewell friends… till next week, keep the supply

144

up. Mustn't fall short of demand... Careful of trickle-down... Bye-bye...

[Leaves café skipping. Honoré now laughing joyfully with each hop. Down the Boulevard de La Villette they go, along the promenade, leaping Martha Graham style to avoid the fouled spots; along past a solitary Sam-the-Man on a bench, bent over and bereaved it seems: has his travestied he-wife taken her pink poodle elsewhere? – but no time to console him; along past an emptied package of lychee jam biscuits, the spine of it ripped out and wagging like a flustered tongue; along past a pair of Algerian retirees awaiting pensions, legs politely crossed to catch their retirement in the crotch; along past the brick guardian's hut, wallpapered with Rastafarian visages, dreadlocks snaking beneath Jiffy popcorn hats woven in tricolour yarn; up to the Trotskyist news vendor hawking Toute la Vérité *at the mouth of the métro which the Mother of Honoré purchases for her mother-in-law at a discount price of €1,50; and now to the right, at last, the great white Soviet dome to which mother and child-in-sling curtsey.]*

For some reason the sight of that gloriously disinterested egg, its brittle white orb protecting the embryonic negotiations to favour communal good over personal gain (and, we certainly hope, more modest wines at Marxist dinner parties), never fails to fill me with a sense of relief. What an antiquated notion disinterestedness has become. It is as mocked and despised, I'm afraid, as the Great Sensibility whose manifestations modern critics of Arts and Letters misjudge as a 'clever distance from the real', when really this exacerbating sensitivity puts one so close to the Burning Thing that stepping back is wise, though not, however, particularly clever. When I think back to that terrible review of

Charles's *Suite #2 for the Holy Spirit and Three Harps* and how the critic derided its thirteen-note serialism as 'post-Christological posturing', it pains me still. The celebratory sincerity of that suite, its Pascalian ambition to marry mysticism and mathematics, and the humility required at its inception to hand over the reins to the Holy Spirit, in short, all that characterizes the genius of Charles's minor masterpiece, was overlooked by our *Le Monde* detractor. Perhaps the de La Rochefoucault family would feel all the more alone in its anachronistic pursuits if that Soviet dome did not herald a higher ideal. It is only natural that we would make our nest nearby, for hens of a feather flock together, isn't it so? In any case, the egg is more than simply a landmark and even Honoré senses this; he kicks energetically whenever we pass by it, as if to push forward the incubating collectivist ideals with his spindly yet sturdy legs; bless him, he is made of good mettle, my son.

Chapter IX

Which recounts a minor literary epiphany as well as other events, mostly of a troubling nature.

Perhaps it is too soon to mention it, dear reader, yet it is hard for me to keep such news from you, because I consider it particularly favourable and enjoy spreading a good word, which in this case is that the Great Sensibility has settled quite solidly in the regions of my mind, where it has been at work orchestrating the narrative of a new operatic venture. It's all very nascent, you see, and I haven't had much time to devote to it, Honoré being the number one recipient of my attention, of course, followed by Special K's communiqués (for we must have bacon around our oysters). Writing comes in third, but better a bronze medal than no medal at all.

My new opera will be based on an urban drama and inter-denominational love tale, a kind of *West Side Story* transposed to Paris's suburbs. Yasmin, a Muslim student at the University of Paris-Saint Denis, takes an inauspicious shortcut through the projects and is attacked and nearly gang raped. Pablo, a Spanish-French youth happens upon the violent scene and rescues the Muslim girl from her captors. Pablo and Yasmin fall in love and their forbidden passion brings two worlds into collision... I think you get the idea. I have decided against the burlesque touches which made *Away in a Manger* a particularly frothy piece in favor of a more dramatic *déroulement*. Why? To be honest I'm not exactly sure; I suppose I'm departing from the comic because the little Cassandra in me insists on my complying with her prophesies. Or could it be because prior to becoming the Mother of Honoré I had an effective lock system, sluiced gates that opened only to happy crews, and that this once flawless system was thoroughly wrecked the night and day I gave birth? Could it be that since the birth no gate is strong enough to hold off the torrent of life crashing through me, and that this great open chasm leaves me vulnerable to the ten thousand ways of dying and living, God help me?

Perhaps it's best not to be too dramatic.

The story of Pablo and Yasmin will probably veer towards the tragic, though who's to say. We shall wait and see. Already I have some ideas about the music which will be a mix of rap, raï and flamenco. Perhaps the Koranoblaster will be of use?

Apart from the opera, I have also been preoccupied with a new change in our family's circumstances, one that has us all reeling and disquieted. If you'd like to listen in, you will very quickly be made *au courant*.

Mathilde called just two days ago with astonishing news. I could tell right away that something was wrong because she began talking a mile a minute about her apiary apparel and not making sense at all. It sounded as if she was near to tears.

'What on earth is the matter?' I enquired. An uneasy silence ensued, then what sounded like a wooden bowl hitting the floor. I believe she dropped her pith hat.

'It's Cousin Constance…' she blurted out at last.

'Yes?'

'Well, she… is in a predicament… what I mean is she came over this morning looking peaky. Then she got sick several times… the last time she didn't quite make it to the bucket…'

'Has she seen a doctor?'

'She has.'

'And?'

'Jane… May God help us… Cousin Constance is with child!'

'Jesus!' I nearly fell over backwards. It couldn't possibly be true! Why, that rope she wore around her waist tied her to the Church and to her Bishop; it kept gypsies out of her girdle.

'Please watch your language, Jane! Especially at a time like this.'

'Christ almighty! You've got to be kidding…'

'I wish I were, Jane. She showed me her pregnancy test; I saw it with my own eyes.'

'But maybe she had someone else pee on it… you know, she could be playing a joke; I had a friend in college who did that to her boyfriend just to scare him. It was her older sister who was pregnant…'

'She would never do that; she has never been a prankster. To think of it! She has just ruined her life as a sister! The doctor said she's in her second trimester already.'

'But maybe she de-confirmed her virginity before she indulged? Did she say?'

'She is still officially confirmed. And now she risks the worse… she

149

might very well be… oh dear, I can hardly say it… she could be… heaven help us! Excommunicated!'

'No!' My dismay at this prospect nearly matched Mathilde's; never in the history of the de La Rochefoucault family has a member been sacked by the Holy See, though admittedly a few misbehavers have come close. Cousin Constance would never get over it, bless her. I felt it my duty to protect her, as I might a teenage mother, impregnated by surprise in an unfortunate case of premature ejaculation.

'Listen Mathilde, no matter what, we cannot let that happen. Promise me you'll support her through thick or thin. We've got to work on the Bishop.'

'I'll do what I can. The Bishop is not known for his leniency though perhaps we can loosen him up with some *bonne chair*. I'll have the demoiselles plan a papal dinner menu – foie gras, caviar-filled eggshells, *homard bleu aux pommes Rubinette*, a dainty Bresse chicken or should it be a *Charolais tête de veau*? Well, that sort of thing. It should soften his sentence.'

'Where is Cousin Constance now? Is she staying with you?'

'No, she's staying in her camper, but she has the mad idea of running off to Naples… to join Rachid and Samir I'm afraid.'

'Oh God, Mathilde, you don't think…'

'Yes, precisely. That is exactly what I think, though she has not revealed the name of the father. Certainly it is one of our magi.'

'Not a gypsy, eh?'

'We cannot know for sure, but I suspect not. They are too much like family to her. To be honest, I think her run-in with the wash-and-dry affected her… rather more than we imagined. She stayed with me the week following the incident, and do you know? She returned to the contraption every day for a full body wash, she was sponged in front and back, then rubbed with vibrating brushes. I know this because she would leave the bathroom door ajar – I caught a glimpse of her face as the sponges closed in on her. Her eyes were closed, her lips slightly parted: she was in the grips of the pleasurehold. I knew then that she had awoken, yet still I did not suspect she would throw her legs up in the air so promptly.'

'She always was impulsive. So easily moved by the Holy Spirit's slightest whim.'

'I suppose so… but we must talk her out of going to join the Muslims. *C'est une mauvaise idée; peu importe* if one of them is the father of her child. They are involved in dangerous business and the stakes have been mounting of late. Last week I spoke with Padre Las Vegas, who you know has become the magi's chief advisor and confidant. Did I tell you the capo has reneged on their deal…? He is now demanding fifty thousand per captive. They'll never have that kind of money. It's impossible!'

'Sounds bad, Mathilde. From what I've understood, they're heavily guarded; the mobsters never let them out of their sight.'

'It is going to require extremely careful planning.'

'Or a miracle. Perhaps we can get to work on that?'

Two things happened just as I hung up the phone: Honoré awoke from his nap and someone knocked on the door. I ran quickly to pick up Honoré who always needs rigorous comforting upon waking. He was delighted to see me and stopped the jaggers instantly once in my arms. Together we went to the door and peered through the peephole. Standing on our doormat was a white-haired gentleman, presumably Chinese. Could this be our upstairs neighbour?

'*Oui?*' I enquired having opened the door. For an answer I got a series of nods and a smile. The man before us manifestly did not speak French, or at least very little. He was dressed in a silky mandarin collar top that floated over matching pants; beneath this white, roomy suit he appeared willowy, though this whippiness belied the peculiar energy I was perceiving quite strongly, a busy frequency that encircled him tightly like an army. I sensed he was made of tough stuff even if a strong wind might blow him up and away.

'How can I help you?' I ventured – in English this time. I wanted him to get to the point. I could feel Honoré getting antsy and irritated that this visitor was taking my post-nap attention away from him.

'Nice baby, Madame. Strong baby,' said our guest as he squeezed one of Honoré's legs.

'Yes, he is very strong, quite a kicker. Say, are you our upstairs neighbour?'

'I live upstairs. Nice flat, very good view.'

'Would you like to come in?' I don't usually invite strange men into the house when I'm about to nurse Honoré, but he seemed harmless enough. And I could tell he was going to be slow in declaring his purpose. Honoré would not hold out if we stood in the doorway much longer.

'Just for one minute, Madame. I bring you something, then I leave you.' I led him into the living room and offered him a seat on Jinn-Jinn, our pouf.

'A cup of tea?' I offered.

'No, only one minute. That is all.'

'I hope you don't mind,' I said as I sat down on our only armchair, 'if I nurse my son.' I'm not sure he understood me, but it didn't particularly matter. I was going to nurse whether this odd little man minded or not. I only wished he would get to his point; he had used up his minute ages ago.

'Yes?' I insisted, to speed up his confession or delivery, whichever it may be. You would think he'd realize the intrusion he was making on our intimacy, but he seemed completely oblivious.

'You can call me Wayne Fellow… that is my name.'

'Well, Wayne Fellow, what brings you here today? Just a friendly visit?'

'Yes, friendly visit.' He nodded his head. I waited for him to say more but he grew quiet again.

'I believe you've met my husband already, right?' He looked at me bewilderingly. 'My husband,' I repeated, lifting my hand to indicate height, a tall man, which Charles certainly is. Still, no light of recognition in Wayne Fellow's eyes. I was about to get up and bring a photo of Charles over to him – the one from our wedding where he's playing his nuptial suite on the gamelon, his sticks only visible as a blur – when I heard the keys in the door. Entered Charles, returning from a job interview at the Cité de la Musique.

'Why hello there! Well! I must say we were expecting you ages ago.' Charles went over to our guest to shake his hand. 'We've been enjoying the tea, I should add.'

Wayne Fellow did his smile-and-nod routine, but said nothing.

'Is everything OK upstairs?' Again, smile-and-nod. 'Anything we can do for you?' Nod-and-smile.

'Why don't you make some tea, Charles.'

'Good idea, Jane.' Honoré had finished nursing; I snapped myself back into place and bounced him on my knees. *Mama's little baby loves shortnin' shortnin', mama's little baby loves shortnin' bread…* We sang, his kiss curl flew, his belly laugh burst forth. We were having a grand time, but then remembered we had company too.

'Now tell me, Wayne Fellow, how long have you been in Paris?' I really do dislike small talk but what else was I to do with this man?

'Please, Madame,' said our guest, reaching into a canvas bag he had set at his feet. 'There is something I must give you.' Odd, I hadn't noticed he brought a bag in with him; had I been more perceptive I would have simply asked him to show me his wares. He then pulled out a fabric-covered box – red with golden arabesque motifs – and set it on his knees. I was waiting for him to hand it to me, but strangely, he made no motion to do so.

'What have we here?' I enquired. I got a nod-and-smile in response. Oh well, I thought, maybe he's waiting for Charles to come back with the tea. Perhaps this red box is for Charles after all – which seemed fair enough. So it is customary in the West as in the East to question the motives of a strange man who offers a gift to the lady of the house. Wayne Fellow was showing us his intentions were gentlemanly; the box patiently sat until Charles returned with a tray.

'I believe Wayne Fellow has something to show you, Charles,' I said just as my husband finished pouring the tea. I pointed to the red box in the expectation that Mr Fellow would take the cue.

'I give you this box,' said Wayne Fellow, though no gesture, no outreaching hand accompanied his words. The box sat mysteriously poised, full of expectation; perhaps we were to make a bid on it? But then our guest undid the hook and slowly, with great care, began opening it. As he lifted the lid, a piece of folded paper sprung out. Wayne Fellow handed it to Charles.

154

'Go read please. Great importance.' Charles nodded to the gentle-man. He cleared his throat and read the following notice out loud.

'Warning for user of magi-mushroom: danger to liver of all kinds, if misdirection. Handle with care. Do not boil in hot water; do not put in freezing zone. For problem with parasite, cannibal happenings, and lowering bowel: one quarter spoonful once per day. Best grind fungus with pestle. After add to favourite fruity liquid.'

Charles and I looked at each other incredulously.

'Uh… What was that part about cannibals? Did I hear you right?' Charles looked down at the paper for verification.

'You did.'

'It must be a mistranslation. I think they're referring to some specific parasite, like a tapeworm. Isn't that right, Wayne Fellow?' But our guest remained silent. Several minutes passed before he lifted the red box, balancing it on the tips of his fingers as a priest does the holy host. I wondered for a moment if he were making an offering to the Taoist sages, but in the end, he carried it over to Charles. We bent our necks and looked inside. The box was lined with bright yellow silk and contained what looked to me like a petrified bear turd (I had stumbled upon one once on a backpacking trip; though it had been rather fresh, not yet drained of its moisture and I had hightailed out of there). We both looked at Wayne Fellow for an explanation. But our gift-giver sat stonily, offering none.

'Listen… uh… Wayne Fellow… You've got to tell us what this is. It looks like dried dung rotting in a treasure chest, and it's supposed to be for parasites or art events planned by cannibals or something. You've got us stumped.' Was he, I wondered, playing with us? Was this all some sort of prank, infringing on our family time? But Wayne Fellow shook his head slowly, brushed aside the nod-and-smile routine. His face clouded up; I could sense his soldiers lifting their rifles.

'You need this! You keep it! The parasite, the cannibal, they are not the worm in the gut; there are people feeding on people. Making money on lives. What I give you, it frees the man from the cannibal!'

'Goodness!' I pulled Honoré in close.

'We accept your gift,' said Charles. 'Even if we do not yet entirely understand its purpose. Something serious is at stake, this we know. We shall wait until we receive further indications.' Wayne Fellow appeared to have calmed; he shook Charles's hand, then bowed to me and Honoré, before promptly taking leave.

'Something serious is at stake?' I questioned my knight once I heard Wayne Fellow close his door upstairs. 'What on earth did you mean, Charles? Is there something you know that I don't?'

'No, it's not that, Jane. Rather it's a matter of deduction. I believe he wants us to get this to Samir and Rachid. The thing is called "*magi-mushroom*" is it not?'

I was impressed that Charles had picked up on the signifiers. I hadn't caught the cross reference.

'I admit it's queer,' said Charles, tossing his forelock back. 'But clearly there is some connection, a kung fu connection perhaps. We will have to wait and see. We're likely to have more information soon.'

'You know, Charles, I had a call from Mathilde, before Wayne Fellow arrived...'

'Yes? And how is Mother?'

'Well, she was upset... she's had some shocking news... just awful, really.'

'What? You must tell me, Jane!'

'OK, but sit down on Jinn-Jinn before I do. You'll need a seat.'

'Good God! What is it, Jane?'

'It's Cousin Constance. Now, are you ready? Brace yourself, feet flat on the floor.'

'Yes, yes, I'm ready…'

'Your Cousin Constance has got a bun in the oven.' I saw Charles's jaw drop, his forelock fall; the news was registering. The impossible was freestyling over to the possible and changing lanes to get there. It would take a moment, I knew. I set Honoré down on the floor so he could practise his speed crawling. He was over to the pouf in no time, grabbing on to Charles's pant leg. Pulling down his troubadour socks.

'No,' said Charles at last. 'It simply can't be.'

'Well it is, God help us. She even showed her pregnancy test to Mathilde. It was really her pee and everything. Pick up Honoré, will you?' Charles was not only shocked but chagrined as well; he needed the cheering up only a child can give. Honoré would remind him of the blessing it is to be pregnant, even for a nun. Within seconds, Charles went from sad to mad (an improvement on the former *tout de même*) thanks to our son's natural therapy.

'How on Earth did this happen?'

'Well, you know, darling… the usual way most likely.'

'What I mean is, Jane: Who is the Culprit? Who did *this* to Constance!'

'I wouldn't put it that way. You're being very old-fashioned. She was a consenting adult… Here, give me Honoré for a minute. I think he wants to play with the Tupperware.' I went into the kitchen and brought out three bowls from the Sheerly Elegant collection; Honoré took the largest of them and put it on his head just as his grandmother used to

157

do to find her salad keepers. Back in those days it was hard to tell the difference between a salad keeper and a multi-purpose bowl, but mother claimed the salad keeper fit over her head and covered her third eye and that was how you could tell them apart.

'To tell you the truth, Mathilde thinks it's one of our magi... most likely Rachid or Samir. But that's only a speculation. Cousin Constance hasn't coughed it up yet.'

'*Nom de Dieu!*'

'I know what you're thinking, Charles. But you're going to have to let it go. They're good men, we both know that. True enough, she's a nun and they're Muslim, but this is the twenty-first century after all. Everything merges and converges these days. In any case, you don't own her virginity, for heaven's sake! She can do with it what she likes. Concretely speaking, the problem is, well... you know... she might get... excommunicated. She forgot to de-confirm her virginity before she threw up her legs.'

'What a way to talk!'

'I'm just putting it as your mother did, Charles. We need to look at this straight on. It would kill Cousin Constance to be deprived of the seven sacraments. I mean what if she had no other choice but to go Evangelical. It's happening all over South America... Padre Las Vegas was telling me about it – it's happening in epidemic proportions!'

'I trust my mother will know how to handle the *évêque*. She has been very good to him over the years...'

'Yes, I'm trying to remember... didn't she pull a few strings to get the Petit Trianon Château for his sixtieth birthday party? Now that was no small feat!'

'That's right, and there's also Dr Delamancha; she had him treat the Bishop for his haemorrhoids. He made a successful recovery and the diocese never saw a bill.'

'Let's just hope for the best, Charles. With so many young people leaving the Church, you would think the Bishop will go easy on her. Maybe he'll let her go with a monition.'

'Yes, yes… perhaps… we'll have to let Mother sort it out.'

Chapter X

On Cousin Constance's visit and its unhappy effect on Jane and which concludes with a sip of sex-on-the-beach.

The following week, while I was translating a recent essay by Special K comparing the displacements of masochistic economies in Proust and Rousseau, and whilst Honoré was napping, there came a rap upon the door. I did not welcome this disruption, for I am always terribly pressed, my office hours being from 10.00–11.00 and 2.00–4.00 Mondays through Saturdays (which correspond of course to Honoré's napping schedule). I nearly refrained from answering, but the rapping continued and a woman's voice called my name.

'*Oui? Qui est là?*' I enquired from my desk, without getting up, for I am posted not far from the door.

''Tis Cousin Constance.'

Constance, I should explain, in her daughterly devotion to Mathilde has adopted her archaic speech habits. Fair enough, it's very catching. Charles tis-es too, and an occasional 'thy' flies out of my

Maraconi mouth as well. A family that pray-tells together stays-well together.

'Oh Cousin Constance! You must come in!' I rushed to open the door, but before I moved away from the threshold to let her pass through, I took a good look at her. My eye could not help but go straight to her middle; the rope was still in place and yet I sensed the beginning of a thickening there, a new tautness to her holy cord as the flesh inched out against it. It was her face, however, that had most changed; a puffiness gained her cheeks and neck, softening the usual sharpness of her features. She looked more womanly but also more fragile and slightly lost. I wondered if her faith had been shaken. Could a couple of rolls in the hay move God away? I suspected she was in the throes of heart-wrenching turmoil, that guilt had her up to the gills.

And so I was surprised to find she took things quite differently.

'Have you any idea what time it is, Jane?' she asked once inside, as if she were in a hurry.

'It should be around three-thirty, I believe. It's good to see you, Cousin Constance. Can I get you a cup of tea?'

'I'm afraid I won't have time for that. But I needed to see you and Charles before I leave.'

'Leave where, dear Constance?'

'I'm going to Italy. Padre Las Vegas is expecting me tomorrow.'

'Listen, Constance, you can talk to me, you know... woman to woman... I mean... there really is nothing to be ashamed about this... your pregnancy. It's a blessing to have a child even if you're, you know... a sister. Do you really think the Lord thinks otherwise? He gave you ovaries and all the fixings – just like any other girl. Listen, you can trust me, Constance. You know how much respect I have for our magi... if it were one of them… I mean if one of them were the father… well, I think it's great.'

Constance looked at me with that strange other-worldly look she has; it is the expression of saints and sages; one that is gained by renouncing the world and dining like gypsies on merguez sausage sandwiches.

'I'm thinking of Mary,' she said, 'a poor carpenter adopted her son, but the true father of the child was the Great Aristocrat.'

'Oh God, Constance. You're not trying to tell me this is a case parthenogenesis…'

'No, I am not. I admit that I have… known a man.'

'And you can't tell us his name?'

'I'm going to be leaving tomorrow, Jane, and need to get something from you…'

'Right. I know just what it is. Let me go get it out of the closet.' I then went rummaging through a duffel bag where I keep my rumpled maternity clothes, mixed in with some size 10 pre-pregnancy items the petiteness of which I find endearing – I keep them around, like one might a photo, as a testimony to thinner times – and pulled out three skirts, two pairs of pants as well as several size 14 Ann Taylor tops that did the job quite well for me while I was carrying Honoré.

'I've got it all here, Constance. I'm just going to put it all in a bag for you. I think everything will fit: it's all elastic-waisted.'

'There's no need, Jane.'

'What do you mean, "there's no need"? You're pregnant, for Christ's sake, and you're going to have to dress like it! That robe of yours has to go. You can't go walking around like a pregnant nun!'

'But that's what I am, Jane. I am a pregnant nun.'

'Well not for long, Constance, I mean… the nun part. You're obviously going to have to renounce your vows.'

'My robe will be perfect; I'll just loosen the belt.'

'Good God, Constance! Have you thought of the Bishop?!'

'He will not be pleased.'

'That's exactly right! You can't think he's going to keep you on the payroll? Let's talk facts here.'

'My needs are meagre. Please dear, Jane, don't burden yourself with this. The Lord will provide; He always has.'

'Provide what? You can't even afford Nivea cream with the pittance you already have! For heaven's sake, Constance, you have a baby coming along!'

'I didn't come here to talk about that, Jane. Do spare me further discussion on the subject.' Very well, I thought. Like Mathilde, Constance has that Gallic way of slapping a conversation shut; it seemed pointless to fight it out with her. Constance has the stubborn streak of a Virgin Martyr, unyielding in her efforts to Godspeed her own ruin. Not even Charles, for whom she has always kept a soft spot, can make a significant dent in her intractability.

'What is it you came for then?'

Constance's eyes flitted around the room, searching the bookshelf, the last stack of unopened boxes in the corner by the window on the right, our book-strewn desks. Clearly she preferred to find whatever it was on her own and simply make a run with it; she was tired of my meddling, of course, but her business had brought her to my home where only I, the mistress of the household, could give her satisfaction. She had to fall back on her skills of obedience, those she acquired at the Bishop's special training college, where she majored in Prayers of the Little Flower – *Les Prières de La Petite Fleur* (St. Thérèse de Lisieux).

'The red box,' she said at last, her voice humble, her eyes again modest and averted.

'You mean… the… Chinese box…? Good God! How on earth do you know about that?!'

'Padre Las Vegas has asked me to pick it up. This is all I know.'

'Right, well you're going to have to wait for Charles; he's the one who knows where it is.' I told Constance an untruth. I knew exactly where the magi-mushroom was, of course. Charles had put it up in the pharmacy cabinet in the bathroom, behind the pain relievers, for it seemed to be a medicinal substance (i.e. treats parasites, lowering bowel) with rather peculiar properties (i.e. also cures 'cannibal happenings'). I was not about to let Constance walk away with the box though; I didn't want that on my conscience. She was in her second trimester and shouldn't be near any kind of toxic fungus. Why on earth Padre Las Vegas would ask this of her I had no idea, but perhaps Charles did. Constance would have to wait. And in the meantime I would put her to work. Honoré had woken up and after nursing him, I gave Cousin Constance a rudimentary course in childcare and Tupperware pedagogy (Montessori style). Honoré loves the rope and the rosary (bless him, little does he know they are soon to go!) and when I left, Constance was teaching him to say the chapelet. He was wetting the wooden beads, Constance was counting the Our Fathers.

Off to the public library I ran, to look for a copy of *Romeo and Juliet* in the tiny collection of English language books they keep in the back. I needed to find a passage quoted in French by Special K to put it back into Shakespeare's English. Fortunately they had a copy of the master's collected works, sonnets and all. I finished my business in record time

165

and continued on with the shopping. The Monoprix for diapers, wipes and pasta; Mme Su-hun's greengrocery for apples, pears, courgettes, onions and tomatoes; and lastly the Boucherie Marboeuf for veal cutlets and a brief discussion on Saucisse de Morteau with Monsieur Marboeuf, from which I gathered the sausage is best prepared with green puy lentils into which one adds a spoonful of peppered mustard. 'And never, ever pierce the sausage before the boil, Madame,' warned M. Marboeuf, lifting his furry black eyebrows. I nodded, hastily writing it all down on my receipt.

The errands took me but an hour. Little did I know as I scurried about providing for my family and increasing my culinary know-how so as to nourish them with flourish, that during my absence, Charles would return home early and Cousin Constance would leave, with the red box in a shopping bag. The mothers amongst you will commiserate with me; for how often it happens that while we work hard to beat the clock, others turn it forward, undermining our efforts with their injudicious decisions. I had not expected Charles home so early; he has just started a part-time job at the Cité de la Musique as an archivist, shepherding over the scores of countless composers corralled in the basement. He normally returns from the range at six; though a last minute call for a strike had shut the doors of that musical city at 4 p.m. resulting in Charles's precocious return. When I found him and Honoré playing a variation of Debussy's *La Mer* at the piano together and no Cousin Constance in sight I suspected she had made her escape with a clueless Charles as her accomplice.

'Charles, Constance was just here. Where is she now?'

'She left about ten minutes ago.'

'Not with the red box I hope.'

'Yes, with the red box…'

'Why didn't you wait for me to get back? We needed to discuss this together… as a family.'

'I'm sorry darling, but Constance was in a great hurry. She's leaving tomorrow and had to make a stop to see the gypsies before she left. They seem to be having some trash disposal problems.'

'Do you realize you let her leave with a poisonous substance? She's very unstable right now; God knows what she's capable of!'

'I had a call from Mathilde this morning…'

'Don't change the subject!'

'Please calm down, Jane. I am not changing the subject. T'was precisely concerning Constance that she called. It seems that Padre Las Vegas has asked her to bring the box with her to Italy. It's for Samir and Rachid…'

'Does Wayne Fellow know them?'

'Apparently so. It's the kung fu connection as I had thought. Remember what Wayne Fellow said about his strange mushroom… how it frees man of the cannibal?'

'He sounded like a lunatic!'

'Don't be too quick to judge. Samir and Rachid are trying to get those men out of a dire situation; they are being eaten alive, worked to death, and now Samir and Rachid are in danger as well. It seems that… this mushroom, or whatever it is… has the power to break the bonds of thraldom. That it liberates. I know it's hard to believe, but…'

'Hard to believe? Why it's positively fabulous! Like something out of *A Thousand and One Nights*!'

'Jane, you believe in the powers of the Holy Spirit don't you?'

'In the Seen and Unseen? Why of course, Charles! What a funny question.'

'Well, just imagine then, that for these Taoist gentlemen, the Holy Spirit manifests Itself in an entirely different form and manner so far eastward of our own as to be unrecognizable. What would the Taoist think if he saw the Eucharist? For him the host would not be the Body and Blood of Everlasting Life but only a see-through rice wafer. I believe it is the same for us, Jane; we just don't see the transcendental properties of the Taoist's prodigious pharmacopoeia. Don't forget we have our own mind-altering drugs which disconnect people from their destructive desires; why, it is entirely possible that Wayne Fellow's fungus works on a particular lobe of the brain...'

'I'm starting to see your point, but if this mushroom thing really does what they claim, it would certainly be a threat to the Chinese government – or any government for that matter! Just think of all the political prisoners there; what if they got hold of it?'

'It is forbidden in China; but there is an effort being made by a group of Taoist monks and medics to grow it in Tanzania, on a very small, controlled scale. Apparently this is the provenance of Wayne Fellow's red box. I really don't know more about it than that.'

'If all this is true, it has tremendous political implications. Just think of what could happen to capitalism, corporate America, the Dow Jones! And all those nasty dictators big and small who throw dissidents into boiling oil...'

'Let's not get ahead of ourselves, Jane.'

'You're right, love.'

'Padre Las Vegas, of course, is keeping cautious; there is the worry that in our pill-popping era, the mushroom might be taken as a quick fix. I am convinced, as is Padre Las Vegas, that the mushroom's emancipating properties only work when accompanied by a raised awareness in its user, and when he is ready for a liberating action. He must be well in both body and mind.'

'Are you saying that if an enslaved man identifies too closely with his servitude or if he's in total despair, this mushroom fix won't fix him?'

'That's the idea... more or less. As for Cousin Constance,' he said clearing his throat. 'We must have confidence in her.'

Charles's forelock was dangling low over his eye, and Honoré, who was now standing on his lap, tugged at it. In return Charles gave a quick tug to his son's. Honoré giggled with each tweak. Ah! The terrible silliness of existence and of resembling one's father!

'Yes, I'm glad you've brought this back to Constance because we need to talk about her. It's clear to me that she's unfit to carry out this task in her current state, not to mention that she's also potentially putting herself in danger. I spoke to Mathilde last week, she feels the same...'

'Mother has changed her mind since; she now feels quite sanguine about it, particularly as Constance will be taken under the wing of Padre Las Vegas once she gets to Naples. Remember, love, how you felt in your second trimester? So energetic, so exuberant...'

'So completely nuts I nearly gave all our clothes away to the Secours Catholique.'

'You were just trying to make room for the baby.'

'I was impulsive, compulsive, given to binge crying; I had premonitions and chronic itching. I wouldn't take no for an answer: when Dr Wannawanna – you remember our obstetrician –

told me no alcohol whatsoever I went home and fixed myself a tall gin-and-tonic.'

'You should not have done that, Jane…'

'That's right! It was terrible of me. That's just my point! And if you want to know the truth, I didn't just slug down one G&T, I…'

'Honoré is a beautiful child!' Charles broke in, cutting me short. 'Let's not dwell on the past. Constance struck me as being well-balanced, both physically and morally… considering her predicament.'

'Jesus, Charles! She wouldn't even take the pregnancy clothes I tried to give her. She thinks she can keep wearing that old robe. I tell you, her mind's not quite right. I had a woman-to-woman with her… you know… to find out who the *père* was, but no deal. She wouldn't spill the beans.' Charles stood up then unexpectedly and took Honoré into the kitchen.

'Is it time for his dinner already? Let me cook up some courgettes for him. And a cutlet…' I followed them in to get his dinner ready, but my mind was still on Constance.

'Have you any idea who the father might be?' I asked Charles. 'We all have our suspicions of course but…' I looked up at Charles who had grown very quiet; he wouldn't meet my gaze and made a kind of vague gesture with his hands, like a conductor who is not sure whether to swat a fly or begin his symphony. 'Say, Charles, she didn't tell you anything, did she?' It occurred to me just then, that against all good sense, she might have recklessly confided in her cousin, just as I had sloshed down the gin. (Let us remember that just a week ago my husband uttered the words 'who did this to her?' with Othello-like undertones.)

Charles engrossed himself in putting a bib on Honoré, who was

170

still trying to pull his father's forelock. Once Honoré finds a good game he plays it obsessively; in this way too, he takes after Charles who will play the same notes over and over again until they suddenly multiply through the friction of repetition into a musical phrase. I looked at Charles straight on, I looked at him until his face flushed under the heat of my gaze.

'She did, didn't she?'

'Very well, Jane,' he said with a sigh. 'She did.'

'And?'

'I'm afraid I can't say.'

'What?! What do you mean, you can't say? I'm your wife, there're no secrets between us, remember? We're united as one in Holy Matrimony, we share the same troth, we're…'

'I promised Cousin Constance. Please don't insist, Jane.'

I can't remember if I turned the burner off or up to high; but I gave the black dial a 360° turn, tossed the wooden spoon on the table and locked myself in the bedroom. I lay down on the bed and cursed the cruelty of the de La Rochefoucault family, railing at the secrets they kept from me. When all is said and done, I am still an outsider, not a tribe member but a tolerated procreator. Was this how Lady Diana felt when Charles and his queenly mother spoke in royal riddles she could make no sense of? All things considered, it was certainly generous of her to have upgraded their gene pool as she did. I was feeling positively ungracious; why be kind to those who betray you? Finding no reason just then that would justify my returning to the kitchen, I threw on my coat, stalked through the living room and left the house. Charles would have to fend for himself with the burner as my slamming the door made quite clear to him.

Along the promenade I walked fast, my feet hitting the pavement hard. I was trying to stamp down the hurtful emotion that had been laying in abeyance in some unsuspecting sinew, and now sprung liquid-like from the muscle, triggered by Charles's secret. Unleashed, it spread through my veins: it pooled about my heart, spooled around my mind. I may have forgotten the emotion for a time, but I knew its procedure well and its pain even better. Mercifully with each step, as my foot heeled and toed the ground, pounded then lifted, the impact opened an empty room in my mind. Small it was, but sufficient to put me above the flood for a time. It didn't remain empty for long though; in strolled a memory of Mother on my thirteenth birthday. She was wearing not the Wrangler jeans she now sports on the mountain, but a pair of high-waisted sailor pants with six golden buttons down the front and a blue-and-white striped long-sleeved Breton-style shirt. Her auburn hair was styled in a Jacqueline Kennedy do; her make-up impeccably matte.

'You look great, Mom,' I admired. She really did look smashing.

'Thanks, darling, I'm on my way out.'

'On your way out? But it's my birthday today, Mom! What about my party? I told my friends I was having a party today.'

'I'm sorry, honey. We'll have to celebrate that later in the week, won't we? I have a business meeting this afternoon, and then a Decorators Anonymous event tonight – I'm going to talk about my theme-based party favours and discuss some of my recent ideas like the cockle-shell shaped bijoux boxes in pink Tupperware-quality plastic. I put a pearl bracelet in each one. Woolworth quality but you can hardly tell. I'll be back late. Don't wait up for me, doll. Remember you go to school tomorrow. Ta-ta!'

This familiar scene projected itself on the wall in my mind's little room. I watched it play out in a string of variations, a montage of shorts that highlighted mother's sartorial history. Her looks swam with the changing tides of fashion. Yet in spite of all the protean panache she never failed to pronounce the same punch line. Her 'ta-ta' could knock the wind out of me. As a child it would toll in my head as I waited after school in the principal's office because Mother had forgotten to pick me up, or as I tooted a broken kazoo at a friend's party long after all the other birthday guests had been collected in station wagons. Many a block-mother had taken me in for an afternoon, added a place setting on her table for my dinner. It is not that I haven't forgiven Mother for her absences – after all, how could she be present for me when she was absent to herself, poor thing. She was forever searching to find who she was but always going about it the wrong way – like when she turned herself blue inside with methylene tablets and pointed proudly at the toilet bowl or bobbed her head with Barbara Eden earnestness whenever I or Father asked about a dinner we knew would not get cooked. Why couldn't she just live in the real world like other moms? Oh I have forgiven her, but this doesn't appease the pain of being 'ta-ta-ed.'

Grandma Maraconi, bless her soul, mothered me in her gruff, old-world way: she drove a golden Cadillac with leopardskin seats and had to sit on top of the Boise phonebook to see over the dashboard. Even when I was six years old I knew her number by heart; she would never get out of the car, instead she'd honk until she saw me running out of the principal's office. She called my mother 'that bird!' Grandma died when I was thirteen, but by then I had other ways of getting home. So all this is to explain why even today I am overly susceptible to exclusions, to being pushed aside, left behind, kept from a secret, and it is why, having embraced the de La Rochefoucault family with even more whole-hearted devotion than I've ever had for my own, I am all the more wounded by the slightest nudge of an elbow, shoving me out of the familial circle.

Having mulled all this over and made some peace with my predicament, I was thinking of heading back, returning home to catch my husband cooking cutlets (oh dear!), but by now I had reached Café Chéri(e). It was a chilly night and the café's red interior glowed like a Chinese lantern. The figures inside appeared darkish, molten, like creatures made of live coal waiting to be stoked. This overall impression of incandescence, so different from the café's endearing daytime shabbiness, seemed both slightly ghoulish and inviting. I decided to go in and get a drink. I decided to be brave; I decided not to renounce entering just because my milk ducts were getting full. I pulled the glass door right up against my nose, but veered around it and into that queer red cavern which immediately tripped up my senses. The assault was full-on, the snaking halos of smoke had me gasping, the raw bass beat tolling out an electric groove popped my ears.

A man with a goatee, jeans belted below his buns and wearing a longish shirt that proclaimed the benefits of skimmed milk, greeted me mysteriously at the door.

'Come get some… *yesseuh, c'est ta soirée, Coco.*'

'Pray tell?' But he would not repeat himself. I wondered about him calling me 'Coco'; I wondered what he meant by 'get some'. I held my hand visor-like above my eyes to see what I could see through the haze of smoke. Miraculously the horizon was almost clear. I could see the far wall, the passage to the toilets, and next to it a DJ at the massive stretch of turntable. I took a good look at our groove-grinder. Manifestly he favoured the layered look: a Ronald McDonald wig sat atop his hip-reaching dreadlocks, several shirt styles (bowling, T, tank) in micro sizes stretched across his chest, which, mercifully for the fabrics, was but a foot in width, but his bottom half was best, for he bulked up in silver tracksuit pants over which he wore a gold lamé diaper with a elastic band in African tri-colour, red-green-yellow.

'*Ca va trancher, Coco. Yesseuh* – with Amar le Terrible… *yesseuh*… jumpy, jumpy.' The gentleman with a belt around his thighs addressed me again, pointing to our music man, who was indeed jumping up and down. The record skipped with each rubber sole landing, which seemed to be the point.

'Excuse me, I'm going to get something to drink…'

'Yeah, Coco, you get your crunk on.' My doorman was getting jumpy-jumpy too. Oh dear, worried the mother in me: would he jump right out of his pants? Honoré did that once, with a pair of Nighttime Pampers. I moseyed up to the bar, next to a young woman sipping a sex-on-the-beach.

'It's good,' she giggled, noticing my eye on it. '*C'est pour les filles, tu sais.*'

I hailed the bartender, put in my order for the same. It felt good to be a girl again. To have sex-on-the-beach again. It tasted pineappley with hints of coconut, like sunscreen.

'*Tu aimes la clap-your-hands musique?*' She asked, wiggling her shoulders like a shivering pup.

'I'm afraid I don't know what that is. Do you mean, gospel music? Like "Oh Happy Day"?' My neighbour was wearing a very low-cut shirt with a push-up bra, and had applied some kind of whitening agent on her cleavage. Her breats looked like plump meringues. Lovely, flawless.

I wished mine looked like that too. Only I wouldn't want to poison Honoré with whiteners!

Amar le Terrible switched to a Johnny Cash remix of 'Folsom Prison Blues' and the crowd started trying to clap to the rhythm. My new girlfriend's pretty manicured hands joined whenever there wasn't a beat. The French never know when or how to clap, but they were certainly giving it a go!

'*Yesseuh...* all right the girls and boys, *maintenant, je vais faire shaker vos French booties!*' The crowd roared, to my left a young man with a gigantic jaw and a diamond stud pierced through one of his ears snickered '*heinhein hin*' into his Heineken. I scooted over to the nearest mirror-studded pillar and grabbed on. The Clash came down hard on us, but already Amar had taken the beat up a notch, and then the Casbah started rocking with a snarly momentum. The riff repeated again and again until it hiccupped. And then there was the doorman; he tripped on his pants, held his arms out glider-style to steady himself.

'*No souci, Coco.* Hey, hey, hey...'

'Cheers,' I said, uncheerfully lifting my sex-on-the-beach.

'*Ne le prends pas si hard, Coco. Y a du feeling.*'

'No, *Moco. Y a du* nothing. But don't take it *si dur.*'

'OK, OK, starlet, but hey, hey... I know what *you* did last summer...' He had his finger pointed at me as he rolled away in a wave of bodies out to sea. I took a sip of my drink and pondered for a moment : What *did* I do last summer? Oh yes, I gave birth, *n'est-ce pas?* To Honoré, bless him! It worried me that I had forgotten, even for a split second. What's come over me, I wondered. Is this what sex-on-the-beach does to you?

Oh dear, now where's the Café Chéri(e) nursing circle? I wanted to get back on track, to see something familiar, a wink of the weekly routine. I looked over at our homey 'sitting section' with its sofa and vinyl armchairs. But no sign of Artie and Tracy, Bettina and Myriam. Good mothers all of them, at home, tending to their babes, answering emails. Our round was now squatted by a group of girls with tattooed ankles nursing mojitos. They all had different sized ankles but shared the same tattoo – a bracelet of roses on a twisting violet vine – perhaps uniting them to a horticultural cause. I was about to go say hello when Amar started some snazzy scratching, then twisted Cheb Mami's high ululating into a 50 Cent rap. My ears perked at this pounding mix. Ideas for my rap opera began popping around in my head. I went to the bar to jot a few down in my notebook. The girl with meringues was having more sex-on-the-beach, 'Heinhein hin,' said the man into the Heineken. 'Oh là là,' said the girl sipping sex.

I wondered if I should stay and go for a second round. I nearly flagged down the bartender, when Amar threw Erik Satie in the mix; I paused like a bird on a branch, head cocked, and then my mind flew home. How could this not remind me of Charles, who in the early weeks of our courtship composed a piece of Satie-inspired *musique d'ameublement* in my honour? I remember listening to it in those nascent hours when love burgeoned bright and curiosity was our comfort. Could it ever be that way again, I sighed, could it? Would it? That whipped cream lightness of love?

'Choo choo, Coco. *Yesseuh… on va kiffer funky…* hey hey… at my ché-ri par-ty… kiss-kiss bye-bye.' The doorman was just doing his job, holding the door open for me. For this kindness I prayed his pants would not drop. The Holy Mother would help him.

'Shoo-shoo, Moko. Flies in the buttermilk. Night-night.'

And when no-one was looking, beneath the sturdy frame of an open *porte cochère*, I lifted my wings and took flight. I flew to my fifth floor nest (US sixth), forgetful of secrets, mindful of love. And I promised myself never to say 'ta-ta'. Not to Honoré, not ever. As the stars are my witness. Amen.

Chapter XI

Which recounts such domestic adventures as
the installation of a country kitchen etc. and how
Special K calls upon Jane to straighten a kink.

'Some coffee, Momo?' I call out to the kitchen-in-progress where Momo is bending beneath our new sink trying on plastic pipes to get the right fit. I'm careful not to disturb him when he's welding the copper ones.

'With pleasure, Madame,' Momo stands up, stretches his back. Prepares himself for the break. He likes our Turkish brew, which I make for him three times a day. The hotplate is currently in the living room, on my desk. I initially put it on Charles's desk but one of the scores he borrowed from the archives (I believe it was Berg) got splattered with pomodoro and we had a near-divorce experience, which we survived thanks to my stain removal skills. I am happy to say that this burner, merely a grade up from its Bunsen cousin, will mercifully take its full retirement once Momo gets our kitchen installed; we pray it shall be soon.

'You know that faucet, Madame…' Momo stands in the doorway. He shakes his head. Doubt draws his lips forward.

'Do you mean our gold water spout?'

'Yes Madame… it's just not going to work… not with the sink you got there.'

'Oh, don't tell me that! It has to work! We must find a way. Let's think about it, OK? Here, have your coffee.' I can perceive the tick-tocking of Momo's mind as he sips his brew silently. Momo, I know, loves to please me. He belongs to that category of workmen whose chivalry is codified by tools: he wields the welding wand to cauterize our crumbling kingdom, the hammer to harden our resolve to set it right. He is our Arabian knight, deploying his pipes to fortify our kitchen. Now he is meditating on our gold leaf spout, topped with a copper partridge oxidized to turquoise blue. I am terribly attached to it, not because of its prestigious association with the Trianon Château, but mostly because of its weathered uniqueness, its castaway status. Honoré too, has a special affection for this stopcock and is forever asking to turn it on and off. In his imagination, it is the very spout the Itsy-Bitsy Spider so valiantly climbs before the rain washes her out. I want to keep it around.

'The problem, Madame, is you need a mixer, you need hot and cold water coming out of the same spout.'

'Yes, I see your point, Momo; there must be a way to do that. Can't you fix it so that the water is cold when the partridge is to the left and hot when to the right, and with a spectrum of temperatures in-between? Something like that?' I appreciate Momo's idea of mixing, of putting together particles so that they diffuse and create a range of surprising outcomes. So much of life is about just this, *n'est-ce pas?* No worthy kitchen goes without a particle passer.

'I will do the necessary, Madame,' says Momo as he sets his empty *demi-tasse* on my desk. The caffeine has given him fresh conviction. He pulls up his pants, which tend to droop, and returns to his pipes. I observe him from my stove. He picks the pipes up, eyes their insides, blows down their barrels. He reminds me a bit of Charles when he prepares the Helvetian horn for guests. I do suspect that if musicians and plumbers were to convene at a wind instrument symposium and share their wares, a fascinating cross-pollination would come of it.

This kitchen remodelling has taken us by happy surprise. We received a call from Mathilde several weeks ago, on Honoré's nine-month birthday, which we celebrated with an Avent bottle brimming with pure unadulterated apple juice, the first bottle he has ever accepted to drink (more on the salutary implications of this in a moment), to inform us that the Countess de Sarry was having the kitchen of her country *manoir* in Bourgogne gutted in favour of a new Italian design affair with lots of chrome plus a snowcone-maker and ice shaver, and would we be interested in taking it off her hands? It seems that at the age of forty-five the countess, a distant cousin of Charles's, has at last found a strong incentive for learning to cook: a love poem plumed by her Italian paramour in the form of forty recipes, each ripe with amorous innuendo, many featuring sea fruits (according to Charles, lots of vongole I'm afraid...) and sweetened ices. Once her kitchen is up to speed, her chef will train her in the basics after which she will brave the burners and ice shaver alone. Good luck Countess; we wish you well with the shells!

So the kitchen we've inherited is country-style with handsomely weathered oak cabinets. The gas oven and range is far from the latest model but we've been assured it works without fault if you have a match at hand. At the moment it is sitting in our bedroom, behaving like a well-adjusted foster child, ready to root wherever hefty arms set it down, in this case, at the foot of our bed, until Momo finishes up with the pipes and gas line. But what I love most is the deep wide basin of the grey-green stone sink. You can set your spaghetti pot in there and have room for dishes plus a small bucket of delicates soaking in Woolite. Just thinking of having a fully equipped kitchen makes me deliriously happy! You might think relief would be my overriding sentiment, for until now I've had to make do with so little (i.e. no kitchen at all!). But my feelings transcend mere palliation. As with any self-respecting cook, I naturally spread my spirits throughout my kitchen, making my pots boil and sizzle madly on multiple burners, froth and sauce bubbling over lids, splattering tile and range in a rude abandon. It is wicked business, this cooking, and you need to have a sorcerer's soul to harness the destructive forces of fire and blade (and ice, as the countess will discover). Thus, I am excited that I'll soon have a full-out cucina with all functional amenities, counter space, plus a KitchenAid mixer and blender – all courtesy of the Countess.

Oh dear, the phone is ringing and it's only 8.50! Could it be Mathilde with news of Cousin Constance? We've been waiting for confirmation that she made it to the monastery. When I think of her riding trains through Italy with that mushroom thing in her knapsack... why she's entirely capable of slicing off a piece of it to stuff in her breakfast bun! Her head's not right, I tell you.

'*Oui?*' I put on my who-on-earth-can-be-calling voice. The hour is early after all.

'Jane! Excuse me for calling before nine o'clock, but the matter is pressing. Are you with the child?' So it is not Mathilde after all, but Special K, calling before we've served the cereal. Odd that someone who so sanguinely rewrites Freud's pessimistic reading of motherhood refers to my son as 'the child'; as if he were more object than subject. Clearly she sees him as the object which precludes her from getting my undivided attention. There is no grande dame who accepts coming in second. Special K is Solid Gold.

'My son,' I am careful to articulate these two weighty words, 'is with his father this morning. How then may I help you?' I keep my voice upbeat and professional.

'I need you to call Homeland Security, Jane. My visa has been refused and I am to leave for Boston in a week… Harvard has tried to rectify this, but it seems we must resolve the problem on our side. You must, therefore, contact Homeland Security.'

'Call Homeland Security? Goodness! Is there a number for that?'

'You are the American, Jane, not I. You must do something.'

'I'll give the Embassy a call. But I need to know a little more, like the reason they gave for denying you a visa.'

'They say my FG14 is invalid. I have no idea why; there are no further specifications…'

'What about your V91222? Did they mention anything about that?'

'No, but there was mention of my 150024… that it was… illegible. Do you know what this means?'

'Let me call the Embassy. When I get some news I'll call you right back.' Jesus! I think as I hang up the phone. What a fucking nightmare! I had spent nearly a week with her filling out those damned visa forms and verifying with the Embassy that all was completed according to their wishes. We were given the green light then, and now they've come down hard on the breaks. Why on earth would Homeland Security bother with Special K? It's hard to imagine how she could be considered a threat unless HS has been hiring right-wing Ph.D. candidates.

The Embassy is long in answering so while I'm on hold, perhaps now is as good a time as any to break my latest news.

I have weaned my son.

At nine months, falling short of my optimal nursing goal by three months, but no matter. The truth is, I had reached my limit. Nine months of enduring Laughing Breasts Syndrome is quite sufficient. Don't get me wrong; I have not been a martyr suffering my way through the laughter; overall I've found nursing beneficial – nutritious for him, calorie-clearing for me and bonding for both of us. I don't feel I've made any lost sacrifices. But I began noticing that whenever I contemplated stopping, I felt my spirits lighten, my body crave freedom from its habit. And there is important information to be gathered from the sensate, is there not? We should watch our feelings just as we watch the evening news. To keep in the know.

I had a discussion with Honoré about this; it made him uneasy at first (he tossed a Clear Impressions Tupperware bowl into the toilet) but when he finally understood that he could suck upon a rubber teat and drink up the sweetest of nectars (apple juice as I already mentioned, other fruit flavours soon to follow) he agreed to make a deal. The first morning of our pact, it was I who panicked. I could feel the milk coming down, and deep in my bosom an anguished Madonna moaned in quivering agony; I had no idea who the hell she was but figured she must be some Maraconi ancestor, perhaps a Neapolitan wet nurse, whose very livelihood depended on the fruitfulness of her founts.

184

It was a bit rough drowning her out, putting down her plea for perseverance.

'Charles!' I cried out. 'Pick up Honoré, please!'

'What's wrong with you, Jane?' enquired my knight, most concerned.

'I'm afraid of her!'

'Afraid of who, dear?' Charles was getting worried. 'You're not getting delirium tremens, are you?'

'No, for Christ's sake! That's when you stop boozing, not breast feeding. But I've got this milk woman gnashing her teeth in my breasts… I can't stand it!'

What Charles did next was entirely impulsive, commendably intuitive. He prepared the aforementioned bottle of apple juice cut with Evian water and pushed it gently into Honoré's mouth, squeezing the teat so that he got a prelibation of the sweet juice. It took a few minutes, but Honoré did at last fasten on and began sucking away greedily; as I mentioned earlier, it was the first bottle he had ever agreed to take. As I watched my son at the surrogate teat, I could feel that ancestor's angst as if it were my own; she had me pulling at my shirt, pounding my breast – I flushed bright red and began itching all over. But Charles did not give in to her; he sat with calm solidarity, holding Honoré in his arms. Bless Charles, it felt almost cruel at the time but he was holding out to help me over the last hurdle. Mercifully, it was all a matter of minutes: the madonna wailed her last lamentation, beat her bosom, then withered away, while, simultaneously, my milk supply began its dwindling; a day later there was not even a trickle left. I must admit it was a bit of surprise to find weaning harder on ma than on babe; but little is predicable in this adventure of motherhood. Which is why the caring arts require something of a routine, not a rigid one – God forbid!

– but enough regularity so that the swerves of the unforeseeable can be... Excuse me, someone's on the line again...

...Visa problem with visiting professor... No, not V91222 – that seems to be fine... yes, visiting professor... FG14... apparently it's... not valid? I don't know... Harvard says... may she? Review her 150024, you say? Right... at two then... red line? No, green line, right. Ask for visa officer... Roger.

Some people have a knack for dealing with bureaucrats and Uncle Al was one of them: he knew how to take the FBI for a ride. He'd get them in his golf cart and take them out swinging clubs. 'You got to talk to them, Janie, like they was children,' he confided to me at an Italian Catholic Federation dinner while we were waiting for the spumoni. Invariably a couple of FBI agents were always in attendance at these banquets and easy to spot, despite their efforts to be like us. They gave themselves away by wearing big gold crosses – our men wore Madonna medallions only – and by cutting their spaghetti. I always felt a bit embarrassed for them. I learned a lot from watching Uncle Al operate: he really did speak to them like infants, with endless patience, offering a soft, encouraging smile. He was strangely loving and at the same time, unflaggingly firm. He never, ever gave a straight answer, but would cast his line far out into the altered reality of childhood where instincts and affects swim unabashed, and reel in a story that would have them hooked by the fin.

Now it's hard to do that without seeming to condescend, or without getting your line snagged: Uncle Al had an easy genius for it. He could deflect an Agent Tom's suspicion, by reassuring the little Tommy in him. He was loved by almost everyone, particularly by the ladies. They say that those who love us the most are also the most likely to precipitate our fall, which was the case, most unfortunately, with Uncle Al; he was brought asunder by his girlfriend Juliana. She loved him more than life but had to share her time between Uncle Al's golf cart and Enrico Dececco's. The capo (Enrico) had a hold on her (think bank account) she couldn't shake. He also had a margarita bar in his cart, equipped with a bartender named Bula. I remember Pops shaking his head at Uncle Al's funeral, saying, 'He didn't even love that dame, the son of a bitch. A damn pity.' But I think he did love her. In the pocket of Uncle Al's favourite jacket, my father found handwritten *pizzini*, crumpled scraps of paper hidden among the pocket fuzz, manifestly written by Juliana. They were sweet testimonies of a mistress's love mingled with anxious domesticity: *Darling, please don't be upset about Enrico. You know that I love you and only you, my heart! Did you enjoy the pasta al forno even though it was kind of burnt? Was there enough pecorino?* And on another occasion: *My darling Alfredo, Why did you send back the tiramisu? I saw Guido leave it on the doorstep this morning. Was I too heavy on the mascarpone? Oh I love you, Al. I do! Tell me when and I'll meet you at the cart. Carissimo mio!*

In the end Juliana, that woman-who-loved-too-much and overcooked everything did not fare any better than Uncle Al. She was pushed over the side of Mount Jason, and tumbled to her death in a ravine as deep as her love. When she was found there were no *pizzini* in her pockets, poor dear.

And so, now whenever I have to deal with bureaucrats and functionaries, I try to follow Uncle Al's inestimable injunction: *treat them like they was children*. I'm not very practised at it, but I'm usually up to the challenge. Like today. I'm waiting for Charles to return home with Honoré so that we can leave. They went out for the morning and then to lunch at La Rotisserie, the neighbourhood co-op. It's run by some very fine Trotskyists who love to roast things on skewers – mostly chicken and lamb, but also tofu, shrimp, duck, merguez sausage and rabbit. Anything, really, that you can pierce with a stick. You can get a whole plate of roasted things plus pilaf and green salad for five euros, which is frankly unheard of in this day and age. I think I hear them in the stairwell – they must have finished their skewers…

'Jane… give me a hand here… Honoré needs a change… yes, yes… well, just a little mess… Honoré loves to toss his pilaf, you know. And we did spill some coffee on our neighbour's copy of Negri's *Empire*... Chicken? No, no… it was beef I believe… or was it pepper pork? No, no, not too spicy… ate a couple of bites, yes… *[brrrring, brrring]* …and lots of pilaf… no, not all on the floor actually… *[aing-gee, aing-gee…]* please get off the phone Jane… *[aing-gee, aing-gee…]* I must leave for work… Honoré must be changed…what's that, dear? To the Embassy? With Honoré? I do wish you luck, love… oh, and Mathilde is coming for dinner tonight… I couldn't, dear, I just found out myself, she called me only an hour ago… Please don't worry about the food… she said she'd bring some angels-on-horseback… yes, yes, I'll pick up some wine and… oh bother! I'll get some Indian take-out then… do quit insisting, you're making me late… we'll just have risotto then… as you like… with peas and parmesean? No, no I'll pick that up, Jane…'

I'm always happy to have Mathilde over, but, for reasons obvious to all but Charles who has never noticed our lack of a proper hearth (the pomodoro incident did open his eyes for a moment, but only long enough to move the burner from his work space to mine), I would rather do this when the kitchen is completed.

'Now that you're all clean, love, we're going to take the métro to meet Special K. She's a celebrated lady but she's having Homeland Security challenges. Shall we try to give her a hand?' Honoré loves nothing more than seeing the city from the kangaroo pouch, nestled against mother, eyes and senses taking on the world from this privileged vantage point. I don't mention the Embassy yet and the distressing fact that we will be momentarily separated and depouched by a security check at the entrance; I will tell him that on Line 1.

We are almost out the door when Special K calls again. 'No, no, you have to come… I can't do this without you… in fact, they might not allow me to assist you during your interview… it's highly confidential… what? No, they said at two. You're going to have to cancel… I mean if you want to make it to Harvard… pray tell? Umberto Eco? Goodness! Well bring him along, then… you can catch up while you're waiting behind the green line… I'm sure there's a coffee machine… Oh, and I'm going to have to bring MY SON along… yes, yes, you'll get to meet Honoré… well, yes, we'll do our best. Oh dear I almost forgot the diaper bag… thank you for reminding… *A toute!*'

Special K has a way of further complicating already complex situations; she's inclined to the kinky. I'm not referring here to her reputation as a libertine, but to the manner in which her mind hooks its tendrils around thoughts and notions so disparate, so seemingly unrelated, and climbs up the metaphysical mountain like an alpinist straddling several peaks at once. She reaches the top, always, but following her footsteps requires twists and turns and sleuthing of the most trying sort. What she lacks at a basic level is the lens of practicality. Why could she not anticipate the incompatibility of having coffee with Mr Eco at the leafy Closerie des Lilas and getting herself to Boston? The truth is, I can see plain when I have to, and I suspect Special K can too, but she'd rather I take up the slack or go in her stead, in a word, fix the problem for her.

I quickly prepare our outing: bottle of juice, crackers, cubes of Gruyère cheese and sliced apple in a Fridgesmart one-half cup container. That should do. Plus all the rest: passports, photocopies of Special K's visa forms, diapers, change of clothes, Itsy-Bitsy Spider book. Honoré is kicking his feet with glee and we are off!

Chapter XII

*Which recounts a trip to the Embassy and
the difficulty of eating apples whilst being
interrogated – and fingerprinted, ma foi!
– by Homeland Security etc.*

'Now that we're on Line 1, Honoré, I need to tell you something,' I say to my son, for whose sake I've remained standing on this longish, crowded métro ride. He jaggers his heart out if I sit while he's pouched against me. The ride is so much more amusing when Mother is jerked to-and-fro by the train's stops and starts, pushed from behind, elbowed by unloading passengers with oversized bags, forced to back-stroke as seas of incoming Parisians roll in. For Honoré, Mother's wild movement, her near loss of footing and verticality provide a splendid half-hour of entertainment. I suppose he is getting a hint of amusement park fun. For the moment Mother is the roller coaster. Seeing as I'm to secure his foundations, his sense of rootedness in the world this is perhaps not such a good thing. I'll have to discuss it with Special K when we get a free moment, perhaps when Umberto excuses himself to use the gents?

'It's this, Honoré,' I resume, speaking softly above his ear and breathing in his warm baby smell, 'we're going to the American Embassy, which is a high security area, like a fortress. This means they need to check everyone at the gate to make sure no-one has explosives hidden in their bags, pockets, underwear and shoes. Actually they don't check your underwear really, but if they suspect you, they sometimes pat you in that region...' Here Honoré starts to get a bit fussy.

'But there's nothing to worry about. They will not check in your diaper, love. Mother won't let them!' I have to resist telling Honoré the story Artie (of Nursing Circle fame) told me about a trip her family recently took to visit her sister in Chicago. As they were making their way through security at O'Hare airport, decalced like Carmelites, lipsticks, bottles, and all gel-based sundries naked in Ziploc baggies, Artie was actually required to de-diaper her six-month-old daughter for nappy inspection after the detection bells went off when they stepped beneath the security canopy. In a divine stroke of retribution (of the innocents and all modern travellers), airport security found therein a sizeable poop, harmless but horribly pungent. As Artie explained, 'I had fed her fish for lunch, wild mackerel... it's so good for you and for the brain... she ate the whole fish... even tried to eat the skin but I took that away... it was burnt. But she really ate the whole fish...' Bless Artie and her holy mackerel. I must give her a call soon, since I won't be returning to the circle. Unfortunately Honoré has not had any fish today, just skewered meats at Trotskyist prices (which perhaps ferment with equal pungency? Though I doubt digestion complies to egalitarian notions); but there will be no diaper removal, I will make sure.

'The worst that can happen, love, is that they depouch you for a moment. It's likely that they will, so please, try to prepare yourself. Whatever is required, you will not leave Mother's arms.'

Fortunately, we've arrived, and will hit fresh air in a moment; it'll whish away our anxiety, put our mind back on the elements. We emerge at street level.

'Why look, Honoré, the Place de la Concorde! See the Obelisk of Luxor – it was climbed by Spiderman, did you know that? And listen, the birds are tweeting in the Tuileries… can you hear them?' But in truth it is hard to hear the fledglings over the commotion of cars speeding in all directions. As I do not want Honoré to confuse chirping with traffic, I swiftly head us Embassy-ward, across the rue Royale onto the Avenue Gabriel. A short line greets us at the gates; we queue, but also peer in through the metal bars to see what awaits us. Much to my surprise Special K has beat us to it. She's already inside and will be going through her security check shortly.

'Hello!' I call from the grille. 'Madame K! We're here now!' I wave my hand high and vigorously; this seems to do the trick. Special K turns around and spots us. Her bothered face suddenly relaxes into a smile of relief. She is all alone, I see, and she's relieved to see us; Umberto, it seems, took a raincheck.

'Be sure to take a number when you get inside,' I remind her. 'We'll meet you in there.' I made a point of reminding her about the number as she was liable to sit down and expect to be called. She's far too used to being sought out and may very well be losing her survival skills.

'*A tout de suite!*' calls Special K over her shoulder as the officer waves his detection wand over her, insisting, a bit too conspicuously, over the lower region. She is standing cruciform like the Lord, and like him, is subject to public humiliation. But she refuses the humbling and takes fast action. With her index finger, she delicately lifts her skirt high up the thigh to reveal her garter belt; it is a metallic hook that has sounded the alarm. But her elegant display of *cuisse*, of plump but shapely thigh has piqued the officer's manly curiosity; he waves the wand over her thigh, up and over the garter, to double check. She drops her skirt, holds her head high. She gains entry into the citadel.

'Only a Frenchwoman,' I say to Honoré, 'can get away with that. If an American tried, she'd just be vulgar. Why, look at Sharon Stone!' Of course Honoré has no idea who the Stone creature is, but one day he will, and I am preparing him for that very moment when his heart could well be lapidated by her kind, if I'm not very careful now. As I've already mentioned, a mother must prepare her son for his hour of reckoning with womanfolk, when he goes to acquire a bride. It's painstaking to teach him the difference between the wrongs and rights, between the dos and the don'ts of girl grazing, yet it must be done, even at this early stage.

'In just a few minutes, Honoré, you are going to meet the owner of that fine leg. But first we must pass through security. We're nearly there, chin up!' I feel Honoré getting a bit antsy and swing my torso left and right. 'Let's hope Special K picks a number, we don't want to be here forever, do we? I mean it's a nice place, Honoré, don't get me wrong; I wouldn't take you anywhere disreputable but...'

'Passports please.' The demand is made by an officer who looks uncannily like Lewis as Louis XVI in *Away in a Manger*, only minus the 'fro. He has that same bumbling look of ursine ferocity. Lewis is an endearing fellow, but if you hugged him – and the temptation was always strong, for he is irresistible – he could squeeze the lights out of you. I believe Jimi Hendrix had this same quality, bless him, and heroin certainly didn't help matters. Those who possess this particular bear energy which the Taoist sages call 'fire-in-water', should stay away from narcotics, which inevitably tip the scales in favour of fire over water or vice versa, upsetting an already fragile balance. Such people should also avoid jobs in security, but I've only just realized this now as I sense something brewing in our officer. I hand him my passport and our *livret de famille*, give him a motherly smile, remembering Uncle Al's injunction.

'Where's the child's passport?' Though a simple question, coming from an officer's mouth, it worries me. What is he getting at?

'He doesn't have one yet. But I have a copy of his birth certificate if you like?' I am doing my best to speak slowly as if to a beginner, in the style of Mister Rogers, the Presbyterian minister turned kiddie show host. A beginner in life and security enforcement.

'No entry, ma'am', unless you have a valid passport to show for him.' I perceive a sadistic steam trail behind his words; his fire element is up in flames, the water roiling with boil.

'Well, I'm afraid there's some confusion here, sir. Let us look together at the *livret de famille*, at the Family Libretto, shall we?' My voice is encouraging and earnest. I open this blue velvet repository of our family history, a gold-embossed gift from the French Republique, like I do Honoré's Itsy-Bitsy Spider book, slowly, expectantly. I am trying to rebalance the fire-water paradox. What he needs is some cooling down; what he needs, like all overly stimulated wee ones, is reading time.

'"Deliverance of the Family Libretto", I translate the first heading, a bit too freely, but so it happens with simultaneous interpretations.

'"The Family Libretto is given to the spouses by the officer of the state who celebrated their marriage." Shall we turn to the wedding page then?' I flip ahead five pages or so, skipping the more sombre explanations of how to declare the deaths of children and spouse (God forbid and Holy Mother protect us!), to our happy wedding day document. 'Look here,' I point out. '"The Tenth of June, two thousand and three at four o'clock". That was the day I married Charles! And while I can't say it was the happiest day of my life, we certainly threw a fabulous party at the castle.' I feel myself light up with this memory of feast and fest. I get excited. My pedagogical ambitions fall by the wayside. Next thing I know, our wedding story rushes out of me, bidden by the mnemonic flash.

'We had champagne a-go-go – Dom Pérignon, mind you! It was a wedding gift from one of my mother-in-law's bosom buddies who's married to the brother of that Arnault fellow. We had a fabulous spread of Russian dishes and caviar coming out of our ears… And boy did we dance! Even Padre Las Vegas, that's our priest you see, was out shaking his cassock till dawn. He led the soul train through the rose garden at three a.m. We all got pricked and scratched, our clothes got torn. I mean, we were *bleeding* – it was a beautiful moment; my dress got ripped to shreds and I had to leave the bustle on a branch of holly… but what are wedding dresses for anyway, right? You only get to wear them—'

'Next,' said our officer, rudely interrupting my narrative. He ushered us forward to stage two, where his wand-waving colleague awaited us. Though I hate being cut off mid-sentence, I am relieved. Somehow I have managed to put out the fire. My words worked like rain. Wedding talk will do this.

'That was a close call, Honoré,' I whisper in my son's ear. 'But we made it through stage one, and now we're about to embark on stage two. I think they're going to depouch us, so prepare yourself.' My prediction is accurate; the second security officer remains silent though he gestures his meaning. His hands do the talking. I take out Honoré, hand over the Baby Björn for inspection. The carrier, unhooked, opens obscenely, displaying its bright red belly and crotch. Honoré and I walk beneath the security canopy; mercifully no bells or buzzers sound. We pick up our belongings and are inside the fortress.

Special K is seated, legs crossed, on one of the adjoining chairs, immersed in reading; her silver lamé Marc Jacobs shoe is dangling off her toes. She snaps her heel back inside it when she sees us.

'I hope this will be quick,' she says, glancing at her watch. 'I have an appointment at five… coiffure…'

'Oh, we'll be out by then! Honoré would never make it that long.'

'Yes, what a darling child you have, Jane,' she says, noticing my son at last, and beaming him with her rays. 'What is his name?'

'Honoré,' I repeat. Patience is always the best policy in dealing with children, security personnel and great ladies. I glance at what Special K is reading, expecting to see the latest issue of *Tel Quel* or *Europe*, a publication with a stake in the Life of the Mind, but instead spy the glossy cover of *Glamour*. Who would have thought!

'I'm reading about Angelina Jolie,' she says in response to my surprised look. There is not a trace of defensiveness in her voice. Here is a woman who knows no shame, who could parade proudly like Lady Godiva and never bat an eye. There is a decidedness about her, and one senses a hermetic meaningfulness to her actions; though their sense might escape most, a Tupperware tightness protects them from the

197

outside agencies of ridicule and judgement. I do have a great deal to learn from her! And if only my mother could take a lesson or two…

'She is to play the role of my heroine, Penelope, in the adaptation of my latest novel.'

'That's fabulous news! Goodness! Your book is going to Hollywood! And Angelina, well, she's quite big isn't she? What does *Glamour* have to say about her?'

'*Quod me netrit me destruit.*'

'Oh! Does she parlay in Latin?'

'Her tattoo does.'

'Pray tell?'

'She wears a tattoo across her lower stomach that spells this out.'

'It means, "What nourishes me also destroys me", is that right?'

'Precisely. And this is the crux of our predicament, is it not? How does one nourish without destroying? How does one give life without giving death as well? This brings us back to the subject of maternal madness, Jane, and how Freud failed to take into account that THE DESTRUCTIVE DRIVE CAN BE REDIRECTED THROUGH SUBLIMATION TO BRING ABOUT A RETURN TO THE CARING ARTS…[ringing of cell phone to the tune of the Stones' 'Satisfaction'] Hello? Umberto! What's that? *Mon Dieu!* It didn't! Oh my!… Was she hurt? Both her legs? Oh dear… yes, well. I understand. I'll cancel our reservation for dinner this evening. Yes… yes, we'll catch each other in Rome then. Not to worry. *Au revoir, cher camarade.*'

'Is everything OK?' I venture to ask, for Special K looks rather upset, and though her conversation is certainly none of my business, I have just been made privy to half of it. Naturally, my curiosity craved a report.

'A terrible thing has happened.' As she utters these words, Special K undergoes a kind of eclipse, is suddenly separated from her brilliance. 'It seems,' she resumes, managing, slowly to slide back into the open, 'that Umberto's assistant accidentally pulled a bookshelf down on top of herself while dusting some of his most ancient volumes. She is alive, thank God, but her legs are quite unwell. Crushed really.'

'That's horrible! Why wasn't the bookshelf affixed to the wall?'

'The bookshelf itself is a Venetian antique and much too fragile to put hooks and nails into. She never should have climbed upon it like she did. She took a great risk, you see. And now what is Umberto going to do? It's so difficult to find good help these days…'

I feel a bilious reaction to the term 'help' arising in me; fortunately Honoré is here to distract me from indulging my ire. The Embassy is certainly not the place to get bitter; it only incites the civil servants to incivility. But even before I married Charles and his communist principles, I had a strong dislike of this idea of 'help'. Of paying someone to do your dirty work and, as it transpires in numerous cases, of lording it over them. In a proper society, of course, no-one would be exempt from doing a bit of dirty work. I have to say Special K is sounding like Shirley, my father's second wife. When not shopping she is 'organizing the help' and complaining about these good folks until she's near to asphyxiation. Shirley too reads *Glamour*, but only in the powder room.

'I'm sure he'll manage. Our concern should be with that poor woman. Will she be able to walk again?'

'It doesn't look hopeful. But she'll get a pension most likely. Perhaps I should see if Rachida has a cousin who might be available for work. I'm sure he'd be happy to import…'

Rachida, I take it, is Special K's help, probably an import herself, a Tunisian helper with hennaed hands, staunch on stains. Might Special K consider me a member of her 'help' crew too?

'Can I see your number?' I ask Special K, for one has just been called, and I suspect it might be ours. She waves a pale green ticket stub. Fifty-six it says. 'That's us!' I pick up my bags, hitch Honoré onto my hip. Special K slips *Glamour* into her briefcase. Now we find ourselves before a Homeland Security officer who stares at us both unblinkingly. All creases of emotion have been carefully ironed out of his face. I try to imagine this is merely a child's visage, perhaps an unloved child who has not yet learned to mimic the expressions of conviviality and delight. I will have to proceed carefully, I see. I will have to teach him how to care.

As I explain Special K's predicament, I make deliberate pauses to enquire about our officer's health – to show my solicitousness (Are you sure you're getting enough vitamin D? You know there's not enough sunlight here, too many fluorescents. You really must be careful!); about his summer vacation plans (Is it a Riviera rendezvous this summer? Or perhaps a Brittany bash? Surfing at San Sebastián? Wherever it may be, remember you deserve it! You've been serving your county behind the consular counter for months. It'll do you a world of good…); and about his wife (why don't you make this a special day for the two of you? All it takes is roses. There is nothing like being popped a bouquet.). And yet I have the impression we are not moving forward, that his paralysis of expression has the same effect as a brick wall: it is barring our way. My attempts to show him that we care only add bricks to his firm partition, and now, alas, Honoré is losing his patience. It must be frustrating to see his mother manage so badly. He starts a fretful jagger.

'Oh, the Child!' says Special K with dismay.

'Honoré… he'll be fine,' I reassure her. 'But let's get back to the documents…' I am about to ask our officer if he would like me to fetch him a cup of coffee from the Nescafé vending machine before we continue, when I perceive someone right next to me. The hair on my arms stands to attention. Goodness! It's Uncle Al! He's coming in loud and clear all right! Perhaps you wonder if I actually *see* him. I can't say I do exactly, though during the onslaught of labour he did appear wearing his polka-dotted bow tie – I saw him, no doubt about it, a fluke we can chalk up to the pain which pushed my every pore of perception to extreme protraction; my vision must have pierced through the boundaries of time and space affording me a glimpse of my ancestor, golf-clubbed and dapper as ever. Since then, on Uncle Al's subsequent visits, I've perceived his presence very clearly without seeing him or the putter, and of course, I hear him loud and clear.

'Naw, Janie, forget the coffee. If he wants to play with bricks, you gotta give him some building blocks. You gotta help him out, you know, like he was a stupid kid or something. By the way, he don't look too good.'

'Yes, he's very pale, isn't he? He's a functionary, Uncle Al.'

'Jane! Please! The officer is asking you for the 150024 form.' Special K unknowingly interrupts our conversation. How annoyed she seems and is getting a bit huffy-puffy. I give Uncle Al a wink and return to our officer.

'That form, I believe…' I say as I'm shuffling through our papers with one hand, the other occupied with holding Honoré safely against my hip. 'Yes, it's right here.' I pull out the paper in question, turn it around carefully so that it is facing our officer, right-side-up, enabling him to understand its function. Our officer looks carefully at this rectangular document, his absorbent concentration sponges up the information directly into his psychic life, creating – and not just passing through – the very structure we call the mind. It is fascinating to watch this happen in a civil servant, perhaps even more than with a child of whom we expect such wonders, and witness them daily. Even Honoré calms as he feels my own temperatures cool with Montessorian observation. Honoré too is absorbing, taking in impressions that will form his mind (which God be willing will not pattern itself civil-servantly, after our officer's).

'It's the fingerprints,' our officer pronounces at last, after three minutes of reading.

'How's that?' I ask.

'The fingerprint matches have been impaired by what seems to be an anomaly of the index digit. Did the visa candidate cut her finger the day before the prints were taken?' He asks me. I translate the question to Special K who pauses for a moment to think it over.

'Even a slight paper cut on the finger will invalidate the results,' the officer continues. 'We will have to try again.'

'Oh dear! Will this cause further delay? She has to get to Harvard by next week. You must try to speed this up!'

'Hey Janie,' comes a voice from the left. 'That's no way to talk to a kiddo.' It's Uncle Al again. I thought he had left already, but it looks like he's decided to stay around and see us through this. God bless him. Really, with ancestors like Al, you're never alone.

'Give him another building block, Janie-girl.'

'Right, Uncle Al. I'll try.'

'What is happening here?' demands Special K.

'They're going to have to take your fingerprints again. Let me have a look.' I take my boss's hands and examine the tips of her fingers. The skin is plump, pink, with uninterrupted lines forming domes within domes, these rings marking identity not age as in trees. No sign of a cut or scratch. 'It looks good. We can go ahead with it.'

'Officer,' I begin in as much of a Mister Rogers voice as I can muster, 'What if you tried to get your senior officer to verify the new set of fingerprints we are going to make right now? We have great faith in your connections and negotiating abilities, sir. Clever men like you are hard to come by behind these counters…'

'Knock off the flattery. Just a building block, Janie,' interrupts Uncle Al.

'Thank you for your help,' I finish off. I didn't realize I was heading down the flatulent road of flattery, a path full of potholes and little explosions, hardly smooth as one might expect. My mission is to give him a building block, as I just have, in the form of a suggestion. Will he take it? Without a reply, our officer gets out his ink pad and invites Special K to dip her digits and roll them carefully on specially designated squares on the paper. Then he shuffles all the papers into one pile and leaves us at the counter.

'With a bit of luck,' I tell Special K, 'this will all go through now. You wait here. You'll be fine, won't you? I'm going to take Honoré for a little stroll around the premises.' Special K looks at me somewhat bewildered. This fingerprinting may be chimed as a routine procedure, but protocol can bring us down, just when we most need to bat.

'Yes, take care of the child, Jane. I will stay here and wait for the officer.' Special K proves herself stoic; she will wait until her lack of guilt is duly proven and stamped into her passport. I turn around to see if

203

Uncle Al is still with us, but he is nowhere in sight. Perhaps he has gone off to aid my father in curbing one of Shirley's shopping sprees. Dad is helpless at managing her demon drive to buy; he could certainly use an equestrian pep talk from Uncle Al – he always knew how to hold the reins.

'Come along, Honoré, let's go to the vending machine and see what's for sale.' I take us both into the adjoining room where, to my surprise, there is not only a Nescafé machine, but a rocking chair with a quilted pillow. Above this homey site is a sign that reads 'Nursing Station: Reserved for mothers'. I cannot quite express how the sight of this family-minded civility floods my heart, brings me near to tears. How strange and contradictory a place America is, harbouring that rudest of hosts, Homeland Security in one room, whilst offering child-care comforts, a cushioned rocker to nurse famished babes, in the other. I suppose there is no sense to be made of it. The behemoth commands the world with its contradictions.

Yet being so kindly invited, Honoré and I take a seat in the rocking chair and begin rocking away as we sing through our repertory of favourite tunes, starting with The Itsy-Bitsy Spider as always and ending with Humpty Dumpty. *Poooor Humpty Dumpty*, says Mom. *Baah, baaah, baaaaah*, says babe. Which leads us into a good old Bah Bah Blacksheep as an encore. 'We make a good team, Honoré, you and I… perhaps one day we'll be like the Partridge Family with you on drums and Dad on the horn… I'll be the lead singer if you don't mind.'

As we nibble happily on apple slices and crackers fresh from our Tupperware, I hear a most surprising thing. My name is being called over the loudspeaker. 'Jane de La Rochefoucault, window eight. Jane de La Rochefoucault, window eight.'

'Oh dear, Honoré, that's us! Let's put all this away and see what's going on. Special K must be needing our assistance.' But just as we put our Tupperware back in the diaper bag, Special K comes out waving her passport triumphantly.

'Did you get it?' I enquire.

'It's all settled. Thank you for your help, dear Jane. I must run off now. Coiffure…'

'Well, have a lovely appointment. Farewell.' But I'm wondering now why in the world I'm being convened to window 8, if business has been settled. Perhaps there is a last paper I must sign as her 'visa guardian'? Honoré and I arrive at window 8, where the officer points to a door on the right.

'Step right in,' says the no-nonsense officer.

'Roger,' we say with a salute. Honoré and I open the door in question and walk into a stale-smelling green room – I believe the colour is called mint though there's little fresh about its sickly hue – furnished with but a table and two chairs. A nearly nude light bulb, scantily covered by a tiny metal conical hat, floods the room in a stark white light. There are no shadows here, there is no place to run or hide. Could it be, *ma foi*, an interrogation room? So it seems and I am wondering why on earth we've been invited into such an unsavoury chamber. We are merely mother and child, Special K's helpers, baptized and rinsed of original sin; surely we are clean (shower this morning) and moderately innocent (communion last Sunday). What could Homeland Security possibly have on us? I can think of nothing, but my Maraconi instincts get the better of me; I'm feeling like a caged fox and must sit down before I start pacing like one. I take a deep breath, remembering that Honoré's sense of well-being depends on my own;

I must tame the feral Neapolitan impulse to flee. It's just a routine question–answer session, surely a follow-up on Special K's dossier. I take a seat in one of the metal backed chairs and sit Honoré on the table. Together we pat out our cakes, flatten them with a rolling pin, then put them in the oven for...

'Mam?' a voice calls me. An officer with a gleaming bald head, quite magnificent and of *The King and I* calibre (think Yul Brynner with a briefcase), walks in briskly. He drops his heavy attaché case filled with a stack of rainbow coloured folders on the table in front of us. I pull Honoré onto my lap and wait. I now see that he is wearing a Western shirt and bootlace tie. Why, he could have just stepped off the plane from Boise, Idaho! Could he be a fellow countryman? From the family of one of those cow herders Mother is always grumbling about?

'Howdy,' I say, for his dress incites this greeting, and I am delighted for this occasion to employ that familiar Western salutation. I wait for a smile of recognition to crack the serious surface of his face, but quickly realize that like baked clay, his visage has lost its moisture and hence its motion. I'm beginning to wonder if all civil servants aren't put through the kiln before swearing in; truly the stiffness is astonishing!

'Ma'am, I'm going to ask you a series of questions. You are to answer them truthfully.'

'I assume you mean the truth, the whole truth and nothing but the truth so help me Mother of God?'

'Our conversation will be taped,' he warns me.

'Just a moment,' I say. 'My son needs to nibble on something. Otherwise he'll never hold out.' I pull out the Tupperware again and hand Honoré an apple slice. He pushes it up against his mouth rather than into it. I help him get it between his lips. Such a supple little face he has! So full of life and expression! 'There, that should keep him busy a bit. I hope this won't be too long…'

'I'm going to ask you a series of questions. When they have been answered satisfactorily you may leave.' I'm half waiting for him to say 'etceteras, etceteras, etceteras' like Yul does in the movie, and would have welcomed such excess verbiage, this pleasure of saying words for the sound of them; but he instead shuffles through his papers until he finds the one he's looking for. He takes a pen in the other hand, flips on the switch of the recorder. Our interview has begun.

'Are you Jane de La Rochefoucault, née Maraconi?'

'That I am.'

'Are you married to Count Charles de La Rochefoucault?'

'With both a civil and a religious ceremony, sir.'

'Are you of the Muslim faith?'

'I'm a Roman Catholic, sir. But we too believe in the one God.'

'Do you have Muslim friends or acquaintances?' Oh dear, I'm beginning to catch his drift. Or am I? Still I feel it is best at this point to lie. In any case, are my frequentations any of his damn beeswax?

'No sir. Unless you count Samira, my hairdresser. She's quite talented and even works during Ramadan when her calorie count is so low. I do admire her…'

'Have you ever been contacted by a terrorist cell?'

'You mean, like al-Qaida? Heavens no!'

'Have you ever agreed to transport objects for men or women who appear to be of the Islamic faith?'

'Well, let's see… I once helped my upstairs neighbour Fatima carry a ten-kilo bag of couscous up the stairs. That was in our old flat.'

'Have you ever heard of the organization Muslims without Borders?' So there it is. Of course I am right. This is what he's been getting at all along.

'Yes, I've heard about them. I've read about them in the newspaper… Or was it the radio? I'm not sure, but it's a non-profit organization that protects the interest of Muslims in Europe. Something like that.'

'Did you know that it has links with terrorist organizations?'

'No, I didn't.'

'Have you ever seen any of these men?' Here he pulls out the mug shots, the very same that Starsky and Hutch pushed before my nose some months ago, of Rachid, Samir and Ahmed.

'No, I haven't.'

'Do you know that it is a federal crime to aid and abet terrorist groups?'

'Yes I do.'

'The interrogation is finished. You may now go back to window 8. An officer will take your fingerprints.'

'My fingerprints? Goodness! Whatever for?'

'At this point it's standard procedure, ma'am.'

'At this point? But… what… whatever do you mean?' But our officer has already stuffed his briefcase with his business. He's at the door, waiting for us to file out. My heart is beating in my ears and Honoré is whimpering for another apple slice. I open the Tupperware to get one out for him, but my hands are trembling and I drop the slice on the floor. Honoré screeches; I fish for another one and this time grab it firmly between my pinchers. Honoré takes it and lifts it to his mouth, or tries to. The slippery slice misses his mouth by an inch, rubs against his rosy cheek and tumbles to the floor. Honoré stretches out his arm pointing to our fallen apple, crying out in condemnation. 'Now that it's on the floor, we can't eat it, darling. There's one more slice – let us try again.' My hand is still trembling and I nearly fail to hook that last slice for it is sticking to the Fridgesmart container and even feels a tad slimy though it shouldn't (Fridgesmart keeps fruit fresh for up to two weeks), but in the end I manage to get it between index and thumb, and, rather than hand it to Honoré, which would have been risky, I slide it into his open mouth. The simpering subsides. And I now notice we are in the room alone again, our examiner has left us. Honoré is momentarily contented but I feel myself sinking into a feeling of aloneness. The examiner has ta-ta-ed us, Uncle Al too. Where are you Al? I cry out. What do we do now? I look at my son, chomping away *sans souci*; he has no clue we've been abandoned in the examiner's room and won't realize until his apple runs out. This feeling of abandonment brings to mind the Lord on the cross, for he too felt forsaken, not by his uncle of course, but by his Father. And yet he held out, submitted to the terrible trial with the happy result that he became not only his own saviour, but the Saviour of Mankind. As always, thinking of the Lord renews my courage and I realize that in abandoning me, Uncle Al has given me his vote of confidence. It is as if he were hiding behind that veil separating the living from the dead, out of sight but rooting for me all the same: Don't let them snoopers scare you, Janie-girl. You ain't done nothing wrong. Now remember that. You're doing good.

The main thing, of course, is to do good, to give them what they want and get the hell out. What do they hope to gain from having my

209

fingerprints, *ma foi*? Surely Muslims Without Borders has no links to terrorist cells. Homeland Security must be on the wrong track and headed for a dead end.

'Come along, Honoré. We must get to window eight. After that, it's adios…' I put him back in the Baby Björn, facing frontways as always. Knowing little of penitential practices, Honoré will look at the fingerprinting with the curiosity of the innocent. I see no reason to hide this from him. It is a bit like finger painting after all and he'll be into that soon enough. I shall try to turn this situation into a pedagogical experiment, in the Montessori approach, demonstrating the activity with the child observing and learning.

'Hello again,' we say to our previous officer. 'It looks like you need these.' I wiggle my fingers Itsy-Bitsy Spider style in the air. Honoré pats his hands for patty-cake, patty-cake then shoves his hand-crafted gâteau at the officer (i.e. the oven) who offers Honoré a weak smile, displaying more self-control than any self-cleaning capacities. He then lifts from some shelf beneath the counter the same paper he had presented to Special K, with the ten compartments. Next comes the ink pad.

'Your right hand please,' he requests. I surrender my hand and he begins by dipping and pressing.

'I could do it myself,' I suggest.

'No, ma'am. That's my job.' Very well, I am thinking. So much for the Montessori lesson in autonomy and observation. Still, I refuse the humiliation of this handling.

'I'll be happy to do yours afterward, sir. We are in a hurry, of course, but we could stay an extra five minutes…'

'I don't appreciate your joke,' he replies icily. His pasty complexion begins to blush ever so slightly. What I have said seems to bring out the best in him.

'Well, it's not a joke. Perhaps you could appreciate it as a suggestion… a kindly one…'

'Left hand,' he commands. I hand it over, though not before inspecting my nails and noticing the chipped nail polish.

'I'm sorry about the dreadful state of my hands. Had I known, I would have had my manicure done. It's so hard to find the time when you're a working mother, I mean, time to take care of yourself, you know. Do you take care of yourself, sir? More and more men are going to the beauty institutes these days for maintenance – facials, massages, that sort of thing, but also for tanning. Personally I would never set foot in one of those fryers, but they say that…'

'You may wash your hands now, ma'am.'

'Ah! We're finished, are we? Well, if you won't change your mind on our offer, we shall leave now. Goodbye, sir.' We turn our heels swiftly and head to the ladies' lounge.

'I think you need a change, Honoré. Look, they have a changing station with Winnie the Pooh motifs! How thoughtful of them! They really do think of everything, don't they?' I find upon removal of Honoré's diaper a compact poo, easy to clean and dispose of. Thank goodness, for we are running low on wipes! Buttoning Honoré back up, I put him in the baby carrier once more and wash my hands with soap that smells of gardenias and something else a bit mineralish – perhaps petroleum?

Our journey back to Colonel Fabien is uneventful, though the crowds are thicker and more pungent, for many at this hour have finished a day of toil and are returning home like us, all the worse for wear. Honoré doesn't mind the local colour, the Parisian armpit stench, nor does he flinch when a plump and very pretty *midinette* nearly lands upon us as the wagon lurches. I'm afraid he's not insensitive to the lovelies and their curves, which soften these collisions. How am I to steer him away from such temptations? I think of the Ancient Greeks who deemed women spongy because they are filled with more liquids than men and hence perfectly suited for doing the cleaning. But this erroneous conception is washed away by a song from one of my favourite rock operas. Its gravelly, below-the-belt refrain comes back to haunt me: 'the bigger the cu-shion the sweeter the pu-shin'…' I'm tempted to sing along but mustn't! Mercifully, we've reached our stop and the song now retreats beneath the noisy exiting, the grunts and sighs emitted from the bulk of bodies mounting the stairs, dishing out the daily fare of *c'est pas vrai!, putain-merde!,* yes the shitty-whores and isn't-trues of heading home.

'They will wash their mouths out with soap when they get *chez eux,* Honoré. We mustn't worry about it.' As soon as I uttered these words the SJLYM (Sounding Just Like Your Mother) alarm went off. Mother always had a bar of Dove on hand; it was her one and only punishment, cruel, corporal and, I must admit, quite efficient.

'On second thought, perhaps they just need a big kiss,' I corrected myself, giving Honore's sweet smelling head a motherly *bacio*.

Mathilde is already at the flat when we return, seated upon Little Miss Muffet (formerly Jinn-Jinn) sipping a glass of wine. She is toying with the Koranoblaster and it is sounding scratchy.

'It's dreadful! Much worse than trying to get the BBC from the latrine,' she says as she holds out her arms for Honoré. 'Oh the Sacred

Child! Come here, Honoré. We will learn the nineteenth Surah together, in spite of the static.'

'Is that the one about Mary?' I query, for I seem to remember Ahmed mentioning this particular chapter during one of our brief interfaith chats. 'And how she was surprised by the labour pains at the foot of a palm tree. And then the Lord tells her to shake the palm tree and eat the dates, but the pains are so bad she's sure she's going to die before the babe is born and the last thing she wants to do is chomp on dates.' As I say this I think about my own desire during childbirth to clamp down on a bone while in the midst of my agony. But bones are one thing, dates another and there is always the risk of accidentally swallowing a date pit and choking. I suppose Allah was trying to reassure Mary that he would provide for her, but his timing was certainly off.

'To be honest, I do not know. I'm simply trying to learn it.'

'But you don't understand Arabic, Mathilde.'

'The sound first, *ma chère*, and then, if necessary, the meaning.'

'Right,' I say, for after all, she is Charles's mother. Then: 'Where's your son, by the way?'

'In the kitchen, Jane. He's preparing us dinner. Risotto I believe. With perhaps some mussels or something'

'Some what? Oh dear…' I rush into our soon-to-be-kitchen and find Charles has moved the burner onto Momo's worktable. 'Why aren't you stirring?' I yell, for Charles is standing several feet away from the pot, clearly involved in his ears and the queer, brassy noises emerging from the Koranophone next door. My accusation startles him out of his tympana.

'Oh hello, Jane. Yes, I thought I would make a bit of risotto…'

213

'In the pressure cooker? You've got to be kidding! Risotto requires tender care and wrist action, stirring and stirring and adding broth. Now we're going to have to start all over! Is there any rice left?' I peer into the rice bag; there is less than a cup left. As the *cocotte minute*'s jiggler valve madly spins away, the rice molecules are being reduced to mush. I bang the fridge door shut, then sift angrily through our boxes of canned goods for another meal. Honoré kicks in with the jaggers; he senses my distress, poor dear. And now Mathilde, determined to concentrate her ears on learning her lines come what may (so like her son!), turns up the Koranoblaster so high that the imam's voice crackles and spits in our craniums. Charles, who by now is suffering acutely from the discordant rise in decibels – the howling of babe, the screeching of mother's tutor, the self-righteous banging of pots and pans of wife – leaps over to the burner in a rash act of *sauve-qui-peu* and makes to twist open the knob on the pressure cooker…

'Good God, stop, Charles! Not the knob, for Christ's sake! Pull the jiggler valve! The jiggler valve!' Rushing to the rescue, I push my husband out of the way and pull the whistling jiggler valve to release the steam. Mathilde enters the kitchen with Honoré in her arms just as the blast of steam shooting from the pot's vent pipe peters out.

'Why these vapours… how extraordinary! It reminds me of the Hammam A Bab El Oued in Algiers and how pink my cheeks were after those baths! And how they would scrub me and then perfume me…'

'Must have been grand,' I mutter as I unscrew the top knob and peer in at our dinner. The sight leaves me aghast. 'Pure mush! It's ruined, damn it, and I'm starving! I didn't get any of those Trotsky-a-babs for lunch like you did…' I look at Charles accusingly.

'The store is still open, I'll go down and pick up some spaghetti,' offers Charles.

'No need. I think we've got some in the cupboard. Put the pasta pot on the stove, will you? And there's some frozen fish in the freezer – get that too.'

'Charles tells me you went to the Embassy today…' Mathilde, I can tell, does not like the way I'm ordering her son around. Wisely, she changes the subject.

'Yes, how did that go, Jane? Did Special K get her visa?' Charles is splashing water all over the floor. He is oblivious to the mess but sensitive to its sound.

'She's all set, but I had a bit of a scare there…'

'How so?' asks Mathilde.

'Well, once they let Special K off the hook – by "they" I'm talking Homeland Security – they called Honoré and me into a room and interrogated us. At first it was sort of like at the airport when the security folks ask you if you've packed your own bags, but then they brought out the mug shots of the magi… and took my fingerprints.'

'Of course they work hand in hand with the DGSE…' says Mathilde pensively.

'This is terribly disturbing, Mother. What exactly does the French secret service know about us? Jane might very well be in danger and I will not have it!'

'Why, nothing at all, *mon fils!* They don't know a thing about us and have failed to prove we have any connection to the good trio of uncles. Of course they are tapping my phone and we have had some odd visitors surreptitiously question the demoiselles, who I've made sure know nothing at all about our mission. We have monks staying with us so frequently – to dry out, you know – that the girls assumed the magi were yet another crop of holy men on the mend. We will not worry about Homeland Security. They were just trying to frighten you, Jane.'

'Well, then they failed. We weren't scared a bit though we didn't appreciate having our fingerprints done. Do you suppose they'll send a copy of them to the FBI? Or even the CIA?'

'Certainly. But now that this has been made clear, we will take the necessary precautions. Let us thank Homeland Security for its heavy-handed actions.'

'I wouldn't go that far… But do you have any news from the magi, Mathilde? Or Constance? Did she make it with the mushroom?'

'That she did. And she is fine. But she has already left the monastery and should be on the Azure Coast by now to do some fund-raising for the gypsies. Padre Las Vegas and I speak twice a week from public phone booths. He has intercepted the fungus and now Padre Negri, the monastery's abbot, has begun negotiations with the capo who has engineered this slave driving, a man who goes by the name of Crescenzo Barra. Which sounds so familiar to me for some reason… isn't Barra a brand of pasta, Jane?'

'No, you're thinking of Barilla,' I correct her. It is shocking to me how little the French know about their next-door neighbours and how willing they are to frequent lousy pizzerias run by Tunisians – but we will save this topic of conversation for a time when less urgent matters prevail. 'What exactly is the nature of these negotiations?' I ask to get us back on track. 'Money for men?'

'Yes, Jane. Money for men, but that is not all because, as we know, the magi will never have enough for the ransom. Padre Negri has asked

216

for the capo's permission to feed the enslaved men whilst they negotiate a price. The idea is to play for time and…'

'Spike the food with a sprinkle of the fungus, right?' I interrupt. 'And wait for the psychotropic change to occur. One that will get these men's minds on the freedom train.'

'Something like that, Jane.'

'Does Padre Negri stand a chance of getting the ransom price down?' asks Charles.

'No, we cannot be sure of this at all. In fact it has become more and more apparent to both padres that because we risk failing on this account, we will need the help of the mushroom. The spirit of freedom is contagious, you see. If we can infect the enslaved men with this liberating virus, so to speak, it might well spread to their captors. Why who knows… perhaps the guards will even hand over the keys!'

'Let's not be naive, Mathilde. We're dealing with the mob here. But what's working in our favour is that we have a priest on the scene – these guys'll go soft on the Church. Barra will probably go along with the plan to let the monastery feed the slaves – that shouldn't be a problem. But I have doubts about this mushroom thing… serious doubts. And if the magi can't cough up enough funds…'

'Let's not jump too far ahead, Jane. What Mother is saying is that Padre Negri is ironing out the kinks and feels sanguine about the possibilities of the magi-mushroom. We must put our trust in it, I'm afraid.'

'Well go ahead if you like. But I'm not sure if I can.'

'Jane?'

'What's that?'

'I believe the Sacred Child is hungry,' says Mathilde, making to hand a fussy Honoré over to me.

'No, not here,' I say, twisting my arm toward the freezer. 'Give him to Papa. Mama's gotta cook.'

I whip out a package of frozen fillet of sole, dig out a bag of porcini mushrooms – here's where I put my faith! – from one of our kitchen boxes and begin cooking dinner on the one burner. Charles with Honoré slung over his shoulder follows Mathilde into the living room. I hear the Koranophone resume its scratchy recitations and can tell from how the chapters jump and collide that Honoré has his fingers on the buttons. Let us hope, dear reader, this is the last extended family dinner requiring me to make-do with a single range while being accompanied by a Koranoblaster. God-be-willing, better culinary times shall lie ahead with a countess-equipped kitchen.

Chapter XIII

*In which Jane discovers her mother is
psilanthropic as well as other revelations
for the betterment of Mankind.*

My unabashed enthusiasm for our newly installed kitchen prompted me to sit down last week during Honoré's afternoon nap and pen a profile piece: 'A *cadeau* from a countess: the making of a country kitchen in Paris'. I immediately sent this off to my mother, suggesting she forward it on to *House and Hedges Magazine*, where she has a friend on the editorial committee (a former *Tupperware Times* journalist). I'm certain we can tempt the *H&H* folks into doing a special number on Parisian apartments, since most of their readers have or at least foresee having a pied-à-terre in Paris. I really want to give Momo all the advertising he deserves, especially as he is trying to enlarge his American client base.

A *cadeau* from a countess:

the making of a country kitchen in Paris

When Jane and Charles de La Rochefoucault moved with their newborn son into their fifth (US sixth) floor flat in the heart of Paris's colourful Belleville district, there was something major missing: a kitchen! As Jane de La Rochefoucault put it 'We had an oxidized copper partridge spigot from the Petit Trianon Château that stuck out from the wall and a blue washbucket beneath it: this served as our sink. We added a mini-bar and sat a Bunsen burner on top of that. It was primitive to say the least. Of course it didn't stop me from cooking!' But when the Countess de Sarry, a cousin of Charles, offered them her Burgundy Manoir kitchen, Jane and Charles could not have been more thrilled. They loved the idea of having a French country kitchen in Paris. 'The warmth of the oak cabinets with their naturally aged patina and the generous proportions of the limestone farmhouse sink sold us on the idea straight off,' explained Jane. What Jane and Charles were after was a kitchen that had it all: efficient prep areas, smart storage, a place for intimate family meals and an elegant, eye-catching ornamental design. 'We didn't work with an architect,' Jane confessed. 'But we did work with a fabulously talented Muslim plumber. He conceived the superb layout – with the prep island; it's perfect for my chopping needs! – and the Islamic touches, like the Moroccan Ali Baba tiles.' This careful blend of traditional terroir and native North African sounds a subdued echo to the neighbourhood's vibrant cultural mix. The signature area is the harlequin pattern of terracotta, green and blue Ali Baba tiles forming the backsplash behind the cooktop. 'We definitely wanted a

warm, cosy kitchen for our interdenominational dinner parties. I
think the Ali Baba tiles will help make everyone feel more at home.
And we love the built-in banquet seating area. No more fussing with
chairs, except for the high chair of course. Thanks to Momo, our
plumber, we managed to integrate the partridge faucet. We felt it
was important to keep a sense of the place's history.' Contacts:
Momo (only after 8 p.m.) at 06 44 57 39 27

As I've said, I sent this off to Mother last week. Seeing it is spring, she
is herding down in the valley, plumping up her lambs for their Day of
Judgement. I rarely hear from her, but oddly, as long as she is not in
the High Country, she will invariably call upon the receipt of a letter. I
think the genesis of this phone reflex dates back to her early post-
divorce years when she responded to every attorney bill she received
(including Dad's) by calling her analyst. She was doing a Jungian
telephone analysis back then and was working strenuously on muscling
up her deficient animus. She began seeing the world through the lens
of symbols; milk bottles now signified the blank page of her life – she
drank litres of it to fill herself with whiteness upon which the 'inscrip-
tions of her inner life could be jotted down'; our backyard bluejay
became a metonym of life's larger pecking order – 'Oh the bluejay! The
deadly, deadly bluejay,' she would tisk-tisk while reading the finance
pages of the *Wall Street Journal*; even her Tupperware Stackables were
invested with metaphoric signification; she saw them as heralding an
economy of cooperation in which people would construct inter-
dependent 'stacks' of knowledge and expertise with all players reaping
the rewards more or less equally. 'Get ready for the stackables, Janie.
This is the Age of Aquarius and humanity is finally stacking up.' I have

no idea where Mother came up with such notions or what they really meant, but she managed to convince herself of their immanent reality. The most persistent symbol, however, the one that impressed itself upon her dreams and her waking hours was of a bleating sheep. The shape and appearance of this night-time apparition remains a mystery to me, but perhaps it resembled the prototype that soon inhabited our house by way of linens and drapery. All our towels, sheets, dishcloths and curtains had a sheep print motif – fluffy, cloud-like puffs of woolly beast outlined in black with stick legs and narrow muzzle, those rudimentary markers of its species, emerging timidly from the cumulus. Like most symbols, this sheep was sky-bound, impervious to gravity; its feet never muddied. That is, until some hungry part of Mother's psyche pulled it deep down inside her for ingestion wherein the symbol provided the necessary calorific intake for embarking on a new livelihood. When Mother told her analyst of this, and of her intention to go into sheepherding, he argued that she was confusing the psychic message of the archetype for vocational counselling. She hung up the phone on him. I remember her telling me that day, 'That's when I realized, Jane, that I had balls.'

'So you're finished with your analysis?'

'Done,' she replied as she tugged at her pants, pulling up perhaps the imagined jewels that would help start her life anew, out on the range, in Wranglers and, God love her, a Wonderbra.

Anyway, Mother's call came in the early evening, as I was giving Honoré his bath, singing the Rubber Duckie song with a French accent. Children are shamelessly tacky creatures. Honoré was dying for me to do an Italian Rubber Duckie, and I would have given in, if Mother hadn't burst into our bathroom singalong with her ringing.

'Jane! I just got your letter. How is everything? How is the baby?'

'Honoré is doing great, eating with his fingers, laughing with his toes… Everything is going well, Mom, especially since we've got this new kitchen. It's changed our lives.'

'It sounds fantastic, Jane. I'll send your piece right along to Susie at *H&H*. Would you happen to have the address?'

'Don't you have it, Mom?'

'You know I don't take *House & Hedges* any more. Just *Sheep Talk* and the *Wall Street Journal.*'

'I'll see if I can track her down on the net. I thought you were regularly in contact with her.'

'Oh, I was for a while. But you know how hard it is for me to stay in touch with the life I lead.'

'Well, you must come and visit us, Mom. And bring a rack of lamb with you… I can do a beautiful job with it now that we have the Countess's range.'

'Yes, yes, I'll look into it… only now, I'm in the midst of converting…'

'Converting? What are you talking about, Mom? From alfalfa to switch grass? Oh, nothing like religion I hope!'

'Yes, Jane,' Mother retorted with that deep voice she always uses to anchor a surprise announcement. 'That's exactly it: Religion. I am in the process of shedding my Christianity.'

'Do you mean that you no longer believe in one Lord, Jesus Christ, the only Son of God, eternally begotten of the Father?'

'No, Jane, I don't believe I do.'

'Mother!' Her confession nearly knocked the wind out of me. I felt as if Samson had brought down the pillar that had held up home since my childhood; I was not crushed by the cave-in but left strangely suspended as though on the verge of being dropped down an abyss. Sunday mass was the one appointment Mother never missed; it was our sole family outing. This communion took mother away from her Tupperware tribulations, father away from his advocacies. It put me at the centre of their love, for an hour, until the Priest uttered his exit, 'The mass is ended, go in peace,' to which we, the parishioners, retorted 'Thanks be to God!' And got the last word. Truly I could not fathom Mother leaving the fold: what could have possessed her? But I had to get Honoré out of the bath quickly and therefore hung up promising to call right back ASAP.

As I diapered and dressed Honoré in his pyjamas, I turned this news over in my mind. What mother had said was that she was in the midst of converting, from which I deduced that at least she had not become an atheist. Might she have turned to Buddhism, I wondered. Or even Hinduism? But I thought not, for her attraction to the exotic never strayed beyond the confines of American sitcoms. She may have loved *I Dream of Genie* but a trip to Cairo would have blown out the little wheels in her head. The foreign, the far-flung radiance of the world only excited Mother with its distant, glimmering sheen. She needed to keep the wheels of her imagination on Idaho roads. I selected and eliminated choices until I arrived at what seemed to me the obvious answer. Immediately I called her back.

'Mother? I was thinking about what you told me... that you consider Christ was uh... mere man. Is that it?'

'Yes, Jane. I'm afraid he is but that, though a very fine one to be sure.'

'So He didn't die for our sins?'

'Now, Jane, I know this is hard for you to accept…'

'Tell me, Mom,' I said cutting through her cautious patronizing. 'Are you trying to become a Jew?'

'That's right, Jane.'

I sighed deeply. This is exactly what I had suspected; Mother wanted to turn back the pages of the Good News, until she reached the shores of the Chosen. Perhaps this would be a salutary change for her, but it made me worried on one account. The Chosen People were, after all, careful about who they chose. Naturally Elizabeth Taylor made the cut, but would Mother? With her background in kitchen containers and sheep? I did not feel hopeful. And the possibility of Mother's ever learning Hebrew did seem slim, though she was certainly trying very hard to learn it, she explained.

'But where does this leave Manuela and Carlotta? You always took them to mass with you. Don't tell me they are going to convert along with you!' I remembered mother telling me that her adopted ranch hands wore little golden crucifixes in their noses for Sunday mass. They were devout, but clearly their sipping of Emerson's hyrid brew with Hindi undertones had influenced how they jewelled up for the Eucharist.

'No, Jane.' Mother made a confessional sigh as if obliged to reveal something that pained her. 'It's been so long since we've spoken, hasn't it? I didn't tell you about Mani-Carla I guess.'

'No, Mom… Did something happen to her… I mean them? Back in the high country?'

'Not exactly, but in a way, well… yes, that is where our trouble started. You see Manuela contracted the West Nile Virus when we were still back in Camp 86. She was way too sick to saddle up so I went to get help from the Johansons' dude ranch – the one with all the celebrity guests and plastic surgeons, I think you remember, Jane – anyway, there was a doctor there from Beverly Hills who kindly offered his services. I thought she was in good hands at first, but as her fever rose he seemed to get kind of kooky. Like he was a bit daft or something. He even starting talking like Jethro from that show, *The Beverly Hillbillies* – remember how we used to watch that together, Jane? You always loved Miss Margaret Drysdale, the banker's wife, didn't you? Something about her tweed suits, that high voice, the RP English… Anyway, he was falling for her, of course, but at the time I didn't see it. Not until he bought her and Carlotta a one-way ticket to LA. Yes, both of them! Clearly it's a *ménage à trois* situation. The doctor may have fallen for Manuela first, but I spied him in the hot-spring with Carlotta while the other was up to 104°F in fever. God knows what that doctor sees in those ungracious girls! Any charms or intelligence they might display, they certainly owe to me! Why, I spoon-fed them Emerson; I taught the Helen Keller story, had them read Laura Ingalls Wilder by the light of a kerosene lamp. I was grooming them in independent womanhood, the pioneering spirit! And now they're sitting like fat hens in a doctor's villa, licking caviar off a tongue depressor!'

I let Mother vent even though she was wrong to say Manuela had no natural charm. In fact she was very pretty when she washed up. Her wavy auburn hair shone with coppery highlights when not dulled by trail dust and her blemish-free skin was dramatically pale. This contrast of dark hair and milky complexion made her appear at once haunted and vulnerable, a combination men lap up and certainly appreciate more than any home-schooled knowledge of transcendentalism. Carlotta on the other hand, possessed Romanish looks; her blonde hair, again, after a wash, hung straight and dutifully, with her fringe forming a little ear of golden corn over her brow. She had an olive tint and could go without moisturizer for days. Mother of course does not want to realize that she had kept them too long; she felt they owed her eternal allegiance for the hours of homeschooling, which of course is rather silly of her. Perhaps she is trying to sublimate this rejection by becoming one of the Chosen People. Only I'm afraid she has unconsciously put herself into yet another situation where she'll harvest more bricks than bouquets. Though I do hope I'm wrong.

'Mother? Do you have someone helping you with this Jewish thing?'

'Not yet. I thought I should learn some Hebrew first. I think it will make me a stronger candidate. I bought all the tapes; I've been working with a very nice textbook. You know my philosophy of self-reliance, Jane.'

'You've been telling me about it, Mom.' I didn't mention the Protestant connotations of this philosophy and how the Jews probably preferred a team player to an Emersonian individualist. Mother would have to find out about that on her own.

'I hope you can make it over sometime, Mom.'

'Jane, you know I can't leave my lambs, particularly with Mani-Carla gone... and I'm twisting my tongue around this new language.'

'Well, then we'll try to come over to visit you, but it won't be this year. Our finances are awfully tight. And I've heard Homeland Security is hard on babies in airports. I'd rather wait a bit.'

'Do be a good mother, Jane. Remember this is the most important thing you'll ever do.'

'Roger.'

I suppose I should be used to Mother's betrayals by now; yet they continue to hit me like a fat dodgeball in the gut. I've certainly had enough practice to expect her hits, which begs the question: why am I always a sitting duck? Mother's Catholicism had long been the staple that joined the thin sheets of our lives. I can't say she was a particularly good Catholic; she certainly had none of Mathilde's mystic devotion, but she did go to mass regularly. And though she rarely spoke about her faith at home, I never once doubted her religious conviction. It is childish of me to feel deceived and even more foolish of me to think that she would never shuck the cross for a more satisfying alternative, one that invited her into a shared history of a people who pledged loyalty to one another. Who knows? Mother's conversion might root her more firmly in a community and an identity, for she has always sought both, without much success. I only hope it is not yet another pose, that she is not going to walk the tightrope of belonging balancing a Torah on her head. Oh dear! With Mother one never knows.

But her phone call did upset me and left me in a foul mood for a few days; I was short tempered with Honoré's Tupperware tossing and imposed a two-day suspension on all plastics (stowing them away in the utility closet) including the Gervais ice-cream containers. Honoré jaggered his heart out but I held firm, at least on Wednesday and Thursday. I was equally irritable with Charles. I stuffed his dirty troubadour socks into his Helvetian horn and then shoved the horn, which had been lounging in the living room for the past two weeks, into the same utility closet where he stores a hoard of other instruments, many of which he invented himself (more on this at another time). It didn't quite fit and I was obliged to open the little window in the back and push the horn outside a bit. I had had it with tripping over that giraffe neck bugle, with not being able to set my legs down when sitting on the couch to read the *Guardian* in the evening. There is nothing more uncomfortable than reading the news in the lotus position; moreover, it is bad for one's health as news of world crisis and misery enters the nervous system directly, aided by the receptive posture. As I pushed the horn up and out of the window I cursed Charles for the nightmares I'd been having, the nightly wake-ups caused not by Honoré but by the anxiety of dodging world-class criminals (namely a jogging George W. Bush but also Pinochet in an electric wheelchair – simply terrifying!) who pursue me during my prime time REM sleep. With hindsight I will admit that blaming this on Charles was slightly unfair, though at the time the accusation felt more than justified.

Now, it would be an understatement to say that Charles was unhappy to find his horn hanging from a window ledge (it wasn't exactly hanging but this was how he put it); he came unfastened. The forelock flapped up and down in sync with his snorts of anger like a paddleball, only the thin elastic string enjoining ball and racket had snapped, suggesting my knight had skipped chivalry's corral. Had I forgotten that instrument was an extension of himself, an outward symbol of the timber of his soul? Of course not. When I'm mad, I like to hit where it hurts. Charles is the kind of artist who is unable to separate his Self from his Creation, a situation for which he has suffered and will continue to do so, even at the hands of his wife. Granted, I actually went easy on him; it was just the brassy ass of the instrument that butted out in the Parisian sky. What did it risk? Certainly not rain or any extremes of climate. At worst a random shot from a passing

229

pigeon. But to Charles, it was as if I had pushed his very own legs out through the utility closet window; in short, he saw my intention as murderous. Let us remember, dear reader, that the splattering of pomodoro sauce on his borrowed musical scores provoked a near-divorce experience replete with dangerous gesticulations (my own; I was armed with a ladle) and oaths (also mine) so offensive to the heavens we frightened the Holy Spirit away. Keeping this in mind and comparing my most recent, and apparently egregious offence with the accidental nature of the pomodoro misadventure, you can well imagine the high drama that followed our bugle episode.

To think that a call from my mother could be the source of our marital strife – for was it not she who put me in the foul, murderous mood? – is simply astonishing, and yet I am sure that mothers throughout the ages, with a nonchalance suggesting an ignorance of their own offence, have triggered such instincts in their progeny. I do wonder if I will have a similarly devastating effect on Honoré and his future wife, towards whom I am already guiding him; it is quite unpleasant to think about and yet I suppose one must if there is to be any hope of steering a different course. I shall ponder on it tomorrow.

But let us get back on track, for I promised to offer *revelations for the betterment of mankind* and my bugle blunder is certainly not one of them. Mother's conversion may prove to be to her own betterment, however. I shall try to remain hopeful. Most importantly, we should be getting news of our magi soon; Mathilde has convoked us to the castle this weekend for various revelations. May the word by good, inshallah.

Chapter XIV

Which recounts a luncheon in Sans Peur and the post-prandial reading of an epistle from Padre Las Vegas reporting on events at the Monastery of San Matteo as well as a romp in the rosary etc.

We spent a glorious Saturday at Thrushcross. An early spring had coaxed the daffodils up from their winter's naps; their brightness warmed and blanketed the ground up to the driveway. Above their sunny heads a pink and white canopy of chestnut tree blossoms dropped petals with bridal grace. There was a quickening to the air, a rousing energy that made us all feel somehow more vigorous. The demoiselles, arms open wide to Honoré, welcomed him with their cuisine-scented adoration. They had set up a playpen area in the bailey with lots of blankets and cushions and attended to him while I sat up on the *chemin de ronde* with my laptop, finishing a translation for Special K – a speech she is to pronounce on for Freud's centennial anniversary. I could hear the squeals and laughter below, the delight of women and baby sunbathing in the bailey. For those two hours before lunch, I felt enraptured with the world, seated up high looking out over the burgeoning foliage of the Fontainebleau forest. I sped along quickly with the translation and for this unexpected celerity was awarded with an hour of free time. Yes, a marvellously uninterrupted hour! I drank it up and as I did so, the minutes lost count, they expanded into liquid sensations, transmogrified from drumbeat to whisper of water and blood. My spirit roamed within, coursing through the murmuring channels, awaking my forgotten corners till they tingled with recognition, but also beyond me, soaring above, below and all around me, reaching outward to sky and land. I felt strangely as if I were a conduit uniting the heavens and the earth, as does the tree, though this was not an ecstatic experience; it was the quietest, most intimate encounter imaginable. It offered neither head rush nor excitement, but pleasure, yes. A sobering pleasure redolent of the raptures in St Teresa's sixth chamber. Yet whatever the whys and wherefores of this moment of grace, it renewed me, replenished my dwindling reserve of patience and yes, even of love, which after a week of domestic tension and battle had blown its own little fuse.

We lunched in Sans Peur, our family much reduced what with Constance and Padre Las Vegas gone. It would have been more lively to dine with the demoiselles outside on the bailey's communal table and benches, but Mathilde convened us to this separate repast: there was news to report which was for our ears alone.

'I've just received a letter from Padre Las Vegas in Naples,' Mathilde announced once we had set ourselves down to lunch. The demoiselles had prepared a salmon *en croûte* which they sent to us by way of the dumb-boy waiter, a crank and pulley affair which Mathilde claims was the brain child of Voltaire conceived on one of his visits to the castle

232

alongside Madame de Châtelet, both of whom signed the castle's *livre d'or* – I have seen their ornate signatures myself.

'Are they still at the Monastery of San Matteo?' Charles asked.

'Indeed they are,' replied Mathilde. 'The brothers have been of inestimable help. Samir and Rachid have taken a genuine liking to them and seem to have no more qualms about the robes they must wear. But let me read the letter to you. We shall feel as if Padre Las Vegas were here with us now, bless him.'

Mathilde pulled out of her pocket several pieces of crepitating onion-skin paper. She ironed each sheet down with her hand, cleared her throat for the reading to follow.

Dear Mathilde,

Blessings of the Lord! Hallelujahs of the Holy Spirit! We now sit in the Monastery of San Matteo retiring for a moment from the great efforts we have deployed to liberate the captivating men, nuestros hermanos moros. Today I bring you the Good News. As we know, Lord Almighty works in most mysterious ways through his Son, Jesus, delivering mankind from Mankind, taking the monies of the Few to spread to the Many etc. With my brothers, these sons of Ishmael, and with Lord Almighty's help, we just today administered the medicine which I beforehand soaked in the Holy Waters of Lourdes. This small piece of medicine looking so poorly; it was such a doubtful specimen. But the Ishmaels insisted with Levantine pleadings that this estrange mushroom be hydrated. Though they did not know the water be so Holy, from Lourdes. What they don't know, don't hurt them.

233

The Padre Negri – a fearless man wearing the garter of Jesús Christo – has taken care of preliminaries by making negotiations with the capo, these dealings most concerned with vitals and feeding the captivating men who so suffer from vitamin deficiencies. I accompany the Padre Negri on one or two such expeditions while remaining most silent. Here is how it happens:

'Greetings from the Lord,' says Padre Negri to boss-man. 'We come in peace to offer food to the workers of our countryside.'

'Our workers eat well, Padre. They do not need your charity.'

'Men cannot live on tomatoes alone, my son.'

'We'll give them ham.'

'But we, my son, will provide them with lamb.'

'Then you are a fool, Padre, for wanting to save us money. What is in it for you?'

'What is in it for us is the joy of the Lord. Any rewards we reap are His.' Etc.

Such negotiations happen until at last we bring them dinner every evening. This kitchen effort made possible by the sweaty brow of Padre Negri who like the Lord must make the fish and bread of life multiply to feed this nightly reception of captivating men. Indeed, we feed them delicious vitals of meats, fishes and sauces omitting the temptation to season with pieces of pork; we feed them back to health to better administer our medicine. Having prepared thus the fungus by way of Holy Water, we then succeed in cutting it into the smallest of pieces, which we then prepared in the way of Spanish omelettes, sprinkling the medicine throughout.

Our life-saving omelettes have been consumed in their entirely this past night in the camps by our captivating men, without a drop of wine as indicated in the instrumental manual provided by Maître Jian who has offered us this panacea from the secret gardens of the Lord to promote peace amongst men. And the men say to us, 'Thank you, good Uncles, for this food which will put flesh back on our bones.'

Now we shall await. Let us pray that their freedom be won from the inside, through the transubstantiation of fear and slavery to freedom and courage. Praise be to God!

Please pray for me night and day.

Your ever Faithful Servant in the cradle of the Holy Son,

Padre Las Vegas

Mathilde held a corner of the letter up in one hand and let the crinkly parchment sigh like a falling gonfalon; she wore a pensive expression. Charles set down his fork, which had just speared through a golden morsel of *croûte* and took the surrendering epistle from her to read over.

'It's all a bit weird, this mushroom business,' I said. 'I mean, how can we possibly believe that mushroom sprinkled on an omelette is going to free these men? It might make them hallucinate – I'll give you that – but allowing them to "win freedom from the inside?" The whole thing is simply too far-fetched!'

'No Jane, you are wrong. It is not far-fetched in the least,' Mathilde corrected me. 'We have not had to fetch anything at all; through the most intimate chain of connections uniting faiths and philosophical practices, the keys have been deposited in our laps; we have merely to open the doors. Nay, what is far-fetched, Jane, is precisely the madness of enslavement, the crossed logic of inhumanity founded on a fetch that twists and corrupts the signs of Christ into instruments of our lowest drives and impulses. We are made in the image of the Lord, are we not? But what is this Sacred Image? It is both a divine energy and a portal, a window through which the Sacred pushes us into resemblance: the endemic distortions, corruptions, enslavements of the Image cast the lines of men into far-flung brackish waters where the soul withers, where the Vital Principle putrefies and the refinements of its ceremonies suffocate from the pestilence of hate. You are wrong, Jane, to believe the madness of the world banal and our means of restoring peace eccentric. Oh, if only we had madness in our grip! Why we would channel it to the divine quarters, filter its follies for the nugget of truth!'

'Well, now that you put it like that…' I didn't want to rub Mathilde the wrong way when she was on a Christological rampage. I learned early on that it's best to ride along on her theological thoroughfares. Once I did make the mistake of likening St John of the Cross's dark night of the soul to post-partum depression and received a harsh verbal warning for recklessly speeding ahead of theological debate and overtaking on the right.

'It does seem, Mother,' began Charles, his eyes still on the letter, 'that Padre Las Vegas has come around on the mushroom…'

'Clearly!'

'Reluctantly though,' I added. 'It sounds like Samir and Rachid had to twist his arm a bit. But I have to say, I'm a bit surprised they're such advocates of this mushroom business. I guess their belief in it has something to do with their kung fu practice, you know, the blind trust a student puts in his master…'

'I had a long talk with Maître Jian about the specific properties of this medicinal fungus,' resumed Mathilde. 'I wanted to know how it affects neurological functioning. But Maître Jian is a man of symbols, which is to say he speaks a language of unification, not dissection. He rearranged the principle of *wei wu wei* to fit our particular quarters: he explained that it – meaning our medicine – is a matter of freeing and not freeing at the same time. And it is from this perplexing paradox that our "captivating men" as Padre Las Vegas so eloquently refers to them, shall re-emerge as subjects of their own lives once again. I assume, therefore, that this curious medicine works precisely upon that nook of the brain in which the binary battle of opposites is fought, defusing that fight for dominance by a tireless play of doing and undoing.'

'It sounds like Sisyphus rolling the boulder up the mountain endlessly,' I remark.

'But no, Jane. What Jian is pointing to is significantly different. Sisyphus is trapped into ceaselessly doing and having his efforts undone. He is unable to do and not do *at the same time*, perhaps because he has been committed by the mythological mind to the stronghold of habit. He can only apprehend repetition, but never constancy. A Taoist would transform such enslavement to a stone by an effortlessness arising from the practice of their paradoxical equation. But this extraordinary notion is not merely the appanage of Taoism, for it also illuminates the Christological mystery as well: what is the nature of Christ but to be both God and Man *at once!*'

'You've got a point there,' I agreed. Mathilde was sounding a bit like Professor Jeremiah Haliburt with whom I was obsessed in college.

Capped with wavy, head-adhering hair resembling the Golden Fleece, he spoke in gnomic tirades as if his thoughts were sputtering in a cauldron, sparking the surface of some notional brew with illuminating precisions. I loved his ragged rigidity, his muttony helmet of hair, and how one could sense the little lights of his mind flashing like the expansive dashboard of the Star Ship Enterprise. Mathilde was less hermetic than he, but was equally equipped with a cauldron of conundrums.

'I'm wondering about how this is going to happen though… concretely, you know. How are these captives going to get out beyond the barbed wire fences?' I asked, trying to bring us back to the basics.

'That we shall see. For the moment such concerns must remain accessory…'

'Accessory!' I cut her off. 'This is the whole point! To get them the hell out of there! We've put ourselves in danger – I mean, I might just have the CIA on my back – and now we've got to have a solid game plan. Why has no-one mentioned money? Is Barra still asking fifty grand per head? Let's stick to what matters for Christ's sake!' I had humoured Mathilde long enough; I wasn't going to take another mystical evasion. Even Jeremiah would not have shrugged off my question so cavalierly; true, he might not have answered it either, but he would have at least cocked his head quizzically and, out of respect for an enquiring co-ed mind, pretended to ponder.

'You still have not understood, Jane, how the outcome is always an accessory, or a decorative by-product as it were, a *tape à l'œil* manifestation of… the process, you see. What interests us now is the course being constructed by this encounter of the metaphysical and the physical – this meeting of mushroom and mind.'

'You mean matter and mind. But let's talk about what really counts here – like the do-re-mi. Has Padre Negri got the price down? Can you just answer *that?*'

I received no response apart from a frosty glance. I was beginning to see why the commies wouldn't have her. It wasn't because of the noble 'de' in her name, nay. The persistent letters of pleading she sent them over the years were enough to dissuade them, for these missives revealed her inability – or is it outright refusal? – to rationalize her way to a communal goal and for the sake of that goal. Mathilde was all about mystical tangents and tasks; her reasoning did not proceed from logical development but seemed to emerge of a sudden, propelled by the energy of cosmic forces that randomly hurled stars down from the heavens, advanced the achievements of asteroids. Only when one understood that her meaning couched itself in an articulate sensibility, a manner of binding sensations with thought, of treating thought as feeling, could one see beyond the nonsensical visage of her ideas. I happen to know this because I too am inflicted with the Great Sensibility. I am guilty of streams of non sequiturs and the usual pitfalls of our ilk. But I'm also a Maraconi, endowed with a cagey pragmatism inherited from Neapolitan ancestors who needed the grit of logic to dodge the law and later (Father and his law practice) to uphold it. The logistics of how to free our men formed a firing line of questions in my mind. But I also thought of Constance, who by her absence in Padre Las Vegas's letter, became all the more palpable and present to the worries that were working on me.

'There's no mention of Cousin Constance, is there?' enquired Charles, taking the words out of my mouth.

'No, I'm afraid there is not, but seeing she is in Cannes, Padre

Las Vegas probably has no more news than we do. But I don't believe there's cause for alarm. All of the Padre's exertions to bring about the liberation have left him little time to focus on Constance who I am sure is making herself useful to the convent where she is staying.'

'Well, that won't be in the kitchen!' I add, for I don't believe Constance has ever set foot in one. The camper she once inhabited contained a kitchen sink which she used as a lavatory and a broken mini-bar in which she kept her vials of holy water; she hid her stipend from the Bishop in the ice-cube containers.

'No, she has never learned to cook,' Mathilde went on. 'But she is proficient on the barbecue. And impervious to the sting of smoke in her eyes, bless her…'

'There must be a way to call the monastery,' said Charles.

'I'm afraid not,' replied Mathilde. 'They have no phone whatsoever. Padre Las Vegas has called me from pay phones in nearby villages, but I haven't had a ring in several weeks. You may only reach them by way of epistle. Telecommunications compete with the Lord's; they will have none of it.'

'Mathilde, could you give me the address where Constance is staying, or the number – assuming the nuns have one…? I'll try to get in touch with her. She's probably acting as the convent gopher, making deliveries, that sort of thing. Didn't you say she was an excellent driver, Charles?'

'She's a queen behind the wheel indeed. She once drove a mobile home down to Orléans for a gypsy family – as intrepid as St Joan.'

'And got a speeding ticket, too, didn't she?'

'The Bishop had it annulled,' Mathilde replied.

'Now how on earth does the Bishop manage that? I mean, you can't annul a ticket… Uh-oh… I hear Honoré! Can you hear him? Oh dear… the jaggers…' The *Aing-eee* refrain scaled the castle walls with full-lung force; he had no need for Rapunzel's braid, my son. The ladder of his vocal chords levied him up. 'He needs a breather,' I deduced from the timbre of his plea. 'The demoiselles are a bit over-stimulating. Let's go down and have our coffee outside. We've talked enough business.'

I excuse myself from the table, relieved to leave prior to the cheese course with its opaque etiquette of slicing.

'Meet you down there…' I mutter over my shoulder before I speed down the spiral stairway.

Below in the bailey, Anoushka rocked Honoré in her arms, shh-shing him with a Russian lullaby that only made him jagger with more abandon.

'Here, Anoushka,' I stretched my arms out to take Honoré. 'Thank you so much for looking after him. It's so dear of all of you.' The demoiselles were clearing their lunch table, though some were lounging on the blankets in *Déjeuner sur l'herbe* type poses, sensually soaking up the gentle spring sun. It was time to show Honoré other vistas. He didn't calm his crying until I began walking with him; movement, better than anything, even sound, will calm my boy, settle his sorrows; he has, as do many of us, the heart of a hobo, a craving for chug-chug locomotion, that Alka-Seltzer of the heart. I take him to the rosary. Few varieties are in bloom though there are some Lively Ladies preparing to flaunt their vermillion trusses. I keep moving through the bushes, avoiding the thorns, which upon my wedding night tore into my satin hand-me-down Dior dress and clawed its tulle bustle to shreds. How queenly that festive sacrifice made me feel; it testified to my faith in life, a willingness to let go, perhaps even to perish, but to return again. Yes, to return again! And here I am now, the Mother of Honoré, taking my son through the stations of the thorns, showing him how to hold while releasing the rose, how not to be petal greedy, or vain of velvet, but the truest of lovers, a Groom of Life. Don't fear the thorns, son. Now there's the key! To know how both to take the prick and elude it.

'Good, my darling,' I whisper to him as he reaches with a finger to caress an ivory petal. An aphid catches his attention. Its pale greenness, its honey-dew decadence renders it slow to the point of immobility. Why, imagine a diet of roses! How could there possibly be fuel for speed in it?

The effect of rose gardens on the wee is similar to that of poppy fields on the grand; Honoré grew sweetly somnolent, he curled his head against my breast, fell fast asleep in the crook of my arm. I led us carefully out of the fragrant rosary and back to the bailey where Charles and Mathilde were seated at table having coffee. The demoiselles had vanished. I did suspect that Mathilde might have shooed them away to assure herself quality time with the Sacred Child. For when she saw us approach and realized her grandson, deep in sleep, would not be up for chat and play, she immediately rang out.

'Oh my darling boy! Look what the demoiselles did to you! I will have a talk with them. How dare they tire the Sacred Child so!'

'Please don't bother, Mathilde,' I replied. 'As the mother I have no complaints. They are of inestimable help to me and in any case Honoré always naps at this hour. Don't worry, you'll get your chance before we leave…'

'My chance! What a way to speak to the grandmother of your child!

As if you've put me on a waiting list to see my grandson!'

'Mother, Jane did not quite mean it like that…' Charles interceded on my behalf. 'Would you like to hold him while he sleeps?'

'Forget it! If I move him one inch he'll wake up. He needs to have his rest and he's staying right here with me!' Though I spoke to Charles I caught a glimpse of Mathilde: she was indignant. How dare I override her request!

'Sorry, Mathilde,' I added. Though I felt no compunction whatsoever; when it came to choosing between humouring my mother-in-law and caring for my child's well-being, my choice could not be clearer.

'Let him sleep!' Mathilde snapped.

'Any coffee left?' I asked, pushing a demi-tasse towards Charles with my one free hand. A thin stream of steam snaked out of the puckered lip of the family-size stovetop espresso maker, the kind with which every French country home is equipped. Charles poured me a cup of the dark brew, stirred in a spoonful of sugar with husbandly know-how. I must give him credit for that extra gesture – the sugaring – because it shows he is sensitive to my habits and preferences. My own father was oblivious to my mother's inclinations and hence to the possibilities of catering to them. He never once thought of hiring a cook when Mother was in her colour-swatch stage though if he had, he would have spared us those uncomfortable bouts of indigestion brought on by the consumption of stewed cardboard. I don't know if Father does much better with Shirley, but as she has the hold on all his credit cards perhaps it doesn't matter.

Sipping the coffee, I thought over our earlier conversation about Padre Las Vegas's letter concerning our captivating men. And it occurred to me that Mathilde had mentioned an encounter with Maître

Jian, which got me wondering how on earth she had met him. I had to marvel that she continued to implicate herself in this extraordinary affair in manners unbeknownst to us. Why, we had had no idea that she befriended our magi after that dinner party all those months ago, that she had embraced their cause like a French Dorothy Day and had become so deeply involved in their plot that she risked sheltering them and their stolen Vegans. How on earth did she manage this? Perhaps if we were not fledgling parents, fighting sleep deprivation and only just barely managing to uphold our side of the bargain in this 24/7 job that is parenthood, we would not be so estranged from her manoeuvring or find it bewildering.

And so I put the question that was nagging me to my mother-in-law directly.

'How is it that you know this Maître Jian? You never spoke to us about him before. Isn't he the magi's karate master?'

'Kung fu, *ma chère*. And you know him just as well as I, Jane,' she sounded strangely sibylline, like the Good Witch of the East announcing the bright news that Kansas has only ever been a click of the heels away. Not that her voice bubbled over with the froth of goodness, mind you.

'How's that? I'm sure I've never met him.' I glance down at my feet. No ruby slippers there, only mud-flecked Keds from the rosary walk.

'He was your upstairs neighbour for a time.'

'Oh yes, that'll be Wayne Fellow then,' commented Charles, nodding his forelock.

'Yes, it seems he goes by that name when he's… off duty.'

'Off duty?' I ask, raising an eyebrow.

'I mean at the end of the day, when he has finished mentoring his future Shaolin champions. When he is able to untie his belt and devote himself to the science of sino-pharmacopoeia and television dramas. Did his telly bother you, by the way?'

'We didn't hear a peep out of him. Perhaps he put down carpeting,' suggested Charles.

'That's unlikely seeing as Madame Li is the owner of the flat. She might put down easy-to-clean linoleum but carpet, no. A most pragmatic woman…'

'Yes, with her all-you-can-eat menus,' I added. 'But goodness! Is Madame Li involved in this too?'

'No, she's quite unaware of what is happening; she agreed to rent the flat to Maître Jian at a weekly rate at my insistence. She grossly overcharged him, I'm afraid, but Muslims Without Borders will cover the costs.'

'She must have rented the flat to the police too, then?'

'No, not at all. They snuck in there without her even knowing. When I told her that she had some freeloading guests upstairs, she had her door and lock changed straight away. She needed a renter immediately which is why she took in Jian.'

'My God, Mathilde, have you been masterminding all this?'

'I've just been giving a little help to my friends,' replied my mother-in-law. 'Do you remember the evening when the magi came bearing gifts for the Sacred Child? Well, I think you noticed how splendidly we all got along and how the Koranophone evoked some of my finest memories of Algeria and its good people. As we were leaving your building, I offered to give them a lift in the *Deux Chevaux*, and it was during this ride to Saint Denis that I became privy to their organization's ambitions, though not, mind you, their plan to steal away with the Vegans – not just yet. They did, however, inform me of their intention to free a group of brothers imprisoned as agricultural slaves. I assured them I was committed to helping this cause in any and every way possible, that I would fight the scourge of slavery like St Michael battled the dragon. I even offered them the keys to the castle as a temporary headquarters if need be. Four days later I received a call from Rachid requesting just this. I was delighted to oblige. There is nothing more salutary to the soul than aiding a worthy cause. Moreover, I am the perfect ally in this humanitarian mission. Yes, the police have been sniffing around, it is true, but they don't actually believe me capable of availing a Muslim organization. I am an aristocrat and a Roman Catholic, two credentials that in the final analysis will numb any suspicions.'

'Speaking of suspicions, have you heard any more from Starsky and Hutch?' I ask. 'Now we know they're in cahoots with Homeland Security, we need to be careful. Or maybe it's just me who has to watch her step… since I'm not an aristocrat myself! Honoré would never get over it if they flew me to Cuba…'

'Oh, I'm sure there is nothing to fear. The French secret service is overmatched. I have asked the Sacred Heart of Jesus to pump our noble name out of the veins of their investigation, to cut any thread of police conjecture that ties us to the plot to which we have, in all good conscience, lent our wholehearted efforts…'

Whether or not, dear reader, the Sacred Heart shall answer Mathilde's supplication with efficacy and speed we have yet to find out. We do hope for the best and must buckle up for the ride ahead, *ma foi.*

Chapter XV

*On the sacredness of naptime, the progress
of Jane's opera as well as news from Cousin
Constance in Cannes.*

As any mother of babe or toddler knows, the regularity and temporal boundaries of naptime must be spared upset and intrusions at all costs. On a day of all-around discontent, of sore rashy bums, of tears at the drop of a silver spoon, of an irritable mother fatigued by the fussiness of her wee one, naptime's cottony insulation offers a truce. On a good day of rhymes, quickly cleaned bottoms and giggles, naptime enforces a propitious separation that only quickens the mutual desire of mother and babe upon waking. And while the benefits to the babe make the headlines of the parenting press, little is said about the advantages, equally salutary, it offers to the mother. Maria Montessori pleaded for a moratorium on unnecessary naptimes and it was her enlightened opinion that parental sleep deprivation is compensated for by the life-giving energy of the child. What a lovely idea really, yet how far from the truth as those of us concerned do know! Lacking the help of a nanny or even a babysitter, I am entirely dependent on the three hours Honoré's morning and noon naptime allots me for my writing exercises. Why not in the evening once he's in bed, you ask? True enough, there remain four good hours to fill with my plume, yet my mental faculties fade, alas, after seven p.m. Perhaps cooking dinner has something to do with this. And my habit of nipping at the bottle of kitchen Sancerre while spreading myself thin between prep island and sink-and-stove peninsula undoubtedly dims the already muted energy I have left at that hour. But so be it; my family must eat and I refuse to serve up frozen dinners or revert to the Hamburger Helper reflex like Mother during her *I Dream of Genie* phase.

I am fortunate, I suppose, that Honoré likes his naps and agrees to go down for an hour in the morning and for two more after lunch without much fuss. He does get tired from overextending himself with the Tupperware (and has become a whiz at decanting exercises). His favourite activity involves using a spoon to pick up walnuts from the nut basket, which he then drops into a Tupperware Thatsa bowl. He has Charles's imperturbable concentration and can go on decanting nuts for nearly an hour. No wonder he's ready for the Land of Nod by ten and gives me forty winks at one p.m. Once I put Honoré down, the first thing I do is boil up a pot of Turkish coffee, and sick that Ottoman guard dog on the cat nap tendency, after which I can confidently pick up my pen, or rather turn on the computer, and get to work. Special K has few transatlantic conferences planned this spring and, as a consequence, my workload over these past weeks has dwindled down to translating her email correspondences with international luminaries as well as handling her online shopping at the Galeries Lafayette where she buys her linens (Egyptian cotton bedsheets only) and intimates (merriwidows and knickers – I'm given very careful instructions!). She has entrusted me with her credit card information, bless her. Had she been from Boise, Idaho and known the name Maraconi, she might not have been so trusting. Such are the benefits of living abroad, starting afresh as it were with a slate clean enough to eat off – or almost. I charge her fifty euros per hour for the shopping, which, in comparison to the cost of hiring a professional buyer is certainly a steal. Special K can't complain, plus she gets her undies delivered by UPS – right to her drawer.

Now, dear reader, in regard to the second topic mentioned in the chapter heading, namely 'the progress of Jane's opera', I'm afraid I will not be able to deliver. I do have ideas as to how the story will proceed, but ideas are a dime a dozen. Anyone can have them and everyone does. The art is in the doing and I, quite simply, have not managed to pen the next development. Though 'simply' is a misleading word, for it implies that it is incumbent upon me to plough ahead while it fails to take into consideration the constraints and halts put on my progress by motherhood. To demonstrate how inauspicious my current situation is to producing art (and the artists among you know what a demanding babe *that* is), allow me to list a week's interruptions – briefly:

Monday: Special K call at 8.30 a.m. for a rush translation – 'Libertinage: a Humanist Perspective'.
Tuesday: Honoré ran a fever. Two-hour trip to Dr Delamancha. Refused his bed; therefore held babe in arms until 9 p.m.
Wednesday: Mathilde dropped by at noon. Fed her lunch. Baby too worked up to sleep (damn it!).

Thursday: Day of teething and consoling. Consoled until I could console no more. Then consoled again.

Friday: Bumped into Artie at health food store; went to the park with babes, got my ear talked off.

Saturday: A formidable fight with Charles over who cleans the toilet bowl. Washed my own mouth out with soap.

Sunday: Lunch at Thrushcross. Finished translation on Enlightenment adultery.

Voilà, c'est ce que j'appelle une semaine typique!

In some ways, though, this week was far from typical and our visit to Dr Delamancha furnished more than simple relief from a fever. As Honoré and I waited for our turn to see the thaumaturge, we read through *Paris Match*, that waiting room staple imparting juicy gossip I suspect even Special K gobbles down when similarly stationed. We quickly sifted through the requisite Sarkozy pages, which were nevertheless instructive for teaching Honoré political dos and don'ts (in this case all the don'ts) until we reached the great *pipol* highlight if there ever was one: the Cannes Film Festival!

'Oh look Honoré – we're at Cannes now! Look, love! That's the swanky Hôtel Majestic where the stars sleep. It's so convenient for them. All they have to do is roll out of bed, coffee up, have a bit of powder room time and cross the Croisette and they're there at the Palace! It's simply magical, Honoré!' I could feel my son grow excited, for he was perceiving as I narrated the photos that energy emanating from the collective projection of aspirations and dreams upon the Starry Few whereby all disappointments, failures and mortal shame are erased in a transcendent moment by goddesses wearing jewels that come with a bodyguard. As the vedettes slow march up the red carpet, they wave at the crowd who receive the vicarious fairy dust with sighs and moans. I wanted Honoré to feel the excitement and yet not be an earnest partaker; I wanted him to remain grounded yet somehow enlivened by the spectacle of these fantastical creatures.

'Here, Honoré,' I said taking out a slice of apple from a Tupperware container. Apples, I thought, would anchor him down, put weight in his belly while giving him a slight fructose buzz. That seemed the right combination. Honoré shoved the piece into his mouth and began chomping with his newly arrived molars. The key was to keep him content in the stroller so that I wouldn't have to spend my appointment time chasing him around and underneath Dr Delamancha's kidney shaped mahogany desk. Honoré moves fast on all fours and if ever there were such a thing as the Baby Olympics, chances are high he would win the five-metre dash. I gave him one more slice before turning the page again to continue our Festival tour. Next we had Sophie Marceau looking quite on the go in a white silk trouser suit. I explained to Honoré that women wore trouser suits to make a statement about their past and present. A trouser suit expresses that a woman may not have been taken very seriously but now insists on being taken so. I also explained to Honoré that though we must commend Sophie for her commitment to *sérieux* we should be dismayed that it takes a trouser suit to confirm it. The next page showed Catherine Deneuve in YSL, smiling demurely. 'You know, Honoré, I have never seen her teeth,' I admitted while Honoré tried to pick her nose with his pinkie. 'Maybe she's got some reason to hide them…' I hinted. Honoré turned the page, nearly ripping it in half, but no matter.

'Oh my! It's Sharon Stone!' Indeed there she was, her platinum tresses artificially extended to mid-back level, a leg scissoring through the thigh-high slit of a fire-engine red backless siren gown. 'The problem with a dress like that, Honoré, is underwear. You can't wear any with it…' I was about to add a dismissive remark about how intimates mattered little to this brainy beacon of Hollywood Heights when Honoré sat up in his seat and began pointing at something in the picture to the right of Stone.

'What's that, love?' I asked, picking up his finger and kissing it. I took a closer look at the photo now and saw what Honoré was fussing about: to the left of Stone amidst a group of clapping Romany girls was a nun. 'Oh my God, it can't be… No, I can't believe it! She must be a lookalike – they say we all have a clone somewhere…' The woman in the photo was young, wimpleless, with short blonde hair and a solemn yet pretty face. Her habit was roomy and sans waist rope: undeniably it was Constance. Her expression of subdued bliss and ambitious abnegation was unmistakable: I knew that look well and how humility and spiritual determination pulled it into such tidy shape. In all likelihood she was about to levitate, perhaps only an inch or two off the ground, discreetly, so as not to steal the limelight from the Stone. 'That's not just any sister, Honoré, that's Cousin Constance! *C'est pas vrai!* It can't be true! I mean… good God! What on earth is she doing there?' The context, clearly denoted by the caption, was a fundraiser event for the charity Genius Gypsies. The Stone, being an egghead herself or at least a certified member of Mensa, felt the cause commendable and delivered a rousing speech (according to caption) of such brilliance that *her genius glimmered as bright as her gems.* I began to make the connections. A few years back, in an effort to promote the scholastic achievements of several

252

outstanding Gypsy catechism students, Constance had become involved in Genius Gypsies: the charity provides scholarship money to a hand-picked group of high-achievers. Rallying for her straight-A students, Constance rolled up her habit sleeves and dug her hands into the organizational sink of Genius Gypsies, acting as treasurer for a time. I remember her telling us last year over dinner in Sans Peur that she was having some trouble keeping her ledgers straight. In the end she'd had to make an appointment with the Bishop's CPA (Certified Public Accountant) to learn more about VAT (Vatican Accounting Techniques) vigorously practised in Rome, which she assumed would help her expedite her reckonings of debit and credit.

Seeing her picture at the gala event made perfect sense then and yet her proximity to the glamorous Hollywood loaf and this unlikely appearance in *Paris Match* amazed me no end: would Constance's debut in the *pipol* press usher in further occasions for prime time visibility? Might she appear on talk shows, say, or perhaps on a reality show – such as the one called Star Academy where competing youngsters croon outdated American pop songs translated into French? The losers of this ruthless competition could cry on Constance's shoulder, find succour in her chapelet of peas, and even feel self-esteem-boosting pity at the sight of Constance's dry, flaky skin. Perhaps gypsies, thus far excluded, would push open the doors to the Academy with her help and win over the jury with a Hindi version of *La Vie en rose*. Spotting Cousin Constance in *Paris Match* made me believe that anything was possible; who knows, maybe there is more in store for her than Warhol's fifteen minutes of fame.

A couple of days after the magazine sighting came a phone call from Cannes. It was Cousin Constance herself, *ma foi!* The line was crackly and we had one of those girandole conversations, firing off subjects from a revolving centre of common concern: there was talk of our troops on the Neapolitan front (so far so good, but more on this later); a few words on the Stone (who claims the pope has kissed *her* ring); an extensive report on the pregnancy (going well though the doctor has prohibited merguez sausage and all barbecued morsels – the staples of her sandwich diet); a firm pronouncement on the benefits of pregnancy fashion and the inappropriateness of nun's wear for the nine-month stint; and finally, The Revelation. Actually, I shouldn't say 'finally', for our conversation did not occur in the linear order I've outlined, but spun from subject to subject and this revelation was made somewhere in between utterances on dietary constraints and Chinese mycology.

'Where are you staying now?' I queried Constance, who had just lamented the sausage constraint. 'I can't imagine the Majestic has put you up. Are you with the gypsies?'

'No, the gypsies pitched a tent for me – they are dear, but I'm staying with the father of my child… at the Couvent de Notre-Dame de Toute-Protection.'

'Pray tell, the father of your child, you say? Now, let's see, who can that be? Sister Huguette?'

'Please don't play with me, Jane. I did not want to tell you about him before as I wasn't sure he would recognize the child. But he has – he has even offered to marry me, which of course I cannot accept as a sister…'

'A sister! Come off it, Constance! We're talking motherhood here, not sisterhood! Do you really think the Bishop is going to keep you on his payroll? He's already supporting ten virgins – I mean real ones! –

and you all are costly, even if you do forgo moisturizer and deodorant. Do you realize, Constance, that you can be excommunicated for this? Cut off from the Holy Sacraments, forbidden to genuflect before the Eucharist even! Mathilde is doing all she can to keep your sentence down to a minimum – now you sure as hell had better cooperate and toss that habit before the Bishop gets wind you're still wearing it. Sisterhood is over, Connie, you're heading to Madonna land now. And frankly you'll never be able to breast-feed with that damn robe – it won't work. What you need are cotton tops that you can pull up discreetly and a good Playtex nursing bra. You want to be able to feed anywhere, even at mass, assuming that the priest will still let you in…'

I ranted for a while, feeling entirely justified, the cause being the worthy one that it was, until I realized that Constance had been on the point of divulging the name of Papa. Upon this remembrance I quickly backed up and out of the cul-de-sac of my tirade to park myself alongside her earlier avowal.

'But what was it you were saying about the father? That he asked you to marry him? May I ask, pray tell, who the blighted knight is?'

'I thought Charles might have told you…'

'No, he's true to his word, damn him.'

'Well, it no longer needs to be a secret: it is Ahmed.'

'Ahmed! You don't say! The man with the moons on his cheeks…' There was a moment of silence between us as I took in the news. I had suspected Samir for a time, but Ahmed never. To be honest I didn't find Ahmed particularly amiable; his religiosity, though certainly well-meaning, struck me as rigid and I had suspected a certain antipathy towards womenfolk distorted his perception of our kind. Constance was proving me wrong, however. Not only had he offered to marry her,

255

showing himself a gentleman, he also agreed to bend his Islamic principles generously enough to embrace a Christian wife. Admittedly it is my own judgement that has been clouded, largely, I now realize because Ahmed had no sense of humour, or none that I could discern; he wore his moons with the deadly seriousness I tend to associate with a flatness of spirit. Could it be that what he craves is the lightness of Constance's levitations, her defiance of gravitation and hence an alleviation from the gravitas that weighs him down? Let us leave the mysteries that unite hearts in abeyance for the moment and hear Constance out.

'Yes, the moons; those lovely crescents… though I'm afraid he has had to shave them off for security reasons. In time they will grow back; once the whole affair has subsided and we have settled down…'

'So let me get this straight: you are going to live with Ahmed, but not marry him? You are going to be a mother with a regular sex life (perhaps best not to exaggerate?) but remain a nun? Don't you think that is preposterously contradictory? Don't you see that what you envision is impossible because life demands we make choices? That you must say goodbye to the old to make room for the new. You know what I'm mean, right Constance?'

'The Lord died for our sins and gained everlasting life. His death is our life. Tell me, where is the contradiction there?'

'I'm glad you've brought that up, because religion is another thing. How are you going to rear this child? As a Catholic or a Muslim? Have you given this any thought? Ahmed is no lightweight Mohammedan; anyone who trims his facial hair into a religious symbol means business and I doubt he'll go in for any of that *Bless us Oh Lord and these Thy gifts* routine before every meal…'

'There is perfect honesty between Ahmed and me. He is far more tolerant than you are making him out to be.'

'But think about the kid, going to Catechism on Thursdays and learning the Koran on Fridays – that's enough to blow anyone's mind. You'll be setting the wee one up for theological schizophrenia. He'll confuse the Son of Man for a prophet, refuse to draw pictures of the parables and then depict Jesus in geometrical abstraction!'

'Well, look at Honoré, Jane, learning two languages at once. Don't you see this as a richness, a blessing that will put him ahead in life, teach him how to see the world through two tongues?'

'Yes of course! But that's language, for Christ's sake! We're talking religion here, Constance! Two traditions that have been crusading against each other for centuries and…'

'But what is the Lord, Jane, if not the Word made Flesh.'

Well, she got me there: I had to admit that Constance had a point. And to be honest, though I did foresee battles ahead on the theological front, I trusted deep down that Cousin Constance would have her way in the end, that somehow she would turn the contradictions into kissing cousins. But God help her. Marriage and parenting are challenge enough without the quotidian strain of managing interfaith negotiations. I'll leave her to find out on her own. *Courage, Cousin Constance!* I passed the telephone to Charles who had been trembling at my language, and he, being already in the know, merely queried after her health and asked to have a man-to-man with the father-to-be to whom he spoke as if to an old buddy with whom he had *raised the cows together* as the French pastorally put it.

Maybe it should be a relief to us, dear reader, that Constance and Ahmed are now comfortably ensconced in the retreatants' dormitory under the wing of Our Lady of Total Protection; they keep separate rooms, I should add, for the sake of the sisters. I have to give credit to Mathilde for having found Ahmed the post of convent cook; never will the secular-minded police dream of looking for a renegade Muslim in a Benedictine kitchen; even in the unlikely event they were tipped off, they wouldn't believe it. And they would be right not to, for what die-hard Muslim would agree to cook for a Catholic cloister? Only one, we must concede, whose loyalty has been won over by Mathilde's undaunted commitment to our common cause. Yes, only Mathilde could have operated such a disloyalty in the name of loyalty, only she could make a man renounce his deepest instinct and belief for the sake of self-preservation and the grander scheme of saving the lives of innocent men. I could continue on happily with this panegyric of my mother-in-law, adding praise to her prize-winning comportment, but I'm being called away by the jaggers; Honoré has woken up from his nap. Oh my little darling! Here comes Mother! Away!

Chapter XVI

*Which recounts the turn for the worse in
the thraldom affair and Jane Maraconi's valiant
attempt to rectify wrongs with the help
of her cousin Guido etc.*

I knew the phone was going to ring before it rang; that happens frequently with me, in fact I am more surprised when this premonition fails to prepare me for the call. It was Mathilde on the horn, nearly out of breath as if she had been running up the stairs, which as it turned out, she had. She was calling from the *chemin de ronde* on her cell, and the combination of the physical exertion it took to get there and the disturbing news she had to relate caused her voice to rise to a high, panting pitch.

'What's wrong, Mathilde?' I asked right off instead of getting Charles as she requested.

'It's the prisoners… Jane, a terrible thing has happened…' She paused to catch her breath. I could feel the adrenaline, hers and now my own, streaming through the blood, putting our lungs to work.

'Oh God! What terrible thing?' I gasped.

'They are gone!' she cried out. 'They have disappeared. I just got a call from Padre Las Vegas. Samir went to deliver the food yesterday evening and found the camp empty – a ghost camp, not a soul around, just the filthy mattresses they once slept on, a couple of threadbare sleeping bags…'

'Gone? Good God! Where on earth…?'

'We don't know, Jane. We have no idea. The capo moved them it seems – just as the situation was turning in our favour, alas! Our strategy was working, the mushroom-sprinkled meals were transforming the men; they relinquished all tension and despair, continued the gruelling work but without worry or resistance; they no longer considered themselves slaves, you see, but free men inching their way out the door, awaiting the ripe moment for departure. And this shift in energy, in the perception these men had of themselves, began to work on the guards; the brutality to which they had given free reign retreated for wont of the easy, enfeebled targets they once found in the prisoners. Just the night before last Samir discovered, as he went to deliver their dinner, that the security gate surrounding the camp had not been locked by the guards: the captives could have escaped that very eve had they known! Only Samir did not inform them of it; he felt doing so would have been precocious. You see he thought the firmer this trust between guard and prisoner grew, the easier the escape – when the time came. He had no idea Barra had other plans – none of us did…'

'Oh my God… this is just awful…'

'God help us, it is even worse than you think, Jane. The Franciscans who have with generous, courageous hearts welcomed us into their community, given us their protection and aided our men in this dangerous exploit have now become a target of the mob. They've received death threats; one of the friars was held at gunpoint in the vineyard, then kicked in the head and nearly strangled with his waist rope. He's recovering thank God, but now we know that no-one is safe. It is all a terrible, botched up mess, Jane. The friars and our magi, not forgetting Padre Las Vegas, are in as much danger as the enslaved men – and God knows where they are…'

'I can't believe the mob is going after the Franciscans; I mean, they just don't do that! The Church is sacred. I remember Uncle Al saying the difference between a judge and a priest is that if you confess to a padre you pave the way to heaven, but confess before a judge and you pave your way to the pen. If the mob can't trust the church, who can they?'

'That, Jane, is only on condition that the Church remain mute, turn a blind eye to their evils. The Franciscans, by virtue of their collaboration have turned the floodlights on their crimes.'

'Well, in that case… it looks pretty bad, Mathilde. Bad all around… Let me give it a think. In the meantime, don't panic.'

'I'm going straight to the Sacred Heart, Jane. What else can I do?'

Before I hung up I promised Mathilde to call Charles right away, but instead I sat upon the couch for a moment to gather my wits. Honoré was on the rug at my feet, deep in concentration with his decanting exercise. He was spooning out orange lentils from a Clear Impressions container and dropping them into a Sheerly Elegant bowl. I noticed he was making very few spills, that his hand–eye coordination sharpened as he went along. His progress was perceptible; it was not unlike watching a seedling sprout and unfold on film at increased speed. How odd that in this moment of crisis a slice of time was cut out for us; I was granted an uninterrupted moment to marvel at my son in the way that other, less frantic mothers probably do daily. The wonder of his little hands, plump and shaped like baseball gloves yet so agile; the straightness of his back as he sits with legs outstretched before him; the way he constantly wiggles his toes and feet in continuous spirals; indeed the mystery of every inch of his being so alive with intelligence and movement nearly bowled me over. I saw not only my babe, but received a vision of the man he was to become. I was witness to the whole of human potential which starts off so small yet so immense. A child is so bare, so fresh and its soul so unabashedly plain to see which explains the unwounded but fragile innocence pooling in his eyes. Honoré's soul craved meaning and I saw he was making sense of his eleven months of life with a spoon, repeating a gesture that was building little bridges inside him, links connecting the different quarters within. He was surprising himself with his own wholeness.

What I was feeling just then was an expanding mother's love. My feelings for Honoré provided the molten core, but the heat issued forth and alighted on humanity as a whole. Such visits of cosmic connectedness pass in and out of us; we happily submit to their fleeting performance as we might to the invitation of casual sex, yet unlike the latter, they mark us for life. They pursue us till we act on our awareness. Such as it happened on this occasion: to be honest I would have gladly, albeit guiltily, put the whole affair with the magi and the vanishing prisoners out of mind, and busied myself with my duties as mother and translator, only I could not shrug it off. I could not forget that the enslaved men as well as Samir and Rachid and the priests were all sons of mothers, that their lives were in serious danger; and just as I would do anything to save Honoré's life if it were ever in peril (Holy Mother protect him!), so would I now do all I possibly could to save the lives of my brothers. There was no turning back this time; I felt it in my bones. What is operating in the maternal heart? The solipsistic madness Special K describes, or this protraction of love arising from maternal nurturance yet spreading beyond its borders? Might this dedication to the caring arts make one care all the more – for humanity, for salubrious air, for a healthier earth?

I knew I could – if I really had to – draw on my family connections and find out where Barra and his Foggia mob were hiding the men. With the magi's ransom money we might be able to get somewhere. Barra didn't think it was enough, but if we told him to consider it a down payment and promised him a share of the Idaho market, he might take the bait. I could rib up a deal and add a piece of American pie – but I'd have to play my cards right.

'Honoré,' I said to my son who now had the spoon in his mouth; he had finished decanting and returned to the ever-ready oral pleasures. 'I have an idea, love. What we need to do is call cousin Guido – I believe he has the connections to help us here. The only problem is, I don't know where he is. Maybe Montana? I'm going to have to call your grandfather and get his number...' I picked Honoré up as I went to get the phone on Charles's desk. Then I sifted through my address book for Father's number; we call him so infrequently I've forgotten it. Shirley does make an occasional call, to acquit herself of her step-motherly duty. Inevitably the conversation turns around to her latest shopping odyssey; it seems she has made several to Toys R Us where she purchased the most wonderful learning toys for Honoré. None of these we have seen, however, for she never gets them to the post office.

She stays far away from federal buildings because of terrorist attacks. But the truth is the post office has no appeal to a shopaholic: there is nothing to purchase but US stamps. Honoré will have to wait until our next trip home to come into this inheritance of plastic playthings; for the moment he's content with decanting lentils.

Fortunately I found Father's work number, which allowed us to bypass talking shop with Shirley. The timing was right: he would be back in the office after lunch, sober – he never drank anything but Crystal Geyser at noon though he did have a martini before dinner – and slightly somnolent with digestion. He usually caught his second wind at around four and it was best to reach him before that, when he didn't pay too much attention to what you said. Frankly, I didn't want to discuss why I needed Guido's number; I hoped to get it out of him with the least amount of explanation possible. Nevertheless I made up a story to cover my real motive just in case; it was a simple one: our Saint Mercy High School reunion was coming up and would he be attending? No matter that I have never once attended a reunion and have no intention to do so ever: Father's natural lack of curiosity about my intentions, the whys and wherefores of my choices and the depths of my daughterly mysteries meant he would be satisfied with almost any alibi.

As it turned out, however, I didn't even need one.

'Janie! Good to hear from ya! How's the baby doing?' Father's speech was slightly slurry, a bit like Dean Martin in Las Vegas, but only because he was on peptic overload – pomodoro will do that to him. I could hear in the background the strains of muzak from his Trivoli radio – it sounded like the Beatles' 'All You Need is Love' but the synthesized violins sent shivers of pathos through the usually jolly melody.

'We're fine here, Dad. Honoré is almost a year old... it's hard to believe.'

'Good... good... and uh... how's the weather there? Raining?'

'No, it has actually been surprisingly warm – very little rain this year. It's disturbing... no doubt we're seeing the effects of global warming...'

'Don't worry about that, Janie... it's a lot of nonsense. What we need is to tap into our own oil reserves; we need to drill the hell out of Alaska, but those damn conservationists want to keep us dependent on the A-rabs...'

'Yes, damn them,' I humoured him, hiding my politics for the sake of my brethren. In any case I knew he was referring to Mother, who he believed a die-hard environmentalist because she once participated in an ecological rally and spent two nights in a sycamore tree. She wore a diaper, which was humiliating but necessary. Her picture appeared in one of the Boise dailies, rapidly earning her the reputation as an activist. In fact, that was the first and last time she ever hung out of a tree in nappies for the conservationist cause. From then on she minded her own business and has never, to my knowledge, voted green.

'Listen honey... Shirley and I might be coming to France. I'm looking into one of those D-day trips to Normandy... Shirley wants to stay in some château she's read about, a kind of bed and breakfast deal...'

'That's a wonderful idea! You'll have to spend a few days in Paris to visit us.'

'We'll see what we can do,' said Father, sounding a bit doubtful.

'But you really must!' I insisted though my heart had sunk to my toes. What is wrong with my family? How is it possible that Father prefers to visit the hypnotic rows of white crosses at Omaha Beach to meeting his own grandson? Is his love so thin and threadbare that it can't wrap Honoré in paternal warmth? I nearly launched into a sales pitch of Paris, highlighting Napoleon's tomb under the gold dome of Les Invalides which Father was sure to admire, but anger shot my heart back up into my breast pocket. Before rage got the upper hand, and remembering the *raison d'être* of my call, I quickly put my question to him.

'Listen, Dad… I'm uh… trying to get a hold of cousin Guido. Would you happen to have his number? Isn't he in Montana now?'

'Guido? No, no, he's in Chicago… been there for a while. Guido, eh?' For a moment I thought he was going to pry and so readied my alibi, but instead he hummed along with the dolorous strings, apparently looking through his address book. I could hear him turning the crisp pages – all of Father's paper supplies were razor sharp, smooth as silk, porcelain white; no speckled recycled papyrus on the premises – and realized that he himself did not care to discuss Guido in any length. That my cousin kept the longstanding Maraconi tradition of mobstering alive no doubt shamed him. He must have been relieved that Guido now hailed from Illinois, far away from the Idaho range. As I've said, Father prides himself on whitewashing the family name with the rhetoric of tax law. Though he had as little to do with his brother and nephew as possible, he knew where they were and how to reach them. You can whitewash a name but the blood will always be crimson, and like Lady Macbeth you won't be able to Dove-soap your hands of it.

I managed to get both the work and cell phone numbers of Cousin Guido and hung up feeling relieved, but also saddened a bit.

'Don't worry, Honoré, you'll meet your grandfather soon. Now that

I know they might be coming over, I'll work on them. We'll start calling Shirley once a week. We can even pretend we are Ekaterina, her buyer at Saks Fifth Avenue. She probably has a Russian accent, right? We can do that! We'll practise tonight with the Rubber Duckie song… Oh we'll find a way to make it fun, Honoré! And they'll be tickled to see you when they come!' Honoré seemed genuinely delighted to practise a new accent, and though it was hard for him to imagine his maternal grandparents as he has never seen them, he did his best, I can tell, to show excitement at the prospect of meeting them one day. Yes, perhaps one day…

I got back on the phone then and dialed Guido's office. No answer. As dusk was falling, I tied on my apron and got our dinner going: fillet of sole with lemon and olive oil, penne with pesto, and sautéd broccoli. Charles would not be getting in till late; he was staying at the Cité de La Musique to attend a concert. Lucky him. A night out on my own, even if only a *viré* to the claret-coloured Café Chéri(e) for a sip of sex-on-the-beach would have lightened my spirits. Oh to heave-ho the weight of changing diapers, spoon-feeding, Itsy-Bitsy Spidering, and saving lives! For just one evening! Since the possibility escaped me, I poured myself a consoling glass of a nice Faugères and sipped as I sautéd. At dinner, Honoré got fussy and refused to eat the green things on his plate, a caprice which left him solely with the sole, and even the delicate fish flesh he shunned after three bites. While I tried to keep my cool, this rejection of my good cooking – the painstaking preparation delivered dishes that can only be qualified as delicious, I promise you – frustrated my expectation of supplying gustatory satisfaction and put me on that tippy edge where I could easily tumble into Mother Trouble. Which I did. While prying Honoré's lips with a spoonful of sole. With his baseball glove fist he punched to the right, knocked the spoon out of my hand. The fish flew, white and glistening, smacking the countess's Miele refrigerator, leaving a shiny splotch of oil before landing on the floor.

'That is it, Honoré!' I roared. 'No-one throws fillet of sole! Not even Marie Antoinette, not even Bill Gates, not even…' I knew my last example had to make an impression on Honoré. I held my breath to let an angel deposit a name on my brain (a trick taught to me by Mathilde). 'Not even… Sharon Stone!' With the mention of the starlet's name Honoré seemed to hit rock bottom; he broke into jaggers and grand-slammed his entire plate against the wall. Florets of broccoli and basil splattered the pale lemon glycerol paint. Seen in a certain light, in a moment of calm, I might have considered the pattern and yellow-green palette of aesthetic interest. But I was not calm just then: Mother Trouble wound me up; my anger, repressed earlier on the phone with Father for the sake of the brothers, tightened its spring, steadied its aim. I was about to lose my cool, do something I would regret no doubt, but somehow Nurture appeared on the stage just then, a deft Master of Ceremonies, ushering Natural Instinct to the left behind the curtain. In the bathroom with the taps turned up full blast, the toilet flushing, yes, beneath this cry of wasting natural resources, I yelled at the top of my lungs till the effort doubled me over. I sobbed all the anger and frustration out, my eyes a baptismal fount promising salvation from the Trouble. Which did, at last, pass in this purge. I ended the ceremony with a slap of tap water on my face. Oh dear, I thought, I've left Honoré all alone!

I could now hear him wailing, the jaggers more jagged than ever as if his spirits neared the pinnacle point where there was nowhere to go but down. I ran and unbuckled him from the high chair, held him in my arms and sang the song of Wynken, Blynken and Nod, the fishermen three. 'Why, imagine, Honoré, casting your nets at the stars! Forget throwing dishes, love. You can rock in a wooden shoe and know just what to do!' But it took Honoré more than a Dutch lullaby to settle down. A bottle of almond milk at last did the job, soothed the smite of angst, took that bite out of the bitterness that had been dinner. 'Poor little dear,' I cooed as Wynken, Blynken and Nod carried him away on the sea of dew. My feeling for him deepened almost miserably. Guilt is a lead sinker, a weight the pressure of which bears down on the seabed of sentiment, until an emotion releases like a groan of exertion. At first it is deep, inarticulate from nesting fathoms below, but once air-bound its visibility begs a welcome. The greeting always distresses me at first, in spite of (or is it because of?) the change of heart it effects. Guilt, as any good Catholic knows, is both a can opener meant to grind down our metals, our iron defences, and a compass keeping us on the right trail as we wander through the woods.

My own dinner was cold by the time I had put Honoré down and I simply ate it that way. Exhaustion hit me hard: end-of-the-day fatigue plus the outpouring of frustration, anger, despair as water streamed out of the taps left me limp. I poured myself another glass of Faugère and went to sit down on the couch. I sifted through the *Guardian* for a while, but my mind would not focus properly, not enough even to read my favourite section, the Nancy Banks-Smith telly report. Chalk it up to exhaustion if you like, but I knew this wilting had just as much to do with avoidance. I needed to ring Guido and was parrying. The key was to put in my call ASAP – on the cell not the tapped land line – before I chickened out. Moreover, I had to do it before Charles got home; neither Charles nor Mathilde could know anything about it.

I was on my own from here on in – but only if I picked up the phone.

The kitchen clock's ticking marched on the living room: the army of seconds nearly unnerved me but I held on to the receiver. Guido's secretary had put me on hold, dammit. If Charles walked in just then I would have to hang up.

'Yeah?' I heard a husky voice on the other end at last. That 'yeah' said a lot: it meant business, it meant *who the hell are you*? It took me a moment to downshift back to Maraconi semantics, the codes of the clan.

'Hey, Guido, this is your cousin, Janie…'

'Janie? No shit! It's been years! Hey, cousin, how you doin'?' Now I could hear that his voice was not only husky; it had gotten hoarse, like Uncle Al's. Due to a hereditary problem that afflicted the glottis no doubt.

'Doing good, Guido. We're living in Paris, you know…'

'Yeah, sure I know that. But what the hell you doin' in France when you got Italy right next door? They got the better bread, the better wine… they got a hundred different kinds of pasta. And they got the Pope, Janie. They got the fuckin' Pope!'

'Don't remind me!' I pretended to be full of longing and regret. I led him to believe that France merely fulfilled a duty, that I was dragged to the land of the Gauls by a Tramontane husband. A good Italo-American wife, I obeyed and kept my trap shut.

'They got the leaning tower of Pisa, they got the Mona Lisa…' I nearly interjected a 'not true' but let him continue. He seemed to enjoy himself and I wanted him in a good mood. 'It's unbelievable there! I mean, they got prosciutto comin' out of their ears, they got gondolas and Masaratis, they got…'

270

'When were you there last?'

'Oh I dunno, maybe ten years ago. But I got my contacts there. Yeah, I'm doing some business, you know. Some *good* business…'

'I'm glad to hear it,' I said, making my voice a bit hoarse too. I tried to think *Dove soap*, to remember the Maraconi patois that had earned me the bitter wash. Had Mother really cleaned it out of me? Can you treat language like a stain when it is the very fabric that clothes you? I spat out the soap and continued.

'…'cause I got some business too… over there, you see.'

'What kinda business you talkin' about, Janie?'

'With the Foggia clan… you up on them guys?'

'Sure. They're into red gold. Got a bumper crop this year. And some stuff goin' down in Spain.'

'Ever heard of one named Crescenzo Barra?'

'I might've…'

'Listen, I need some help with him. He's holding some of my friends in his pen. They're good friends and I want 'em out.'

'So… what do you expect me to do?'

'Maybe you could, you know, offer him some business, make a trade-off. I get my friends back and you give him a bit of terrain… in Chicago. Listen, I got a good offer to make you too. How does two hundred K sound?' I probably shouldn't have offered the magi's money, but since this was our last hope…

'What makes you think I want this Barra guy on my turf, Janie?'

'OK, not Chicago. Let's say Boise. Couldn't you give him…'

'The Ferrara family works that now – they're doin' the golf courses and those gated community developments. I'm out of there. In any case, cyberextortion's the way of the future, Janie. That's where it's at…

271

been workin' with the Russians a bit on the digital shit…'

'The Russians? Well, uh… Listen Guido, things look bad here – in Italy, I mean – and they're only going to get worse. We've got some Franciscan priests involved. One was held at gunpoint and beaten up pretty bad. Barra's overstepping. You don't do that to the Church.'

'Does sound bad, Janie. Sounds real bad…'

'Listen, think about it, will you? I can promise you two hundred grand…'

'Yeah, all right. I'll look into it. But let me ask you something: who are these friends of yours?'

'Good guys, Guido – they just got caught on the wrong side of the fence.'

'Yeah, well, I'll see what I can do, but only 'cause they's your friends, Janie. I don't usually get into that shit.'

'Believe me, Guido, you'll be doing right by Uncle Al. I think about him a lot you know…'

'Yeah…he was a good man, did good business. The problem was the golf carts…'

'The girls too, bless him.'

'I sorta wish he were around today…'

But he is! I almost blurted out. Then thought better of it. It was unlikely Guido channelled like I do. After all, the ability is a recent acquisition since the night I gave birth, limited, I've discovered, to the avuncular line. As far as I know I am incapable of channelling for other family members and equally incapable of explaining how I get on the psychic lines with Uncle Al. I'm just happy that Al is still around and avails himself in times of need. It would have given me even greater delight to share this news with Guido, but I knew doing so would have distracted us from the dire matter at hand. Our conversation ended on this wistful note of ancestral longing; it was as if we had both cast our lines out to uncle land. I had a feeling we'd get a bite soon.

Charles came home at around eleven in good form; the concert had clearly inspired him in some way. In any case it drove him straight to the kitchen where he poured himself a nightcap of Calvados. The apple brandy tended to heighten the Great Sensibility; I joined him for a nip of it.

'The concert was… how should I say it? Decomposed. It was as if the composer had rubbed out and written over his score – like a kind of palimpsest… you could hear the remarkable texture, the fadings and scrapings… I can't say it was entirely successful, but it has given me ideas,' said Charles looking reflective, forelock loosely coiled against brow.

'Is it ideas you are looking for, dear?' I asked.

'No, not exactly, Jane, but I have been struggling to make a post-Stravinskian statement using an entirely invented instrumentarium, and perhaps this idea of erasing, scratching out could be extended to the notion of washing, cleansing and the particular blurring it creates… I have in mind to work with a series of harmonics…'

Now it is true, dear reader, that I don't often talk to Charles about his compositions. Not because I am uninterested, quite the contrary. In truth I don't want to bump into or (heavens!) burst his acoustic bubble while he is in the throes of creating. My discretion is a sign of respect, of keeping that proper distance, when the bonds of marriage want to narrow and rope *right* in. But when Charles opens the little door to his bubble – which he will, suddenly, almost miraculously –

and invites me to visit his workshop, I'm an eager guest and collaborator.

And so we spent the late hours discussing our respective projects while sipping apple brandy. Perhaps this is when I feel closest to Charles, when we find ourselves soaring on the same wing, dreaming and scheming in the metaphysical heights where we map out our future in harmonics and colours, threads and arcs. Yes, we chattered away like larks and after moved onto other frolics, which will not be mentioned herein.

Goodnight, dear reader!

Chapter XVII

Which recounts Jane Maraconi's disquieting dealings in Foggia.

'**D**on't you worry now, Janie, you just keep on the road there. Thatta girl.'

'Thanks, Uncle Al. I'm doing my best; I just haven't driven with a gear stick in a long time...' The Fiat jerks as I shift into third, then slip smoothly into fourth. I am on the freeway and the slow lane suits me best. To my left, cars whizz past, weaving in and out of lanes, giving full reign to their inner Mario Andretti.

'Why don't you kick it up there a bit?'

'Listen, Uncle Al, I don't need a backseat driver. The main thing is to get there alive. Honoré needs his mother.'

'You got that right, Janie.'

I sigh as I think of Honoré back in Paris... Ah my little Lutetian! My darling love! We will be apart for two days: be strong my boy! I send him words of encouragement and try to imagine him top-of-the-daying with the Tupperware. I tell myself I have left him in safe hands with Fatima and almost believe it. I found Fatima at La Ruche, a convent of busy bees across the Canal St Martin that houses female students. She's studying to become a paediatrician and has a natural way with babies. I watched her teach Honoré how to toss Servalier tops like a frisbee and though he didn't quite get the wrist technique, he belly laughed and hugged her with admiration. Her natural Maghrebi warmth and humour combined with her medical professionalism and Mère Marie-Thèrese's strong recommendation won me over. Mathilde promised to drop by tomorrow and Charles, of course, will take over in the evening. I told Charles that I was accompanying Special K to London for a conference, and I had told Special K that I had to attend to some family business, as I put it – insisting I would only be reachable by e-mail so that she wouldn't call just as Charles served up the cereal, and risk foiling my plans.

So far so good. My Air France flight into Naples arrived on time and I picked up my car at the Hertz counter without a hitch. Now in front of me: a two-hour trot to San Marco in Lamis where the beleaguered Franciscans have their monastery. It's a shame not to have time to visit Napoli where my ancestors – God help their souls – once racketeered throughout the Quartieri Spagnoli, and where my distant cousins now control the garbage business. I would have liked to lay a rose at Virgil's tomb or climb the slopes of the volatile Mount Vesuvius, a bottle of San Pellegrino and a bag of biscotti tucked into my backpack. But business urged me forward; with girl-scout *sérieux* I had plotted my course on the Michelin map as I once mapped my cookie sale rounds. After a thank-you to the Hertz man for his tip-off on how to get on the right *autostrada*, I was ready to go. Uncle Al showed up as soon as I got into the compact rent-a-car. It was about the size of a golf cart. It must have made him feel at home.

'I'm glad you're here, Uncle Al. This is my first trip to the homeland, and you know, I don't even speak Italian…'

'Your father shoulda taught you, Janie…' says Uncle Al with disapproval.

'But he doesn't speak Italian himself! How could he have?'

'Your grandma shoulda taught him,' Uncle Al reproached.

'Well, what about you, Uncle Al? Do you speak Italian?'

'Kitchen Italian, Janie, good kitchen Italian. You know, like *passa il sale*…'

Well, that's America for you, dear reader. The cost of belonging. People will sell (or salt) their tongues for this hot commodity. But back to the Fiat.

Uncle Al and I don't speak again for some time; we listen to the radio – a stream of Italian pop songs peppered with advertisements for products unbeknownst to us. We peer out at the stretch of fields around us, the ubiquitous citrus trees coiffed in wooden trellises, the villages in the distance, the usual roadside eyesores.

'What the hell is this music?' Uncle Al trumpets, indignant. 'What happened to all the good songs? Like "Volare", you know. "O Sole Mio", "Return to Sorrento"… the old songs… I want to hear one of them tunes. Change the station, will you?' I press the hide-and-seek button; music barks then skitters away. But nothing of the oldie-but-goodie sort: the stations must be keeping a muzzle on Domenico Modugno. A soprano then ferociously arias over the air waves. 'Yeah, yeah, that'll do, Janie. Keep it there, will ya?' I hit the finders-keepers button. Verdi's *Aida* is now ours.

Opera gives me courage as I drive; the monstrous virtuosity of the voices climbing and descending the ladders of feeling inspire me to push hard on the accelerator and pass a Winnebago with a German license plate. The sunburnt sixty-something woman driving it holds the wheel with her right hand; she shows off her thick naked upper arms, the red flesh of which flaps with the Winnebago's vibrations. Her morbid devotion to Apollo expressed by coconut scented pilgrimages to his sandy temple along the shore is shining on her florid face. Might she be a modern-day Frau Gerber returning from an Adriatic vacation? My mind hops a few rocks, then lands upon a steady stone: Cousin Constance. I picture her maneuvering that mobile home down to Orléans with the determination of St Joan crossing the Loire. She took that hazardous trip in a straight shot, bless her. Her constancy inspires me to equal firmness, just as Verdi is pushing me to the pedal. And so I drive, not stopping for the loo, not stopping to eat, though I am hungry and hope the friars will kindly heat up some macaroni frittata or at the very least proffer a prosciutto plate. I'll be needing something in my belly before my appointment.

'Can you believe all these lemon trees, Uncle Al? They make me think of Grandma Maraconi's lemon crostata. Now wasn't that the best!' I expect to hear Uncle Al express some degree of gustatory appreciation; though he often rejected his mistress Juliana's misshapen yet lovingly-made dishes, he would never turn up his stately Maraconi nose at Grandma Maraconi's cooking: it put Juliana's to shame. Uncle Al chowed down at Grandma M's almost as often as Pops and his regularity at that table perhaps explains in part our current closeness. He was as much a fixture of my childhood as my grandparents and the dented aluminium pasta maker screwed into Grandma Maraconi's kitchen counter. But unlike Pops, Uncle Al genuinely enjoyed my company and took my kiddie concerns very seriously: whenever I needed a Big Bad Wolf he would drop down on all fours and howl; whenever I climbed Jack's beanstalk, he would fee-fi-fo-fum till I screeched with terror and delight.

Yes, I expect Uncle Al to second the motion, to praise the perfection of Grandma's lemon crostata. But he is not on cue; I hear no gravelly *That was somethin'!* and I sense suddenly, in the atmosphere, an emptiness and only the faintest tremble of a presence alighted and left. *Damn, he's gone! Oh, Uncle Al! Why did you have to leave me now? Promise you'll come back... in my hour of need!* It is strange how it happens: one minute he is there, the next he is gone.

Alone now in the car I try to convince myself as I had once before when interrogated at the Embassy, that Al's absences bespeak an affirmation. It is his way of telling me that all will be fine, that I'm in the driver's seat, heading in the right direction. I mentally go over Guido's instructions which are simple enough: collect ransom money from the magi, drive the monastery's van to appointed destination (directions given over phone and committed to memory), gather prisoners, hand money to Barra, return to France with freed men immediately. I'll probably never know what Guido negotiated or what flavour of pie Barra got on his plate. Guido didn't take the money I offered him, though. I'm left to assume he's found another way to make out smelling sweet, like setting up a joint phishing scam with Barra to invade the Italian market. Samir and Rachid are still holding on to the two hundred thousand grand: it's my job to deliver it and buy back our men.

Fortunately, my inner compass avails me just as Uncle Al evaporates: I attune my needle to magnetic north and keep my bearings. Surprisingly, this talent for orientation, refined by Girl Scout map exercises and wilderness training in the Blackfoot Mountains, derives directly from my mother whose sense of direction in field and forest has proven infallible; never have she and Pinesol strayed, never has a llama or lamb led her off the trail. It's a curious thing that she possesses such a faculty for hugging the right road while being so fickle, so intransigently unreliable in orienting her commitments. Mercifully I've only inherited the compass, not the confusion.

At last I reach the Monastery of San Matteo surrounded by woodland that slopes down to embrace a medieval village below. By now, dear reader, my bladder is strained to the point of excruciating discomfort and my stomach is growling for grub, though I'll try to hold out just long enough to give you a brief tour. Apart from the pretty, Romanesque church, the monastery itself is a boxy, sun-baked affair, more glazed than painted, in a custard yellow hue with the edges of its fissures a dark brown as if the sun had spilt morning coffee down the cracks. A neatly groomed vineyard surrounds the buildings; the expectation of fruit hangs delicately from the vines in immature clusters of hardened peas, opaque and green. But there is no-one tending it now. There is no-one anywhere it seems. I look at my watch: it is three and time for nones. The brothers will be in the chapel saying their ninth hour prayers. I walk up to the monastery's front door, a sort of *porte cloutée* that has been left ajar and so I assume it's fine to enter. The foyer opens on to a long corridor with a concave ceiling, low and tunnel-like and exceedingly white apart from the dark wooden doors smelling of Turpentine and beeswax that dot the narrow passageway. Towards the back, voices and a reassuring stream of sunlight emanate from one of the doorways, and as I draw nearer to it, the sounds become almost recognizable. The mass ditchers are not speaking Italian, that is certain. I slip into the open doorway and find myself in a bright, spacious kitchen where Samir and Rachid are taking a postprandial Fanta.

'Uncles!' I call out in greeting. Then remembering my elementary Arabic add, 'Asalaam Alaikum.' The relief I feel at finding them almost surprises me; I have only seen these men on three ocassions, yet our shared commitment has bound us with ties of near kinship.

'Wa-Alaikum-Salaam,' the men respond, rising from their chairs, tapping their hearts in the North African manner. We give each other the kiss of peace, and from this vantage point I see their faces bear the marks of strain: a deep furrow wrought by a train of worried thoughts runs across Samir's brow, and even his smile of welcome, genuine though it is, seems painfully to disrupt the straight line of the track. Sometimes a distraction from a worry – such as my arrival – will make a man worry all the more. Now, Rachid looks altogether different from his previous Parisian incarnation: the shadows of his face have shifted slightly and darkened considerably; what was once a thin sliver of shade beneath the luminous grey light of his eyes has now become an almost purplish wedge dimming the illumination above. It looks as if sleep now eludes him, as it had Ahmed in the oubliette. Night's ink bleeds beneath his wide-open eyes. Bless them both.

'Welcome, Jane... please sit down. Here you are God's guest...' Samir pulls out a stool from underneath the kitchen table. A dish of leftover antipasti with a few slices of prosciutto, an odd artichoke heart, some confit tomatoes and a bouquet of pickled cauliflower catches my eye.

'You don't mind, do you?' I say pointing to the plate. 'God's guest

281

is famished. To do His work, she must eat.' Samir pushes the plate my way; Rachid fetches silverware and some bread. 'Thank you, my friends,' I say before I dip a piece of hearty bread into the olive oil. The rich perfume of the oil dresses up the rustic *pane*, just as a new coat will make the man; and I feel renewed, as if wreathed in olive branches. I gobble down the good morsels and would have happily continued if my bladder had not pressured me to find relief. No longer can I stave it off, but mercifully I'm in a monastery and not a tree (Oh when I think of mother in the sycamore!) where restrooms are required by Holy See writ. Though new to these quarters my nose spotted one on my way up the corridor behind a silent dark door. I excuse myself politely *pour me rafraîchir* and sniff my way back to the *cabinet*. Unfortunately, but not unsurprisingly for this is a monastery, I find there is only a urinal in that small chamber, but its basin juts out enough from the wall for me to sit upon it – uncomfortably I might add. I hoist myself up, straddle the strange demi-bowl; like a saint I fear neither germ nor STD (surely the monks don't have them!). Nothing will get in the way of my relief though I do wonder if the screws affixing urinal to wall will hold. I pray to the Virgin Mary that my weight will not bring it down, and mercifully, for she was once a woman incarnate faced with surely worse potty prospects in the manger, she ensures the porcelain prevails. Thank you Holy Mother and thank you dear reader for your support in accompanying me to the monastic latrine where no woman has gone before. Let us wash our hands and return to the kitchen.

Samir has set a generous serving of carne al Ragu on the table for me, a dish that Grandma Maraconi would rise early before mass to make. It was our dominical treat and led us all to believe there is something about meatballs that fortifies faith, as if they hit the spot where doubt lurks and punch it away with protein.

'So,' I ask sopping up stray puddles of ragu with my bread, 'any last minute news? Anything I should know before teatime with Barra?'

'Yes, something you should know,' says Rachid. 'You will not be going alone. Samir will accompany you.'

'That's out of the question!' I snap. 'This is family business. Strictly. At least to them. Guido has it lined up. All I have to do is deliver the package and bring the twelve men back with me. But what you can help me with is the van – I'd like to test drive it before I head off…'

'We cannot let you go alone.' Rachid looks at me unflinchingly; the gravity of his expression plucks a nerve in me.

'Listen, I won't be in any danger. Promise!' I insist, making a cross over my chest for emphasis, following the lines of my Playtex cross-your-heart bra. I'm surprised to feel that criss-crossing ribbing; I had forgotten I was wearing it. The bra was given to me by Mother and is only put into service when we are behind on laundry.

'My cousin would never let anything happen to me,' I continue confidently; the firm embrace of my armature worthy of Jane Russell – or Special K for that matter – heartens me. 'I've got the cash and that's all they want. Plus their market share in Chicago… Guido's worked that out.' Seeing their faces remain as resolute as ever, I am compelled to add: 'Listen, Uncles, the deal is I can't bring anyone else along, least of all a North African Muslim. Talk about putting me in danger! I'm sorry to say it so bluntly, but this business is blunt, isn't it? So let's drop it. I'll make some coffee.'

Rachid grunts his disapproval but does not challenge me further. I put the *caffettiera* on the counter to work. Three cups of

283

percolated brew seem to settle matters; they tune our intentions in unison.

'How about that test drive?' I ask after taking my last slug of coffee.

'We should wait for the brothers. The car is theirs…' says Samir, playing cautious.

'No, I think we should give it a try now, while they are praying. I believe their orison will help me.' True enough, prayers do help – particularly in the absence of power steering. Our getaway van, I discover, is a silver Odyssey mudcaked from some friarly expedition in the fields. The experience of driving it, of sitting up so high and majestically distant from the hood's nose, surrounded by windows – for the designer of this model supplanted steel with glass – makes me feel like a true American mother in an oversized gas-guzzler on her after-school rounds, picking up her boys from the Little League; scooting her girls to their scout meeting: a mother with a mission and the big wheels to prove it.

Unpractised, with only a Fiat run for a warm up, I am surprised to find the driving smooth; this great glass panelled leviathan responds sprightly to my accelerating; the gears shift almost gracefully. I'm even more surprised to find the lack of power steering causes me but little grief; my arms have been muscled more surely by motherhood than by the practice of pumping barbells. I have Honoré to thank for this as well as the bags of groceries I haul up to the fifth (US sixth) floor daily.

'In the house of Honda I am also God's guest,' I remind myself.

'Al-Hamdulillah,' harks Rachid. He has just belched and hits his heart.

I drop Samir and Rachid back at the monastery and cross myself before I turn out onto the road. It is more like a dirt path, really, cutting through the fields and fraught with potholes, just wide enough for the van to pass. My nerves hold court in my hands, which now tremble on the wheel: I grip as hard as I can. Twelve apostolic identity cards – all counterfeited with care – lie stacked in the glove compartment; in the far back seat is our haberdashery stocked with the dun-hued habits Samir slipped in before wishing me *bonne chance*. The captive men shall have new names, changed visages and their christening fount will be this mobile fishbowl streaming with liquid light. It is a pleasure to drive an aquarium though the bumps are causing some spillage. I think of the Lord returned to Galilee after a quick romp in Heaven; his face unrecognizable, his words predictable.

The zipperless moneybelt Samir gave me has been chafing my waistline. I'm lined with cash: a hundred K strapped against me like the explosive-lined vest of a suicide bomber. It would certainly be a relief to take off this mazuma belt and give myself a good scratch.

'Janie?'

'Yeah? What is it?' I tune in to channel Al.

'You're gonna have to be careful here. Pay attention.'

'Jesus! Holy…!' I hit a pothole that was more like a crater; the whole right side of the car plunges down. I floor the accelerator to get us out of the rut.

'Thatta girl, Janie.'

'I'm *trying* to pay attention, Uncle Al! Can't you let me know ahead of time when you're going to pop up?'

'Nah… I never know myself. It just happens… I come when you need me, Janie.'

'Yes you do, Al, and I'm so grateful. Not many women have uncles as sweet as you…'

'You always were a good girl, Janie. Never had to tell you to finish your plate…'

'Tell me this is going to go all right, Uncle Al,' I blurt out. I'm seized by a sudden terror.

'Like I said, you gotta be careful. The guy's a son-of-a-bitch; used to know his grandfather – he was a bastard too…'

'But Guido has everything taken care of, right?'

'Yeah, yeah, Guido… the kid thinks he's big stuff up there in Chicago. Freezin' his ass at five-below just to schmooze with the Russians…'

'Listen, Al, just promise you'll stay with me till the end. You've got to see me through this.'

'Don't worry, Janie-girl. I'm right with you. Watch out there!' I swerve to the left just in time to miss a rut that was about as wide and deep as a hot tub.

'Thanks, Al.'

'You got it. Nice drivin', Janie.'

Now the road is growing narrower and runs down a gulley with a terraced incline rising on either side of it. Vineyards. Crucified vines. And they are towering over us. Guido had said grapes, that's all. I begin to doubt I'm on the right trail. Did he say ravine? Maybe not, but he did say turn right at a graffiti-covered shack. I spy a wooden shelter up ahead but no graffiti. Continue on. More vineyards with no grapes, which is worrisome; more shacks without tagging, which is defeating. The sight of urban defacement will set everything right; it'll be the scribble of civilization that steers us to the path of redemption. What did Guido say, a mile? Half a mile?

'Look up ahead there, Janie… to your left,' says Uncle Al. I crane my neck to get a better look, but only barely make out a structure of sorts.

'You can see it from here?!'

'You gotta have good eyesight in this business. Foresight we call it. That's our baby. You get ready to take a turn up there.'

The shack comes into view and looks like someone went at it with paintbrushes not spray. White paint. The message is mute to us; we don't have time to read the literature. A ninety-degree turn and we're on the right road. Two hundred yards, Guido said. And the grapes will subside.

He was right: the vineyards recede and give way to a long abandoned fig orchard. To our right is a semi-derelict barn in a tangle of vines and brambles. A Mercedes is parked out in front.

'Here we go, Uncle Al... Stay with me, now!' I pull over to the side, park some twenty metres from the other car. Cut the engine. Everything is statue-still outside; no-one emerges from the house – or the car for that matter.

'You got yourself a bean-shooter, Janie?'

'Of course not, Al! Good God! I wouldn't even know how to fire one if I did! I'm a pacifist for Christ's sake!' I can hear Uncle Al tsk-tsking me.

'Well, ankle over there now, why don't you...'

'Yeah, OK.'

'He's inside there, all right. Be sure to knock on the door. You gotta be polite... this guy ain't no *capo di tutti i capi*, but still he's a boss.'

I get halfway to the barn when someone steps out of the doorway, a man dressed unseasonably in a black leather coat. Presumably it is Barra. Certainly he looks the part. By which I mean he looks almost like a Maraconi. The square Neapolitan forehead and pronounced widow's peak, the way he has combed back his hair. But his nose is not stately like ours. It's a disappointment that doesn't merit the publicity of a widow's peak. There is nothing hawkish about it, no hump to see it through times of duress; it is extraordinarily average, straight, in a word, undistinguished. To each side of its bridge, a beady, opaque eye looks me up and down quickly. He has earphones in his ears.

'You just don't say too much, Janie. No small talk, you hear me? Just keep it quiet,' says Uncle Al prepping me. Now we are face to face, at arms' distance. I want to cross my heart – the way men tug on their jewels for reassurance.

'Guido's cousin,' I say offering my hand. We shake. His hands are slightly clammy. Or are mine?

'Barra,' he says, crushing his cigarette butt with his foot. 'You got the cash?'

I nod my head, then gesture to the barn. 'Are the men in there?' Barra nudges his head toward the barn, giving me the go-ahead.

'Say, Uncle Al… this isn't any kind of set up, is it?' I ask my ancestor as I turn my back to Barra.

'Looks OK, Janie. I have my eye on that guy… sort of got the sense that something's not quite right with him… he's nervous, does some nose-candy… but let me worry about it. Go on.'

I reach the barn and heave open the large wooden door. The sensation of walking into near total darkness makes me more than a little uneasy. It takes a minute or so for my eyes to adjust to the penumbra, and when they do, I make out the men sitting against a far wall, not in a huddle but in a line. None of them seem to be wearing shirts, though it's hard to make out their faces. I count the crouching figures: there are eleven men.

'Aren't there twelve of you?' I ask them, bewildered. Something is wrong.

'Eleven,' says one of the men – I can't make out which.

'And the twelfth?'

'Dead,' says a different voice.

'Killed… shot in the head.'

I want to cry out but stifle the scream; my knees are near to buckling beneath me.

'I've been sent by Muslims Without Borders to release you and take you to safety.' The calmness of my voice surprises me. It is like a friend come to encourage me. 'Please get up and go to the van. You will be fine.' I direct these shadowy figures out the door. The men file past me, attached by a common chain at the ankles, and out of the doorway, into the light. Now I see them well. They are shirtless as I had thought and their skin cooked to the colour of beets. Their shoulderblades jut from their bodies, sharp and outspoken like a pelican beak. The chain clangs in ominous communion as they walk. That they have been physically ravaged is evident; that they have been humiliated by chains and abuses is undeniable. And yet looking at these men was like standing in front of a door and guessing from the clarity of the light piercing through the cracks around its edges that sunlight floods the unseen room behind it. What they keep hidden surrounds them like a buzzing aura. I watch their march across the yard, their ascent into the Odyssey.

Alone now in the barn, I lift up my blouse and start to undo my armature – a Velcro strap and two buckles – and push the wads of money into a nylon Monoprix shopping bag I had also stuffed into the belt. To avoid wasting time putting the belt back on, I stuff it into my pants against my back. The bulge is surely unsightly, but my roomy painter's smock will hide it. I put the shopping bag over my shoulder and head out. Barra makes towards me like he wants to conclude the deal in the dark. I put a step on it; we will finish off in the light of day, have a garden party if necessary.

'It's all here,' I say pushing the bag towards him. From the corner of my eye I notice the last two men getting into the Odyssey. Barra wants to count the cash, so I follow him to his car. He opens the trunk and puts the bills into a suitcase, keeps counting. I have to fight the impulse to flee, to jump into the driver's seat and haul us all out. I dig in my heels. The ground is unyielding, however, so overbaked that it does not absorb the solicitations of an approaching vehicle; instead it rumbles and vibrates like an informer giving me a scoop I'd rather not hear. But there is not even time to brush off the message or put it on hold; a car lurches into the driveway.

'Watch out!' I scream at Barra just before two armed men wearing balaclavas leap out of the car and make to open fire. I drop to the ground. Sheltered on the left side of the car, I quickly inch my way under it, away from the bullets. Barra drops too, but not alive like me – I'm sure of it – not after the spray. The assassins approach the car, I hear the thump of their footsteps.

Oh My God! Take whatever you want but let me live. I have a child, a baby, not even a year. Spare me for the child. A child needs its mother. Don't you have a wife? Children? What would you do if ever she… please don't shoot me! Step-mothers ruin the lives of their step-children even with the best intentions and men will always take new wives – it's in all the fairy tales… Take whatever it is you want – my wedding ring, the gold bracelet – but leave me alive. Don't take my life!

And they do. And they don't.

Though I can't see their faces, I see their eyes – or the eyes of the one who kicks me so that I roll over, the one who estimates the cost of my life in several seconds and decides I'm not worth the kill. His eyes are sea-green and dark lashes canopy over them. It is an unwise habit to trust beauty blindly, yet I cannot resist. Because of his jewel-like eyes I might stand a chance. I imagine that salvation and death are colour-coded and that the former has a Mediterranean hue. I plead breathlessly, nearly to the point of asphyxiation, but my outpouring of words does not produce even the slightest flicker of comprehension in that placid sea. He has no idea what I'm saying, but my urgency, which is ugly, makes him step back from me. And now I lie there, hands crossed over my chest, until I hear their car engine rev and the sound of wheels pulling out of the drive.

'Are you all right, Madame? You must get up if you can.' I hear one of the former captives saying near to my ear. The chain gang has left our getaway van to help me back on my feet.

'He's been killed,' I say, pointing to the front of the car where I saw Barra shot down. The former captives tug at my arm to pull me away from the sight of Barra's body. But I must see for myself and tug back until we are all standing at the foot of the man bathing silently in his own blood.

'What can we do for him?' I ask, averting my gaze. The car's trunk is still open and now emptied of its monies.

'We must leave him,' say the men. 'It was he who enslaved us. The earth will take him back in its own time.' And I know they are right. We do not have time for a burial. We will have to leave Barra's death to its own fate.

'Let's get back to the van then,' I say, but my legs buckle under the weight of the murder I've witnessed and just barely escaped. Two of the men catch me before I hit the ground.

'Come on, Sister,' the men say gently, coaxingly, 'God is on your side. And we are here to help you. Thank you, Sister, God be with you, Sister, there will be rewards in heaven for you, Sister…'

'No rewards required,' I say, pulling myself up into the driver's seat. 'Just luck. So say your prayers, good uncles.'

Chapter XVIII

*On how Jane and the monks risk the road and
become guests of France in the dark of night.*

I'm driving fast now, up the boot of Italy, chauffeuring eleven men,
eleven pseudo Franciscans, for they have all put on the robes which
Samir left neatly folded in a duffel bag. One of the men – Mohammed
but rebaptized Frère Marc – is busy sawing off the shackles. We have
decided that the ankle rings will have to wait for a subsequent date and
more careful handling. We made a quick stop outside Terni to purchase
a saw at a large commercial centre – an indispensable accoutrement we
discovered, having earlier made a collective pit-stop at a gas station
where the fetters, of course, incommoded us. I led the chain-ganged
monks to the loo and wearing a most serious face, hushed the odd looks
directed our way with a papal air: *'Penitentes,'* I explained in a one-word
summary. *'Pellegrinos – pilgrims,'* I then added for extra clarification,
nodding my head sharply to snip us free of their gawking. Those who
believed the Church capable of almost anything accepted docilely, only
moderately fascinated; others glared in horror. One cackling man of

an insalubrious mind tried to follow them into the gents. I blocked the door and threatened him with a hot cup of Nescafé from the vending machine. It seemed wise to avoid another episode.

No-one drives this recklessly in Idaho, no-one would think of taking the road for a slalom course, hike poles and rear buts skyward to increase velocity. But when in Rome do as the Romans. I am driving like a bat out of hell though thankfully my radar is sound. I am pushing into another dimension where fatigue, hunger, the bodily riddles untether as gravity retires. We are all floating in place in this fishbowl, but the parts of us on the job – our feet and our hands – find no impediment to their purpose. Frère Marc saws, I step on the accelerator and change lanes for no good reason. I drive. But what is driving me is the man I saw die today. He pursues me as the dead will do – until buried and mourned and still, even then. It's the sorry sight of him lifeless next to the radial tyre that is haunting me. And I have the strangest feeling, a gut feeling, that while I know he's dead, he does not. He was cleaved too quickly from life to know what hit him.

So here I am, the depository of Barra's undainty demise and whether I like it or not I've got the album of testimonial snaps: I remember the crisp white shirt sponging up his blood, colouring to claret, the chest beneath perforated with bullets; then a close-up of his widow's peak and plainspeaking nose pointing down to his wounds; then below his belt, the memento mori of his death, a casket spray sprung from the loins, gorged with blood, bulging against his fly, defiant, and God help him, as hard as a rock. How can such a thing be possible? To give death the bird like this? No wonder he doesn't realize he has passed: what man with an erection can think otherwise? Mercy!

'Let's put some music on. Any CDs in the glove compartment?' I ask the monk next to me in the front seat, Frère Pierre I believe – I am just getting to know these lads and I've never been good with names. If I continue to drive like this I will have us all killed.

'Cheb Mami?' I ask, recognizing the treble of the Algerian crooner.

'*Vous le connaissez?*' Pierre-Mohammed looks at me, surprised. *You? An American?*

'*Plus fort!*' I nod my head. The music must be loud enough to drum death away, shake off not only Barra but also the sacrificed brother, our twelfth apostle, whose name would have been Brother Thomas, had he not been gunned down for doubting, for making a pre-emptive scramble when salvation was at hand. The captives knew of the monastery's plans and were expecting a liberator, not Barra's thugs. I try to imagine this Brother Thomas's despair, when on the brink of freedom, he saw the guards come to shackle and take them away. In a split second he made the decision to run for it. There was nowhere to go but down.

'Chase them away!' I tell Cheb Mami under my breath – 'May they be free at last!' I proclaim, borrowing the rhetoric of the freedom fighter extraordinaire, Martin Luther King. 'Free at last!' Cheb Mami's voice twists upwards, snakes around the tree of life until we are all a-quiver and shorn up by the living rhythms, the ululating synthesizers. The apostles are clapping to the darbuka, applauding this seated performance: a dance-a-thon to expel the devils of the dead. I swing my head left and right, rock my hips in rhythm: Terpsichore, the muse of dancing, keeps me awake and alert at the wheel and though she whirls away fatigue, I can sense gravity returning to ground control. And drive past the sunset into witching time.

Outside our fishbowl, midnight constellates the Golfo di Genova into garlands of tiny lights haphazardly strung inside pockets of night; beyond these twinkling islands, darkness ravishes the horizon, a pithecoid beast dropping down upon slender Hope, slipping into her bays and beaches to scatter seeds for the dawn. How strange to be driving these men to their salvation through the night in this aquarium, through the land of my ancestors in an Odyssey, fishing for men when my one son sleeps in a distant crib missing his mother's lullaby, missing her bedtime kiss. Oh I mustn't think of Honoré now, I mustn't! But I do, and as I do, an abyss cleaves open just where my foot hits the pedal, an aspirating chasm. *Resist for Christ's sake! Resist!* My only hope for motherhood is to renounce it momentarily, and like Peter before the cock crowed twice, oblige my own survival and that of Honoré with a dirty lie. *I do not know the child you mention*, I tell the chasm; *I do not know at all what you are talking about.*

We are approaching the French border. A sign suggests we prepare.

'Cowls up!' I trumpet to this troop of tawny Moors. 'If they see your Othello-ish faces without the cover of these cloaks we are cooked. Nuked!' I insist. 'Brother Marc, put the saw away please – hide it in the haberdashery. If we get searched, it might look suspicious.' Unfortunately, not all the fetters have been filed off. Three of the brothers are still shackled; I therefore direct them to the very back seat. 'Remember, you are penitents. Drop your heads and look guilty.' Having given my orders I now try to tackle my trembling, which seems to increase with the passing of each kilometre. I remember Katharine Hepburn, her patrician elegance augmented by a quiver, for she had the straight-backed dignity of a tuning fork, sensing the world in middle C and emitting the proper, New Englandish vibrations. *Look upon your weakness as a strength* I hear in my head: but who is this speaking? Certainly not Uncle Al; definitely not Katharine. I suppose it must be my mother then; she does have her moments of pith.

A service station type canopy dotted with night-lights straddles the highway up ahead; traffic – the little there is – slows down. A sign overhead reads Frontiero di Ponte San Ludovico.

'Ready?' I enquire – more to myself than to the men. I keep my eyes on the line of red brake lights ahead of me; the queue has begun. We are lining up for permission to pass; judging from the cars preceding us, there is more formality than investigation involved. Each car is hosed down with harsh illumination beneath the shelter, passports are handed over, but all this appears rhythmed by routine.

'Heads bowed in prayer, good men! We're up.'

I roll in under the shelter. The customs officer who let the Mercedes ahead of us pass through with only a cursory glimpse at the passports proffered, taps on my widow. I unroll, he bends to have a good look into the Odyssey. *I am a fisher of men, dear officer. My nets I have dropped, and in the place of sea, found fields, bodies bought.*

'*Que la paix du Christ soit avec vous,*' I offer him the Lord's peace in French, for we are but five feet from the border. Next to me Brother Marc shuffles for the passports.

'What is the occasion?' asks our officer.

'These good Franciscan brothers, who live close to the crib of Jesus, and as you know, in poverty yet without any deprivation of the wine they labour to produce, are being put into the special care of a "dry" monastery near Cannes. They shall remain within those confines of sisterly care for three weeks, under the strict supervision of the Lord our Father and Alcoholics Anonymous...' As I feed him this baloney and do my best to distract him, he is perusing the passports.

'Who's this?' he asks, handing me back one. It takes me a couple of seconds to register what has happened. 'There are thirteen passports,' continues our officer. 'And only twelve of you.' He aims his military flashlight into the van as he walks around us taking stock; we are drowning in border patrol illumination, asphyxiating on great gulps of floodlight. The enormity of our gaffe hits me: why hadn't I tossed that last passport for Christ's sake, or at least tucked it away somewhere separate from the others? *Good God, we're lost, the gig is up!* I am torn between two equally fatal instincts: one to floor it, the other to raise my hands above my head.

'No it ain't over, Janie. Never say never. You just gotta talk to him like he was a kiddo. Remember that, Janie. You'll do good.'

'Oh, Uncle Al! God bless you!'

'You just keep telling Him that, Janie.'

'Oh but He will, Al, for helping me out. For saving our lives! God knows there's good in it…'

Our officer has just made his full rounds and returns to my window, putting his head nearly inside just like Miss Ida, my favourite waitress at Brady's Drive-in Burgers, used to do. She managed to get most of her face inside and not bump her bun against the window frame. An icon on the altar of my childhood cathedral, that mnemonic edifice made out of all things divine and tasty, Miss Ida invariably would slip me half a buffalo chip cookie to dip into my vanilla milkshake. She was dear, she was sweet, and her bun was always neat… Of course I am regressing here, but this is good it seems. Uncle Al recommends it.

'Yes?' I ask our officer patiently, raising my brows like Ida used to when asking for an order.

'Where is he?'

'Who, pray tell?'

'The thirteenth man,' he says grabbing the passport out of my hand.

'Oh, that'll be Brother Thomas. Yes, well… he was supposed to come with us, it's true, but just last night he came down with a bout of the scruples. You see, he is inflicted with scrupulosity… it's an anxiety that provokes an exaggerated feeling of guilt over something that isn't even sinful – like sex for example! Well, I suppose scrupulating about sex is a bit naughty if you're a brother, but the point here is that he had such a bad case of it last night that his guilt drove him to the cellar where they keep their grappa. It was simply impossible to get him out of bed this morning. I'm afraid in our haste to hit the road, we forgot to return to Thomas what was rightly his.' I speak this last line with the conviction veracity brings to an argument of persuasion; indeed, these were the only true words I've spoken at the Frontiero di Ponte San Ludovico. Mercifully, I'm an unlikely candidate for scrupulosity. I feel no compunction, just relief, for the officer hands me back our proofs of identity, and waves us through.

'Mabrouk!' says Brother Marc né Mohammed beaming me a smile that nearly leads me off the road: such radiance, such white teeth! No stains from mint tea! I'm trembling now more than ever; it's a delayed reaction. I parlayed our way through border control and now am paying for it. Though it's a small price to pay.

'Congratulations,' says Brother Marc once again. 'Now we are at last the guests of France.'

Chapter XIX

*In which Jane finds herself the
recipient of a rare charisma and is bidden to
the Café Cheri(e) by a telephone call.*

U pon arrival at the Gare de Lyon, indeed stepping off the TGV
train onto Parisian pavement, at that very moment of foot to
ground contact, I found myself besieged by a sudden fear that things
might not be the same at home, that in the interim of two days
dramatic changes had taken place as to make my husband and son
unrecognizable. It was an eerie feeling I could neither explain nor
override with my common sense certainty that nothing out of the
ordinary had occurred in my absence. I was sure to find Honoré at
some new trick, standing say, heroically holding onto the back of a chair
(oh to think that soon he will walk!) and Charles perhaps playing a
pastoral suite on the alpenhorn. Yes, in my mind the home front
hummed with its daily tasks and habits while my heart's frantic beating
convinced me I was heading for Hotel California. But if this irrational
fear was born of my first step, walking helped me clarify its intent; as I

marched my way down the quay, I reflected on this uninvited sentiment which clearly arose from yet another fear embedded in deeper soil – that of having so radically departed from my quotidian reality that I might not be able to regain it. What if *I* had become unrecognizable? Did the rescuing stain me with Barra's blood or cut me a widow's peak? What if resuming my life as before had become impossible or at least improbable?

I took the métro to Nation, then changed to Line 2 to arc up and over to Colonel Fabien. The familiarity of the métro, of finding myself seated on a restless *strapontin*, of eyeing the sign showing a little rabbit who gets his naughty fingers caught between the doors, of reading the warning below in Italian: *Non mettere le mani sulli porte rischi di farti schiacciare le dita!* which does make it sound like good fun and games, yes, this return to the recognizable had the salutary effect of settling me. And as the métro reeled forward approaching my stop, it widened the distance between Italy, the home of my ancestors, and France, the home of my family. I began to wonder – a pondering perhaps even queerer than the aforementioned fear – if the whole rescue mission, the high-tailing in an Odyssey, the dodging of bullets etc., hadn't been, in fact, performed by deputy. Of course rationally speaking this is implausible, and in any case, I did still remember exactly what happened – or at least thought I did. When I actually tried to reconstruct the events as I sat there on the *strapontin*, an unsettling confusion, like the kind brought on by extreme sleep deprivation, scrambled the faces, the places, the times, the names. It felt as if a map of the events of the past few days was concealed from me like a risqué tableau behind heavy curtains, that I would have to tug open the drapery to get to them, and that pulling was requiring more muscle with each passing métro station.

A crushing fatigue overcame me; I had slept little the night before. I dropped the migrant monks off at the Our Lady of Total Protection convent near Cannes, having intercepted Padre Las Vegas in Monte Carlo where he awaited us parked in a white Fiat Panda by the Casino. I followed him to the convent, which I never would have found on my own at night, for it was tucked away in the coastal hills where the streets twisted and turned confusingly. Once there, Padre accompanied the men in, for Cousin Constance was not to know or even suspect my involvement in the operation. Then I drove into town and parked the Odyssey near the train station, in a street that appeared relatively safe and *sans histoires*. There I shut eye, or at least tried to, rising at half-past six to check the train schedule. I caught a seven o'clock with an easy connection to Paris, hoping to be lulled to sleep by the locomotive's delicious constancy. But as it transpired I was too wound up by all that had happened; my hands still sensed the urgency of the wheel – it continued to precede me like an overturned halo, not golden but molten red, and perhaps of Mattel make, for it spoke phrases if squeezed: turn me left for Emergencies; turn me right for Urgencies! A confused transference from prisoners to passengers operating in my tired mind, had me believing I was saddled with the lives of those on the train. *Must get them back to Paris, must not fall asleep on the wheel.* From my blue velour seat in second class I was pushing the buttons that would get us all back to the safety of Paris.

Perhaps you think it even more presumptuous than preposterous that I could possibly imagine myself responsible for the lives of strangers on the TGV train; please allow me to explain. This belief I had – preposterous or not – bleeds out from the rivulets of motherhood and is no doubt misdirected, but who would accuse any mom, working as hard as any 7-Eleven convenience store, of being hubristic? Admittedly I had become addicted to the rescuing which is a common occurrence among paramedics and mothers alike.

It wasn't until I got off the métro at Colonel Fabien that I became less beholden to the claims of conscience and it wasn't until I began climbing the five (US 6) storeys to our flat that the adrenaline evaporated and fatigue kicked in. My legs burned with the effort and by the time I reached the door I had to bend down to catch my breath. Yet these physical discomforts disturbed me far less than the greeting I was about to receive.

'Hello…' I managed once in the door, still panting a bit, *ma foi*.

'Did you get the bread?' Charles yelled his question from the kitchen. I wondered if he was expecting someone else. Was Mathilde due to drop by with a baguette?

'I'm home!' I yelled back, plopping down my bag on the floor. In the kitchen I found Honoré in his high chair, his face smeared with creamy crests of a strawbery *petit suisse*. Charles was doing some washing up. I picked up my darling boy and wiped the Helvetian mess off his face with his bib. How good it was to hold him!

'Did you get the bread?' Charles repeated.

'The bread? What are you talking about? *Chéri*, I just got home… from the conference. I didn't know you needed bread. If I had I would have picked some up.'

Charles turned around from the sink and gave me a peculiar look, a mix of irritation and incomprehension.

'Jane, you didn't go to the conference! Whatever are you talking about? You just left here half an hour ago to get some groceries. Now, did you get the bread or didn't you? We're out of it as you know.'

'Good God, Charles, what are *you* talking about? I've been gone since yesterday morning! My train just came in about forty minutes ago!'

'Now listen, Jane, this is a rather sick joke and I am awfully tired – you know I didn't sleep well last night what with Honoré waking up at four and our, uh… subsequent play time…'

'Well if there is a joke, you're the one who's playing it, not me. If you really need bread, then I'll go down and get some, but first I'd like to spend a moment with my son, if you don't mind! I haven't seen him in two days, after all!' Just then, as our hostility was about to bare its claws the phone rang. Nearest to the horn, I went to pick it up.

'Allô?' I barked into the receiver. Rather than commence with a salutation, our caller beat the bush itself, plunged into the heart of the matter, in short, performed a split-second biathalon so that our conversation began at the finish line.

'*Ma chère, je sais tout! Absolument tout!*'

'Well, *bonsoir* Mathilde. How about that!' I turned and gave Charles my 'it's your mother' grimace. 'I just stepped in the door, Mathilde. Perhaps you'd like to speak to Charles. He tells me you were going to bring over a baguette…'

'Jane, did you hear me? I said that I am *au courant*, in the *know*. I just got done speaking with Padre Las Vegas. Tell me, how did you weather that storm?'

'Fine, fine. My hair caught a bit of wind though… looks a mess I'm afraid.'

'I see, Jane… you are trying to keep this from Charles, but you shouldn't bother yourself. I plan on telling him everything. As your husband he must know.'

'That's not a good idea, Mathilde...'

'Pass me Charles.'

'Perhaps we could discuss this more in depth ourselves before making rash decisions.'

'Pass me Charles, I said.' The authoritarian tone of Mathilde's voice resonated down her nobiliary line calling to arms a host of commanding ancestors. I was outnumbered by her ranks, trampled down by the weight of their severity. I passed the phone.

Honoré and I snuggled and consoled each other while listening in with trepidation. Lord knows how Charles was going to react to my duplicity, to my dealings with Guido, to my life-risking exploit and how I almost got shot down along with Barra and then drove like a demon to France with eleven men in the back – even if he did support the cause wholeheartedly. He would remind me – as if such recall were needed – that I am, after all, Honoré's mother, his beloved wife, and because of the natural primacy of these roles my presence on the home front requires constancy; that putting my own life in peril could only jeopardize the well-being of my son – and husband, who in matters of the hearth bears the burden of numerous handicaps; in a word, that what I had done was rash, foolhardy, and in the final evaluation, selfish. Might you feel inclined, dear reader, to defend me against that last, outrageous accusation? I must explain that in its wooden condemnation a splinter of truth stands up against the grain. Yes, I took the risks I did to save the migrant Moors, but I did so knowing that beyond my dread and exhaustion, hovering above it all, a reward awaited in suspension. Neither monetary or particularly moral, the recompense offered me rather a heroic exhilaration, of the kind that perhaps Robin Hood felt as he robbed the wealthy depraved, and I must say that through it all – the gloom, the morbid impropriety of death, the shedding of shackles, the piloting on Italian roads – it was this adrenalin-charged tow that pulled me along, and the eleven men in my wake as well.

Honoré and I held fast to each other as Mathilde put Charles *au courant*. We could not hear her, of course, but listening to Charles we tried to fill in the blanks.

'I'm sorry, Mother, but what you are saying is preposterous! Jane has been here both yesterday and today. Her conference was cancelled. What? How is it possible? How can we be sure? Ubiquity you say? Yes, well, I don't doubt the Padre Pio practised it, but Jane! Yes, yes, I know about the charismas, Mother, please don't be condescending… well, this is a great deal to take in, Mother. It is highly disturbing to me and I will need to hear about this directly from Jane… yes, do come by tomorrow. Or rather don't. We'll come out to Thrushcross. Yes, yes… Goodbye, Mother.' Charles handed me the phone and held his head between his hands. His forelock tipped forward, dangling vulnerable like a lone thought poised before an audience knuckled up to punch it down.

'Shall I get us a drink?' I proposed.

'Yes, Jane, that would be best,' replied my knight. I thought of fixing us a Pimm's but didn't have the fruit. I served up two vodka tonics instead, sans lime, with Honoré propped on my hip. Then I poured him a sippy cup of apple juice, which he proceeded to guzzle.

'Here's to home sweet home!' I proposed. Charles, Honoré and I lifted cups in salute. The forelocks of both my loves were flopping loosely against their brows. I pulled up Honoré's hair to wrap it around my finger.

'I know what you must be thinking, Charles, and realize the risk I took put both of you in a potentially very bad spot… but I saw that it was possible, that I could pull it off with Cousin Guido's help and you know as well as I do that it was our only possibility. So I did it.' I tried to emphasize the pragmatic reasoning behind my act. No-one can fault you on being practical, unless of course you live amongst the French.

'You should never, ever have done that,' he said setting his glass down.

'Now, Charles, I know what you think, but…'

'You are a mother now, Jane. Your life means everything to Honoré and to me… And you know what I think of your Cousin Guido!'

'Of course I do, but he held the key, don't you see? You're right, he's a mobster and into some bad stuff, but let me tell you, on this one, he did us a big favour… he didn't even take a cut of the ransom money – and I had offered him all of it! And besides, we grew up together; he's like the brother I never had. How can you expect me to forsake that? It would be like me forbidding you to talk to Edward – which would only be to our detriment, naturally. Cutting off family is like cutting off the leg of your favourite chair – you just can't sit comfortably afterwards.'

'You've left me in a difficult place, Jane. How will I learn to trust again?'

'Oh, let's not get melodramatic! I didn't cheat on you for heaven's sake!'

'But you lied to me.'

'Oh come off it! I lied for a good cause.'

'I can't believe that last night we were… that I was… good God!' Charles shuddered.

'What on earth are you talking about?'

'Jane, I must inform you that you were here yesterday. You never left, or at least one of you didn't.'

'One of me? What on earth…?'

'What I am trying to say is that you were both in Italy and here with me and Honoré. You experienced, as they say, a bi-location – the ability to be in two places at once – one of the most rare charismas granted by God, and usually only given to those who smell of sanctity. I guess He's made an exception for you, Jane. I have no idea why.'

'You must be joking!'

'I wish I were. To think that we… last night… made… Good God!' Charles wailed and dropped his arms.

'You mean we made love last night?! Or rather you did with – her? Well, maybe I'm the one who should feel cheated!'

'But it was you of course. Or her… Good God! I don't understand.'

'Nor do I.' I thought for a moment. 'Let's be good Catholics and assume we're not supposed to.'

'Yes,' said Charles nodding his head. But in the next breath, he went on, unable to surrender this early in the game. 'Mathilde says the Padre Pio granted you the charisma; that he invited you into the warp where time slides off the back of space…'

'Well, that was sweet of him – to invite me into the warp. Because it all sounds pretty warped to me! It's not that I don't believe it, it's that I don't *feel* it. I have no recollections, no sense of what the other one, the other me, experienced. I have no sensations that lead me to her, that point in her direction. Nothing even subliminal as far as I can tell. It's the weirdest thing…'

'It seems that it happens oft like this – that there's a complete disconnection between the two manifestations of the same person.

Though in some cases, much rarer, the person has cognizance of the bi-location – as with Padre Pio.'

'I wonder why he did it though… I had a babysitter lined up and everything.'

'Perhaps this is what kept you safe and alive, having this other you on the home front, taking care of family business. Never doubt the wisdom of the great saints. If you doubt it is because there is something you have failed to see.'

'Oh husband of great wisdom!' I imitated Mother imitating Barbara Eden in genie attire. 'Tell me, though…' I added with a wink. 'How was I… or she? Passionate I hope?'

'You were… uh… she was quite – how should I say it – *très douée en amour*,' said Charles looking most confused.

'Good in bed, in other words. Well I should hope so! Or should I be jealous? God, I have no idea. It's too weird for words.'

'That it is, Jane.'

Honoré, who I had set loose on the kitchen floor, was by then in the Tupperware drawer having a grand old time. I had to wonder what he thought of the other me. Was her mothering just as mad? Did she sing Mother Goose rhymes with a Japanese accent? What did she cook him for dinner and lunch? Did she julienne his green beans – he won't eat them any other way. But then I felt myself sliding from the elastic heights of wonder to the constrained low-lands of worry. Quickly, I snipped the thread of these thoughts, put my mind to the here and now: what would we have for dinner tonight? What was in the fridge? Several fillets of veal wrapped in the butcher's thin sheets of brown tissue paper, a slab of half-salted butter and a chunk of gruyère cheese of the same provenance, fresh parmesan, aubergines, courgettes, red onions, artichokes, fennel and some carrots with elaborate green headdress still intact. On the table sat a bowl of garden tomatoes marbled red and yellow towards the stem: the fragrant kind. The only kind I ever buy. So she had bought exactly what I would have; she even went to the farmers' market on the Boulevard de La Villette, the only place around here where you can find honest to goodness tomatoes and not the hot-house variety! Today was market day – and she knew it. How extraordinary! It's silly to say perhaps, but I would have liked to meet her – this clone of mine. It's rather mystifying having someone step in for you with such perfection that neither your son nor husband notices any discrepancy whatsoever – not a hair or a word out of place: me to a tee.

I took a nap for what was left of the afternoon, and awoke famished. We would have an early dinner. Charles and Honoré played the piano – a piece that sounded like *Ode to Joy* – while I prepared the veal, pounding it with a mallet, and some quick aubergine. Put the pasta pot on to boil water for the penne. I do love this kitchen, fit for a countess. And although morganatic restrictions preclude me from wearing Charles's title about town, in the kitchen I am Countess Jane without a doubt. I can shave ice without a machine, cook cockles with my eyes shut – Charles's *cousine*, the Countess de Sarry, can only envy me, now that I have reign over her donation. Poor dear, she is probably still struggling through those recipe poems written by her Italian paramour, getting the temperatures right for love.

Over dinner Charles lifted his glass of wine to me for a toast.

'I'm happy to have you home again, dear.'

'Then was she not quite as good as me?' I asked, hoping this meant she in some way fell short of being me. That yesterday's Jane was not up to par with today's. Odd to compete with oneself.

'Every bit as good overall, but…'

'But what?'

'Her cutlets lacked a bit of…'

'Of what?' I insisted impatiently.

'Salt I suppose.'

Brrrrring, brrring, brrring.

'Oh that damn phone!'

'Shall I get it?' asked Charles.

'No, no, I'll pick it up. It's right here… Hello?'

'Jane? It's Tracy. Listen. Could you bring my measuring spoons tonight – the ones I loaned you? I've got to make birthday cakes for the twins next week.'

'Sure, I've been meaning to give them back, but tonight?'

'Well, you're coming, right?'

'Oh! Oh! Oh!'

'We're counting on you, Jane. It's moms' night out!'

'Right… well, I know… it's just that tonight I'm so absolutely exhausted… I've been…' I bit my tongue.

'Nothing that a good drink couldn't fix. Besides you were just glowing at the market this morning. You had a kind of… I don't know… a Mona Lisa look… sort of.'

'Did I? Goodness! Well, thank you for saying that. But that's hardly how I feel now.'

'Listen, Jane,' Tracy put me straight. 'Just throw on a dress, a bit of lipstick, fluff that gorgeous hair a bit. You're lucky that it doesn't take much. And toss those spoons in your purse. Meet you in an hour at the Chéri(e).'

I think you realize, dear reader, that I needed this night out like I needed the proverbial hole in the head, and yet I saw no escape from it. If Tracy had seen me in the morning looking like the Giaconda in trainers pulling a *caddie*, what possible explanation could I give for feeling like a rookie stuntman after his first day on the job. I certainly couldn't complain of an overzealous afternoon workout; I've never set foot in a gym, never will and she knows it. I'd have to go and make the best of it; sipping would be the only requirement once there. Very well. Shall we?

Chapter XX

*Which recounts an evening at the Chéri(e) in
which Jane, Artie, Tracy, Myriam and Bettina meet
P. Diddy in the barnyard as well as the girl who
flunks and the girl who consoles etc.*

Bettina and Tracy stand on the corner of the Boulevard de La
Villette and the rue Rébeval both wearing summer dresses that
reveal a bulge at the navel, a mound once de rigueur for any woman
applying for beautyhood, but now only seen favourably by the
manufacturers of Slim Fast shakes. Next arrives Jane, similarly clad
with the tidy tummy tussock perhaps even more flatteringly displayed
by a dress she calls Miss Haiwa II, a summer version of Miss Haiwa I.
Artemis jogs to her friends jiggling; she is not wearing proper support
and embraces everyone excitedly. At last, Myriam brings up the rear
in jeans, thin as a rod, flat as South Dakota. There is one free table
outside on the terrace but Tracy, the Moses of all the mounds, insists
they begin the evening inside where it isn't so tame, where things
actually happen and women use Neet in the toilets and men lose their

highlighters. Jane leads them into the crowded red den, into the roar of clubbers.

'*Bonsoir les poules, ce soir au Chéri(e) c'est le dress code basse-cour. Yessseuh!*' croons a young man at the door with a cock's headdress sprouting from a mesh of dishwater-blond dreadlocks and an identification T-shirt that says *J'suis P. Diddy.*

'Who the hell is that?' asks Tracy from behind.

'P. Diddy,' I say over my shoulder.

'*Eh, eh cocottes,* are you *prêtes pour la party?*' (Claps his hands.) '*C'est du love à l'apéro ce soir eh eh. Yessseuh!*'

'What's he saying?' asks Artie.

'There's some kind of barnyard theme tonight, a lovers' cocktail…'

'Barnyard!' Bettina sounds more fed up than impressed. I guess they don't do barn-a-thons in Berlin.

'Yeah, like Old McDonald, you know – a moomoo here, a moomoo there…'

'Then let's go milk the bar, ladies!' Tracy charges ahead past P. Diddy, impervious to the clubbies tip-toeing to Henry Mancini's *Pink Panther* theme; like the Red Sea on point their shores recede. We walk straight through. Tracy reaches the banks first.

'Je voodray sank moheetoes see-voo-play.' She yells over the head of a French girl who tries to console another French girl who has just flunked her *capès d'anglais* exam (*Il m'ont posé cette putain de question sur Tristam Shandy… non, je n'ai pas lu, mais même les anglais ne l'ont pas lu, putain! Un an de travail foutu à cause de ce putain de livre que je n'ai pas lu et que personne ne lit. Merde! Putain de merde!*). Tracy flashes five fingers. The French girls flips the bird. The bartender intercepts the order overhead; the French girl scowls at Tracy who has

316

not read Sterne either but who did not lose a year of her youth because of it.

'*Non, que quatre!*' I yell over Tracy, the girl who has flunked her exam, and the girl who tries to console. I hold up four fingers until the bartender registers. Then stick up my thumb. '*Et UN sex-on-the-beach.*'

'Oh no, Jane, this is a mojito night!' Tracy counters me. I shake my head, adamant. It's the mint in the mojito I don't want. Mint is for the morning.

'Sex On The Beach!' I spell it out to Tracy who finally turns to the bartender again and yells over the heads of the French girls – the one who flunked and the one who consoles.

'Bon, new voodrans cat moheetoes ey oon sex-on-the-beach feenallmaw.'

'*Eh eh eh les poules. J'ai ma pudeur* you know, *mais ce soir on* lose control *eh eh eh Yessseuh! On va brailler baby eh eh eh.*' P. Diddy returns, thumbs in his armpits, with more Good News from the poultry pen. He does a barnyard shuffle next to Artie. P. Diddy says, 'Come on Coco, let's see vous shakez that French booty.' Artie says, 'Greek, my Greek booty.' Her half-unpinned underpinnings allow for the highest degree of Hellenic booty-shaking possible. But Artie ups the ante; within seconds she has her entire body shimmying and jiggling, she is like a shapely, life-size jello girl, a gelatine Galatea. P. Diddy says, 'Eh eh eh baby, *y a du* shaking in the town tonight. *Y a du* love *chez les poules ce soir eh eh eh Cocorico! yessseuh!*' In a state of near trance, Artie takes a step forward into the arena and jello whips for all she's worth. People are looking at her; the music is no longer Mancini but Kahled. Myriam says, 'But what is she doing, isn't it?' Bettina says, 'She hasn't even had a drink yet…' Tracy says, 'vooz oreeyey poo meuh deer eskew-zaymwaw!' and looks down at her splashed dress in disbelief. The girl who consoles says, '*Mais elle n'a pas fait exprès, Madame!*' Myriam says, 'But everyone is looking at her, is it not?' Tracy dries her dress with a cocktail napkin. Nearby Bettina says, 'She's scaring me!' Next to her I say, 'It looks like she might implode or something.' At the bar, Tracy says, 'That bitch just bumped into me and spilt half my drink down my dress – and didn't even say she's sorry!' The girl who flunked says, '*Putain de merde, ces américaines. Qu'elles aillent se faire foutre!*' Myriam says, 'Someone must stop her, must they?' I say, 'Naw, let her shake it, it's liberating… you know how much time she spends planning her menus, it's good for her to let loose.' A circle has formed around Artie, the clubbers are clapping in the pig pens, catcalls whistle down from the hayloft. Tracy says, 'She's got her eyes closed. I think she may be comatose…' I say, 'Cheers Tracy…' Her glass is already empty. I sip my sex-on-the-beach. Bettina says, 'What are you doing, Jane?' I say, 'Sipping a sexy drink through a straw, and you?' Myriam says, 'Tracy spilled her drink, isn't she?' Bettina says, 'A mojito… and there's something wrong with it. Do you taste it?' Myriam says, 'I taste it too, something is not right with the green things, aren't they?' Tracy says, 'If they change the music she'll have to stop. She's only dancing because it's Greek music.' 'Not Greek,' I say, 'Algerian.' The girl who consoles says – '*Allez ma grande, personne ne l'a la première fois, tu le sais bien…*' DJ Amar le Terrible, wearing a sheepskin and tricolour boxing shorts tonight, cuts Kahled with riffs of Natasha Atlas; Artie starts twirling like a dervish. Tracy says, 'The thing about Artie is she wears those skimpy pre-teen bras, you know, with a cherry print, a bit of lace around the edges…' Myriam says, 'Cherries? No there is none, just mint and something green too, isn't it?' I say, 'Well, if that's what she likes…' Tracy

318

says, 'What she really needs is a good control top panty and a cross-your-heart bra. You can get Playtex, you know, at the Galeries Lafayette. A bit pricey but worth it. It prevents what we're seeing right before us.' I say, 'But I think Artie is making cellulite exciting. It's redemptive – for all of us!' Bettina says, 'Did you notice I lost ten pounds?' Tracy looks straight at Bettina's E-cup chest. Tracy says, 'You're kidding, right?' Meanwhile P. Diddy struts by again, rearing his rooster headdress. P. Diddy says, '*Y a du people ce soir. Yesseuh! J'ai ma pudeur mais…ça chauffe au Chéri(e). Do you mind? Eh eh eh cocorico!*' P. Diddy undoes his belt, drops his drawers. Tracy says, 'My God, that freak just took off his pants!' The girl who flunked says, '*Mais je ne veux pas danser!*' Myriam says, 'That's his underwear, isn't he?' The girl who consoles says, '*Allez! Allez!*' I say, 'At least they're boxers. Anyone ready for a second round?' Myriam says, 'Yes, but not this one with the green things. Maybe the one you have, isn't it?' Tracy has downed Artie's drink. Bettina says, 'I'll have what you're having.' Artie is still twirling, her arms out to her sides. Someone has hung P. Diddy's pants over one of them. She dances. Tracy says, 'Cheers, girls.' Myriam says, 'Cheese girls.' We are all sipping sex-on-the-beach except for Tracy. Tracy says, 'Now they're using her for a clothes rack! I think we should stop this.' The girl who flunked says, '*Mais c'est quoi cette fille-là!*' Bettina says, 'I think we need to do this more often. Get out, I mean… Jean-Pierre goes out with his friends at least every other week, they've got a rock band…' The girl who consoles says, '*C'est une folle… t'en fais pas…on fout le camp si tu veux…*' Myriam says, 'Yes, yes, Daniel goes out many times a week, but he doesn't have a band, does he?' The girl who flunked says, '*Non, j'veux pas.*' P. Diddy undoes one of his hair ribbons and gently sets it over Artie's other arm. P. Diddy says to Artie, '*C'est mon *chouchou eh eh eh* starchild, I love you, you know… *on va pousser des cris de coq* tonight. *On va faire du* French cancan in the starlight *ce soir, yesseuh!* I say, 'I need to sit down.' Tracy says, 'Already?' Bettina says, 'She doesn't look well.' Myriam says, 'She looks green, isn't she?' I say, 'I'm not so well.' Tracy says, 'Need to go to the ladies?' The girl who consoles says, '*Tu as besoin d'aller aux toilettes?*' I say, 'Yeah, I'll be right back.' The girl who flunks says, '*Oui, tu gardes la place?*'

'*Excusez-moi, excusez-moi, excusez-moi, excusez-moi.*' I rush through the crowd. The stalls are empty, thank God. The choppiness in my stomach has me doubled over, the purge is roiling and yet I'm much neater than the girls using Neet. I go to splash water on my face. Successive sprays that send water flying everywhere – not my fault but the sink's: the Chéri(e) bowl is too small, the pressure too high. I sense someone behind me waiting to use the facility. I finish and say, '*C'est pour vous maintenant.*' The girl who flunked says, '*Vous êtes mouillée madame.*' I say, 'Not to worry, I'll air-dry.' Back in the café Amar has switched to an Afro-Cuban beat. Artie is leaning against the bar next to P. Diddy who has placed an index finger under her chin. Artie says, 'It is wonderful to dance! You know I spent the whole day curing olives…' I say, 'Goodnight everyone.' Tracy says, 'Get some rest, Jane.' Myriam says, 'You OK getting home, are you?' The girl who consoles asks, '*Ça va mieux?*' I say, 'I'll be fine, thanks.' Bettina says, 'We'll see you later, Jane. Get home safe.' The girl who flunked says, '*Oui, oui.*' P. Diddy swings by, his pant legs hang over his shoulders. P. Diddy says, '*Tu pars si tôt, Coco?*' I say, 'I'm afraid it's not my *soirée, ce soir. Bon soir.*'

And head home to my beloved but deceived husband, to my warm but unfaithful bed.

Chapter XXI

Which recounts a last visit from the slyboots
S&H and the joyful occasion of Honoré's first steps,
and which concludes with a brief word on the
sacredness of wee ones.

Shhhhhh! Tiptoe, will you please? Honoré is sleeping; it's his first nap of the day. Don't mind if I take a minute to worship at the cradle a bit, do you? I don't get the chance to venerate often and promise not to be too egregiously adoring – like the mothers Special K warns about, those who CHOKE THE CHILD WITH THEIR OWN NARCISSISTIC DRIVES. I prefer to put any narcissism to pen or penne – and hope we're all better off for it. Though who's to say.

'Tis Honoré's first birthday today. I think it shows! His kiss curl has grown so long it now reaches just below the bridge of his nose. And I don't have the heart to cut it, even though it dangles from left to right over his eyes like a pendulum when he shakes his head in disagreement. Thankfully, no hypnotic consequences have been detected. Now the forelock is flung back over his crown, damp and mingling with his less presumptuous locks. He is sweating a bit, exuding the buttermilk transpiration of the Innocent. His breathing: the susurrus whisper of God addressing all things, when all things began to look good. Everything about Honoré – his tenacious appetites, his ever-moving feet, his determination, his incontinence, yes even his helplessness – converge in the claim that he will inherit the earth. Whether or not the earth will abide; whether or not he will inherit the best or the worst of it, we cannnot say as yet: the inheritance simply happens.

There is a sublime sweetness that blankets the babe once desires are driven down, and wilfulness has winged away to the playground of dreams. Our cradled tots trust with the same regularity and surprise as they pee and poop: the body trusts. Faith is an organ, like the heart and spleen, yet at birth it has already achieved its fullest maturity while the others lag sorely behind, suffer scores of pains and indignities. For the first year of life faith blooms, stretching its petals beyond the tiny body into every danger. A sleeping child may make us want to clasp our hands in delight, but the sight of his trust can terrify us.

Let's close the door now, I just saw Honoré stir. He'll sleep for another half-hour if we let him and I'd rather he doesn't wake up cranky. Funny, this feeling of accomplishment and even relief at his turning one – nature takes care of so much after all. Motherhood is an invitation to follow the child as he performs his aliveness without fear of falling or failing, to return to the language of the living in its earliest shades and shapes – curling the nascent sounds into meaning and rhyme. And it presents perhaps the only occasion to sing 'Baa-Baa Black Sheep' à la Bob Dylan to a responsive, sing-along audience. Never, I confess, have I felt more exhaustion, but also more exhilaration of all the senses and emotions, than this first year of being the Mother of

Honoré. Thank you dear Honoré – my little love, light bulb of my life – you have paid me such an honour! To think we will celebrate our first birthdays together tonight!

I should tell you, dear reader, that we had yet another visit from our sleuthing slyboots, Messieurs Starsky and Hutch, just two weeks ago – and I believe, if indeed my antennae tuned in to the right frequency, that it was also the last.

'*Oui?*' I enquired from my side of the door in response to the vigorous knuckle thumping.

'It's the police, Madame. Please open up.'

'Yes of course,' I said undoing the bolt. Then: 'What can I do for you today?' I stood there nearly eye-to-eye with the darker detective, that swarthy steed of ponyish proportions and detected from the wilted, unstarched collar of his white button-down a hint of resignation, a *laissez-aller*, provoked I surmised by Doubt itself. After all, they have nothing to go on but conjecture. But here Doubt was working in our favour, if I could just get it to hose down the last little flame of suspicion.

'We'd like to know, Madame, if you've seen or heard from these men.' Hutch fanned out three plasticized photos, holding them like a hand of cards. I peered closely to see what he'd been dealt.

'Now, are those the same gentlemen you showed me last time? Or is it someone else?'

'Have you heard from or seen any of these men?' repeated Hutch as if reading some flash card burned to his memory. He wasn't putting the screws on, not really.

'No, no. I'm afraid I haven't. I've never seen them before. But perhaps you would like to come in for a cup of tea?' I wasn't sure

Uncle Al would approve of this suggestion, but I thought I should at least try to show some hospitality; it is preferable to stand in good stead with the posse. Besides, they looked tense, like they could use some. As they followed me into the living room, I could feel their eyes roaming the bookshelf for clues linking us to the magi, but our display merely featured odd toys and Tupperware parts, stacks of books and piles of papers scribbled upon by Charles or me – just notes and poesy. Thankfully the Koranoblaster sat up high on a shelf in Honoré's closet, out of sight. But even if it were in plain view it could hardly be used as evidence against us. That a contemporary composer such as Charles should incorporate divinity toys into his instrumentaria only seems the most natural progression of an artist whose œuvre continues to be inspired by metaphysics and theology.

'Never mind the mess,' I said. 'Oh, do be careful!' I ran to offer Starsky an arm; he had just tripped over Charles's bugle, which stretched its preposterously protracted neck across the living room (I no longer say a word about *that* for the obvious marital reasons though I'd *certainly* like to). 'Please have a seat. I'll put the kettle on.' Honoré stayed in the living room with our guests. He had been crawling around with a Tupperware top in one hand and a rattle in the other, showing off his ambidexterity. He has picked up a great deal from Dick Van Dyke as a one-man band in *Mary Poppins*. Such gusto! Such joy just to grip his transitional objects and scramble at full speed all at once! Perhaps this is how the Lord feels when He's got the whole world in His hands – just before He drops the ball.

'Oh, Honoré! Be careful, my love!' As I sat the tea tray down on our makeshift coffee table, Honoré frisbeed the lid of a Servalier bowl at our guests with surprising force. How, I wonder, did he learn that? Starsky winced with some exaggeration, rubbed his shin.

'Oh dear! You got him right in the shinny shin shin!' I picked up Honoré and gently plucked the soft skin and pudgy flesh around his tibia to cultivate his sense of empathy. 'Are you all right?' I asked Starsky, who looked a tad miffed without any obvious reason for being so – certainly the Tupperware incident was nothing to moan about or enough to make workers' comp kick in. He hiked up his shoulders but his body drooped below them, sagging at the solar plexus and signaling unresolved 'issues'. I was reading the signs of defeat. He had been so crisp on our first visit despite the relentless heat, so certain to establish the connections between the de La Rochefoucaults and the Mohammedan NGO even though these tenuous ties, like the threads of cotton candy, seemed to melt into that summer's blistering mouth. Admittedly this was a rather odd situation: the object of their visit was to pin us to a crime we did not commit, but their failure to come up trumps stirred a sentiment akin to pity in my breast. They looked so out of place in our living room: the smaller man all but disappeared in the spongy marsh of our secondhand sofa; the taller man, whose length was in his legs, sunk low and spider-like in the cushions and peered at us between the twin high-rises of his knees. As a hostess it behoved me to humour them. I poured the tea, passed along the cups and saucers. Small talk would help us all out, I thought.

'My mother-in-law gave us this teapot – actually, it's not really a teapot even though I use it as one, it's for hot chocolate – it was a wedding gift,' I said referring to the oblong, rose print Limoges pot in which the Earl Grey infused. I kept one finger on the golden tulip that sprouted from the lid as I poured. 'Apparently it belonged to George

Sand; she served Chopin his hot cocoa with it – she mothered him so. I have no idea how Mathilde, I mean, my mother-in-law, got a hold of it, but she has all kinds of wonders in her pantry – one of Madame de Maintenant's chapelets, a portrait box belonging to Madame de Châtelet depicting Voltaire disguised as the pope!'

'Your mother-in-law is very *spécial*,' commented Starsky. I ignored his meaning – the French *spécial* – as if she were odd, not quite right.

'Fabulous is the word – as in almost not to be believed. I admire her immensely. She has tried very hard to be a communist, you know, for years she has tried. They still refuse her membership even while their ranks are diminishing, but that doesn't keep her from doing the work.' I nearly made a smart remark about their massage therapy session at Thrushcross, but, mindful of my position as hostess, refrained. Honoré gripped onto Starsky's pant leg, plying his sturdy legs to achieve verticality; and now once up, standing triumphantly, he opened his mouth wide, not to offer us a smile as I initially thought, but to dig his sharp little teeth into our guest's thigh.

'I'm so sorry!' I apologized as I tried to release Honoré's grip by pushing my pinky up inside the corner of his mouth – a nursing technique I used to use to stop the suction. 'I believe he's just trying to learn his anatomy – you know, the thigh bone's connected to the knee bone, the knee bone's connected to the shin bone… Oh Honoré! Let go – that hurts! Ouch! Ouch!' It was the onomatopoeia that did the job, not my pinky. Meanwhile Starsky sucked in his breath as if to stave off the pain, or rather to let us know it hurt and he didn't like it. I did feel badly about this, but babes are twenty-four-hour learners and their on-site education may require testing teeth, tasting legs – I am always surprised by the inventiveness of their pedagogy.

'Do you have children of your own?' I ask our good guests, hoping to earn their parental understanding. They answered in the affirmative. Usually the question breaks any ice, but their professionalism simply frosted it over; they did not elaborate. Hutch had his eye fixed on Charles's blue notebook wherein my knight recorded his verbal compositions; it was sitting open on a chair three feet from us. I peeked at it myself and saw Charles's distinctive print (he never composes in cursive) and the words 'car wash' underlined at the top of the page.

'Please, more tea,' I offered, leading them away from the blue notebook which was none of their damn business after all. 'And some biscuits, you must be hungry...' I ran into the kitchen and pulled out some anis biscotti I had made, set them on a plate in a pinwheel formation. Honoré, unversed as yet in the art of manners, grabbed one off the plate first. Starsky and Hutch followed suit.

'They're homemade Italian cookies and quite nice to have with tea,' I explained. Hutch dunked his into the tea and let it crumble and melt in his mouth. Starsky, however, simply sank his teeth in to get the dry, gravelly consistency: why dip in it tea when it becomes perfectly wet with chewing? I have to agree with him on this – it is the contrast between dry and wet that interests the pallet. We were happily crunching our *goûter* when Starsky suddenly dropped his jaw and began fishing in his mouth for something with his index finger. This uncouth gesture would be but brief, thought I. Best to ignore it. But his line and sinker sunk down in the depths of his mouth and his rod tugged away. Curious to glimpse his catch, I narrowed in on him, forgetting all manners. His frown and furrowed brow spoke of trouble in the mouth.

'Pray tell?' I asked. 'What's the matter? Did you bite your tongue?' In repsonse, Starsky pulled out the fruit of his fishing – a chink of molar, the size of a currant. 'Is that from the biscotti?' I asked, quite worried really – he could sue me for this. 'I promise you there is nothing hard in them, no candied fruits or pebbles for that matter...' Starsky returned to the excavation site and fiddled for the culprit, that something hard enough to break a tooth. His search was idle, nothing came of it.

'The same thing happened to me once,' I went on a bit eagerly. I wanted to clear the name of my biscotti: it was an old family recipe, one of Grandma Maraconi's – they were meant for pleasure not pain. 'I had just finished writing my rock opera *Away in a Manger* and sat down – just like we're doing now, for tea. I bit into a Marks and Spencer's butter-cream biscuit and one of my molars split in two – just like that! I guess it was ready to go and it took but a biscuit to budge it.' I was going to continue on about how teeth symbolize mortality and how dentists of my childhood tried to compensate for the lurid undertones of their profession with consolation gifts – rabbit's feet key chains distributed for bravery – when Starsky moaned in dismay and perhaps some pain too.

'Oh dear! Is there anything I can do for you? Shall I call *S.O.S. Dentiste*?'

'We'd best get on our way,' Hutch said standing up, having nudged Starsky's elbow. Our guest inspectors thus took leave of us, indeed, they seemed all too eager to scram which saddened me a bit, even if we had accomplished our mission. I was proud to discover that Honoré had Maraconi instincts beneath all the de La Rochefoucault refinery. He did his part – yes, his jejune acts of aggression obeyed a family imperative he must have strongly sensed – to send the hound dogs far off our scent. I suppose it would not have hurt us to have them longer, but there really was no point in going beyond the call of common cordiality. What would we have continued to talk about? The new and very naughty novel by Houellebecq? Or might they have been interested in discussing Enlightenment darlings like Diderot? In fact, I doubt they are readers or they might have sniffed us out. If they had read *The Thousand and One Nights*, they would recall how the Christian Queen Ibrizah harboured Muslim mercenaries in her chapel for protection and they might have guessed our little secret. In a word what our sleuths lacked can only be called Imagination, the Faculty of Fancy with its penchant for improbable unions. Undoubtedly, we should not expect more of them; they are impersonators after all, sleuthing with only a sitcom for guidance. Go in peace, lads, I whispered softly as I heard the pitter-patter of their feet in the stairwell. And take a good book with you for the dentist's waiting room.

Please excuse me, dear reader, but I must get back to the kitchen – we're celebrating Honoré's birthday with a family lunch and I still have to wash the *frisée* and whip up the vinaigrette. The meal is mostly finished though: I cobbled together some pollo alla Scarpariello (aka chicken shoemaker's style), prepared homemade gnocchi for starters and made puff pastry for strawberry shortcake. A hot meal on a summer's day could come as a shock to the season, but since the weather has been cool, too cool for my taste, and so entirely in contrast to last year's blistering temps, we actually need the warming up. When I think back to those early months, to the litany of sleepless nights, the erratic twenty-four-hour nursing, the frightening fragility of the baby (they're actually quite sturdy but we didn't know it) and the relentless heat I do wonder how we made it through as well as we did. Actually we didn't do anything particularly well, but perhaps there is some merit in *doing* without the help of a night nurse or nanny, or any of those other surrogates – formula, mechanical swings, guardian angel monitoring systems etc. Were we heroic? Were we stupid? Neither, I suppose. We were average all round. Like any other parents we acquired new habits and concerns, surprised ourselves with gestures of tender efficiency and a love that nearly did us in. We stopped thinking in sentences, learned how to punch with a single word; thoughts became interruptions and their impertinence miffed us. Things are still much the same but we've grown used to them – more or less.

KNOCK, knock, knock; KNOCK, knock, knock; knock KNOCK knock; knock, knock, KNOCK…

Oh dear! Is that Mathilde at the door already? Must be. That's her knock all right – she raps in some code – perhaps she's spelling Mathilde in Morse. God knows. Or could it be the Apostle's Creed?

'J'arrive…'

'Bonjour ma fille. Nous sommes prêts pour la fête!' Mathilde thrusts a platter of angels-on-horseback at me – they are served on their shells this time, not toothpicked, and smothered green in minced parsley. Then she skips blithely around me, straight for Honoré's room. 'Now where's the Sacred Child? He's not sleeping, is he?' Mathilde enters his room, before I can beat her off his track.

'He *was* sleeping…'

As if racing her demoiselles to the finish line of infantile affection, Mathilde bolts from the nursery bearing a pink-cheeked Honoré, a moist Honoré, an Honoré who has produced a bumper crop tripling his diaper size.

'Go ahead and change him,' I suggest. After all, it is the first farmer to the market who fetches the best price. Mathilde ushers Honoré to the changing station where the Bébé Cash diapers sit in a crooked stack. Mathilde ooh-là-làs with admiration at Honoré's offering and rolls up the sleeves of her cobalt blue Chinese worker's jacket.

'Where on earth is Charles!? He's supposed to bring the bread!' I mutter, as I measure out my olive oil. 'He should be here by...' The jolting sound of key mating with lock, that rough, metalic intercourse, announces Charles's return among us. Often it suffices to castigate someone mildly in thought to bring them near in body. My husband's long legs conveyed him quickly to the kitchen. Under each arm a glaive of bread promised our protection – against what danger I'm not sure, but as the man-of-the-house he must always be prepared. Baguettes are shoddy affairs these days and as papery as the modern communion host, but Charles has purchased the nice kind, called *tradition*, with a thicker *croûte* and a chewier *mie*. As broadswords they fare better too, as Honoré is about to demonstrate. He has just returned from the changing station and has nabbed one from his father. He brandishes it with relish.

'Can you take that bread away from him, Charles? It's going to end up on the floor... Oh, and Mathilde, what about Padre Las Vegas? Will he be joining us? I've certainly made enough chicken.'

'Oh no. He won't be coming. I'm afraid he's still not back yet. He got detained in Monaco I believe?'

'Monaco! *Mais quelle idée!* That's a terrible place for a priest – it's just one big seething pit of corruption and Euro glitz...'

'Precisely why a priest is needed... the truth be told, he is taking a bit of a vacation – a much needed one. Why, he is the Johnny

Appleseed of Liberation Theology in Europe, tirelessly sowing the seeds of a Christological Marxist consciousness in the rocky soil of France and Spain…'

'You mean he's playing Punto Banco at the Casino de Monte Carlo?' I interrupt her before the winds of afflatus whip her up into a rant.

'That's right,' she concedes as she lifts the plastic wrap off her platter of oysters – I see she has spiced the angels up by adding red pepper flakes to her recipe. 'He must be indulged from time to time. A penchant for games is not uncommon among the frocked.'

'What's the news of the men?'

'They reside as pensioners at the convent for the moment, until they regain their health and vigour by way of tagines of lamb and saffron prunes, of chicken and chickpeas, stuffed stomach of mutton, confited carrots… Ahmed cooks for them like kings. They are well, or at least better… I daresay a few more weeks of this regaling and they will be on their way, to Paris most likely, to find work; Samir and Rachid will help them find temporary housing in Saint Denis…'

'And what about Samir and Rachid? Will we be seeing them anytime soon?'

'Highly unlikely. Paris is out of the question; they simply cannot risk it. But the Franciscans have bequeathed to them an outhouse on the monastery property. It was once a very roomy Roman latrine. The idea is that they will restore it to standard and set up their head-quarters within. Things could be worse, I suppose. Fortunately there have been no reprisals from the mafia – not a sign.' At this mention of the mob, I jerk my head twice to the left towards the living room signaling Charles to take Honoré out of the kitchen. This subject is not for tiny ears.

'Have you heard *anything* at all…' I put it to Mathilde once Charles and Honoré have cleared hearing distance, '…about *them?*'

'Have *you*?' Mathilde returns the question.

'Not a word. Nothing from Guido. So I decided not to call him. No news good news I tell myself. If he thought we were in any trouble he would have let me know. But Barra was killed – at least I assume he was Barra, but how can I be sure? – and the money was taken. We're out of the picture now – it's their business and their feud. I guess we were just lucky they didn't do us in… the gun was on me and I just kept going on about being Honoré's mother, how they had to spare me for his sake… I might even have been speaking in Italian – I have no idea. The words poured out of me like…'

'The word of the Lord.'

'What's that?'

'It is at such dire times, Jane, that the Divine One speaks for us – if we are able to surrender.'

'Hmmm…' Personally I had chalked my reaction up to good guts and strong Maraconi instincts, but perhaps Mathilde has a point. Who knows, maybe my Babylonian moment was divinely inspired in part. Let us just say that succour came to me from afar and near, in the way that language can arise – urgent, tongue-burning, heedless of Dove soap.

'I suppose they will leave us alone – the money is out of our hands, the men out of theirs. In the end, they didn't want their slave-labour around any more. They had become a liability, you know.'

'I'm sorry you had to go through that, Jane, but you were not alone,' says Mathilde thinking of the Lord.

'No doubt about it,' I add, thinking of Al. 'And Honoré never missed his mommy which is the most unfathomable part of it all…'

'One does not fathom grace, Jane. One either welcomes it or denies it.'

'But I wasn't even given a choice, was I – to either embrace or deny? I had no idea what was going on back at home. It just happened – without my consent.'

'Yes, and I suppose there's a good reason for that.'

'Do you think? I kind of feel like He played a trick on me. Like He used me a bit…'

'Remember what Saint Teresa once said in her Interior Château: "His Majesty knows best what is suitable for us. There's no need for us to be advising Him about what He should give us."'

'Right, well never mind. It's not like I'm applying for sainthood or anything. I just don't care to be cloned, especially when I had a babysitter ready to take care of Honoré. Everything would have been fine…'

The phone rang just then.

'Jane?' I heard through the crepitating wires. It was my mother no less. Calling from the ranger station at Wawona Springs, the connection but a squirrel tooth away from disappearing altogether.

'Mom! It's good to hear from you. We're all here celebrating Honoré's first birthday!'

'I'm sorry, dear,' I hear through the static, 'What's that again?'

'Honoré's birthday! It's today, Mom, his first birthday. I can hardly believe it!'

'What good news, Jane! I had no idea.' Unchannelled electricity rises over her voice with flame-like licks and leaps. She's drowned out, re-emerges. 'Give him a kiss for me.'

'Boy, I wish you could see him, Mom. When are you going to come over?'

'Not until the conversion is finalized, Jane. And that won't be until after next Hanukkah at least. I've got a load of studying to do and I brought the Talmud and the Torah with me out here. Had to bring an extra llama to carry it all.'

'Have you been meeting with a conversion study group or something?'

'I've been doing the whole thing online. It's much more amenable to my lifestyle and you know how I feel about groups… The Rabbi Kohn has been a wonderful help – he's the one who teaches the course. He seems to think I'll be ready for the Beth Din by next January.'

'The what?' I asked just as a bucketful of stagnant electricity drenched our line.

'I am just a bit concerned about the part where we have to commit to raise our children as Jews,' she goes on. 'I mean…'

'Too late now, Mom.'

'But there is Honoré to think about…'

'Listen, Mom, before you even think about converting my child, you might want to meet him. OK? Just meet him!'

'That is unfair of you, Jane. You know perfectly well I can't leave my lambs – this is a tough business! Yesterday I spent most of the day applying and reapplying their sunscreen. Last week I lost two of my fairest lambkins to third degree sunburn, the poor little babes were cooked alive! It's the bog asphodel around the lake – they've been chowing on it and it photosensitizes them. Mani-Carla used to help me with the *Bain de Soleil* but now it's just me and Pinesol…'

'Well, come when you can, Mom. You're always welcome,' I swallow

335

my rising ire for the sake of Honoré. I could well have given her a mouthful, enough to sever our ties for several years at least, but someone wiser in me came forth, stifled the cry. The Mother of Honoré is but a year old, yet more sagacious than Jane for all of her thirty-eight years. Her wisdom is of the umbilical sort; nothing fancy or clever but fastidious in its maintenance of maternal ties. It – this lineal bond – is a breathing thing after all, not a line for hasty half communications but a lifeline.

In a word, I, the Mother of Honoré, realize in the nascent bloom of my age, that we are still tethered to one another in spite of the fact that Mother is and has always been on the run, out on a limb, hanging from trees, diapered and determined, dipping swatches in her stews, too far away from the schools and parties I attended to pick me up when the lights went out – yes, in spite of all her assiduous absences from motherhood. Mother and I stood apart, like many a mother and daughter, on either side of the looking glass but with an immaterial line that not even surgical scissors could cut, gripping us at opposite ends. Perhaps in a year she will make a stopover in Paris on her way to Jerusalem. We will hold out for that, Honoré and I.

'Good luck with the lambs, Mom,' I say in farewell. Then surprise myself with: 'When Honoré finally meets you, he'll be proud to have a grandmother so dedicated to the herd.' Which is more or less true: I think he would be if he ever met her. Not many infants have grannies who shepherd in the backcountry, studying the Torah by the flicker of a Coleman lantern at night.

'How is your mother?' asks Mathilde once I hang up. She has only met her once, at our wedding, though I don't think the encounter marked either woman as particularly memorable. The steadfast, mystical Mathilde would probably not care much for Mother's shifts and drifts, her fits and starts if she knew about them and I certainly wasn't going to breathe a word about her imminent conversion. Imagine!

'She's working quite hard with her lambs,' I reply, checking on the whipped cream in the fridge. 'She sends her hello,' I lie, my head in the chilly box, my finger poking to check firmness. It is silly of me, perhaps; I needn't lie, but I want to cover for Mother's lack of solicitude, if only to maintain appearances of our having family feeling. From across the ocean 'tis the best I can do.

'When will she be coming over? I don't believe she has met the Sacred Child…'

'No, she hasn't yet had the pleasure,' I reply as I light the burner under the pasta pot. 'But maybe sometime after next Christmas I think; She's dying to meet him.' I'm beginning to wonder if my nose is starting to lengthen; I've heard it happens to Italians.

'Jane! Mother! Come here! You must see this!' Charles shouts from the living room. I look over my shoulder and nearly drop the Tupperware full of gnocchi I just took out from the fridge.

'*Mon Dieu!*'

'*Ma foi!*' adds Mathilde peeking through the doorway.

I bound into the living room. Mathilde is fast on my heels. Within a split second we are both squatting down, our arms wide open to welcome the miracle.

Which is this: Honoré stands, yes *stands*! holding nothing but a rattle, his sceptre. Sovereign and standing on legs of Charles's linguini length; he trembles with pride and concentration as he takes a step. A STEP! *Un pas en avant...* The first! He totters, drunk with the

337

achievement, a rivulet of drool gathers speed as it reaches his chin; anything could happen in his mouth, a tooth could cut through its pink gummy earth and he wouldn't notice the pain. Verticality starts with the feet; I watch his mind flooding his toes.

'Oh Honoré, you're doing it!' I encourage him, beside myself with excitement. It is like watching Neil Armstrong softboot the moon, only better. The first step conquers the quadruped in us, sets us up like trees, only unlike our arboraceous kin we are ambulatory conduits between heaven and earth, and our branches more supple, less sturdy. Honoré takes his second step, then a third.

'*Bravo, mon garçon!*' Mathilde chimes in right behind me. Our maternal nets open wider for the catch. Fourth step, fifth step… he's tilting forward, head suddenly leading his feet. Not the way to do it. His excitement has sent his mind shooting up from his toes to the highest branches; top heavy he is, heady. I notice his forelock has swung to the right and sticks to his brow, creased with concentration.

'Come on, Honoré! Come on love!' He's nearly running now, going faster, his feet trying to keep up with his head; his earth with his sky; he has not yet learned about the tortoise and the hare and how slow and steady wins out. But we'll have time for that later.

'*Oui, mon chéri. C'est cela, ma puce. Encore un pas…*'

'You've got it, Honoré, you're doing it my boy!' I encourage him on, applauding his balance. Here we are, Mathilde and I, two outfielders with our mitts in the air, vying for the catch. Mathilde has the advantage of Keds, I, that of kinship. Honoré veers to the right, tipping in Mathilde's direction, his legs nearly running to keep up with the speed of his brow, and Mathilde reaches out to his little heavens to embrace them in her larger constellation, but then just before reaching her galactic bun he abruptly leans left to escape gravity's right hand, '*That's it, Honoré! Oh here my love,*' and rolls into the arms of *maman*, he does. '*Bless you, my boy! You've made it to home base, love!*' Honoré squeals and giggles, giddy with his triumph. And I am just as proud as he, perhaps even more. After all, I know what it means to walk. I know that walking is always a way of discovering, not only the world – that is obvious enough – but the firm yet elusive contact of the body with the world. For Honoré the experience is fresh and without contradiction as yet. A cause for celebration.

'Shall we open the Widow?' Mathilde suggests, rising. She reaches for her bag and pulls out a bottle of Veuve Clicquot champagne.

'Wonderful! Look what your mom has just pulled out of her bag,' I say to Charles, as if admiring a magic act – which pulling champagne out of a purse indeed is. 'Does it need to be chilled?' I enquire, hoping that it does not. I'm more than ready for a toast ASAP.

'I should think not. I chilled it beforehand at the château, though it did go to six o'clock mass with me.' Holding the bottle's wide end against her cheek, she concludes that it is quite cool enough.

'Will you do the honours, Charles?' I pass him the bottle, which indeed feels sufficiently chilled, and go to fetch the flutes. I also put a pot of boiling water on for the gnocchi. Honoré continues his cruising from Mathilde's arm to the sofa, to Charles's knees. He gets unbalanced after six steps or so and needs a landing strip to regain his centre of gravity. I can feel his excitement from the kitchen and I can already tell we won't be having dinner around the table. My son is determined to practise and therefore practise he will. What could be more important after all? Who would have thought of calling Armstrong back into Apollo 11 to eat his peanut butter flavoured Space Stick dinner when he had the moon underfoot? We'll have din-din on our laps in the living room; he will grab bites of gnocchi on the run.

'To Honoré's first year!' pronounces Charles, holding his glass up for a toast.

'And to ours as well… as parents!' I add, making my flute ring gaily against Mathilde and Charles's glasses. Honoré speeds over to me; his balance is improving by the minute. He doesn't fall but grabs my knee and reaches for my glass.

'Oh dear! I forgot Honoré's sippy cup. Come on, love, let's get you a nice little cocktail.' I take Honoré's hand and lead him into the kitchen where we prepare a cup of apple juice. He takes it from me and waves it in the air like one of Hrothgar's men in the mead-hall. And now, I think, he will chug-a-lug like Beowulf the Geat. Which he does, giving the cup a bottoms-up while throwing back his head and downing the juice, walking all the while (and holding my hand) so as to get to the living room in time for the toast. We salute once again, the sound of plastic against glass is less cheering, but we don't need cheering at all. We're happy as clams, feeding on oysters. Mathilde's platter of angels-on-horseback has landed on our coffee table. The salty savouries make us thirsty for more; they whet our appetites.

And I wonder how it is that we can still be so hungry after such a year, so hopeful, so forgetful when we've slept so little but worried so much. Nature hired me for nine months of gestation and nine months of nursing; the Lord's agent Padre Pio doubled me so as to do His Rescue Work. Is it a woman's plight to be a vessel? And if this is so, then surely she changes the very definition of one. Liken us not to Tupperware oh world! We are exponents and interpreters, we magnify meaning when the fear that there is none is greatest. We are carriers of life and of death – it's a low paid business. We'll never get rich, but the world would crumble if we ever quit.

'Mama, mamama mama, mamamama mama…'

'What is it, Honoré?' I look down at my son who is holding on to my knee, his own knees trembling from post work-out fatigue. He wants me to hold him now, for he has pioneered enough and needs to fill up on affection. I pick him up, rest him in the crook of my arm so that he is sitting on my lap facing the world. And it occurs to me that I have always held him this way, even when he was wee, so that he is turned worldwise rather than motherwise. It dawns on me also that this is how the Holy Mother holds her baby Jesus in numerous depictions. The truth is I do want my boy to face this world, to feel enough a part of it, grounded in it so that the desire to care for it will shape his integrity. As so I hold him like the Madonna, looking outward, a presage to the world.

'It's time for the birthday cake!' announces Mathilde jumping up, and collecting the salad plates (*sans* cheese, thank you!). The chicken turned out flavourful and succulent; it slid off the bone and could almost be eaten with the fingers, which is how Honoré and I ate it. The gnocchi I tossed in a light but basil-fragrant pomodoro sauce; not a morsel of it was left. The meal was a success even if we ate it without a table. The strawberry shortcake was made in Honoré's honour, for he loves berries and red fruit most of all.

Mathilde emerges from the kitchen with the cake lit up by a single candle shaped like the number one; Charles turns off the lights. As we sing *Bon anniversaire* Honoré grows quiet, so terribly serious. And with the cake before him, his face lit up by the one candle, he seems infused with wisdom beyond his years; his kiss curl is pushed up into his hair leaving his brow free and placid and he is looking upwards yet inwards, as if witnessing some vision inscribed in the eye which requires, like stained glass, the light of the world to see in full colour.

'It's time now, Sacred Child, to blow out the candle,' appeals Mathilde.

'But make a wish first, Honoré…' I quickly add. We hold our breath waiting for Honoré to blow out the flame. I blow softly to show him how it is done. He leans forward, poises himself for the task, and rather than blow, spits and sputters all over the cake.

'Bless the Sacred Child!' chimes Mathilde.

Sacred Child? Well, who knows? Maybe Mathilde has a point. But how does one keep the child sacred then, through the trials of life, its cruelties and its base temptations, through our own faults and misgivings? Perhaps just by recognizing he is sacred – every day, I suppose. By repeating, relentlessly, this recognition of what is good in him, to the point of appearing 'troubled' (think Special K) if it takes that. Whatever it takes. To keep our children hallowed.

Chapter XXII

*Which recounts yet another surprising turn of
events involving plusses and minuses as well as the
fortuitous visit of Momo in a suit.*

'What brings you here this morning?' enquired Dr Delamancha, twisting the tip of his left handlebar between index finger and thumb while studying me, according to his wont, suggestively. It was an early bird appointment for which I had rolled out of bed at seven, vaguely slurped down a cup of Early Grey, and pulled on a pair of jeans and a red v-neck T-shirt. I hadn't brushed my hair, though my teeth were clean. And I felt weepy and nauseated, my sense of smell so acute I nearly swooned on the métro when a rocker in a Mano Negra tee lifted his arm to hold the bar and set off an olfactory infestation that forced me to recede to the next wagon. What happened to morning showers after an eve of rock and roll? I wondered. Then remembered I hadn't taken one myself.

'I just haven't been feeling well, doctor. Nauseous, moody, tired all the time. Maybe it's just the working-mom syndrome…' Delamancha leaned forward, peering at my face with his X-ray vision. Then the intensity of his gaze suddenly softened; his eyes lowered to my chest, slid over the surface of my skin, perusing my 'balcony'. Oh dear, thought I, perhaps I am showing too much cleavage for the a.m.? In all modesty, I must admit that compliments paid to my décolleté have always been bountiful. I have Grandma Maraconi to thank for that, bless her; she was endowed with what cousin Guido used to call Italian Torpedoes and I was always surprised by how solid and uncompromising they felt against my child's head and how her elaborate manner of armouring this bosom made it appear to be aiming at a FBI-infested target on the horizon. It was as if this suspended jetty were less a landing pier for tired and cranky grandchildren than a self-propelled weapon capable of discharging against a family enemy. Mercifully my own are less menacing, more redolent of grapefruit than military projectiles. But the question remained: Was Dr Delamancha looking down my tee for a bit of Florida vitamin C?

'When was your last period?' he asked, now at the computer typing away. What had seemed perhaps misplaced, now fell into its proper place; he had been gathering information not fanning his lust.

'I've been so busy, doctor, I'm afraid I haven't paid much attention...'

'Perhaps you should be paying attention. You are still fertile, you realize.'

'Oh, but we are very careful,' I shot back, catching his drift. 'There's no way I'm pregnant – we take all the necessary precautions.' Dr Delamancha lifted an eyebrow as he continued to punch at the keys. I left his *cabinet* with a prescription for Sepia Officinalis, spirulina and a pregnancy test, which I certainly was not going to buy.

And I didn't except that…

'Charles!' I called from the bathroom the next morning. 'Get in here!' I was holding a pregnancy test in disbelief. It appalled me that I actually conceded to tinkle on the little tablet which, incidentally, I did *not* go out and purchase; the test I now held was a leftover from the double test I bought for my first pregnancy. Something in me, a defiant streak I suppose, a desire to prove Delamancha wrong (what can be more satisfying than showing up a hubristic, cleavage scoping medic?) motivated me to pull it out of the pharmacy cupboard that morning and perform my task, certain my pee would prove HCG-free. Yes, I was sure Delamancha had misdiagnosed and that I would gloatingly get him on the horn in a minute to tell him so. Hence, when the plus sign appeared with its mathematical and Christic connotations, it hit me like a betrayal.

'What is it, love?' Charles came in holding Honoré's hand.

'Maybe you should set Honoré up with some Tupperware in the living room? I don't think he needs to see this.'

'Right,' said Charles acting promptly upon my suggestion, sensing an important matter at hand. I shook the test as I waited for him to return; sometimes a little shake sets things right. With homeopathy, a shake activates the potion; perhaps rattling the test would stimulate the pee – properly this time – so that the vertical line would fade to white nothingness and let us contemplate a minus.

'What is it, dear?' asked Charles upon his return, brushing his kiss curl back to have a look.

'Well, what does it look like? Remember this?' Charles obediently peers down at the blue cross that has bled through the circle like some divinely inspired image – I could tell he didn't know what to make of it exactly: how quickly he forgets! 'It's positive,' I interpret. '… the pregnancy test… but there must be a mistake. We've been so careful. There's just no way.' I shook my head. Charles remained silent for a long moment, absorbed in some recollection.

'Yes we've been careful… except for that one time…'

'What one time? What are you talking about? We've used condoms EVERY single time.'

'Oh dear,' said Charles pushing back his lovelock, which kept lapping at his right eye.

'Maybe one of them got punctured?'

'No, Jane. There was one time when we did not take the precaution…'

'Listen, Charles, I pay attention to these things, right? And we never had sex without birth control.'

'But we did, Jane.'

'Wrong.'

'We did, I assure you, only you weren't exactly there.'

'What?'

'I mean you were here but it was – oh dear, how confusing it is – it was that *other* you.'

'The *other* me? Oh God!' Befuddlement froze my mind while my heart raced at breakneck speed. My legs trembled, my head began to spin; it took a few moments for words to avail me. 'You don't mean *her!*' I tried to look Charles in the eye but his curl was covering the left one and his right eye was looking elsewhere, deliberately away from me. 'Do you mean, my double…? That so-called *me* who stayed while I was off risking my ass in Naples? Oh, Charles! My God, how *could* you?!'

'Jane, I assure you. There was no way of knowing. She was, I mean, you were… just the same as always. I promise you it was impossible to tell any difference…'

'I still can't believe you had sex with her! With *her*! Good God, Charles! You cheated on me! And what's more you didn't even use birth control, for Christ's sake. Oh how *could* you!'

'You were very passionate, Jane. I'm afraid I lost myself a bit…'

'Lost yourself?! Oh this is too awful for words!'

'I… I really don't know what to say… it is simply…' Charles peered down at the cross.

'Unbelievable!' I finished his sentence.

We looked at each other for a moment in silence. I searched Charles's eyes for something other than the shock that dilated them. For some glimmer of reassurance. My own eyes, I knew, were giving him a prescient reading of our future.

'Get ready, love,' I said at last. 'We're in for another round.'

Just then, a knock on the door.

'Who on earth…? At a time like this!' Charles shook his head in consternation. But it was too late to ignore the rapping; Honoré was already careening around the corner, shrieking in front of the door with excitement. What's more, I secretly welcomed the interruption. We needed the distraction from our queer revelation and this guest, whomever he might be, a door-to-door salesman or a Pentecostal proselytizer, would provide it.

I peered through the peephole to see who was calling. Our visitor was a man wearing dark glasses and a suit. He was swarthy, short and had a purposeful knock.

'Hello, Madame,' said our unknown *ami* in the doorway. 'It's me,' he added taking off the shades.

'Momo!' I stood there staring at him for a moment, marvelling at this transformation in our plumber. Had I not known his trade it would have been impossible to guess it from his current attire and dapper bearing. His hair was side-parted and neatly combed down with the help of Dippidy Do, his face cleanly shaved and after-shaved, the scent of Fabergé cologne preceding him in generous gusts. His suit, though its sleeves swallowed his wrists and its shoulders bulked a bit, was clearly of a sound make. Even the impeccable shine of his wingtips seemed to herald the arrival of an advanced man amongst us. A man promoted to loftier realms of luxury cisterns, as we were about to find out.

'Why, do come in,' I said remembering my manners. 'We're about to have our coffee... you'll have some with us, won't you? Charles, could you get the coffee ready? I'm going to get dressed.' I made a little curtsey and bowed out; threw on Miss Haiwa I – I felt I should try to match Momo's sartorial standards – and washed up. I put the pregnancy test in the cupboard rather than tossing it. I thought we might need to take a look again at this tangible proof of our deputy conception.

'Well this is very good news, Momo. Jane will be delighted to hear...'

'Hear what?' I asked, walking into the kitchen. Charles, Momo and Honoré were all seated around the table. The stovetop espresso maker pointed its puckered lip at me, exhaling a snaking stream of steam.

'Pour me one of those will you, Charles, love?' I point to the coffee. 'So, what's the news?' I ask Momo. In response, Momo clamped his mouth shut as he drew in a deep breath. Then, leaning forward, his nose nearly in his coffee, he reached into his back pocket, presumably to get his wallet. I began to wonder what he had in mind: was he going to pull out wads of cash… to impress us? I was filled with dread for a moment; the sight of a fat cash roll would awaken unwelcome associations of my afternoon with Barra.

'Momo… I think I'd rather not…'

'Look, Madame!' Momo cut me off. He had his wallet open and was pulling from one of its slots not bills but cards. Calling cards to be exact. He waved them excitedly in the air like winning lottery tickets, before setting them down on the table, one by one, for my inspection.

Mrs Taylor James Plimsbury
234 rue de Belles Feuilles
75016 Paris
tel: 01 45 75 94 92

'Hmmm… that'll be the Plimsbury family from Connecticut,' I said recognizing the name. 'They made their fortune with garden sprinklers and hydropathic utensils I believe. I met them both one summer at the Embassy's Fourth of July celebration. Mrs Taylor James had the most amazing emerald green Chanel bag, custom-made from Plimsbury hoses. She was simply euphoric, full of Yankee optimism and kept saying to me, "Isn't Paris just a dream! Just a dream!" and she was waving her sparkler around recklessly. "You're living the dream, Mrs Plimsbury! You're living it!" I concurred. She was getting me quite worked up! I was going to light my sparkler from hers but then she burned a hole in Mr Taylor James's shirt and someone threw their highball at him to put out the flame… then the pompiers came…' I looked up at Momo who was patiently waiting for me to finish: he had something of importance to add.

'They have four Dagobert Thrones which I installed – all of them!'

'Dagobert Thrones? Pray tell?'

'An amazing toilet, Madame, majestic and made for a king. Like a great wooden chair, taller than you! When you lift the lid it plays a song.'

'Like "Good King Wenceslas"?'

'It also has an ashtray,' Momo added solemnly.

'Impressive!' I concluded, though I did wonder if they gave him free reign with the mosaics as we did. Was this illustrious matron a patron of the arts as we were? Or was she just into medieval reproductions? Momo gave me a baby-you-ain't-seen-nothing-yet look and played his second card.

Mrs Terry Winston Welkes III
34 rue du Ranelagh
75016 Paris

'Welkes as in skyscrapers, right? They own about four of them. And a load of freeways too, out West. I remember bumping into her at a Democrats Abroad meeting several years ago when we were campaigning for Kerry. She has the most amazing hair-do, like a Danish pastry with swirls of white strands for the cream filling. She kept saying, "Maraconi… Maraconi, I've heard that name before, Maraconi…" To get her off my scent, I said, "Maybe you're thinking of macaroni… macaroni and cheese, macaroni?" She glared at me. "Oh no," she said, "I meant Maraconi… yes, Maraconi, uh huh… Maraconi!" She must have been from Idaho, but I didn't bother to ask. I skipped. Next thing I knew, Bush had won.'

'A devastating turn of events,' added Charles.

'Japanese design, not beautiful like the Dagobert throne,' said Momo giving us a compte rendu of the Welkes III latrine. 'But better: six soundtracks, electrodes that measure the size of the bottom, and sprays that… No hands needed!' Here Momo lifted his arms in the air to emphasize the miracle of front-and-back aerated spray plus posterior dryer. 'And they sent me to a training course, paid for everything, including lunches. I am now a certified Matsushita repairman. It is a great pleasure to work with the Americans.'

The third card Momo slapped down was not white as the others but boudoir pink. And scented! I caught a strong whiff of a floral carnation fragrance: Fragonard's Billet Doux?

> *Miss Janine 'Esperanza' Elizabeth Cottlebaum*
> *12 rue Champfleury*
> *75007 Paris*

'No, I've never heard of Miss Cottlebaum, but she has a Champs des Mars address…'

'A very, very, very nice lady… no plumbing problems, really. Just needed a screw or two… to affix the soap holder. Momo does the necessary!' An admixture of white pride and red embarrassment converged in a pinkness that heatedly coloured his palette.

'I'm sure she appreciates your… accommodating her so,' I added, reddening a bit myself. Momo returned to his coffee and slurped it up in three little gulps as if he were at the *zinc*. He had more cards but didn't offer to play them.

'We're so pleased your business is flourishing, Momo,' I went on.

351

'This is wonderful, wonderful news, really...' Momo then held up a finger, signalling that there was more to come. He reached into his jacket pocket and brought out a small purse made out of a silvery fabric.

'Here, Madame Jane.'

'Well, what on earth is this?' I hesitated to take it, but Momo set it in my hand. 'Oh! What have you done, Momo? You shouldn't!'

'It's for you,' he insisted with boyish pride.

'Oh, Charles! Look what Momo has done!' Out of the moiré pocket, I pulled a golden hand the size of a thumbnail, a hand with three fingers pointing straight up, a pinkie pointing east and a thumb pointing west. I recognized it immediately; 'It's Fatima's hand! And it's simply beautiful!' Indeed, it was fourteen carat gold, a finely hewn piece of jewellery.

'You must turn it around!' exclaimed Momo. Apparently the hand had a trick up its sleeve. I turned it over and discovered a turquoise enamel eye encrusted in its palm; it looked straight into my own grey orbits promising unblinking protection.

'Hamsa!' exclaimed Momo.

'The evil eye?'

'Hamsa or Fatima. Fatima was the daughter of Mohammed. Hamsa means five...'

'And the eye?'

'Only one is needed to keep evil away.'

'I'm glad to hear it. Charles, will you help me put it on?' I had strung the charm on my thin gold chain so that it dangled next to my miraculous medal. I could tell from the feel of it – the added weight, the pleasant sensation of the charms chiming together – that this marriage of metals was a happy one; not a match made in heaven perhaps, but a testimony of terrestrial cooperation. 'This is too kind of you, Momo. You really shouldn't have done it, and I have to say I can't see why you did…'

'It is to thank you, Madame Jane, for bringing me to the Americans. Your book has opened new doors to your friend Mohammed.'

'My book?'

'The book you wrote about me – all these finest of people have read it and called me for my services.'

'The book I wrote…?' I paused for a moment, puzzling over *The Life of Momo: Adventures of a Muslim Plumber in Paris* – a volume I was to have authored, perhaps by proxy (God help me!). Then it dawned on me that he must have been referring to the article I sent to *House and Hedges* ages ago. I had no idea they had published it! Susie, mother's friend, never even confirmed receipt.

'Oh, you mean the *House and Hedges* article! They could have let me know! I mean, the least they could have done was send me a copy of the issue!'

'It was a wonderful book, Madame Jane, which, inshallah, will continue to bring me more American customers.'

'Well, I'm glad it's worked out for the best, Momo. May more heiresses and wives of industrialists continue to ring your bell. Night and day. Inshallah.'

When Momo had left, nearly skipping I should add – it seemed he had an assignation with 'Esperanza' at noon to affix another soap holder – I went back into the bathroom to take care of a bit of business. Our own throne, once such a miraculous novelty, did suddenly fade in comparison with the dream johns Momo was now installing. But I reminded myself that art transcends technology, that the surprising mixture of mosaics and tile made our little corner unique and therefore irreplaceable, above the petty competitions of the potty industry.

I opened the medicine cabinet and pulled out the pregnancy test. Looked at it hard, not thinking a thing, just peering at it until there seemed to be no difference between my eyes and the blue cross. Then I tossed it in the garbage.

'*Que sera, sera…*' I started to sing, like Doris Day in *The Man Who Knew Too Much*. Playing a desperate mom, Doris finally gets her kidnapped child back by singing this corny song at the bottom of an embassy stairway. The optimism of it is extraordinary, but equally astonishing is Hitchcock's descent into the childish realm of bad taste. What fun he must have had! '*Whatever will be, will be… The Future's not ours to see… Que sera, sera…*'

And I knew then, just how pregnant I was.

Chaper XXIII

Which begins with an entry from Musicopedia and recounts a near drowning, a tangle with red tape as well an auspicious turn in Charles's destiny.

(COUNT) CHARLES DE LA ROCHEFOUCAULT

From Musicopedia, the free online encyclopaedia of musicology written by musicologists

Count Charles de La Rochefoucault (born 24 February 1964) has been called one of France's most original avant-garde composers. Having studied at the Julliard School of Music, de La Rochefoucault returned to Paris to work in collaboration with Pierre Boulez. Breaking with the Schoenberg tradition of twelve-note serialism, Charles experimented with John Cage's conception of chance music, expanding the notion of randomness to include a new alchemy of sound and tempi he calls 'Holy Spiritism'. His *Suite #2 for the Holy Spirit and Three Harps* was the object of much critical controversy when it was first performed in 2006 at the Cité de La Musique.

Charles is also the inventor of a highly eccentric instrumentaria, including the intriguing cariope which he constructed for his *Car Wash Aria in F Sharp for Ten Monks and Cariope*. Based in part on the nineteenth century calliope, the cariope is an organ of steam whistles and car wash parts – outsize brushes, rubber wraps, hoses and cylindrical engines – creating what he calls 'de bruits bruts insonores' (raw insonorous sounds).

Many consider de La Rochefoucault a mystic though he refutes this claim. He and his playwright wife Jane Maraconi live in Paris.

List of Performed Works to date:
- *Symphony for Gamelan and Three Tubas*
- *Symphony of the Seven Dwelling Places* (with alpenhorn)
- *Suite #2 for the Holy Spirit and Three Harps*
- *Ode to the G.S. in F minor*
- *Car Wash Aria in F Sharp for Ten Monks and Cariope*

Charles's Musicopedia bio reads nicely, doesn't it? We are delighted he has made the cut and that at last his music is drawing deserved attention. But perhaps it's best if I backtrack a bit as I imagine you are wondering about the cariope and the *Car Wash Aria in F Sharp*. I have, I know, mentioned that Charles invents instruments. Our one closet bursts with his homespun and rather hybrid variations on the standard acoustic fare, such as the guitar-harp (Honoré's favourite, and perfect for Dylan psalmodies), the drumolin, a sort of violin played with drumsticks upon the knees, and the 'cor-sympathique' a three-loop horn wrapped with cat-gut strings which vibrate 'in sympathy' as it honks, plus many more! The cariope, however, is quite a different species from the rest. It is kept out at Thrushcross because of its colossal size and is a massive contraption of whistles, engines and car wash parts sitting within a steel frame, which, viewed from a distance, seems to have the depressions and elevations of a mountain relief, with rugged peaks of metal and brush fibre sloping down to a central keyboard at its base, and below this, a red velvet-covered seat with gold leaf legs, prim, delicate and entirely in contrast to the bulky machine hovering over it. The cariope, or rather Charles's *Car Wash Aria in F Sharp for Ten Monks and Cariope* made its 'splash' a month ago at the Cité de La Musique. Unfortunately, I was not able to attend either performance, for Honoré had an ear infection that miserably carried on the whole week.

Charles returned home the night of the first performance quite late; I didn't hear him come to bed, but his athletic tossing and turning woke me up.

'What is it, dear?' I enquired, suddenly wide-awake. 'Did the concert go well?'

'I believe it did,' replied Charles in a tired voice. 'At least it went as I had planned it…' I didn't particularly like his 'at least'; it meant some little parasite was chewing on his triumph.

'If it went as you had planned, then it was a success!' I nearly bark to scare off any lurking doubt.

'Yes, of course… it was surely a success… but I can't stop thinking of that critic and wondering…'

'Was he there?'

'Oh yes he was; in the front row. He was… chewing the whole time… a stick of gum I suppose.'

'Well… what can you do, Charles? It's out of our hands now… All we can do is say our prayers.'

'Please do that for me, Jane.'

'Do it *for* you? No, no, no… ten minutes of transcendental med should be about right. Come on, we'll do it together.' And so we both took two de-stress tablets of Indian ginseng and ommmed together till we yawned together. Till sleep became our mantra.

A week later, two days before Charles was to give his second performance, the review we were dreading appeared. Charles had left on his usual Saturday morning run to pick up the paper and croissants.

'Oh I know you're hungry, love, but Dad hasn't come back yet. You'll have your crescent bun soon. He'll be here any minute,' I reassured Honoré, who likes to have his croissant *tout de suite*.

'How about some banana while we're waiting?' I tried to sound cheerful but Honoré didn't buy it. He was a budding Frenchman after all; it was either croissant or *rien du tout*! I might have tricked him into eating a *tartine*, if I had had some bread, or even cinnamon toast, but I could tell that my banana proffering offended his sense of propriety. Oh dear, I thought, will he one day cut his hamburgers with fork and knife, like his father?

'Some hot cocoa?' I offered to make amends. Honoré nodded his head; suddenly we were both feeling brighter. The prospect of sipping warm chocolate in a sippy cup restored our sense of order. I pirouetted to the left towards the fridge with an impeccable *porte-a bras*, then swung my right arm out to open its door while my left one swooped down to grab hold of the milk carton. Only there wasn't one: no milk, only a can of Pelfort beer and a bottle of Thai hot sauce. 'Well!' I said brightly, 'It looks like we'll have to make slimmer's chocolate. Just add water and shake! You'll love it, Honoré.' My son looked at me doubtfully but did not make a fuss; he was waiting to see if I would actually ruin our delicious Dutch cocoa with boiling water. Mercifully, just as the water kettle blew its siren, Charles returned, a bag of squished croissants pinched against his waist by an elbow and a copy of *Le Monde* tucked up under his armpit. His forelock dangled limply over his brow, wanting in energy; his shoulders curved beneath some unseen oppression.

I relieved him of the croissants, fluffed one back up for Honoré to the best of my ability, and flicked off the excess of buttery flakes. 'Is everything OK, love?'

'Oh yes, fine, fine,' he replied absently before dropping down on the couch; his newspaper fell onto the cushion next to him.

'What's the word?' I ask pointing to it.

'Not sanguine…'

'Pray tell?'

'Very well…' Wearily Charles picked up the newspaper and opened it to a page blotted by a coffee stain, undoubtedly acquired at *Chez Fabien* where, when in need of an extra blast, he sometimes stops for a coffee. '"One wonders,"' he began reading drearily, '"where de La Rochefoucault's unprecedented whimsy of daedal contraptions is intended to lead us musically. This preposterous sum of incomprehensible eccentricities is entirely unrelated, even by liberal standards, to what is commonly called music. One is left with the distinct impression that the whole production has been mounted as a farce, a circus attraction for an ill advised and hearing impaired audience.'"

'A hearing impaired audience?!'

Charles set the paper down to take a brief respite from the pundit's attack.

'Do we need to go on?' I asked.

'Just one more thing,' insisted Charles, holding up his index finger like a conductor's baton. He picked the paper back up and read on. '"Surely the most insufferable moments came when a choir of pseudo monks blasted us with deafening Kyrie eleisons and horns. There was no afflatus, though much, I'm afraid, of what sounded like flat out flatulence."'

'That's just a cheap shot!' I pointed out.

'Yes, cheap perhaps... And they were real monks... but it's costing me... oh it is costing...'

The week following that review shifted us into a realm of reverse, where at best we spun our wheels like economy cars axel deep in Idaho mud, and, at worst, we watched, heads twisted backwards, the past ram right into us. Monday morning Madame Li, the wife of Monsieur Li who Charles once fished from the canal, came a-knocking on our door at 7 a.m. Frantic.

'Madame! Madame! My Husband! Please! Come at once!'

'What's wrong?' I asked, still in peignoir and only two sips of coffee into the day. But Madame Li hadn't time to answer; she went running back down the stairs, waving her arms and wailing. Trusting I would follow. Which I did, with Honoré on my hip, and still in my bathrobe. Charles needed a moment to pull on some pants, but was soon on our tail. Down four storeys (US five) to the Li's first floor roost. Madame Li had left the door to her colourful showroom of plastics open for us.

But we were too rushed to take appreciative notice of the acidulated bouquets, 3-D placemats, fire-engine red PVC chairs and strobe light *horlogerie*. Her screeching nasal tone, a curious rhapsody of raptorial and feline shrieks, hailed from a further chamber to the left, next to the kitchen.

'Oh my God, he's drowning again!' I cried out, turning my left hip away from the scene to keep Honoré facing the plastic menagerie and let Charles pass through to get to the bathtub where Mr Li was flailing his limbs, sinking, then mercifully re-emerging as Madame Li pumped his arm hanging over the edge. Her incomprehensible wailing and the steady up-and-down movement of this conjugal piston reminded me of Helen Keller at the water pump upbraiding fate with each pull of the lever for the misfortune of her marriage to deafness and blindness. Mr Li had turned a blind eye, a deaf ear to the lesson he was to have learned that night in the Canal de l'Ourcq when Charles freestyled to his rescue and nearly drowned in the mire alongside him. But Tsingtao beer benders are for forgetting. Neighbours are needed for help. Charles bent his knees to grab Mr Li under both arms and with a tremendous heave-ho, pulled the beer-logged Li onto the bathroom floor where his spouse grabbed hold of his legs. I pressed myself in the small space between toilet and sink as they carried him out to the showroom couch, which incidentally, was not plastic but decorated with bright green blow-up PVC cushions.

'Everything's fine, my love,' I reassured Honoré. 'Your father has saved the day again. Here, let's get a towel. It's not nice to see your neighbours naked.' I picked a rough blue towel off the floor and placed it over Mr Li's loins, or rather over the Robin Hood cushion, which Charles had already placed there. Madame Li was giving his cheeks little wifely slaps to wake him up, but Mr Li only uttered some drunken request that arrested his face in a momentary smile, pushed his eyebrows up high like barbells before he made a lax descent into hops-flavoured sleep.

'I think he will be fine, Madame Li,' said Charles whose jeans had darkened to indigo and whose teal T-shirt was like an archipelago of tiny turtle-shaped isles amidst wide pools of sopping sea.

'Thank you! Thank you!' exclaimed Madame Li excitedly, nervously, clearly eager to see us leave with the same swiftness with which we arrived. But before we did, she rustled in a cookie tin, or rather box, for it was not made of malleable metal but rainbow coloured resin, and pulled out a fat almond cookie for Honoré.

'Very kind of you, Madame Li. Please let us know if we can be of further help to your family,' said Charles as Honoré greedily stuffed the sweetmeat in his mouth. One day he would learn his father's good manners, but in the meantime why not live a little? I bent down to Honoré's level and crunched into the cookie myself. The hard, granular biscuit seemed to explode under my teeth into yellow chunks and a spew of crumbs. I caught as much of the flying morsels as I could before they hit the floor, but the damage was done, and now Honoré belted out the jaggers. I had ruined his reward. What kind of mother would bite into her son's congratulatory cookie and spoil the fun? All I can say in my defence is that I was hungry.

This unhappy episode in the life of the Lis had the beneficial side effect of distancing Charles from the distressing review, at least for a time. He returned to our neighbours' the following day to check on monsieur, proffering capsules of dietary charcoal to help dry out the marsh left from the high tides of brew. Mr Li would not take them, however, and Charles retreated with a bow, wishing them well. His mind then rapidly returned to its wheel of worry. He retreated far into himself and was easily irritated by interruptions of any sort, particularly phone calls. And phone calls we were getting, the pre-coffee-and-croissant kind, from none other than our provider, Special K.

'Hello, dear Jane, excuse me for calling so early – I can hear you are with the child – what is his name? Balzac, was it?'

'Honoré,' I corrected her. I was pleased all the same that she made the effort. 'What can I do for you?'

'I need to renew my visa once again, Jane. I've been invited as a guest lecturer by New York University for the spring and already they have requested I start the process, seeing the difficulties they've been having with Homeland Security…'

'Isn't our last one still valid?' I've come into the habit of using the Queen's 'we' with her.

'I'm afraid not. The whole process must be begun again. And we must not dilly-dally. The last time was particularly drawn out and difficult.' Her tone was accusatory, as if the complications of her last application arose from my dilatory treatment of the dossier, and not, if the truth be told, from her faulty fingerprints, due to some paper cut she acquired from flipping too hastily through Heidegger. This nearly got my ire up but, knowing better than to ruffle all our feathers so early in the day and at such a delicate moment in Charles's career, I let it blow over.

'Roger,' I said adopting the spare but reassuring parlance of Homeland Security officials. 'I'll get on it today!'

'The gall of that woman, calling so early!' Charles said crossly after I hung up the phone. He shook as he poured me coffee. I put my hand on his and steadied him.

'Well, you know, Charles… she's got a busy day. You've got to think of her like an industry, manufacturing mind and text, careful to keep up the brand image. It's a big job.' Charles continued to shake his head disapprovingly, then appeared as if seized by a singularly strong emotion. He stood still for a moment, or at least tried to, but I could detect a tremor, a small quiver ready to threaten his dignity.

'As if art were not…' Charles began.

'Oh it's a big job too, love! And that is why we should be understanding, you see… We are all trying to do too much… trying to do the big jobs, or is it too many little jobs…'

Of course I knew exactly what Charles was saying and I knew he was right: our service to the Great Sensibility required we tightly bundle our energies and direct them with laser-like precision to our respective arts. But the truth was we were in no position to argue our point; we were still getting ourselves out of debt and doing so required we – or rather I – cater to Special K's industrial needs with a professional degree of altruism and efficiency. My own artistic projects, requiring wholehearted dedication as such things do, would have to simmer on the back burner, and it was best, it seemed to me, to accept this predicament rather than to find in it a source of constant and wearing conflict. In any case, I am sure that in some way my shopping and translating for that Great Lady will not have been in vain in regard to the Great Sensibility, which is ever eager to invest in Greatness of all sorts, and in varying shapes and sizes. Special K, of course, is size XL.

I spent all of Honoré's naptime making sense of the myriad visa forms, filling them out, double and triple checking. One mistake, one scribble and the dossier goes into a long remission. At five Honoré and

I paraded down the Boulevard de La Villette to the post office and sent off a manila envelope to Special K.

'How about an apricot juice at the Café Chéri(e),' I suggested to Honoré who then insisted on pushing his own stroller to get there. 'Red tape can make you real thirsty, my son. Your grandfather is old hat at it and drinks litres of Crystal Geyser by day, martinis by night. The thing is to keep hydrated…' Though it was chilly, the terrace was flooded with late autumn sun; we took a seat on the far side, away from the street where it was quieter, and ordered juice and a *panaché*. I craved that little liquid hit after the dry hours at the bureau. A martini would have punched too hard; the shot of beer in my *limonade* gave me just the tickle I needed to shake off the day's tensions. Honoré sucked up the sugary apricot nectar through a straw like a hummingbird at a feeder, in fits and starts. Probably because I kept interrupting him with my wishful thinking, poor lamb.

'You'll get to meet your grandfather soon. He's going to come over with Shirley, your step-grandma, to go on the D-day tour. They'll come to Paris to meet you after they've wept at Omaha Beach and knocked-knocked on the bunkers. It'll be very exciting, love, to meet your granddad at last. And you'll get an idea of what it was like when your mother grew up. Not that I knew Shirley back then or anything about the Price Club. But she's a good companion to Gramps, keeps his credit cards from expiring. Oh! – and she'll probably start bawling her eyes out when she sees you, so be forewarned. We don't pay any attention to it any more… she's a display girl all the way – from the toes of her Marc Jacobs to her tear ducts. We'll just make sure we have a hankie to hand.'

Two days later, another phone call came in at 7.30 just as Charles was slicing Honoré's croissant into bite-size pieces:

'Jane?'

'Speaking.'

'Excuse me for the early hour, but where on earth is the FG14!'

'That'll be in the envelope I sent you. I made sure all the papers you needed were there.'

'Well I can confirm that it was not in the envelope!'

'Right, well, can you tell me which documents you have? Do you have three of them?'

'Yes, there are three: the V91222, the 1500ZY and one called Foreign Visitor's Income Statement.'

'Perfect! You have them all. Foreign Visitor's Income Statement is English for FG14.' Please believe me, dear reader, when I say my intention was not to be in any way condescending to the Great Lady next to whom the Mensa-affiliated Stone is but a pebble. Rather, I wanted to point out an anomaly in bureaucratic procedure whereby, for reasons unknown, the form's numerical moniker only appears in reduced sized script in its lower left hand corner, which, in the course of our telephonic conversation, I explained to Special K with the favourable result of allaying her worry.

But only for a time.

Two days later, I was treated to yet another early-bird special.

'Jane!'

'Yes?'

'Excuse me for calling you at this hour, Jane, but I've been the victim of a theft and it concerns both of us. My attaché case was stolen yesterday at the university.'

'And did it have…?'

'Yes, it did, Jane. All the visa papers I'm afraid. Did you keep copies of them?'

'I did. But I'll still have to redo them.' I sighed.

'Please do, Jane. I'm infinitely grateful. We suspect it was one of the doctoral students who stole my briefcase. A rather troubled girl from Turkey who has been stalking me… it's a case of exaggerated transference I'm afraid…'

'Goodness!' How frightening it all sounded! It must be terrible, indeed, even dangerous to be so floodlit by someone else's psychic projections. She's lucky she got away with everything but her briefcase!

I tried to barricade the freakish grad student from entry into my head as I redid Special K's visa forms, the original versions of which the troubled Turkish girl was now perhaps using for toilet paper or God knows what. It was a tedious job, one which I tried telling myself was no worse than the online shopping I do for her. But because it actually was worse, as it offered none of the perks of the Galeries Lafayette, I found it entirely fair to charge her an overtime rate.

On the periphery of these telephone conversations, I could feel Charles retreating to the lower decks of our vessel where the few existing portholes offer murky views of an impenetrable seascape. It is always salutary when at least one passenger of a sinking boat remains steady and hopeful; sometimes salvation is in sight, and only requires binoculars. In our case, while I kept my eyes glued to the lenses, Charles lapsed into a listless state. Somehow the disappointment was dissolving his sinews, eating away at the might of his tendons. He had difficulty connecting his thoughts, and once, one morning as he was getting out of bed, I swear I saw his left leg unnaturally bend forward like an arc, as if his knee were no longer a hinge but a lax and rubbery knob that could be plied in any direction. I did think of calling Delamancha but instead, I listened in. Clairaudience, after all, is but a strong signal of feelings and intuitions to which the particularly sensitive ear tunes in and interprets. Call me an exegete of the invisible scriptures, the vibratory rhymes that lock into sensation. And what I was sensing gave me the strong hunch that some shift in the crustal plates of Charles's destiny was actually taking place.

Two weeks later, we received an e-mail from an American journalist named Bob Steelman who had attended the July 2 performance and was, as he emphatically put it, *moved beyond words, left utterly speechless!* He requested an interview with Charles, which he intended to publish in none other than the avant-garde magazine *Bomb*!

'This is simply astonishing...' murmured Charles, for whom the news sent a kind of electrical charge through his connective tissues. He lost his rag doll floppiness almost immediately; his kiss curl tightened its screw. I could tell that like me, he sensed – not hoped, for hope is a cumulus of the mind casting deceptive shadows over the senses – more good news would be arriving in the wake of Steelman's e-mail.

And it did.

Chapter XXIV

Which recounts a telephonic invitation and an auspicious guest appearance before concluding our tale with a brief word on our subject of predilection – motherhood.

The following week, on a Tuesday eve, we received via e-mail a copy of a rave review published in the *Village Voice,* written by one of its Paris correspondents:

Not since1974, when French funambulist Philippe Petit danced between the Twin Towers on a cable five-eighths of an inch thick, has France produced another maverick artist of such daring as Charles de La Rochefoucault. His Car Wash Aria in F Sharp *bursts forth, from the very first notes of the cariope – a strangely Javanese sounding and fabulously preposterous instrument invented by de La Rochefoucault combining a steam engine, organ pipes and an automated car wash – with a magisterial explosion of sound that hits the audience like a cascade of Niagara proportions. One has the sense of being showered with music, of being held under a torrent, then vigorously buffed by gigantic brushes, dried by shrill whistles. But this perspicacious parody of post-modernism is rendered with high-minded sérieux and offers a sumptuous aviary of noises – and silences – from known and unknown instruments, that is as carefully constructed as it appears random. De La Rochefoucault has earned himself a controversial reputation for working with a wholly unusual and even esoteric instrumentaria including the Holy Spirit such as in his* Suite #2 for the Holy Spirit and Three Harps. *Daring he is and adamant in reclaiming the sacred 'Holy Spiritism' of silence which he measures by calibrating both its absences and its varieties in compositions that spark with finger-in-an-electrical-socket energy and command you to listen.*

'It's brilliant!' I said to Charles, setting the article down on his desk. 'Oh Charles, wouldn't it be wonderful if you could take your Car Wash Aria to New York where it would really be appreciated? Historically the Americans have known how to promote French exports – cars excluded of course. I think they'd like to have you around, Charles. I just get that feeling.'

'I think perhaps you're right, Jane.'

'Why don't you work on your contacts there? I'll send Lewis an e-mail in any case. He seems to know everyone – off off off Broadway at least. He hasn't done too badly for himself since *Away in a Manger.*' I went to look for my telephone book to refresh myself with the names therein, going down my lists to spot potential contacts – when the phone rang.

'Pick it up, would you?' I asked Charles, as I skimmed the A-B-C listing with an index finger.

'*Oui?... Bonjour Edouard... comment-allez vous, mon cher homme?... Et votre épouse? Oui, oui, tout à fait... Je suis très heureux de vous entendre... Ah bon?... .A New York vous dites... oui, oui... en effet c'est tout à fait heureux... oui oui... le ministère... d'accord, très bien... c'est une excellent nouvelle!*'

'What on earth was that about?' I asked eagerly, my curiosity piqued by the mention of New York.

'Oh it is quite extraordinary...' replied Charles. 'That was Edouard de Landry at the *Ministère de La Culture*... it seems I've been requested to perform *Car Wash Aria in F Sharp* by The New School... Apparently they would also like to invite me over in the spring as a guest lecturer... it's some sort of exchange with the ministry.'

'You've got to be kidding! The spring! That means we'd be there when Special K is! Maybe she'll hire me as an interpreter... or her personal buyer at Saks!'

'It's all rather surprising, isn't it? Only I don't know if it will be possible what with the state you are in... moving to the United States might compromise the health of the baby.'

'What do you mean, compromise the health of the baby? Do you think France has the monopoly on maternity wards? We're built to give birth anywhere, we women – have been known to pop them out in taxis, on planes, in cornfields. Having a baby in Manhattan will be as easy as flipping pancakes on a non-stick grill. You must say yes, Charles. Call him back right now and say yes!'

'Yes, yes, but I must have a night to think about it... all quite a shock isn't it?'

371

It was – a shock, that is, but I was in the mood for surprises. I've often experienced change, even of the most salutary and desired sort, as a slightly unwelcome disruption in my careful rituals, as if there were a small Bartleby in me saying *I prefer not* no matter how marvellous the opportunity brought on the tide of change. Yet, like any reasonable person, I invariably end up stifling the fancy of Melville's pallid scrivener to get on with things. In this case, however, and for perhaps the first time, my Bartleby voiced no opposition to the plans so unexpectedly proposed. And, without the counterweight of contrariety, I was feeling particularly light-hearted and as if on my toes, ready to leap off the flat runway of my ironing board to a mountainous future that promised us the highs of altitude and a sunny perch on the summit. I had lived and struggled in New York as a *célibataire*, but life there as distinguished guests – and as a threesome – would be distinctly different; it would be like returning incognito. No-one would recognize us until they heard our names and voices, for the circumstances would dress us in entirely new attire. We would have the freedom to experiment without the risk of losing our shirts; what more can artists ask for? I was nearly giddy with anticipation.

In the kitchen, as I started to get dinner ready – cooking can help me get a handle on any headiness – there was a knock on the door. Not just any knock, but my mother-in-law's curiously coded rapping; she was sending us one of her knuckle communiqués.

'Were you expecting Mathilde?' I asked Charles as I was gathering my ingredients for puttanesca style penne. 'Listen… What is she tapping? A Hail Mary?'

'No, it sounds more like Mary Had a Little Lamb, listen… she's doing it for Honoré.'

'Oh bless her! Why don't you open the door…'

With Honoré racing alongside him, Charles went to greet our Mother Goose. The tuneless rhymes came to an abrupt stop and now voices filled the hallway. I heard Mathilde and Charles, but also the voices of other men, which I could just barely make out. Could it be? I wondered. Yet it was not until the group of guests funnelled out of our exiguous entryway and into the living room, that what I suspected was confirmed.

'Asalaam Alaikum. Greetings, good Uncles!'

Before me stood a stunning triptych of men swathed in white, all the wiser for their good works, their car heists, their forgeries: our magi! Gone now were the tracksuits and trainers of their suburb days in Saint Denis; gone were the hooded robes of the dungeon and the monastery. Swathed in kung fu apparel, they had the look of champions returning from a tournament at the temple, quietly inhabited by their victory. Curiously, all three had changed their hairstyles from the Caesar cut so common among North African men, to a layered fauxhawk in the case of Samir and Rachid, and in Ahmed's, a Chow Yun Fat coiffure that would have made any pilose signs of piety sprouting from his cheeks appear as phony in contrast as paste-on postiches. To his credit, it seemed Ahmed now eschewed the ostentatious wearing of cheek symbols; perhaps we can conclude that the crescent sideburns and the convictions they expressed grew from a passing fanaticism, now wrestled down by a pressure point attack. He was the handsome sum of the Asian equation of more hair on the head and none on the face, and I hoped Cousin Constance had the good sense to encourage the improvement which was bound to make their lives easier – imagine trying to negotiate a mortgage at a French bank with sickle-pruned sideburns!

It was not the magi who came bearing gifts this time, however. Mathilde stepped forward from behind this trio with a swaddled babe in her arms and Cousin Constance in tow. From the pink blankets, we surmised the newborn was a girl, which Mathilde confirmed in her introduction.

'Behold the Sacred Daughter!' she announced with pride, inviting us to peer into the petals of blankets. The tiny babe was sleeping soundly; wisps of dark, moistened hair clung to her brow in swirling tendrils and her complexion flushed more tawny than rosy. That she was Ahmed's daughter left no doubt (but of course we have never doubted, have we?). I searched her face for some resemblance to Constance's and found none, but perhaps any mother–daughter likeness would take shape later, and, with any luck, there where Constance kept her finest asset, revealed to a happy few.

'Congratulations! Oh, she's absolutely lovely!' I hugged Cousin Constance who was still very much a creature of habit, which is to say, she continued to wear the Bishop's uniform, completely unphased by the impropriety of it. A stubborn girl. But she had grown out her hair and now wore it in a chignon at the nape of her neck, which gave her a maidenly air. Overall she looked quite well and this was surely due, as I was later to learn, to the fact that the Sacred Daughter – named Jeanne, bless her – slept through the night blissfully and was bottle fed. That Constance showed no inclination for nursing surprised me at first, but quickly reassessing the situation, I realized that this was only normal, for historically speaking, neither nuns nor aristocrats have ever been much inclined to breastfeed. Constance and Ahmed were blessed with what many term 'the dream baby', and which really just meant they could continue life more or less as before (hence the habit) missing that rare chance parenthood offers most of us to test the extent of our stamina, and to return from that front of chaotic feedings and night quakings with delirious and thus wonderful stories, for we all know it's the most preposterous story – and not the perfect one – which entertains us in the end.

We all fluttered and cooed around the baby for a time and what a lovely, tiny creature she was, and how unfair, in fact, to call her a dream child. For once awake she struck me as singularly perceptive and wise-eyed, not the stuff of dreams but remarkably real, soulful and almost ready to challenge her parents with her will.

Though this surprise reunion and its sweet epiphany whipped us up in a state of excitement, an anxiety hovered over its edges. Our admiration of the luminous Jeanne had cast the whys and wherefores of the magi's appearance among us in the shadows, but now these questions were creeping into my awareness. As far as I knew they were Wanted Men, and, perhaps, had we been stationed in Boise or New York or – God forbid – D.C., potentially Guantánamo material. I thought I read in the bright whiteness of their attire, a sign of surrender to a fate of incarceration, and yet their ease and relaxed demeanour suggested an entirely different set of circumstances.

I invited our guests to join us for a humble meal of pasta puttanesca. They accepted unanimously and I excused myself to prepare the dish – which is as simple as can be in fact, simple enough for a Neapolitan whore to whip up between tricks it is said. I was soon joined by Samir who offered to give me a hand.

'Thanks, but no need,' I told him over my shoulder as I diced an onion. My eyes began tearing and I went to rinse my hands, which usually helps smite the sting. When I returned to the cutting board Samir had taken my knife and was finishing the job.

'You don't need to do that…'

'What you must do next time is soak the onions in water before you cut them,' he advised me, ignoring my weak attempt to dissuade him.

'I'll try that… the next time. But I have a question for you, this time.' Samir raised an eyebrow but continued to chop. 'And it's this: I'd like to know what on earth you are doing here. Good God! Do you realize you are risking your skins?'

'We came,' Samir volleyed back, with a chuckling sureness, 'for Master Jian's Master Class demonstration. It is a tradition; he hires us to do it every year…'

'And every year you've got Starsky and Hutch hounds on your heels? Every year Homeland Security interrogates your friends and asks them if they've ever held a Muslim's hand and even takes their fingerprints to make sure they have… or not? Do you also organize annual car heists and slave emancipations? These people mean business, don't you see that? They are out to get the noose around your necks!' High doses of anxiety can have the calamitous effect of cracking down my emotional dam and I was doing my best to hold back the retaining walls.

'Where should I put the onion?' Samir asked, every bit as sober and composed. Not even his eyes were irritated.

'In the pan…' I tried to reply but the words got strangled in my sobbing.

'There is nothing to worry about, Jane,' reassured Samir erasing any lingering trace of a smile from his face. He gave me a friendly pat on the shoulder. 'Everything has been arranged… in our favour. We are no longer at risk.'

'Arranged?' I managed to sputter.

'Various deals have been made… trade offs…' Samir was being vague, did not seem inclined to elaborate, but I looked at him expectantly, waiting for more, waiting to be reassured from head to toe. 'Let us just say that because we orchestrated the release of the enslaved men, we've been granted a few favours… by some mighty uncles. Now, Allah be willing, Muslims Without Borders will be able to carry on its outreach programmes and missions in France once again, and soon, in Eastern Europe also, inshallah.'

'I'm glad you're looking ahead, Samir, but what about the cars? They may have cleared you on the terrorism account, but what about the theft? You are still key suspects there.'

'Yes, we were. But now… now we are not.'

I could see Samir's 'now we are not' took us right to the terminus; he wasn't going to offer me another ticket to make the next connection and I resigned myself to getting off the train a bit lost. Some high placed 'benefactor' had stepped in on their behalf and for all I knew it could be the King of Morocco or even that bite-size stuntman, Sarkozy himself, though it was unlikely he'd be partial to a project hidden from the spotlight. It might have been some minister cousin of Mathilde's or even the mayor of Saint Denis… I mulled this over as I diced tomatoes. Samir returned to the living room where Honoré was serenading guests with our Italian version of 'Frère Jacques'.

'Do we have any more champagne?' Charles breezed into the kitchen in high spirits.

'You must have heard the news, then?'

'What news, dear?'

'About out friends… that they've been cleared under rather… mysterious circumstances.'

'Oh yes, yes! Marvellous news, isn't it! I spoke with Mathilde about it on Monday.'

'On Monday! And you didn't tell me?'

'Didn't I?'

'No you didn't! How could you have kept that to yourself?!'

'But I didn't realize that I had, Jane. I'm afraid I forgot myself a bit… because of these reviews. It's all quite disconcerting…'

'And did you also invite everyone to dinner?'

'That I did.'

'Without telling me?'

'I'm afraid it slipped my mind… you know what a critical time this is for me, love!'

I turned my back on Charles, tossed the tomatoes into the sizzling hot olive oil and stirred. But the familiar gesture did nothing to dissipate my emotion. My hurt and anger at being so lightly considered, of being taken for *La bonniche* multiplied at cellular rate. I turned the burner down to low, instructed Charles to watch the stove, then walked silently past our guests in the living room to the bedroom, where I shut myself in. There, into the mute, feather stuffed belly of my pillow I cursed the de La Rochefoucault tribe for its cavalier treatment of its morganatic member, for its symptomatic forgetfulness. Oddly, as my pillow talk gained in virulence, an image of Mother dressed in Barbara Eden-wear came a-visiting, and I felt my complaint merge with Mother's own, all those years ago. Had father ever seen who she was? Did she really have to winterize her face in frosted make-up so that he would notice she was beautiful but feeling blue? Had he ever really paid attention? If he had, perhaps she would not have needed to make such exotic spectacles of herself; perhaps with just average doses of husbandly recognition and appreciation she would have stayed and have been happy. Thinking of Mother and the degree of invisibility she endured and bravely combated in inventive ways – from peeing in Picasso blue to fashioning herself as the subservient Genie (when she could have opted for the brighter Mary Tyler Moore!) – saddened me. I could honestly say that Charles did not ignore me or fail to see who I was. We were a team, Charles and I, a lopsided one at times, it is true, but our devotion to each other went unquestioned. The glue of our mutual adoration guaranteed us a certain elasticity of heart to forgive shortcomings. Remembering this sobered me.

'Excuse me…' I heard from the other side of the door. 'Are you in there, Jane?'

'Yes…yes,' I said quickly fluffing the curse-dented pillow back up. 'You can come in.'

Cousin Constance emerged from the doorway, a stout Avent bottle in her hand.

'I'm sorry to bother you, Jane, but could I possibly heat up this bottle in the kitchen?'

'Why of course! You don't need to ask. Go right ahead!' But Constance did not make a move for the kitchen; she just stood there, waiting, from which I deduced she needed some help finding the pans perhaps. I stood up to lead her to the kitchen, but something about her manner made me pause. Rather than head back out through the door, she sat down on the corner of the bed, as if she wanted to chat a bit. Have a mother-to-mother, so to speak.

'Is everything going well?' I asked. Then ventured on with the usual: 'How is motherhood treating you?'

'Oh very well, Jane. Jeanne is a dear, not a problem at all. But I've been wondering how I might…'

'Yes?'

'How I might manage not to…'

'Not to what?'

'Not to get in that way again… I mean, I don't want…'

'You don't want what?'

'I don't want to get…'

'Pregnant?' I guessed.

'Yes, I don't want that,' she admitted calmly, now that I had sniffed her out. 'And I've heard there are ways…'

'Of course there are, Constance. Just go to your doctor tomorrow and get on the pill. And don't dilly-dally around: since you're not nursing you're probably fertile already.'

'Oh I couldn't do that, Jane! No, no, I'm talking about the *condoned way*,' she said lowering her voice. 'I thought you would know something about it. Won't I be needing a thermometer?'

'Only if you're coming down with a fever.'

'Oh I'm sure there's a thermometer involved, but I just don't know much about it…'

'Ah… the old rhythm method… I see. Oh Constance, it doesn't work, not really. You can't possible listen to the church on this point – it's run by celibate men! And frankly it's none of their business if you pop a pill or have an IUD put in. Of course, if you want to live dangerously and invest in a pricey ovulation indicator – and these things are very *hands on* if you know what I mean – you can get one at any pharmacy. I seriously think you'd be making a mistake, though, and it would be so much simpler if you…'

'Thank you, Jane,' Constance cut me off.

How like Constance, and Mathilde for that matter, to cut the conversation short just as I was warming up! And how typical of her to suscribe to Vatican-condoned methods when she's on the verge of excommunication!

'Tell me about Jeanne – are you both doing well?' I asked, changing the subject. Clearly there was no use going on about the intricacies of gauging *mittelschmerz* and ovulatory time.

'We do the work of the Lord together now,' she replied with her usual assurance.

'You mean, you take her with you to the gypsy camps?'

'Of course I do, Jane. That is my work and I certainly can't leave her at home alone! There is usually a young mother who watches over Jeanne while I make my rounds.'

'You mean you leave Jeanne alone with a gypsy girl?'

'Yes, we are fortunate that help is so kindly offered to us. They take care of Jeanne as if she were one of their own… Why, you look surprised, Jane?'

'Well, I am… I mean… isn't that a dangerous thing to do? Leaving Jeanne with people reputed for kidnapping!'

'Oh no, Jane! What nonsense! Our relationship is based on trust and faith in the Lord, and I've come to know the women quite well. Together we've planted a lovely pea garden in an abandoned bathtub and the crop has been good, which I take as an auspicious sign. And remember, Jane,' she added, before making a rhetorical pause to prepare me for the revelation: 'We are armed!'

I've seen this gig before. Constance yanked out two rosaries, her usual wooden bead affair and another made of fresh peas. She must have strung it together that afternoon, the green pearls had not yet shrivelled. She was quick to the draw but what kind of weapons were these? Even invested with Constance's fervent intentions, the pea chaplet, I had to believe, offered far less protection than a garlic necklace, which we all know is rather pungent but hardly pro-phylactic. Yet there was no use, I knew, in contradicting her: Constance would not veer from a course mapped out by her hallowed cartographer, the Lord. I wondered what Ahmed thought of her choice of babysitters; did he perhaps share her propensity for blind trust? Or maybe he knew nothing about her makeshift crèche. What I do know is that though steadfast and serious in her devotion, Constance can be sneaky.

'Let's get that milk warmed why don't we?' I clapped my hands decisively, in the optimistic fashion of Americans who remedy doubt with action, and headed for the door. Constance rose to follow me; I took the bottle from her hand and led the way. But as soon as we stepped into the living room, I caught a whiff of something burning.

'Where's Charles?' I asked Mathilde, alarmed.

'He's in Honoré's bedroom... They're getting the Koranoblaster down from the closet...'

'But he was supposed to be watching the stove!' I put a move on it and reached the kitchen only to find the base of my puttanesca sauce dried out and burnt to the pan. I spun the knob to off, put the hot pan in the sink where it sizzled against the wetness there. Our first interdenominational dinner party in the countess's kitchen would have to be cancelled. I went into the living room to make an announcement.

'My dear uncles and guests, given the unfortunate plight of my puttanesca sauce which, unlike the phoenix, cannot resurrect from its ashes, I am pleased to announce that Charles would like to invite us all to a Chinese feast at the Lotus d'Or, Madame Li's restaurant. We have a great deal to celebrate tonight, don't we? How about some widow wine before we go?'

Just then Charles walked in with Honoré on his hip and the Koranoblaster in hand.

'That's a wonderful idea, Charles!' Mathilde commended her son. 'How kind of you to treat us. I haven't had Chinese in ages.'

'Oh… well… uh yes, of course. It's my pleasure, Mother.' Charles assumed my little lie with poise and I was proud of him. My aim was not to humiliate him in any way, but merely to make him pay for his misdeed by honouring him as host, which really was a generous gesture on my part.

Little Jeanne nestled in Ahmed's arms, sucking at her bottle while the rest of us, yes even Samir (though not Ahmed!) chin-chined with our glasses of Veuve Cliquot. Honoré took sippy cup chugs of grape juice while playing the Koranophone with one hand. He has talent, my boy, and was showing off just a bit; he had one surah playing in loop and added to this a salsa beat which he shifted every twenty seconds or so to a rhumba-ish style rumble. Then in painterly, staccato strokes, he hit the 'Piaf button', a plain black knob thus named by Charles, of which the incongruence can only be explained as a manufacturing fluke, and *La môme*'s hit 'Non, je ne regrette rien' rang out in strident contrast to the holy chapters. Honoré was rocking back and forth on his diaper-cushioned tush as he played the machine, as much in the groove as the nappied Amar at the Café Chéri(e). Oh bless my boy!

Our evening at the Lotus d'Or was memorable, for Madame Li prepared us an extravagant assembly of dishes – salt and pepper ribs, jade rabbit sea cucumber, fried pumpkin dumplings, lotus seed pod fish, cream fatty catfish and even snow fungus soup – with care and consideration (pork platters were demarcated with parasol toothpicks). And, upon Mr Li's insistence, prior to our dining, the magi agreed to perform a few Shaolin stunts, requiring the removal of two tables near the windows, an effort rewarded by a stupefying demonstration. Samir began with a fluid series of strikes, virtual throws and leaps, his arms flapped and swooped with eagle-like ferocity and his fingers curled into raptorial claws. Rachid crouched like a tiger then sprang, his feline arms and legs mauling the air before landing his prey in a back flip. Lastly, Ahmed showed us the formidable praying mantis with its trademark amen clasped between two hands and imposing legs flexed to leap. He began low, loin nearly to the ground, then sprung in violent yet fluid jabs until at last his whole body twisted in the air like a bladed helix. The diners set down their chopsticks to watch and applaud. The potent qi emanating from our magi flew Mr Li over the moon, where, to celebrate the exceptional views from the orb's front row seat, he popped open a Tsingtao. Each *oh-là-là* we uttered confirmed a mutual feeling that the magi would swiftly land on their feet in Saint Denis. For such men there could be no borders; the walls of the world would accommodate them with cracks and fissures through which to slip.

*

The past few weeks of phone calls and e-mails confirming and detailing our plans to spend spring in New York have buoyed us up. Charles has lifted the orbit of his morale to see eye-to-eye with our ascending horizon in America and none of us is insensitive to the lightening of his load. I would not say he's on cloud nine: it's not exactly that; his head has long been in the clouds and they are too familiar for him to find them diverting. The heights come naturally enough to him; it is the lower – and more fraught – registers of belonging that have been shored up by this happy turn of events. We are being invited after all; we will be guests: New York's guests, which is like being desired by someone grand, almost like being God's guest in a Muslim home, though we won't be asked to take off our shoes.

Our second child will be Manhattan born and Honoré will discover the joys and pains of siblinghood in Central Park. I wonder if, with each pregnancy, a mother has doubts before she doubles her love. Does she fear she might not manage to spread equal measures of tenderness upon the bread of her life, and that the child who first made her into a mother will, outshined by the glaring neediness of those more newly born, be the last to receive the warm, buttered love? I wonder what happens in Egypt, where mothers so often name their first son Mohammed and thus become *Oum Mohammed* or Mother of Mohammed, when this first son is followed by a brood of siblings. Does she always keep Mohammed's name? In honour of the tiny prophet who turned her into a mother?

Honoré and Charles are seated at the piano plucking at the keys; it is a strangely pleasing music they are making. Both their forelocks are dangling over an eye but neither bothers to brush them aside. It is six o'clock, a warm evening, and sunlight streams into the living room windows, soaking my little pots of burgundy-hued geraniums in what is left of the day. Mathilde will be coming for dinner. I'll start the cooking when she gets here; it'll be a light meal of pesce all'acqua pazza, with porcini mushroom risotto and for dessert, a lemon granita now congealing in the freezer. The real treat is the bottle of Lacrima Christi brought down the slopes of Vesuvius by Padre Las Vegas. The bottle is witness to our undying friendship: we will sip the tears of the Lord between mouthfuls of our fish. Mathilde is very proud of her son, but saddened we will be gone for so long. A mother's blessing, a mother's curse; one reaches out to the other.

Listen. Can you hear, dear reader, the soft chiming, now fading pinkly as the peal gently caresses the geraniums at the window? The bells of the Hôpital Saint Louis chapel are making their rough count of the day's sacraments: the births, the deaths, the communions, all the departures from and towards the living within its *enceinte*, just before nightfall, when families huddle together in rooms that are never big enough, around tables with missing chairs, to keep the harm of the world away. A purplish sunset cloaks the domes of Sacré Coeur in regal finery that will transmute to midnight blue soon, and I imagine these cupolas nursing some gigantic night child, a constellation of need and hunger in the sky. Will our new adventure be as fraught with blind exhaustion? Undoubtedly. Will we console the pains of colic with any more efficiency? It is unlikely. Am I ready for it? No, I am not. Do I welcome it? Yes, I do. You do not have to be ready to welcome; the warmest greetings require no preparation – just presence. Hail, my little one. Know that your coming gives me pleasure. Know that just the thought of you fills me with reckless joy. We will welcome you with an aria; we will treat your simpering with a symphony, an alpenhorn will applaud your developments. You who are to be Honoré's sister or brother, who will join the arc of light that illuminates our hearts, welcome.

And to you, dear reader, farewell!

Acknowledgements

A warm thanks to the gracious hospitality of Ledig House and the Château de Lavigny where portions of this novel were written. My gratitude to the good souls who have helped me along the way: Violaine Huisman, D.W. Gibson, Susan Marson, Ray Watkins, and Charlotte Sheedy, my agent. Et surtout, mes remerciments les plus chaleureux à ma chère éditrice hors pair, Laura Barber.